GOLD PROMISE

GOLD PROMISE

Through the Canvas: Book Three

NINIE HAMMON

SPRING & STONE

Chapter One

LIKE SWARMS of some winged creature, all her fears wheel around and around in her belly and a great buzzing sound fills her head, the voice of a thousand flies drowning in unison. She is running faster than she has ever run in her life, terror thundering through her, a stampede of monstrous beasts, crushing everything in its path.

A dark hallway, a maze of shadowed corridors, a rabbit warren.

Her feet are bare. Shoes make noise and she must be so quiet she passes like a shadow through the hallways, running to—

She's not running to, she's running from. Here, she will be killed. Out there where the monsters are … maybe she has a chance.

She can't think about the monsters, though, because if she does, she will lose her courage. The monsters can hear what is only whispered. They watch you everywhere, can see down from the sky, find you where you hide — can see through walls, into cars or buses or airplanes, find you hiding in the woods or a cave or …

No, she can't think about that. She will find a place to hide where the monsters can't see her, can't hear what she says only to herself. She has to. She will make it through the monsters' kingdom and go back home and warn them about the Others who steal little girls and take them to a world full of terrors where their parents can never find them.

As the young woman flies past the closed doors, she makes no sound except for her heavy breathing, and she opens her mouth, tries to make her panting softer.

Her heart hammers in her breast, but it is strong. She is young and strong and she will survive.

Her heart is young, strong ... yes, it is. That's what the monsters want, the ones out there who will rip her beating heart out of her chest. That's what they do, pluck out her eyeballs and leave her blind — the monsters like blue eyes — but keep her alive so they can feast on her insides, taking her heart and then her—

No! She can't think about that now. She must only run. Escape!

Another darkened corridor leads off to the right. Should she turn down it? Is it this way? Or straight ahead?

She doesn't know.

She can't remember.

Think! What did it look like? Think!

She hears a sound behind her.

No, no, no!

There are footsteps behind her. Not soft, light footsteps like hers but lumbering, pounding footsteps.

Clump. Clump. Clump.

It's one of them!

Oh, dear God in heaven, please, oh please, no.

Clump. Clump. Hammering feet behind her. She has to run faster. The pain from the stitch in her side flashes up her body with such force she can feel it in her jaw, but still she runs.

Dark hallways. Turn here?

Another hallway. That one?

So many and she is lost now, running wildly in horrified panic, no destination in mind except away.

No longer looking for the hallway that leads to the gold archway with words on it — that's where their world begins. On the other side of the archway is where the monsters live. But she's not even looking now.

Gasping. Can't breathe. Run!

Suddenly, light blinds her. The dim shadows of the hallway vanish and she can see clearly — walls, doors. She looks back over her shoulder to see who is behind, and slams into something, hits so hard she smashes her lip and her whole body recoils. It's a person, a man, who grabs her by her left wrist, but her forward momentum swings her around him to the side. He doesn't let go, merely yanks her backward with a snapping motion and a bolt of pain shoots up her arm from her wrist that takes the little breath she has. She would scream, shriek from the pain but she has no air in her lungs even to squeak out a cry. She collapses, her knees buckling under her and he lets go of her wrist and lets her tumble to the floor in agony. She writhes there, trying to cradle her broken wrist.

It hurts so bad. Trying to gasp for breath but she is too frozen by the pain to breathe in. The world begins to gray out at the edges, the pain softens in the fog. Her face settles in slow motion down onto — carpet. It's carpet here, not cold stone. It's soft carpet. She feels it gently tickle her nose. The world grows darker. Darker.

In the dimming world, a hand reaches down for her, slowly. The stone in the ring on his finger sparkles in the bright light. The tattoo of a skull on the inside of his wrist stares menacingly at her with its black-hole eyes.

He yanks her off the floor to her knees by her hair. The world brightens. The man holding her upright is …

It is him. The Beast.

An enormous man. A beast — broad, square and massive, built like a refrigerator. He shakes her by her hair and she cries out, tries to hold her injured arm but it flops out of her grasp when he shakes her and she screams from the pain, the nauseating pain.

"Stand up or I'll drag you."

His voice is a rumbling horror, gruff, as if there is gravel in his throat.

She tries to get her feet under her, but can't. The man holding her hair yanks hard. She wails as he pulls out a huge handful and drops her honey blonde curls on the floor in front of her.

When he grabs her hair again, he pulls her all the way up to her feet, continues to pull until she is dangling in front of him, his huge paw tangled in her hair.

Her world is only pain.

He sets her feet on the floor.

"Stand up! I said I'd drag you and I meant it."

She manages to keep her balance this time and stands swaying, cradling her left hand and forearm in her right. Blood drips down her forehead and into her eye.

"Come on!"

The Beast grabs her upper arm and marches off with her, yanking her along because she can't keep up. Her broken wrist dangles, her hand flopping at the end of her arm and every movement grates bone against bone and the pain threatens to consume her. But she doesn't have enough air to scream.

He turns on the lights as he goes and she is barely aware of passing doorways and halls leading off into darkness. When they get to the stairs, she loses her balance and stumbles into him.

"Stand up!"

He slams her into the wall face first, smashing her lip, and a new agony stabs through her from her nose. The world is spinning. He holds her up, yanks her forward and she staggers. She can't get her feet under her before he yanks again.

At the bottom of the steps he turns down a dimly lit hallway.

Yanking.

Dragging.

Blood dripping into her eye and off her lip.

Her wrist has swollen so quickly that it is like a splint. Movement doesn't grind the bones so fiercely.

When she trips and falls to her knees, he lets go of her upper arm and makes good on his threat to drag her by her hair. Grabbing a handful of her long, golden curls, he snaps her head sideways as he pulls her body along the floor.

The pain in her scalp is ...

Her broken wrist drags along the floor, bouncing with each step forward.

Pain is her whole world. She can no longer tell where the stabbing agony comes from. It comes from everywhere, every part of her.

Then he drags her over a threshold and tosses her to the room. Her *bedroom, clothes in a pile, the closet door ajar. Lying by the bed, the shoes she slipped off so she could run silently. Looking along the floor, she sees … Jeni!*

The Beast kicks her in the hip, the pointed toe of his shoe digging into the scar left by the dog that bit her when she was five. The scar is ugly. It was once the only imperfection on her flawless body.

"Jeni," she whispers.

Then he kicks her in the face, breaking off teeth, smashing her nose, the force of the blow knocking her over onto her back. Blood gushes down her throat from her nose and mouth, so much she can't breathe. She manages to roll off her back onto her side, choking, coughing out blood, spitting out pieces of teeth.

He kicks her in the face again as she lies curled on her side. She actually hears her cheek bone snap.

"This year, you won't need a mask to go trick-or-treating."

Everywhere is only pain, such pain that she steps back away from it. Leaves herself and retreats down into some inner darkness, runs as she ran down the dark hallway. Deeper and deeper.

From a great distance, she feels blows. He is kicking her, but the pain is all one thing now, a blanket covering every inch of her so that she feels the blows like you feel pressure when you get a tooth pulled, but no pain because your mouth is numb. She is not numb, she is the opposite. So much agony that it is a kind of numbness.

A voice full of pebbles speaks from the place she left when she ran away into herself.

"I would cut you into little pieces with a chainsaw — a finger, a foot — but this is not the place to make such a mess. Too much noise. You are a lucky girl that I cannot do to you what I would like."

He laughs, a sound like rocks in a landslide.

"So I must be merciful."

He leans over her, grabs her by the neck and lifts her off the floor. With both hands around her neck, he holds her out in front of him. Then he squeezes. She takes a breath, only she doesn't. Nothing happens.

She struggles to inhale, tries to suck air in, desperate for breath.

Turning her head, she opens her ruined mouth, squirms, frantic, has to breathe!

Her eyes bulge as her diaphragm pounds into her neck. Her throat is blocked, closed. Shut.

Darkness closes in from the outside of her vision, like curtains drawing across a window.

Blackness takes the world away.

Chapter Two

Bailey Donahue lay in the dark nothingness of death.

All the pain was gone now.

Her eyes snapped open.

She screamed! Except she didn't.

Had to get away.

Run!

Nooooo!

Her heart hammered, the rattle of a snare drum. She made a little grunting sound. That was all she could—

The man with the shiny ring and the skull tattoo … where was the big man with the gruff voice and the huge hands who had …?

It hurt so *bad!*

She drew in a deep breath. Where … where was she?

She was in her studio.

One beat. Two. It took that long to sink in.

In her studio!

No.

Oh, please no.

Her hands trembled so violently she couldn't hold onto the

paintbrushes — *brushes!* — in her hands and they dropped to the floor, splattering red and blue paint onto her shoes.

She stared at the splotches of color on her new shoes. New Balance. Running shoes. She'd been about to go run—

There was a painting on the easel in front of her.

Seeing it, her heart kicked into another gear altogether, pounding so hard each beat detonated like a bomb, blood exploding through her veins, each pulse bludgeoning her temples from the inside, as if looking for a weak spot where it could burst through and squirt blood, spew blood—

She turned and raced out of the room without lifting her eyes to the portrait she'd painted there *with both hands*, and slammed the door shut behind her with such force it must have sounded like the gunshot T.J. and Dobbs heard months ago that she didn't. The concussion of door against jamb was so jarring it shook the shelf on the wall beside the door and a small ceramic London phone booth teetered there, almost regained its footing, then toppled over and kamikaze-dived onto the floor where it burst into shards of glass that spun out across the hardwood floor like figure skaters in competition.

And she ran.

Out the front door without closing it, letting the screen bang, across the porch, down the steps, across the yard Dobbs had paid some kid ten dollars to mow and out into the street. Not the sidewalk, *the street.* She ran down the street as hard as she could go, as fast as she'd ever run, a full-out sprint.

Run! *Get away.*

Obeying the ultimate primal necessity — fight or flight. She'd chosen Door Number Two and was no more in control of her own body than if she'd boarded a bus with a meth-head driver who was bouncing off parked cars and lampposts and mailboxes on a downhill race to a cliff.

Unlike the girl who had just been savagely beaten and strangled — with Bailey along for the whole ride, every excru-ciating second — Bailey wasn't running from a brute in a shadowy hallway. She was running from a painting on an easel in her studio. A painting she'd been *compelled* to paint.

No!

Not now. It'd been months since that … that whatever-it-was out there reached through her canvas, hijacked her body and left a vision of the future behind. It had been so long since she'd drowned with Macy Cosgrove, that she'd come to believe maybe it was over. You know, one and done. That the lone dead child would be the total of her contribution to this madness.

Well, okay, there'd been the horror of the painting she *chose* to paint, the one that was supposed to help the police find a kidnapped child but didn't. The one that had thrust her into the mind of a monster and that very nearly got the three people closest to her killed.

But she'd *decided* to paint that. She volunteered because she thought she could help.

This was different, this out-of-nowhere BAM! She'd actually begun to believe that maybe she'd never again …

To quote Rocky the Flying Squirrel, *wrongo, moose breath!*

Somewhere, she catalogued the sights that flew by as she ran.

A car slammed on the breaks and laid on the horn to keep from running her down at an intersection.

A dog penned up in a yard chased her from fence line to fence line barking. Not precious Sparky the Wonder Dog but some mutt that appeared to have inherited characteristics from several breeds — not their most pleasing attributes. Its legs were only a couple of inches long, holding up a spotted fat torso on which rested a head with the smushed snout of a boxer but with none of the charm.

There were children kicking a soccer ball in a yard beside a gigantic blow-up Dracula and assorted ghosts dangling from tree limbs.

A man sitting on a park bench looking at his cellphone.

A cat walking the tightrope top railing of a balcony. Not a black cat, though, but there were plenty of those around in the various decorations that also featured witches and zombies. Brice had pointed out the other day that he hadn't seen many spiders in Halloween decorations around town. Shadow Rock had had its fill of spiders, thank you very much.

Gradually, Bailey began to run out of steam.

She staggered.

Stopped.

Managed to duck her head behind a big oak tree to keep from grossing out the passersby as she heaved, sent flying chunks of breakfast and the bitter bile of too much coffee.

Then she moved on a few steps, *upwind* of her vomit, and stood with her hands on her knees, still gasping. She rubbed the mark on her left arm below her elbow — not even really a scar, but she still felt phantom pain there from the tarantula bite two-and-a-half months ago.

She had gotten up before sunrise feeling good. Rested. *Not a single nightmare about spiders.* That in itself was a strange enough phenomenon that the paparazzi should have shown up with cameras blazing to capture the moment for posterity.

She had a busy day all mapped out for herself that included waging war again with the attic, the one she'd been cleaning out the day Brice had blown out of her driveway, lights flashing and siren wailing, to answer a "child missing" call at Corruthers Elementary School. She'd abandoned the task for almost two months after that, but now that Brice's arm was no longer in a cast, he could help with the heavy lifting, and she'd decided to give it another go — determined to dig through the layers of generations of junk in search of artwork painted by Sophia Watford, the mysterious original owner of the Watford House.

And she was going to watch Sparky this morning while T.J. kept his — drum roll, please! — *final* appointment with the skin graft specialist who'd repaired the damage wreaked by a brown recluse spider on T.J.'s left leg.

Without even bothering to brush her teeth, she'd run her fingers through her hair, pulled it back into a ponytail with a red scrunchie — which she wore with blatant, in-your-face defiance because some teenager in the mall had disdainfully commented that scrunchies were *like, totally out of style.*

She'd gotten her brand new running shoes out of the box, planning on following the four-mile route that would take her through downtown and out to the dock, put on socks—

And everything ended there.

She had no memory of putting on her shoes, but clearly she had. She looked down at them now. There were splatters of red paint on the right one and blue on the left. Another wave of nausea swept over her and she was afraid she was going to upchuck the lining of her stomach and other nearby internal organs, which was all she hadn't already throw up.

"Excuse me … are you all right?"

Ah, the obligatory good Samaritan, who always seemed to show up just when Bailey felt least capable of refusing help without sounding like a sociopath herself.

Wanting to scream at the old woman with a bent back and a purse dog on a leash: *I was just beaten, kicked and strangled. I've had better days.*

But she bit it back, smiled weakly, babbled about running too fast, morning too hot, and staggered away, aware that something about her was drawing the attention of others. Bailey did not want the attention of others. It was possible there was not a single person drawing breath on the planet who wanted the attention of others less than Bailey Donahue did.

Then she saw the smear of red down her leg, from when she'd dropped the paintbrush — *paintbrush!* — and realized it looked like blood. She pointed at it, announced like a babbling magpie to anybody and nobody. "Paint … haha, it's just *paint.*"

Then she smeared it around so it was a blob of red rather than what appeared to be leakage from her femoral artery.

Her breathing had returned to normal. She looked at the nearest street sign and groaned. She had run almost five miles — in a straight line, and now she had to walk back, sans the flash of rocket fuel that had propelled her forward.

She reached for her cell to call — who? T.J. He was probably on his way to her house right now with Sparky.

Well, then Brice. Or Dobbs.

No, she couldn't call T.J., Brice or Dobbs or anybody else on her extensive contacts list which contained a grand total of six names ,and that included the place that changed the oil in her car and the pest control service she'd called so often to spray her house for spiders they now refused her calls. And, of course, U.S. Marshal Bernard Jordan, the man who moved her around like a knight on a chessboard. He had given her all three of his numbers — office, home and cell, insisted on being on her "emergency call" list. She couldn't call him, though, even if she'd wanted to and she absolutely did *not*. She couldn't call anybody because she hadn't stopped to gather up her cellphone when she bolted out of the house.

No phone. No house key either. Fortunately, that wasn't a problem since she had left the front door standing wide open when she ran out.

She turned and headed back toward her neighborhood, smelling the crisp autumn air, trying to enjoy the splash of riotously beautiful gold/crimson/yellow color on the foliage. Trying not to think about the still-wet portrait that waited for her on the easel in her studio. The portrait of a girl who had been murdered.

Chapter Three

T.J. MARCHED across the yard and up the Watford House front steps with as severe a look on his face as he could muster, prepared to fasten a leash to the little apricot-colored golden doodle's collar and drag him back to the car and make him do the whole thing over. Only way he was gonna learn.

The front door was open, so T.J. called in, "I'll be in directly, Bailey," and bent to hook the leash on Sparky's collar.

There was no sound from inside the house.

It was quiet, too. No sound of music. That girl did like to play loud rock songs that T.J. thought sounded like the wreck of a silverware truck.

"Bailey, you in there?"

Sparky yapped once. Just once. That wasn't the same thing as barking. One yap was communication. And it was as handy as those human words that had lots of meanings — like "aloha." The one yap could mean: "Help, there's a splinter in my paw." It could mean: "You set my honking pig toy on the counter last night so you wouldn't step on it when you got up to go to the bathroom and scare yourself to death — can I have it back now?" It could mean: "Let me out — quick, or clean up doggie pee off the floor."

It could also mean "Something's wrong but I don't know what." That's what it had meant when T.J.'d left the house a couple of months ago to walk into a living nightmare. Somehow, Sparky'd known somethin' was comin'.

Right now, it meant, "Open the door, Bailey, so I can come inside and lick your whole face."

But Bailey didn't answer either T.J.'s call or Sparky's yap.

Then T.J.'s mouth filled with spit and the copper taste of fear, like he was chewin' on pennies.

Ever since the warm June night he and Dobbs had sat out front of this house and heard the gunshot when Bailey'd fired a bullet into her brain, he had watched the return to humanity of a lost soul. In the beginnin', he'd feared every time he opened his eyes it'd be to a day Bailey wasn't in, that she'd made good on the suicide attempt. But in the handful of months since then, the four of them — him, Bailey, Brice and Dobbs — had logged enough living to fill up a handful of lifetimes. He knew she no longer wanted to die.

But Oscar might have other plans. Oscar was the name Sheriff Brice McGreggor had given the bullet her suicide attempt had lodged in Bailey's brain. The doctors had said Oscar might never cause her a moment's trouble and she could live to be one hundred. They'd also said Oscar could move just a hair, get dislodged by a blow to the head, or a sneeze. If that happened, Oscar would kill her instantly. She would never know what hit her.

T.J. flung open the screen door.

"Bailey! Bailey girl, you answer me. Where you at?"

Crickets.

He started to run through the house, calling for her. Instead, he looked at Sparky.

"Find Bailey," he commanded.

That was the game they played. Sparky would run all over the house, lookin' and sniffin' until he found her hidin' somewhere holding his favorite treat in the whole world — a hard-boiled egg.

Sparky didn't go runnin'. He just stood lookin' up at T.J. with that face that somehow managed to look like he was smiling.

Bailey wasn't here. If she had been, Sparky would have gone lookin', woulda found her even if she'd been … even if Oscar'd bit her.

He felt a breath whoosh out and supposed he might have been holdin' it. Relief flooded through him in a warm tide that felt like hot chocolate on a snowy morning. Or straight Maker's Mark whiskey from a shot glass in the darkest ditch of midnight when the memories came screamin', pullin' him back into the nightmare he'd escaped all those years ago, and from the more recent one that'd provided his still-healing spider bite.

So Bailey wasn't home. Where was she? He considered that as he went from room to room — just lookin' around, not scared anymore of what he'd find. The door was open and her car was in the driveway. He went upstairs and seen her purse on the nightstand by the bed. Her cellphone was beside it.

Back downstairs, he went into the kitchen, where a cup of half-drunk coffee sat cold in the sink.

Only one other place to look. And if he found there what he suspected he might find, it'd explain why Bailey'd gone runnin' outta here like her pants was on fire.

On the floor in front of the door, he found broken glass, one of Bailey's collection of miniatures — a London phone booth. He stepped over the glass into the room where north light flooded in from the bank of windows, which was why Bailey'd picked the room to use as an art studio.

Sittin' on the easel was a painting. A table with a bowl of fruit — way down at the bottom, totally dwarfed by the out-of-proportion window that took up almost the whole canvas. There was a … girl in the window. The paint was still wet.

Chapter Four

When Bailey turned the corner and started down her street, she saw T.J.'s old Ford pickup parked in her driveway.

She'd have to tell him about the painting.

And then they'd have to decide what to do about it.

T.J. was sitting on the swing on her front porch with Sparky beside him, and as soon as the dog spotted her he leapt off the swing and dashed across the newly-mown grass toward her, his tail a wagging blur, a look of utter delight on his face. Could a dog's face show such things? Well, Sparky's could! If he'd been a big dog, he'd have bowled her over. But just twenty pounds of fluff that looked like thirty pounds of dog could do no more damage than to jump at her, begging/demanding to be adored.

She obliged. Dropping to one knee she folded the wiggling, squirming animal into her arms, buried her face in the soft fur on the top of his head, and felt the horror of the living nightmare of being *murdered* retreat into the shadows where the wild things are.

T.J. got up out of the swing and came across the grass to greet her and to peel Sparky off her.

"Sparky, sit!" he told the dog, and the animal obediently

plopped his backside down in a spot of bare dirt, his tail wagging so furiously it sent up a small cloud of dust. T.J. laughed and Bailey waved the dust cloud out of the air in front of her face and rose to her feet with what resembled a genuine smile.

"Have a good run?"

"No."

"Didn't figure you did."

"You saw the portrait." It wasn't a question.

He put his hand on her shoulder.

"I'm sorry." The affection in those two words brought unexpected tears to her eyes.

"It's awful, isn't it?"

"You don't know?"

"I know what I … lived." She shuddered and he guided her up the porch steps to the swing.

"Sit," he said and she obeyed as obediently as Sparky.

"But I didn't look … I, you know, woke up with paint-brushes in my hands."

In some ridiculous way she couldn't have explained, the fact that she painted portraits of "what hasn't happened yet" with *both hands* amazed her almost as much as the content of the portraits she painted. She let out a long breath as he sat down beside her and Sparky leapt up into her lap. She ran her hands through his fur. "T.J. … I was murdered …"

"Strangled. I know. I saw."

"I guess I need to see, too. I—"

"Not just yet."

"You don't have time to sit here holding my hand. You have a doctor's appointment, remember? You're going to be late—"

T.J. patted his left leg, the site of half a dozen painful skin grafts.

"I done spent half the mornin' lookin' for an excuse not to

go. Ain't no way I'm passin' this up. You and me'll just sit here for a spell."

She smiled a little. "I bet 'spell' was a word you had to exile from your vocabulary when you 'lost' your dialect."

"It was for a fact."

The smile faded. "Here we go again, T.J. It's been months since Macy Cosgrove. Just when I thought—"

"It was safe to go back in the water …"

"The great white is still cruising out there, waiting to bite me." Of course, she already knew the answer to the question before she asked it. "It always will be, won't it, T.J.? That shark is going to be circling my life … from now on. I'll never be rid of it."

"Nope, I don't 'spect you will."

T.J.'D studied the portrait for a long time when he'd walked into the room and found it there on the easel with the paint still wet. The initial shock was staggering and he was glad he got to be there with Bailey when she seen it "for the first time."

He'd left the door to the studio open. The two of them walked together into the bright room, the cheeriness of the yellow sunshine belying the horror of the dark portrait that sat in the middle of the room, with two paintbrushes and gobs of paint splattered on the floor beneath it. She'd been avertin' her eyes 'til they stood in front of it and there was nowhere else for her to look. Even then, she lifted her eyes slowly — backing up emotionally from what she knew she was gonna see, digging her heels in.

When she finally did focus on the painting, she looked like somebody'd slapped her. No, like somebody'd drawn back a boot and kicked her square in the belly with it.

Bailey's hazel eyes, that was the color of a still pool reflecting the woods on the shore, widened until there was white showing all around. She stopped breathin', then let out a little squeak that carried with it a weight of horror and denial that musta been a strain for the tiny sound's shoulders to bear.

Before them on the easel was the portrait of a nightmare. Literally.

The center of the picture was a girl's face, though she'd been so badly beaten she was unrecognizable. Her hair was honey blonde, hangin' in long curls, and her eyes was open, a startling sapphire blue — but bulgin' out, with red stippling in the whites of 'em. Petechiae, the medical examiner on all the cop shows called it. Hemorrhaging in the blood vessels caused by the pressure of strangulation. Her pale skin was dotted with tiny brown freckles, like she'd been dusted with cinnamon.

Hands crushed her throat, the thick fingers and wide wrist bones of a very large man. Her neck was so slender the man's fingers encircled it and lapped over, almost looked like he was holdin' a baseball bat. He had a pinky ring on his right hand, small and oddly delicate, with an intricately ornate gold band and a single diamond, a perfect oval stone, mounted to be flush with the band's surface.

T.J. thought that the diamond made a statement — large, but not ostentatious, almost understated. The ring was tasteful, designed for somebody with a discerning sense of style. Its presence on the fat finger of the callous murderer was offensive, like findin' a single white rose in a pile of vomit.

You could see the girl's neck and shoulders below the hands. And it appeared that the man was literally holding the girl out at arms' length in the air in front of him as he squeezed the life out of her with them fingers diggin' into her flesh.

Her face was a ruin, nose smashed over onto her right cheek, lips split. Blood poured out her open mouth over broken, splintered teeth, too. That'd struck an emotional chord with T.J., almost seemed worse than any other horror.

He had hit her, more likely kicked her, in the mouth so hard he'd knocked out most of her front teeth. That was either an act of a homicidal rage or of total indifference. T.J. figured the safe money was on indifference, a blow delivered casually by a man who'd done that before. That and worse.

"Another man was chasing her." Bailey's voice sounded small and vulnerable. "She was running away and crashed into this one, the Beast, and he broke her wrist."

She turned to T.J. "Have you ever broken a bone?" She didn't wait for him to answer. "I haven't. Worst injury I ever had was stitches on my knee after I fell off a bike when I was nine. I had no idea how bad a broken bone hurts." She swallowed. "Brice's arm when Melody broke it, I didn't appreciate the pain …"

She took another breath, staring not so much *at* the portrait of the dead girl as *through* it, to a scene that was playing out in real life right behind it.

"The broken wrist bones ground together when he dragged her along the floor by the hair."

T.J. was more horrified than he was prepared to be, and he almost reached to stop her, to tell her we can talk 'bout this some other time, or how 'bout I fix you a nice cup of hot tea. But he stopped himself. However difficult it was for him to hear, it was a whole lot harder for her to tell. And indescribably harder for her to live it along with that poor girl with the broken teeth.

Bailey was ramblin', rememberin' bits and pieces, not makin' a lot of sense. Didn't matter. She needed to tack words onto it, look the monster dead in the eye and now was the best time, while the wounds was fresh, so wouldn't be openin' them up again to recall details later. Though she would. She'd remember a whole lot more about this experience than she wanted to.

T.J. had thought 'bout that when he was a boy and his mama was paintin' the portraits that drove her mad. He could see she'd changed, was different from the moment she woke up after she was knocked unconscious in the Watford House kitchen. But at the time, he hadn't really understood that she was livin' the experiences with the people she painted. Toward the end, he figured it out, though. As an adult, he was introduced up close and personal to Post Traumatic Stress Disorder. Lived with it himself after … after what happened. He couldn't imagine that livin' an experience like this wouldn't leave Bailey so stricken with PTSD she couldn't get out of bed.

But then, she blinked in and out of the mind of a monster a couple of months ago. She was a lot stronger than she looked.

There was so many layers to this. So many layers.

"She only says one thing … just looks across the floor and says, 'Jeni.' Like she was calling to someone, maybe … saying goodbye."

Bailey turned to him and let out a shaky breath. Even so, when she spoke her voice trembled.

"So now what? I swear, T.J., if you hadn't been here when I got home, if you hadn't already seen this painting, I would have taken it out into the back yard, hacked it apart with an ax and burned the pieces."

"I ain't sure you coulda done that."

"What do you mean?"

"When my mama first started paintin' them pictures, she hid 'em from my daddy 'cause he told her he'd kill her if she ever painted another one. She was takin' an awful chance doin' that."

"Why'd she do it, then?"

"I think she *had* to keep 'em. I don't think she could destroy 'em, until …"

"Until what?"

"Until they let go of her."

"Meaning?"

"You know what I'm talkin' about. The connection. 'Til

the thing you painted happens, you's connected to that person. This girl here," he gestured toward the painting but Bailey'd looked away and she didn't look back, "she's still alive ... ain't she?"

"I suppose, I ..."

Bailey took a breath, tried to center herself. Then she looked like she was listenin' hard to hear a soft sound, or maybe tryin' to recall the recipe for bean dip.

"Yes. She's still alive. I can ... feel her. This," she waved her hand toward the painting but still didn't look at it, "hasn't happened yet."

"There's your answer, then. You can't destroy this picture long as she's alive."

Bailey burped out a little sob then.

"That's not the right answer because it's not the right question."

"Meaning?"

"Meaning the question ain't 'Can I destroy the picture?' The question is 'What do I do about it?' Am I ... are *we* ... s'posed to try to help her, to keep her from being murdered?"

"What do you think?"

"Dobbs would say we have to try."

"I didn't ask what Dobbs would say."

"*You* tell *me*. Answer the question your own self."

"I don't know. When I painted the portrait of Macy Cosgrove dead, *drowned,* we were hellbent for leather to keep her alive."

"And we did."

"Did we?"

"Oh, there you go—"

"I have to go there. *There* is what it all comes down to. Yes, we rescued Macy Cosgrove from a flood. But there wouldn't have been—"

"You don't know that—"

She held up her hand.

"Okay, it's at least *possible* there would never have been a flood in the first place if we hadn't meddled in the affairs of …"

"Of …?"

"Of whoever … *whatever* … if we hadn't tried to stop the painting from becoming reality. I decided then I wasn't ever again going—"

"But you did."

"Not that kind of painting, I didn't. I didn't just get hijacked out of my life and wake up with paintbrushes in both hands. I *decided* to paint that portrait. And it didn't do any good. The boy still died, so did two other children."

"How many times we got to have this conversation? I done pointed out that you *saved* the lives of who knows how many other children by catching the kidnapper."

"But if we interfere this time, leap on our horses and ride off to rescue this girl … in the process, we could get her killed. We could *cause* her murder." She pulled in a breath and he realized she was on the brink of tears. "If I caused … if it was *my fault* … I don't think I could live with—"

He put his hands on her shoulders.

"All them pictures my mama painted for all them years… every one of them things happened — just like she painted it. And she never done a thing to *cause* 'em. What that tells me is that this here," he pointed at the painting and stood there, waited 'til she finally turned her eyes toward it, too, "is gonna happen. Onliest way it *won't* happen is if we stop it."

"This isn't as simple a thing as finding a little girl … This is a murder. How do you stop a murder?"

He felt her wobble slightly, realized how unsteady on her feet she was.

"Okay, that's enough for a while." He turned her around and marched her out of the room.

"I broke the phone booth …"

She was looking at the glass on the floor, delayed shock

firin' off random synapses in her brain. He'd set her down, put some warm tea in her belly and then they'd call the sheriff. There wasn't nothin' else to do, but her mind hadn't got that far yet.

They'd only taken a couple of steps out of the room when Bailey stopped and whirled around. All the color had drained out of her face.

"Halloween."

She said just the one word, but it was slathered in all kinda meanings. Before he could ask, she blurted it out.

"He told her she wouldn't need a mask to go trick-or-treating on Halloween."

"Halloween is Saturday."

Chapter Five

KAVANAUGH COUNTY SHERIFF BRICE McGREGGOR opened the little box and stared at the contents.

He wasn't the kind of man who second-guessed himself. A total waste of time. Life rewarded action. Doing something was always preferable to doing nothing. And a worldview like that precluded looking back over your shoulder to rehash the last thing you did.

But as he looked at the little box in his hands, he thought for the one zillionth time that maybe he should have gotten something else. Not that the decision to get the earrings had been arrived at precipitously. Hardly. First, he'd agonized about whether he should get Bailey a birthday gift at all. He'd been the one who'd let the cat out of the bag, mentioned to T.J. and Dobbs when her birthday was. He'd seen it on her driver's license more than three months ago when he was identifying "a suicide victim." Only she hadn't died, of course.

Dobbs had come up with the idea of a celebration dinner at the Nautilus Casino in Whispering Mountain Lake, dragged him and T.J. into it, then dumped the whole load on Bailey — who had, in T.J.'s words, "pitched a conniption fit." They'd only gotten her to agree to attend by informing her that the three of them were going to the casino Friday night to celebrate her birthday whether she joined them or not … but she was welcome to tag along if she so desired.

She'd finally agreed to attend if they'd agree not to get her gifts, and they'd all nodded their heads like good little bobble-head dolls. None of them meant it, of course. And Bailey was nobody's fool. She knew they were faking.

That hurdle surmounted, he'd suffered through deciding what he should get, and after he finally decided on earrings, he'd agonized over which ones out of the plethora of female ear dressings available in just one jewelry store. He had limited himself to only one — it was a wise man who knew his own limitations. Now that he'd purchased them, he was revisiting his earlier angst. They were green, the color of her eyes — which were hazel with golden streaks in the center. He couldn't find any green earrings with gold streaks, though, but these were close.

The sales clerk — Cassandra Jacobs — had gone to high school with him, had suffered through Mr. Bergman's mind-numbing American history class seated next to him, and she had gone out of her way to be helpful. While he was going out of his way to pass the decision off as a casual thing, no big deal, just a birthday gift for a friend, emphasis on that — *friend.*

She hadn't bought anything he'd tried to peddle, of course. Women figured those things out fast. But he had managed to conceal his mental anguish about the purchase until he left the store, after which he battled surging waves of buyer's remorse.

He snapped the box shut. This was absurd. The deed was done and he needed to move on. And moving on was not at all an unpleasant thing because it involved anticipation of the birthday celebration her three friends had jammed down her protesting throat. They were having dinner at the fancy restaurant in the Nautilus Casino, which Brice had toured in his official capacity with other area law enforcement officers before it opened. He was looking forward to spending time with her. And with Dobbs and T.J. as well. He'd known *about* T.J. his whole life, everyone in town did, but getting to know the man personally was … delightful. No, that word was way too foofy. Eye-opening and mind-expanding were more appropriate. And who wouldn't like Dobbs, an affable giant of a man who, oh by the way, happened to be worth millions.

His cellphone rang and caller ID showed it was Bailey.

"Hello, birthday girl. Want me to sing to you now? Hint: the answer is no, you don't want me to sing to you. Not now. Not ever. I sound like a walrus giving birth to a forklift."

"Can you … come over — now?"

He reached up and touched the scar on his right cheek where he'd been bitten by a "widow" spider — red, black or brown, take your pick. That was what'd happened after the last time Bailey had painted one of her "portraits." And that's what the call was about — a painting. That much and more had been conveyed by the simple question.

"Half an hour."

Chapter Six

Raymond Dobson fished in the pocket of his overalls for a treat.

"Sit!"

Sparky obediently plopped his backside down on the floor in front of the big man. T.J. had told Dobbs he wasn't allowed to give the dog a treat unless Sparky did something to earn it, so it would reinforce his training. Dobbs didn't care what the dog did or didn't do. One way or the other, that pup was going to get this treat.

T.J. returned to the room from Bailey's kitchen carrying a tray with a pot of coffee and mismatched cups and saucers. He set it down on the coffee table in front of the couch.

Popping the treat into the fur-ball's mouth, Dobbs patted the couch cushion. Sparky hopped up next to him and lay down on his back, his tail wagging, his front paws flopped over in a perpetual beg, his belly displayed for scratching. Dobbs smiled, then looked up to see the others weren't smiling, had nothing to smile about and his own joy drained out of him.

There was another painting.

Dobbs had known it was going to happen. They all had. He cast a glance at Brice. Poor man, when he'd first been confronted with the reality that Bailey could paint a portrait of the future, he didn't know whether to wind his watch or take third base. Maybe it was easier for Dobbs and T.J., because of what they'd experienced as children. The young were always better able to embrace mystery and magic.

"We all seen it," T.J. said. He handed out mugs of coffee as he talked. Dobbs's with cream and sugar, Brice black. Bailey had shaken her head when he offered her a mug. She sat in the recliner, an old, ugly piece of furniture that was the most comfortable place to sit in the room. Curled up in the big chair, she looked like a little kid.

T.J. poured himself a mug and settled on the couch with Dobbs on the other side of Sparky. The dog quickly abandoned Dobbs and put his head in T.J.'s lap, where the man sat unconsciously rubbing the special spot behind the dog's ears that rendered Sparky almost comatose from pleasure. T.J. didn't tell everybody that he slept with his dog, but Dobbs knew. There wasn't anything about T.J. Dobbs didn't know. Except what'd happened to him for all those years in Special Forces. T.J. didn't share that with anybody. And he suspected T.J. *thought* he knew everything about Dobbs, too, given the two of them had been friends since they were four years old. But T.J. was wrong about that. Very wrong.

"So now we got to decide what we gonna do," T.J. said.

"This isn't like trying to save a child from drowning. It's one thing to try to prevent an accidental death," Brice said. He was seated in one of the set of wingback chairs at the far end of the couch, but not relaxed back into it. He was seated upright, on the front edge of the chair. "It's something else entirely to try to prevent a crime."

"*Should* we interfere?" Bailey sounded wrung out, as well she should have given that she had been beaten and murdered — before breakfast.

"We have to," Dobbs said. Every one of them knew he'd always come down on the side of trying to change the fate of the people in the future paintings — maybe as penance for all the times when he and T.J. were kids that they knew what was going to happen ... but didn't dare interfere.

"All I know for a lead pipe certainty is that that girl's gonna be murdered — unless we figure out a way to stop it. All them paintings, all them years, my mama wasn't never wrong. Not once." He looked at Bailey. "Do we run the risk of *causing* what we's trying to prevent? I guess we do. But it's better than turning our backs and walking away ... and lettin' that man with the pinky ring and skull tattoo kick that girl's teeth in and then strangle her."

No one spoke. In the end, the decision was Bailey's. She was the one with the "gift." And with the gift came the curse of responsibility.

The silence hung heavy. Might have seemed awkward among people who hadn't been through together what the four of them had.

Then Bailey let out a pent-up breath and squared her shoulders.

"First, we have to figure out who she is." She tried to make her voice sound stronger than it was. "And we've certainly been there, done that."

When she'd "tried" to paint a portrait of a kidnapped child two months ago in hopes of getting a clue to what had happened to the boy, Bailey, T.J. and Dobbs had tried to track down the child whose picture she *did* paint — a little girl they thought had died in a traffic accident eighteen years ago. The search had led them into a nightmare.

"Should we just start out this time with a private investigator?" asked Dobbs, because that's how they'd finally located the little girl.

T.J. shook his head. "We ain't sniffing down a trail that's eighteen years old this time," he said. He cast a sideways glance at Dobbs, who'd hired the private investigator. "Or hacking into hospital records we ain't 'lowed to see."

"If we're going to figure out who she is, we have to start at the beginning," the sheriff said. "What do we know about this girl?"

Bailey looked miserable. "She's got three days to live." Then she told them about the murderer's reference to Halloween. "It's Tuesday, Halloween's Saturday. Sometime between now and then …"

Then they watched her cue up a horror movie in her mind and set it running. It wasn't as horrible as living the event with the murdered girl, as she had done while she painted it. But even remembering such a nightmare was fuel for PTSD.

"Any other physical characteristics besides her hair color?" Brice asked. "A mole? A tattoo?"

"She has freckles, but not like yours. Just a little dusting of them … like cinnamon. And she has a scar on her hip — a dog bit her when she was a little girl. The man kicked her in that spot." Bailey paused. "I didn't see any marks or tattoos on her arms or hands. I … I think she's beautiful, though. Before he … ruined her face, I believe she was lovely."

"Pretty young girl tryin' to get away from … what?" T.J. asked. "Do you know?"

"No, just that she knows she's about to be murdered and she's running down a long hallway with doors on both sides."

"Like a school or a hospital or a hotel?" Dobbs asked.

"I don't know which. She was so terrified she wasn't paying attention to where she was going and so the images are vague. And she's barefoot. She took off her shoes so she could run without making noise." Bailey thought for a moment. "And she's wearing a white gown. She's afraid she might trip on it."

"That'd tip things toward a hospital or a hotel. Not likely she'd be running down the hall in a school barefoot, in her white nightie," T.J. said. He set down his coffee mug on the table. He hadn't even taken a sip.

"And she's … she doesn't make any sense. I don't understand what she's thinking."

"What?" Brice asked.

"Okay … she's running away from somewhere, something, some*body* she is certain plans to kill her. But she is terrified of where she's going *to* as well and that's the part that's weird. She thinks where she's going is a land filled with monsters who have super powers, who can hear what she's thinking and see through walls."

"Superman?" Dobbs said.

"Goody," T.J. said.

"She doesn't know how it's possible to hide from that, but she's so scared she's willing to face it and try — so she can find her way back home."

"Dorothy wanting to get back to Kansas," Dobbs said.

"Yes, something very like that. She wants to warn the people … in 'Kansas' … about the others — monsters who kidnap little kids and carry them off to some strange land where they never see their parents again."

"Sounding more and more like a fairy tale," Dobbs said.

"Fairy tales are closer than Marvel comics. Not so much superheroes as mythical beings, like out of a story. And the monsters who have these powers want to catch her so they can eat her — rip out her beating heart but keep her alive while they eat the rest of her."

She paused for a moment, concentrating.

"And her eyes. The monsters want her eyes most of all because they're blue and the monsters prefer blue eyes."

"So this young woman … *believes* in fairy tales," T.J. said.

"If she genuinely *believes* superhuman beings are out to get her, that's a variation on wearing an aluminum foil hat so the aliens can't hear what you're thinking," Dobbs said. "She's delusional."

Bailey shuddered. "If she is crazy, it's garden variety mental illness. Nothing like a … split personality."

The room was silent for a beat. Every one of them thinking their own thoughts about the insane child whose personality had so fractured she had turned into a real-life monster.

Dobbs held his hand up, his index finger about two inches from his thumb. "I know about this much more than the average layman about such things, but sounds like paranoid schizophrenia to me." He'd minored in psychology in college, but only because he wanted to factor human nature into his passion for business and finance. "And nothing I know is current. But I've read some things."

In truth, he'd read extensively about all things related to the functioning of the human mind and emotions, about mental diseases and disorders. Partly because the subject fascinated him and partly because he'd spent his life in psychological self-diagnosis, trying to self-medicate away the gnarled tangle of horror and terror planted in his mind when he was a child forced to look at future tragedies before they happened, the demons that still stalked the deserted hallways of his dreams.

"I'd say we're talking serious mental illness here, and that narrows down the search. If she's clinically mentally ill, it's likely she's institutionalized. That would fit in with the white nightgown, bare feet and the long hallway with doors."

"If we stickin' with what we've figured out so far — which is that these paintings ain't 'bout some crazy woman in Des Moines — then there ain't but a couple of places she could be. She's either in Forest Hills Sanitarium in McKinley or Westminster Acres." T.J. turned to Brice. "Am I missin' anything?"

Brice had grown quiet when the conversation began to center on mental illness and sanitariums. Dobbs wasn't surprised. He had almost been killed two months ago by a woman with a split personality, had spent a week in intensive care on a ventilator and had only gotten the arm she broke out of the cast a couple of weeks ago. He was entitled to be creeped out by mental disorders.

"Westminster Acres is the more likely," Brice said, the words coming slowly. "Forest Hills is older, and as far as I know, they kind of specialize in long-term care for … the chronically mentally ill. Not treatable."

"Both these places are right here in Kavanaugh County?" Bailey asked.

"Westminster is," Dobbs said. "Forest Hills is one county over. Still within our imaginary circle." They'd figured out when they were looking for the little girl Bailey'd painted that the events she and T.J.'s mother painted were "local," not disasters in Bangladesh, but somewhere within something like a hundred-mile radius of Kavanaugh County. "It's closer than driving to Huntington."

"So we're sayin' we think some mentally ill woman, hospitalized, got away somehow, and was tryin' to escape 'cause someone … on the staff or an orderly, somebody like that, threatened to kill her?" T.J. said.

"Hate to sound like a fortune cookie, but it's not paranoia if the world really is out to get you," Dobbs said. "She wasn't hallucinating or dreaming up the threat. Someone was out to get her—"

"And they got her," Bailey whispered.

"Not yet, they ain't."

"How do we go about finding her … how do we look? It's not like Westminster Acres is a petting zoo." Dobbs took the final swig of his coffee and set the mug on the tray on the table. "We can't show up and ask to talk to every female patient between the ages of—" Dobbs looked at Bailey. "How old?"

"Early twenties. That should narrow it down."

"I can come up with some plausible explanation for needing to talk to some of the patients," Brice said, but didn't look a bit happy about it.

There was a silence.

"What if it's tonight?" Bailey's voice was barely audible. "What if that man is going to—"

"It ain't tonight," T.J. said.

"How do you know that?"

"Cop's gut. Ain't never lied to me. They's times I didn't listen …" He looked pained, and Dobbs wondered if T.J. had been suspicious about the kidnapper who'd snatched the three children but hadn't done anything about it.

He reached over and patted Bailey's knee. "Trust me, it ain't tonight."

Her smile looked like she'd affixed it to her face with roofing nails.

Chapter Seven

THE GAUZE OF SLEEP, falling away in tattered skeins, was still fuzzy-ing her brain when Bailey opened her eyes … and smelled perfume.

Perfume? Here … in her bedroom … why …?

Then she knew.

The girl in the portrait in her studio whose ruined face would haunt Bailey for the rest of her life, was at that moment smelling perfume. Maybe wearing it. Maybe just near someone who was.

And the two of them were … connected.

The smell wasn't overpowering, not like some woman in Walmart who'd doused herself with Blue Waltz, which they sold there by the quart. If this had been the real thing, rather than a knockoff, it was *expensive* perfume. Bailey didn't recognize it specifically, but she could probably have guessed what the real thing would have cost.

Clive Christian No. 1 sold for more than two thousand dollars an ounce, and the Imperial Majesty version cost six times that. This wasn't that, but it was definitely seated in the front of the plane with those fragrances, in first class.

Caron or Chanel or Baccarat. Francis Camail or Annick

Goutal. One of those great houses had created it, and the aroma was … sigh … *enchanting.*

Oh, how Bailey loved perfume, and that was why she never wore it. She was a perfume snob, her tastes waaaay beyond what she could afford. She and her little sister, María, used to spend Saturday afternoons browsing the perfume aisles of high-end department stores just "window shopping." They'd sample one scent after another, dab a little on a wrist or behind an ear, until they finally went nose blind and couldn't tell one from the other. And, of course, the only thing on display for customers to sample were the synthetic knock-offs — often knockoffs of pricy knockoffs — certainly not the four-and-five-thousand-dollar-an-ounce fragrances like Joy, which was made from the oil of ten thousand jasmine flowers.

Lying still, Bailey inhaled deeply — even though she knew that wouldn't enhance the fragrance because she wasn't smelling it through her nose.

This was like the morning she had awakened to the smell of bacon and coffee and for a disorienting few moments had thought her whole two-year nightmare had been just that — a nightmare — and that Aaron really was in the kitchen making breakfast and Bethany was asleep in her crib down the hall. That was before she realized that she was smelling what the little drowned girl in her painting smelled.

The tasteful, understated fragrance slowly faded away and Bailey lay in the still-warm sheets, thoroughly confused. T.J. had been right. The girl whose portrait she'd painted hadn't been murdered last night. She was definitely still alive, probably getting up about now and getting dressed.

And putting on perfume.

So how did a mental patient, institutionalized because she was so out of touch with reality that she believed monsters wanted to eat her eyeballs — how did that girl come by perfume as expensive as what Bailey'd smelled? Even a good knockoff was pricy. Oh, it was possible Bailey had been wrong, that she'd smelled some *cheap* knockoff. But she didn't think so. Bailey knew her perfumes!

She sent out a group text to Brice, Dobbs and T.J., telling them that she still felt connected to the girl who was going to be murdered, knew the girl was still alive. Right now. They still had time …

But the sand was sliding rapidly out the top side of the hourglass.

When Brice picked her up to take her with him to Westminster Acres, she told him about the perfume. He didn't have any explanation for it either, but in truth he didn't appear to be concentrating, seemed distant somehow. That wasn't like him.

Right. Like she knew for certain what was and what wasn't "like" the man she'd met only four months ago — in earth-revolving-around-the-sun time. More like half a lifetime in shared experiences. Only right now … Oh, he was cordial, but as cold as a salmon washed up on the shore of Nova Scotia. They'd have ridden along together in silence if they hadn't passed the entrance to a coal mine. Bailey pulled the handle on that conversational slot machine — "Did you ever work in a coal mine?" — and was rewarded with a lap full of tokens.

"That'd be a *big* no!" He burped out a bleat of laughter. "Guys like me usually don't make very good coal miners."

"Why not?"

He looked surprised.

"You don't know a lot about coal mining, do you?"

"Only what I've seen in movies."

"Ahhh … movies, the source of accurate information about all manner of things. Like police officers and bad guys in shootouts who never run out of ammo. And coal miners — some big dude with his face blacked out slings a pick over his shoulder and rides in an elevator down into a long dark tunnel deep underground. That about right?"

"About."

"Not even close. West Virginia coal mines aren't under the ground beneath your feet." He gestured out the window at the steep mountains rising up all around them. "They're under the mountain you're standing next to."

"So you don't go *down* …?"

"You sit on a train called a mantrip and ride straight in."

"Like a ride at Disneyland?"

"Except longer. Six or seven miles."

"*Miles?* Underground? How do they breathe in there?"

"A fan—"

"What kind of fan can blow air six mi—?"

"It doesn't *blow*. It *sucks*. Bad air out, good air in."

She couldn't imagine what a contraption like that must look like, but she let it go.

"I still don't see why you'd make such a lousy coal miner."

"The miners in *Lord of the Rings* were dwarves — there's a reason for that."

She still wasn't tracking.

"The roofs in these mine shafts are only fifty-two inches off the floor."

She almost choked. "A little over four feet tall? You're kidding! You *are* kidding me, right?"

"Coal miners — even short ones — work bent over, squatting or on their hands and knees."

"Bent over *all day?* Why is the roof only fifty-two inches high?"

"Because the coal seam is *only fifty-two inches thick* and no coal company on the planet is going to dig out the rock above the seam just so the miners can stand up while they work. Moving rock costs money; miners with bad backs can be replaced."

"So you're saying there's no place in the whole mine where you can stand up?"

"Oh, there are places where the roof's taller — but they're usually not a miner's favorite place."

She watched him as he spoke, his face more animated now than it'd been before the mine discussion. His features looked like they'd been chiseled out of stone, solid. No carrot head, his red hair was wine-colored, almost burgundy. Surprisingly, his eyes were brown, not blue, almost caramel-colored. And his face and hands wore an overlay of freckles so close together there seemed hardly any space between. She recalled watching his face as he lay in intensive care after the spider bite that almost killed him. His freckles then had stood out on his pale skin like pepper on a fried egg.

"Okay, I am officially confused. Why wouldn't you like a place where you didn't have to bend over?"

"The roof of a mine shaft is unstable, *caves in*. When that happens, you use the scoop to dig the rock out of the shaft and haul it away. But there's a hole in the roof there, and it's a place you can stand upright."

"Yeah, but you're standing right where the roof just caved in!"

"Now you're getting it. And sometimes, pieces of roof *do* keep falling in the same spot. Roof falls, haul the rock away. Falls again, haul it away again. By the time the roof stabilizes, it could be fifteen, twenty feet off the floor in that spot."

He smiled and she saw the faint hint of a dimple in his right cheek. Funny that she'd never noticed that before.

"One of my deputies told me about a spot in Harlan #7 where the roof was so tall they just left the last pile of rock that fell. It made a little island in the shaft and the miners'd climb up on it to eat their dinner. Called it the 'Break Room.' I think there are a couple of places like that in Last Hope Ollie."

"Last Hope Ollie?"

"After Oliver Northfield lost his shirt in the mining business half a dozen times, his wife finally laid down the law.

'This is your last hope, Ollie,' she told him, so when he filed his claim and mining papers, that's what he named the mine. Made his first million there. Now Mr. W. Maxwell Crenshaw owns it."

"Of Crenshaw Coal Company fame?"

"One and the same."

The impound dam at the top of Turkey Neck Hollow had been owned by C3. Brice had to be thinking the same thing. He'd been right there when the dam exploded. Bailey had been in the hollow below.

They could have died that day, both of them. And very nearly did die the next time Bailey painted a portrait. Would their lives be in danger every time they tried to … change destiny?

Her arms suddenly pebbled in gooseflesh, like ice water was dripping down her spine. She felt an uncanny — and unpleasant — certainty that it would, indeed, be so.

The man with the tattoo and the pinky ring — *that* was a dangerous man. And they were about to mess with him.

Chapter Eight

Brice turned off Miller Pike and wound down a smaller road that had no sign but Brice said it was Cedar Stump Road — which, of course, he knew because he grew up here, while she was an intruding interloper from Away From Here. Half a mile down Cedar Stump Road, they came to a black gate in a wrought-iron fence. Imposing, architecturally at least. Gave a gothic feel to the place. But if there were any other barrier than that, any other fence to keep the crazies in and the rest of the world out, Bailey couldn't see it.

Bailey waited outside while Brice was shown into the office of the hospital administrator.

Hello darkness, my old friend. I've come to talk with you again.

Bailey froze. The music was faint but distinct. Simon and Garfunkel.

… vision softly creeping left its seeds while I was sleeping.

Brice came back, saw the look on her face and asked, "What?"

"'Sound of Silence' … you don't hear it, do you?"

"No, but apparently you do."

The sound faded and was gone.

"Not anymore."

He understood, was silent for a beat, then handed her a lanyard with a tag that said "Visitor" on it. At the door leading into the facility, he punched a button. Bailey heard a dignified buzzer sound on the other side of the door and the knob released.

A woman in a nurse's smock was waiting for them. Bailey was grateful that her smock was not decorated with cartoon figures, as had been the attire of the nurses when she woke up in the hospital after her suicide attempt. This nurse's smock was surgical green.

"The residents are eating lunch right now and they'll be wandering in here as they finish." She gave Brice a look that made it clear she thought he had no business here. "If you need anything," she pointed to the video cameras in all the corners and over the doorways, "big brother's always watching."

After the nurse left, there was only one other person in the room — a smartly dressed woman about fifty-five, wearing a business-style gray pants suit. Her hair was blonde, cut short, and her face looked tired and care worn. But when she saw them, she smiled a small smile.

"Here to see someone in particular, officer, or did you just come to bust the whole lot of them?"

"There are several people we want to talk to," he said in his official Sheriff Brice McGreggor tone, which was off-putting and probably designed to be. Bailey tried to soften the moment.

"Who are you here to see?"

"My daughter, Stephanie." She brightened a little. "You'll probably recognize her when you see her. Everyone says she is the image of me, though I can't see it." She paused for a beat. "She won't recognize me, of course. If we stood side by side in a mirror, she might remark that we kind of look alike, don't we, and isn't that strange."

"She doesn't know you're her mother?"

"If I try to tell her, it upsets her. So I just let her think I'm whoever she wants me to be today. Maybe I'm her mythical friend Martha, who is a fashion designer in New York and who wants her to go there and model clothes. When you see her, you'll know why somebody might actually want her to be a model ... but she doesn't have a friend Martha."

The woman started to speak again, then seemed to realize that she was the only one speaking.

"I'm sorry. I didn't mean to intrude. But there are seldom any other visitors besides me. Chronic patients like these don't have many people left in their lives who haven't given up on them, written them off because of their behavior, or just want to pretend they don't exist." She put out her hand. "I'm Miriam Callahan."

Bailey shook. "Bailey Donahue." Brice just stood there, so Bailey covered for him. "How long has your daughter been here?"

"Almost ten years," Mrs. Callahan said. "There were other institutions before this one. When it first ... started happening, we had her committed — had to, we couldn't handle her. She was only fourteen. My husband and I—" She looked sheepish. "Just me now, he falls into the category of 'pretend they don't exist.' We didn't want to believe someone so young could ..."

The woman looked into Bailey's eyes.

"Is it hard for you? That they change, become somebody else entirely? Don't you think that's the hardest part?"

The sheriff had been standing silently beside her, not a party to the conversation, just in the presence of it, which wasn't like Brice at all. But when she started talking about changing, becoming somebody else, he looked uncomfortable and discovered he wanted a drink of water from the fountain on the other side of the room.

"Actually, we don't know the person we've come to see. I mean, we're looking for someone."

"Who?"

"Uh … we don't know."

Bailey hopped behind the wheel of the cover story they'd concocted and gave it a test drive.

"There's a little boy in Kavanaugh County Memorial Hospital who was in a wreck and he will need multiple surgeries. But he has a very rare blood type, AB negative. Only .6 percent of the population has that type."

"Can't they just give him, O negative? I thought that—"

"The doctors say his weak little body doesn't need to be dealing with non-matched transfusions on top of everything else and they're looking for an AB negative donor. One of the nurses remembered a little girl who was treated for a dog bite in the emergency room there years ago who had that blood type. We're trying to find her."

"And you're looking here because …?"

"We know almost nothing about her. There was a fire in the administrative wing of the hospital about ten years ago that destroyed thousands of records. All we know about the child is what the nurse remembers — her blood type, the fact that she will likely have a good-sized scar on her backside from the dog bite … and she might be mentally ill."

Bailey claimed not to know the details, only that the nurse had said the child had displayed extremely bizarre behavior, might have been autistic, paranoid schizophrenic … who knew?

"And she was a beautiful little girl." Bailey added that part, knew in her gut it was true. "Strikingly beautiful, with honey blonde hair, golden curls. This search is a total shot in the dark, but it's worth a try."

"The person you described could be a lot of people," said the woman. "Could even be my daughter except she's type A positive and she was never bitten by a dog so there's no scar on her butt. Tattoos, but no scar. At least, she believes there are tattoos, thinks she's covered in them, can tell you where she got every one, what the weird symbols mean — she's drawn pictures for me. None of it's true."

She gave Bailey the scraps of a smile.

"Her reality is a pleasant one, not difficult. Life's not difficult when you don't have to deal with the real world."

Bailey nodded, wondering if Stephanie would, indeed, look like her mother. But no one came out of the cafeteria except an old man and a black woman, both of whom looked like they were taking serious medication.

Bailey crossed to where Brice stood like a sentry guarding the water fountain. She tried to engage him, lure him out of the thousand-mile stare he'd worn since he picked her up this morning.

"If Mrs. Callahan's daughter is any indication, the girl we're looking for could be so out of touch with reality it's useless to ask her questions."

"She was lucid enough to—"

He stopped as the nurse who had shown them in came in through the entrance door. But she didn't approach them, and went instead to talk to the woman waiting for her daughter.

"Mrs. Callahan," she said, in that particularly patronizing voice some nurses used, "they're looking for you in C Wing. You should have told someone where you were going."

"I'm waiting for Stephanie," the woman protested, sounding as sane and rational as … as Bailey herself.

"When she comes in, I'll bring her to you. Now, come with me."

The nurse grasped the woman's arm firmly and she went along docilely enough, but turned to look back at Bailey and Brice.

"I hope you find the woman with the rare blood and the butt scar," she said.

Bailey and Brice exchanged a look.

"That was instructive," Brice said.

Other people began to file into the room. None of them could possibly have been the young woman in the portrait. There were several girls about the right age and body type. But one had brown eyes, not blue, and another had real tattoos from head to toe, without a bare spot to call her own on her whole body.

Maybe Stephanie did exist after all.

The most likely candidate was a young woman who immediately began walking around the perimeter of the room, her shoulder dragging along the wall. When Bailey tried to talk to her, the young woman told her that cranberries were out of season and she couldn't have them with the turkey and that was final.

Clearly, that woman was not in possession of enough of her faculties to have decided she was being stalked by a murderer or the presence of mind to run from the threat. They had brief conversations with half a dozen others who only marginally fit the description. Nothing.

On the way back to town, Brice was as taciturn as he had been all day. She couldn't get him to bite, no matter what conversational bait she dangled. Finally, she gave up and they rode in silence. Everybody was entitled to an off day.

"Same time tomorrow for Forest Hills?" Bailey asked when he pulled into her driveway late that afternoon.

He nodded, offered a perfunctory, "See you then," and drove away.

Forest Hills was the old facility, the one where chronic, "incurable" patients were warehoused. Clearly, Brice wanted to go there even less than he'd wanted to go to Westminster Acres.

Bailey shivered, even though the unseasonably warm October weather was holding. The chill she felt had nothing to do with the weather and everything to do with a girl in a white gown running in terror down a hallway.

Would the girl with the golden curls survive the night, wake up to another sunrise in the morning? The clock was ticking. Tomorrow was Thursday. Halloween was Saturday.

51

Chapter Nine

THE SHERIFF DROVE AWAY from the Watford House where he had dropped Bailey off in the driveway, made it down Sycamore Street, turned off on Beckwith Drive and made it almost all the way to Route 27 before he finally had to pull over, fling open his door and vomit violently on the asphalt. The oily fingers of nausea had begun to coil in his guts at the mere mention of Forest Hills Sanitarium yesterday. He had barely eaten anything all day, which was a good thing, because there was less of it to come back up when he couldn't hold onto his visceral response any longer.

He sat there with his car door open, gasping for breath, straining tears rolling down his face. Then he slammed the door. The stink of his own vomit was threatening to make him start heaving again. He sat there then, in his cruiser, listening to the dispatcher.

"Unit Four, see the white female at the Shell Station at the corner of Oakmont Drive and Pearl Avenue. Possible 10-17."

A 10-17 was a domestic disturbance. The Rosewood Apartments were behind the gas station. Ben Phillips in Apartment 3C was obviously already drunk, shoving Sylvia around, and she'd run. Ben must have left work early today.

"Unit Two, respond to a 10-10 at Jeter's Tavern."

Fight in progress. The natives were restless and it wasn't even dark yet. Bet tonight there'd be a full moon.

Listening to the calls soothed him some, helped him swallow back not only the bile in his throat but a bit of the fear in his belly. But not all of it. Not even enough to keep his hands from shaking as he pulled his cruiser back into traffic. Not heading to the sheriff's department in the courthouse. He wasn't ready to face anybody who knew him well, who would instantly spot his pale face for what it was — the face of a man who had just been confronted by the Boogeyman from his childhood that had stalked him day and night since he was seven years old.

HE IS BUILDING A CASTLE, no a fort … yeah, a fort where the good guys in the white hats, like the ones in the vintage western movies he watches with his dad, can make their last stand against the cattle rustlers.

He's building with the special blocks his father made for him. They're wonderful blocks, not the pitiful little things you can buy at a toy store, made out of some kind of pine probably, small enough to fit in your hand and so light and flimsy that building with them is like building with a deck of cards. He used to have a set of those. But then his father, Brice Creighton Drummond McGreggor Jr. — folks called him Drum — had stood in the doorway watching him build, then disappeared into his wood workshop in a room off the garage.

After that, for the next six weeks until his eighth birthday, Drum McGreggor worked in the wood shop almost every night after supper and didn't emerge until hours later. No one was allowed to see what it was he was making, but it was clear he was making something. You could hear the grumble of his heavy table saw, and the shriek of his circular saw eating into a piece of wood. Then the grumbling and shrieking were replaced by the high whirring sound his electric sander made when he used it to smooth some wood surface.

All Brice's life, his father had built things. Drop-leaf tables, chairs, shelves, even a desk — anything to satisfy the woodworking lust of a man who had yearned to be a carpenter but who had been forced into the coal mines to support his family.

Brice only begins to suspect that what his father has been working on for so long has something to do with him when he is shunted off to his grandmother's house to spend the night the day before his birthday.

The next day, he's led into the big basement playroom with his eyes closed.

What he sees at first defies description. It's a set of blocks, of course, but what a paltry description for such a wonder. His father has taken oak two-by-fours and cut them off into six-, eight-, ten- and twelve-inch lengths, then sanded them smooth. There are wooden arches, circles, half arches, triangles, every shape imaginable.

And it isn't just that the blocks are twice as big as a store-bought set of blocks or even that they're made of heavy, sturdy oak rather than pine. What's the most astonishing thing of all is how many there are. Stacks of the different sizes of blocks fill one whole end of the playroom, floor to ceiling, ten feet deep. He thinks there must be ... at least ... six hundred blocks. A later count shows there are actually 850.

There's absolutely nothing Brice can't construct with the blocks. He makes structures big enough that he can fit inside, has a whole town of block structures that he can assemble and disassemble at will. Every kid in town wants to come to his house to play.

The blocks are the best birthday gift he ever got!

And the last one he ever received from his father.

It was after his eighth birthday that his father began to change.

Months pass. Years.

Now, as he sits making a wall out of blocks, he listens to the sounds from upstairs. But he doesn't listen. They don't exist. Except they do.

Screams. Cries.

A human voice making a sound that doesn't have a name.

All the noise comes from the guest bedroom upstairs where the man who'd made Brice the set of blocks, who'd helped him construct the first few buildings with them — where that man lies tied to the bed as he goes completely mad.

It began innocently enough. Always an agile man, his father slowly becomes inexplicably clumsy. So clumsy, in fact, that he cut his hand severely, had to dash to the emergency room for ten stitches, and after that his mother begged him not to work with his tools anymore. At least not until the doctors could figure out why he had suddenly started to walk funny, in a jerky-jerky fashion that didn't look like anything Brice had ever seen before.

Over time, his father began to shake, to twitch all over. He could barely feed himself because the random movements splattered food all over the room.

They were calling it a name by then, but Brice didn't listen and didn't want to know the name. If it had a name, that meant it wasn't something like a cold or the flu that was going to hang around and annoy you for a time and then go away. If it had a name, that meant it was permanent and Brice flatly refused to believe his father would remain as he was forever.

Brice is right about that part. His father doesn't stay like that forever. He gets worse.

His arms fly up, his legs kick out, he has no control over them. He becomes too unstable to walk. Mama puts him in the bed in the guest room upstairs then, and stays home from work to look after him. Without her working, there would have been no food on the table if his grand-mother — his father's mother — hadn't stepped in. She wasn't wealthy, but she had more money than anybody else Brice knew and she kept the wheels on so his mother could stay home and care for his father.

Brice heard his mother and grandmother talking about his father only once. He had come home from school early because of a power outage and found his mother on the back porch sobbing and his grandmother trying to comfort her, saying she understood, she knew how his mother felt.

"I know, I know," she'd said. "When I done it with my Mac, I didn't have nobody to stand with me. You got me. Nobody knew what it was back then. Everyone was afraid of him. At least, now folks under-stand that it's not his fault."

Grandma had looked after his grandfather the same way his mother was now looking after his father, put off for as long as possible "taking him to the asylum." Eventually, his father'd have to go there, too, of course, just like his grandfather, but his mother and grandmother would keep him home as long as they could.

His father forgot Brice's name, called him "Whoopie." He'd go into the guest bedroom where his mother had strapped him to the bed so he couldn't fall out, and his father would make those strange noises and grunt, and then call him Whoopie.

After a while, Brice had stopped going into his father's room at all.

The family moved to Lexington, Kentucky, to his grandmother's house there, where everything was on one floor and they could move his father around in a wheelchair. Brice's mother had told him how sorry she was to move him away from everybody he knew, all his friends. Brice didn't tell her he was glad to move! He hadn't allowed any of his friends to come inside and play with his mountain of blocks since his father started acting crazy. He was ashamed of his father, embarrassed by his condition, and enormously grateful to leave Shadow Rock to live somewhere nobody knew him.

The day they moved his father to the nursing home his grandmother still called "the asylum," Brice hid in his room, hunkered down among the shoes and snow boots in his closet while family members called for him and searched the whole house.

When his cousin Joe found him and ratted out his hiding place, his mother came and kneeled in the closet door, telling him he had to go with the rest of the family to help his father move in.

Brice pitched such a fit, his aunt stayed home with him so he didn't have to go.

But he couldn't avoid going to the asylum to visit his father, walking past the doors of other patients who were tied to their beds like his father was tied to his, people who made horrible, strange sounds and who couldn't control their arms and legs. Or people who didn't move at all, didn't talk, didn't look at anything or anybody.

The man he saw on the few occasions when they forced him to go for a visit was nobody Brice recognized. He was a stranger who only vaguely resembled the man who had made the mountain of blocks for Brice when he was eight.

He was skinny, so thin he might have been one of those prisoners of war he'd seen pictures of in the history books. His hair had gone from carrot-colored red to a dull gray that was the color of nails or the clouds that settled over the valley and drizzled rain for days in the springtime.

The man didn't know Brice's name, didn't recognize his mother or the nurses or his own mother. He was a mean man who screamed obscenities when he used words at all, which wasn't very often. He tried to bite the nurses, so they'd had to use surgical tape around his jaw so he couldn't get it open far enough to hurt them, and then they'd hold him down and take it off and try to feed him, but he never ate a bite that Brice ever saw. He just drooled and slobbered and sometimes cried unconsolably.

When his mother came to pick him up at school in the middle of the day when he was twelve, he knew why. They'd been saying for a long time, whispering so he couldn't hear — as if he were deaf as well as stupid and hadn't known for weeks that his father was dying.

His mother took him out to the car that day, got in, turned to him and said quietly, "Your father is dead, Brice."

Brice's first thought was, "I wonder if I'll be able to cry at the funeral."

HE HAD TRIED NOT to hear the name of the thing that had stolen his father, but over the years it was impossible not to. It wasn't until he was about sixteen, though, that it began to seep into his consciousness the significance of what he'd heard that day he'd come home early from school and found his mother and grandmother talking on the back porch.

His grandmother knew how his mother felt because she'd had to take care of Brice's grandfather when the same thing happened to him.

His grandfather'd had it.

His father had it.

When he was older, Brice looked it up. The thing he wouldn't call by its name for years was a disease with onset between forty and fifty that destroyed brain tissue, taking away faculties, physical abilities, memory, personality and eventually the whole mind. It was caused by a defect in the DNA, on chromosome number four, making it repeat too often. In normal people, it repeated ten to thirty-five times. In people like his father — up to 120 times. The more times it repeated … well, big number, bad case. And the bigger the number, the younger you were when you got it.

The name of the thing was Huntington's disease.

It was hereditary.

Years ago, scientists had developed a test, a way to determine if a person carried the defective gene. If you were a carrier, you would develop the disease. One hundred percent of the time. No exceptions.

Brice had never taken the test.

Chapter Ten

Jocelyn Farrington looked out the big window at the end of the hallway in her wing at Forest Hills Sanitarium, seeming to study the view of the mountains, a stream and the woods beyond.

That wasn't what she was looking at. She wasn't looking at anything, was just staring out into space, trying to organize the jumble of thoughts in her mind, trying to *think.*

It was hard to think when she was so scared!

He would come for her tonight. He'd wanted her to know that, to be terrified all day, waiting. She'd seen him right after the shift change this morning. She'd crept out of her hiding place behind the mop bucket in the storage closet before anybody even reported she was missing, and there he was. The huge orderly had swapped his white uniform for street clothes, was wearing a King's Island Amusement Park t-shirt with the picture of a huge rollercoaster — the Beast — on the front. And bling. Gold necklaces he couldn't wear at work. In his hospital whites, he was only allowed the one ring with the bright, shiny stone. He spotted her, checked to see that nobody was looking, and then drew his finger slowly across his neck.

He'd be back when his shift started tonight at eleven. He'd wait until everyone was asleep … and then he'd come.

She heard the echo of geese honking. She wouldn't have heard them if she'd really been listening to music on her iPod Touch as she appeared to be, the earbuds snug in her ears. She never listened to it, of course. It'd been sent to her like everything else — the watch, earrings, new shoes — by the people who pretended to be her family, but weren't really. She'd been kidnapped from her *real* family and the imposters only sent her gifts to trick her. Of course, she never wore the watch! There was something hidden in the mechanism that would … do something to her. She didn't know what exactly, but something bad.

The iPod had come loaded with music, and she had never listened to any of it, not one time in all the months since the crafts room nurse had shown her how to operate it. Who knows what would be piped into her head along with the music if she actually listened! Did they think she was stupid? So she had loaded her own music, old songs, ones she could remember from when she was little — the ones her *real* parents had liked in her *real* home. She only listened to those, only those! But she pretended to listen to them all, kept the earbuds in her ears all the time so the nurses would think she was listening and couldn't hear their conversations.

The geese overhead honked their lonely song and she looked up into the sky where they flew in a V formation. Why did God implant in birds the ability to fly like that, and yet he allowed only a handful of humans to see the world the way it really was? Only a few knew that the world was inhabited by monsters — real ones, the Revenants. And the Others, who'd brought her here and locked her away in this place. Only a few had been born with Orion's Brand, a red mark that identified them as Ones Who See.

And the number of the few was dwindling daily.

A nurse padded up behind Jocelyn.

"You didn't eat much of your breakfast, Jocelyn," she said.

Had the nurse been trying to sneak up on her, to catch her searching for Revenants in the trees? Jocelyn had learned by bitter experience that when she was scanning for the Revenants that stood in the shadows waiting for nightfall, for a full moon, her own eyes glowed golden, and it was a light "normal people" could see.

The spies the heart-eaters had planted on the sanitarium staff looked for the light, tried to catch you using it. If they did, they'd find a way to take some small piece of you to mark you — a lock of hair, a fingernail, anything that would identify you so the Revenants would know you were not just One Who Sees but a *warrior*.

Revenants could see through walls, find you wherever you hid, hear what you said even in a whisper. And they slipped in sometimes now, stalked the hallways in the moonlight.

It hadn't always been like that. Jocelyn could remember when she had first come here as a child, kidnapped from her parents by the Others to use as a slave for their experiments. Though the Others did terrible things to her when she was strapped down, gave her drugs that made her crazy, this place was at least safe from the Revenants. But days became months that became years and the world darkened. The ancient runes on the doors and windows were losing their protective power. It had been too long since the ancients had put them there, painted in their own blood. Nowhere was safe now.

She turned toward the nurse, removed her earbuds, and smiled. They liked it when you smiled. They thought it meant you were happy.

"I wasn't hungry is all. I don't like oatmeal."

"I saved some fruit for you, in case you get hungry before lunch." The nurse smiled, too, and maybe her smile did mean she was happy. Jocelyn didn't know about that but she could tell she hadn't been caught. Either the nurse hadn't seen her eyes glow or she wasn't a spy.

"What are you listening to?" the nurse asked.

"'Flawless,' by Beyoncé and 'Blank Space,' by Taylor Swift," she said. Jocelyn had never heard either one of those songs, but she'd seen the names listed on the playlist.

"I like Taylor Swift," the nurse said, and went on talking about the singer. It was clear she wasn't a spy for the Revenants, but she might be in league with the big orderly who had caught her last night, knew that she'd seen. The orderly who would come for her tonight if she couldn't escape. Escape *where?* Outside these protected walls were the Revenants! But in here was certain death at the hands of the orderly with the Beast on his shirt.

Her heart began to hammer, her palms grew wet with sweat, but she couldn't let the nurse see. If you got emotional, if you showed fear or seemed upset, they would give you a shot and you'd wake up in that room with leather straps that tied you to the bed. Jocelyn couldn't be tied down! Not now, not tonight, not after what she'd seen when she was on patrol last night.

She crept out of her bed every night after lights-out, stalked the shadows of her ward, made a circuit, checking the dark corners, the puddles of moonlight in the unlighted crafts room and the cafeteria. Always wearing the magic necklace of paper clips she kept hidden in the hollow base of a lamp. Virginia had given it to her. When she wore it, white leopard marks appeared on her body — like thousands of scars — that made her blend into the shadows if a Revenant looked her way. She'd never been in the other wings of the huge hospital. The doors at both ends of her ward only opened from the other side at night.

Her advantage was that Revenants didn't know she could see them in the moonlight. Actually, she couldn't see them, but she could see the spot where they were. She could tell a Revenant was there because the light around their invisibility was different from the light everywhere else. It was a very subtle thing, had taken her years to figure out, but you could see little ripples in the air where a Revenant was standing in the moonlight. A little like looking at the bottom of a still pond and then you toss a pebble into it and the bottom of the pond is still visible there but there are ripples in the water that distort what it looks like. When a Revenant stood in moonlight, the normal light did that, it made ripples as it passed over their crooked, misshapen bodies.

Of course, Virginia could see Revenants anywhere, light, dark, hiding, disguised — it didn't matter. More than that, though, Virginia didn't have to fight them as Jocelyn did. She had the power to kill Revenants with her blank stare. Jocelyn had watched her do it once, stood in awe in Virginia's doorway as she melted a Revenant without even leaving her bed!

So whenever she could, Jocelyn would sneak into Virginia's room and coax her out of bed into a wheelchair. Virginia never looked at anybody — perhaps because she might melt normal people, too, but Jocelyn didn't think that was it. Virginia had never spoken a word to anybody the whole time she had been here, but she talked to Jocelyn, didn't say words out her mouth, of course, but she spoke inside Jocelyn's head.

But Virginia hadn't joined Jocelyn last night, wasn't there when she spotted the Revenant standing in a shaft of moonlight streaming in the crafts room window. She wouldn't engage it unless it tried to take someone's eyes, then she would fight. One on one, she had killed many Revenants. She couldn't fight more than one at a time, though. Even Virginia, the most powerful warrior she'd ever known, couldn't stand up to a hunting pack of them.

When Jocelyn had been in the Dark Place, where she'd hidden for months after the Others kidnapped her, she had watched a pack of Revenants kill the old lady in the room across the hall. They looked at her with their yellow eyes, her blood dripping off their fangs, and listened to her scream as they ate her heart while she was still alive. They'd plucked out her eyes first — they liked blue eyes best — so the old woman couldn't see, but Jocelyn had seen. Jocelyn had screamed and the nurses gave her a shot and locked her in the room strapped down to her bed.

The Revenant last night had been small, though. Jocelyn had been certain she could take it if she had to.

And then the red-haired nurse with bad breath had come in the door at the end of the hallway, left the heavy door to close slowly behind her and lock. But the Revenant slipped through before it did. Jocelyn had followed.

She didn't know any other part of the hospital, but she'd followed, winding through the maze of hallways, around corners, down carpeted passageways and stone floors, down stairs. They passed the big gold archway that led to the glass atrium on the front of the building. She paused to look up at it. Through that archway and beyond was the lobby that opened out into a world full of Revenants.

When they reached the hospital basement, there were no windows, no moonlight, no light at all except for what shone beneath a closed door on the far side of the basement, beyond the metal doors where she could hear the boiler. She moved silently toward the door ... and heard human voices behind it. Men's voices. And the high, keening cry Revenants made when they were hungry.

She was frozen to the spot in terror and horror as soon as she understood. She turned to run, but the door opened before she could get away and the big orderly saw her.

"You, hey you. What are you doing down here?"

He was huge, a giant with hands the size of shovels, his footsteps like hammer blows on the concrete floor as he chased her — clump, clump, clump!

He caught her, grabbed her and demanded to know why she was there, what she'd seen.

What she'd seen, of course, was a room where humans were making a portal for the Revenants, a way around the protective runes on the doors and windows.

She had gotten hysterical, cried, sobbed, begged him not to hurt her. She promised him if he'd let her go, she wouldn't tell anybody what he and those other men were doing in that room.

"You're right about that, sweetheart. You're not going to tell a soul." He had started dragging her back toward the doorway. "I will cut you into little pieces and feed you to—"

To the Revenants!

She fought him, twisting and squirming until she managed to wiggle out of his grasp. She ran away, hid behind boxes in the basement while he looked for her, yelling that he would shut her up, that he'd find her, kill her to keep her silent. She'd sneaked out of the basement, came back up to her ward before dawn, hid in the broom closet.

" ... Jocelyn, did you hear what I said?"

The nurse had been talking about that singer but Jocelyn hadn't been listening. She'd been trying to figure out how she could sneak out of the ward tonight. She could put a piece of tape over the part of the heavy door that locked automatically when it closed. If nobody noticed the tape ...

"I asked if you'd mind having some company after lunch?"

Jocelyn froze.

"Company? Somebody's coming to ... I got a visitor?"

She didn't want to get too excited, expect too much. She'd had visitors before, thought she would have time alone with them so she could explain that she'd been kidnapped, was a prisoner here. Time to plead with them to take her through the land of the Revenants — back home.

But she'd been watched every second so she had no time to tell anybody anything.

"Yes, you do. I told them they could come and talk to you

if you didn't mind, but if you don't want company, I will send them away."

Not want company! Of course, she wanted company. Today! She would tell the visitors about the orderly who was going to kill her and they would rescue her and take her away from here.

"Who is the visitor?" She asked the question as if she didn't care.

"There are two of them. One of them is Brice McGregor. He's the sheriff of Kavanaugh County, and the other is his friend Bailey Donahue. I don't think you know them."

She didn't know them. But a sheriff! Could it really be true that a sheriff wanted to talk to her?

"I don't know them," Jocelyn said, looking at the floor. "But I'm glad for the company if they want to come sit for a spell."

"You need to eat your lunch first."

Ah, that was it. Tell her she had company so she would eat the drugged food and then she wouldn't be able to tell the visitors anything. But she was onto their tricks. She knew where she could stuff food, down into the flower pots in the dining room, into her pockets and then go to the ladies' room and flush it. She knew how to make it look like she'd eaten when really she hadn't.

"I didn't eat much breakfast so I'll be hungry."

"Good. I'll bring them to you when they get here after lunch.

Then the nurse went away and left her alone. Her mind was spinning. Maybe she wasn't going to die tonight after all! Maybe she was going to be set free!

Chapter Eleven

"Just so we're clear on this," said the rodent-faced man who glared at them across a broad cherry desktop that looked like an operating table without a patient — and probably was as clean. "I tried strenuously to dissuade Ms. Strickland from allowing you to come here today."

A sign on the door, "Roderick Styles, Administrator," had identified the office but there was no name plate on the desk. In fact, the office looked as sterile and impersonal as a room at Motel 6. Not a book out of place on the bookshelves, which Bailey suspected were just for show anyway. The titles she could see, *The Complete Works of Shakespeare*, *Moby Dick*, *The Sun Also Rises*, *Paradise Lost* did not seem to her to be the kind of reading material the man in front of her would have selected. He looked more of a Marvel comics kind of reader. Definitely not John Milton. She was sure the interior decorator who'd been hired to make the place seem like the domain of an intelligent, educated, erudite man, had better taste in fiction than Mr. Styles.

"Obviously, you weren't successful," Brice said, cold.

The man bristled and flushed, highlighting the patch of beard on his lower lip that was supposed to look sophisticated.

Without sufficient testosterone to grow out more than a tuft of fuzz, though, it only looked ridiculous. His raging case of Little Man's Syndrome was exacerbated by the presence of a man Brice's size in his office.

When they'd all discussed the local mental hospitals she and Brice should search, Dobbs had suggested they go directly to the owner of Forest Hills — a personal friend of his — bypassing the puffed-up banty rooster sitting in front of them now, which was likely what had ruffled his feathers.

Brice had spoken to the owner earlier in the day. The sanitarium had been founded by her great grandfather, Anthony Garfield Strickland. He had built it here in this out-of-the-way place as a secluded retreat for the wealthy patients it housed, offering the privacy the uber-rich and much-respected East Coast old money crowd demanded for their precious loved ones. Wouldn't want it to get out that there was, ahem, mental illness sprouting somewhere on the family tree.

Though Brice could probably remember the place before it began its decline — and perhaps T.J. and Dobbs could comment upon it in its prime — the 2015 version of Forest Hills Sanitarium in McKinley County, West Virginia was old, seedy and depressing.

Once Brice dropped the name Raymond Dobson, the current owner, Andrea Strickland, couldn't have been more accommodating. Bailey intended to ask Dobbs about that. In truth, she knew little about the histories of the old men who'd shown up at her house in the rain the night she tried to commit suicide. She imagined there were some stories to be told there! But you couldn't very well dig into someone's past without expecting them to dig into yours.

Ms. Strickland didn't ask a single question about the full-of-holes story Brice and Bailey had cooked to explain why they were looking for a young woman whose name they didn't know and whose description they didn't have.

The administrator, however, was not inclined to be so easily satisfied.

"You need to understand that the blood types of our residents is proprietary information which we cannot release to a third party without violating the provisions of the Patient Privacy Act."

"We don't want their blood types," Bailey said. "We just want to ask them a few questions. A dog bite isn't such a casual injury you'd be likely to forget it."

"I don't understand why you have come to believe that one of our residents is the person you're looking for."

"I don't mean to offend," Brice said, though clearly he absolutely *did* mean to offend. Or at least to put the man in his place before he could shoot more holes in their story, which already looked like a colander. "But you don't really have to understand why we want to know what we're asking, Mr. Styles."

The man's face colored again and a vein began to throb in his temple, but he kept his squeaky voice level.

"You're wasting your time, Sheriff. If you had called me instead of Ms. Strickland in the first place, I could have saved us all a lot of trouble. I can assure you there is no one here who can help you."

He started to rise, as if dismissing them.

"Actually," Brice said coldly, "Ms. Strickland gave us the names of two residents who fit the profile of the person we're searching for. We'd like to talk to them."

Styles sat back down before he ever got completely to his feet. A thin glaze of sweat now covered his brow and his upper lip.

"Which two?"

"Jocelyn Farrington and Virginia Mason."

Styles looked like someone had pulled his chair out from under him and he'd landed on his butt on the floor.

"Jocelyn Farrington's mental state is such that ... you can

ask all the questions you want but you can't believe her answers."

"We'll decide what we can and can't believe," Brice said.

The man backed up to punt.

"Very well. I am glad to cooperate with the police in any way I can. I will ask Miss Farrington if she would be willing to talk to you. Her family … can afford her care, but they never visit, no one visits, so she could refuse to see strangers. She can refuse to answer your questions, and even if she does … you don't really understand what you're dealing with here. She has been diagnosed with paranoid schizophrenia, has a whole construct of reality that is totally delusional. Everything she says is a total fabrication."

Brice said nothing for long enough to make the moment uncomfortable. When he spoke, his voice was soft.

"Why are you so determined to discredit whatever Miss Farrington says before the words even leave her mouth? What is it you're afraid she'll say?"

<h1 style="text-align:center">Chapter Twelve</h1>

As Brice and Bailey followed the orderly Styles had summoned to show them to Jocelyn Farrington's room, Bailey inquired under her breath, "Is it a crime to cause somebody to have a stroke — because if it is, you just committed it."

They went down the hall to an elevator and rode it to the second floor. This hallway had more the feel of a "nut house" than Westminster Acres. People crying out, others making unintelligible noises. Bailey glanced into a room as they passed it and a woman there was strapped to the bed, writhing and making sounds that were almost words but not quite.

Brice looked neither right nor left. His face was utterly devoid of expression. Not the look of a face in repose, but a face where every facial muscle was held rigidly in place.

They paused in front of Jocelyn's closed door, thanked the orderly and stood silent until the man was out of earshot.

"You ready for this?" Brice's voice sounded strained, like it was hard for him to engage his vocal cords.

She nodded and started to knock on the door, but he touched her arm.

"You think you'll connect to this girl if she's the right one?"

Bailey had been wondering the same thing herself. The

flashes of connection had been more brilliant with Macy Cosgrove than the ones she'd had after she painted the strangled girl, and there was probably a reason for that, though Bailey couldn't think what. Maybe children were just better connectors; they felt things more easily and more purely. When she'd smelled breakfast cooking, and heard "Country Roads," that wasn't really playing on the radio, it had been distinct, clearly not a real sound from the real world, but a sound that was unmistakable, like a memory.

This time, her flash images had been more vague. The perfume smell had faded so quickly, if she hadn't been a perfume junky, she might not have noticed it at all. And if there'd been an image of some kind to go with it, she hadn't seen it. The music a few minutes ago had been so faded and washed out it was difficult to picture and recall. If she hadn't concentrated, the image would have receded like a dream that's only stored in temporary memory and fades so fast you can't grab hold of it.

She'd heard music a couple of other times, too, but it was so distant it was barely audible. Either it was far away or in another room. She had heard sounds like distant buzzers. Were they the sounds of nurse call buttons in a hospital, or something else entirely?

She could fit all the flashes of connection to the girl who was beyond this door and to this mental hospital, but they would likely fit other places, too.

"Maybe I'll connect. Maybe not. Let's just see what happens."

She knocked and a small voice called out, "Come in."

It wasn't really a hospital room, had more the feel of a dorm room, though the furniture was old and worn, like it had been expensive when purchased and kept in good shape. A standard-sized bed with a flowered bedspread, a desk, two chairs, a book case.

Bailey called up the images the girl saw when the man

threw her to the floor. There'd been piles of clothes on the floor, the closet door ajar. This room was neat, not a sock out of place. Still … change a couple of details and it *could* …

The room definitely had an aroma, a distinct bottled fragrance — Pine-Sol. Smelled like somebody had just used a gallon of it on the floor. The girl could have been wearing the most expensive perfume on the planet and the cleaning compound would have masked it.

There was a girl sitting on the edge of the bed, her back as straight and erect as a piano teacher. She was looking at her hands in her lap, which were wiggling and twisting, like she was trying to get something off them. She had long hair and it was blonde, though it seemed to be a lighter shade than the girl in the portrait. But now she was sitting in the sunlight streaming through a high window. It would look darker with less light.

The girl was coiled as tight as a watch spring.

Bailey waited for the hammer blow of connection, or even a thin tug of recognition. She felt nothing at all.

"They didn't want to let you talk to me, did they?" the girl said. Her voice was soft and she didn't look at them when she spoke. She never stopped wringing her hands, either.

"You're Jocelyn Farrington, is that right?" Brice said.

She looked up then, but didn't meet their eyes, kept her own eyes roaming around on their faces, always moving.

"Yes, and you are a sheriff and his friend and they said you were coming to visit today but I didn't tell them how bad I wanted to talk to you or they would have given me drugs and tied me down with the leather straps in the bed in that room like they always do when they know I've seen something they don't want me to see."

She said the whole thing in one long stream, a single sentence without stopping to catch her breath. Brice and Bailey exchanged a look.

Brice gestured toward the only two chairs in the room and

asked if they could sit. She nodded. Brice sat in a worn wing-back and Bailey sat in the desk chair beside the girl's desk. The desktop had a gooseneck lamp and a pile of papers. The only one she could see was filled with strange shapes, like hieroglyphics. On top of that was an iPod with earbuds attached.

"My name's Brice McGreggor and this is Bailey Donahue. We're glad to meet you."

"Jocelyn. I'm Jocelyn."

She stopped wringing her hands. It seemed to take a great force of will to do it, like she had to grab hold of herself and make her hands be still. Then, with an equal force of will, she moved her eyes slowly up Brice's face until she met his eyes. She only held the look for a second, then looked away. She turned to Bailey then and did the same thing, moved her eyes slowly upward until she was looking Bailey in the eye. She instantly looked away. Then grabbed herself and made herself look back, look deep into Bailey's eyes.

Her eyes were a startling shade of light blue. Then the eyes darted away, like pulling a hand away from a flame. They landed on the papers on the desk and the girl looked alarmed, glanced at Bailey, back at the papers, clearly afraid Bailey'd seen them and …

And what?

Bailey tried to divert her.

"You like music, do you?"

She was looking at her hands again, shook her head, paused, then nodded.

"Some. The old ones."

"Old? Like … Simon and Garfunkel old? 'Sound of Silence,' maybe?"

Jocelyn let out a little cry, a mouse squeak, and relaxed. Something like a strangled sob escaped her and she started to rise. She didn't, though, just sank back on her bed, no longer tense.

"Yes!" she whispered. "And the 'Bridge over Troubled

Water' and 'Eleanor Rigby' and 'Heard It Through the Grapevine' and 'Pretty Woman' and all the old songs ... you're *human*." There was awe and wonder in her voice.

She sat then, just looking at them.

If she'd been listening to 'Sound of Silence' and Bailey heard it through their connection ... why didn't she feel *something*?

Brice looked at Bailey, as if handing the ball off to her.

"I guess you're wondering why we have come to see you today," Bailey began.

"I don't care why you're here. I've only had a few visitors since I was kidnapped and locked up — anybody who shows up is welcome."

"Who kidnapped you?"

"Not the Revenants. The Others."

The Others. The strangled girl had wanted to go home and warn them about the "others."

"All that matters to me is that you *are* here. You're here and you're human and you'll listen to what I have to tell you. You won't let that man come tonight and kill me."

Bailey shot Brice a look.

Yes," she said, "we'll listen."

And for the next half hour they heard a strange tale of creatures that could only be seen by some people, special people, creatures that stalked invisibly among humans, pale lions that took from the herd of humanity those who could not defend themselves. They also hunted people like Jocelyn, the Ones Who See. When they caught you, they took your internal organs, pulled your beating heart from your chest, and ate your eyes — they especially liked blue eyes.

Bailey listened in horror and fascination, wondering what it must be like to see the world as a place with monsters lurking in every corner, waiting to attack and kill you, eat you alive — literally — while you begged them to kill you. She tried to tune out the actual words and concentrate on the girl and the emotions. Tried to connect somehow to this person, tried to match whatever she sensed from her to the panic, the terror of a girl racing down a dark hallway—

Brice squeezed her arm and then interrupted the girl.

"I'm sorry, Jocelyn, would you please repeat that part? Tell me what happened to you last night when you were hunting Revenants in the moonlight."

"It slipped out of the ward and I followed it out into the hospital. I've never been in the other wings, but I kept track of where I was, where to turn, so I could find my way back. We went past that arch, the one you have to pass through to escape."

The girl was searching for a hallway with a golden arch.

"Tell me about the orderly," Brice said. "Describe him."

"He's huge and ugly.

"Does he wear jewelry?"

"Not when he's in hospital whites. Then he just wears the one ring with the sparkling stone."

Bailey tensed.

"He has holes in his face, like he had the measles or acne maybe. And this morning, when he threatened to kill me, he was wearing the Beast."

The girl was running from the "Beast."

"A t-shirt. It's a rollercoaster, I think."

Bailey tried not to flinch, instantly saw the hands encircling the girl's throat.

"He threatened to kill you?"

Jocelyn described her adventure the night before, how the orderly told her he would cut her up — *I should cut you into little pieces with a chainsaw* — and ended by describing the "throat-slicing" gesture the orderly had made when he saw her this morning.

"It's a good thing Virginia didn't go hunting with me last night. Nobody knows what Virginia knows or sees," Jocelyn said. "She's in there in the darkness by herself and she won't let anybody but me in." She paused. "Sometimes we change places with each other and nobody can tell. Identical twins."

Virginia was the other girl they'd come to see, the one who was catatonic.

Jocelyn reached out tentatively and touched Bailey's knee.

"You are ... real," she said. "I can feel it."

Bailey, on the other hand, felt nothing at all. While the girl was talking, Bailey had glanced around the room, looking for anything like the images she'd felt from the connection to the girl in the past few days. She'd been listening for the "sounds" ever since she entered the facility, and it could be that the discreet nurse-call buttons were what she had heard, but she couldn't be sure.

Jocelyn's medical records were sealed so they couldn't find out whether or not she had a scar on her backside, and they couldn't very well ask her to drop her drawers so they could check for themselves. Only one way to find out.

"Jocelyn, I'd like to ask you about scars. Do you have—"

Jocelyn's head snapped up and she looked at Bailey as if Bailey had slapped her.

"No," she said in the pitiful whine of a little child. "Oh, please, no." She began to shake her head. Tears welled in her eyes.

"Jocelyn, are you alright? Did I say something to upset you?"

"You're looking for the necklace that protects me. I should have known. I shouldn't have hoped."

Her lip was quivering but she forced a brave smile. "But you won't find it. Tell the Most High Revenant that you failed, just like the other emissaries he sent to steal it from me."

Jocelyn returned to the rigid posture she'd held when the two of them entered the room. Wound tight. Not looking at them.

Bailey looked at Brice and he shrugged.

"Thank you for your time, Jocelyn," Brice said.

Silence.

The two got up and went to the door. "Let's see what Virginia has to say," Brice said as he opened it.

Jocelyn lifted her head but never made eye contact.

"She won't tell you where it is. Jeni is too smart for all of you."

Bailey's breath caught in her throat.

"What did you call—?"

"Identical twins: Jocelyn and Jeni."

Chapter Thirteen

As soon as they closed the door of Jocelyn's room behind them, Bailey squeezed Brice's arm.

"Did you catch that? Jocelyn and Jeni. That was the last thing the strangled girl said. She called out, '*Jeni.*'"

"Is Jocelyn the one? Did you feel anything?" Brice's tone was brusque, almost demanding. He wanted this hunt to be over!

Well, so did she. But she wasn't sure.

"She ticks a lot of boxes. The song … I heard 'Sound of Silence' in my head while I was waiting for you to bring me the lanyard. And that's what she listens to." She paused. "But I didn't feel anything, no connection."

"Makes sense now that Styles didn't want us to talk to her. He must be in on it."

"In on what?"

"Down in the basement, I'm thinking a meth lab, but maybe just a distribution point for oxy. It's something drug related, and that orderly thinks Jocelyn knows about it. He'll have to silence her."

"But why would he care? Nobody'd believe her if she told."

"The guy who murdered that girl kicked her teeth in. This isn't his first rodeo. Men like that don't take chances."

He pointed down the hallway. Virginia's room was two doors down. Clearly, he wanted to get this done and get out of here.

"Maybe you'll connect to this girl."

But she didn't.

Virginia Mason proved to be exactly as the hospital administrator had described her. She was completely catatonic. No light of any kind in her eyes. She had retreated down so far into herself she probably couldn't even see daylight above.

Bailey couldn't help feeling her skin crawl, looking into those lifeless eyes. She'd painted a catatonic child and the portrait had led her and the others into an unimaginable nightmare. She shrugged it off, tried to feel something, any kind of connection. But there was nothing, though Virginia met the minimum requirements for inclusion on their search list. She had blonde hair, not quite the right color either, but that could be the quality of the light. Her eyes were a muddy blue. It was hard to imagine a girl like this — who walked if you led her, sat down where you put her, opened her mouth for you to feed her and sat where you left her — would be able to summon the mental wherewithal to run from a killer.

Still, looking deep into the girl's vacant eyes, Bailey had a sense that there was an awareness there that understood very well what was going on around her, an awareness that had not been shoved off the deep end into psychosis but had willingly leapt off into nothingness rather than live in a reality too horrifying to countenance.

It was impossible to say what that awareness might or might not be capable of.

The two of them got into the elevator alone and Bailey reached past where Brice's finger hovered over the button with 1 on it toward the green button marked B.

"Let's go have a look at what's in that room some guy's willing to kill for."

"We can't. Our visitor's passes only allow us to enter the public areas of the hospital and specified private rooms."

"Like I give a rip about obeying the fine print on our visitor's passes."

"We can't go barging in like Sherman marching on Atlanta," Brice snapped. He held up one finger. "One, I have no jurisdiction here, absolutely no authority."

"Then we call Sheriff Oliver and—"

He held up a second finger. "Sheriff Oliver has no right to search these premises. And you'd be hard pressed to get a judge to sign off on a search warrant based on the testimony of an institutionalized mental patient."

"But—"

He held up a third finger. "Operations like this one don't exist in a vacuum. It's a sweet setup — a rambling old building out in the middle of nowhere — where a heavy traffic flow in and out wouldn't be noticed by nosey neighbors. This county has a reputation ..."

"You think the sheriff is being paid off—"

"I didn't say that! But I'm certain there's somebody up the food chain from our weasel-ly Mr. Styles who's powerful enough to make things happen. Or make things go away."

"So what do we do?"

"*We* don't do anything. *I* will have a chat with Mr. Styles."

Brice strode through the frosted-glass door marked Offices toward the dignified wood-paneled door marked "Roderick Styles, Administrator."

When she realized he intended to barge right in, Styles's administrative assistant leapt to her feet.

"You can't go in—"

Brice opened the door and found the administrator in a meeting with two men wearing hospital whites. Doctors, probably.

"Excuse me, gentlemen," he said, "I need a word alone with Mr. Styles."

Styles turned the color of a ripe tomato, so outraged he couldn't even find his voice.

"You can't come barging in here like this—"

Brice went to his desk and leaned over it, using all six feet six inches of his body to intimidate.

"I just did. And you *do* want to talk to me … *alone*."

He glared at the little man, who wilted like an out-of-season rose.

"If you'll excuse me, please," he said to the two men, who'd already displayed the good judgment to get up and start toward the door. "I am so sorry for the interruption." He hauled out as much bravado as he could muster. "This won't take long." Tried for authoritative and in charge. Missed by a mile.

As soon as the door closed behind the last white-coated man, Brice said, "I know what's going on in the basement of this building."

The man should definitely never take up the game of poker. All that bright red color drained out of his face and his lip literally began to tremble. He sat, probably because his legs wouldn't hold him upright any longer.

"I don't know what you've heard, but I can assure you—"

"Put a sock in it! Here's how this goes. I talk. You listen." Brice was leaning over the desk again and the man actually looked up at him like a mouse at an eagle. "We clear?"

The man said nothing.

"That was a question. Are. We. Clear?"

"Yes," he said, his voice airless. "Say what you have to say so I can go back—"

Brice had learned from experience that when you were

trying to put the fear of God in a man, less was usually more. Get to the point, blunt and harsh.

"Two things."

Brice looked at his watch.

"Thing One: In exactly twenty-four hours, some good friends of mine in the West Virginia State Health Department are going to conduct a 'surprise inspection' of *every inch of Forest Hills Sanitarium*. Shingles to foundation. Flies on roadkill. With me so far?"

The man couldn't speak.

"You got twenty-four hours to dismantle your little basement enterprise. If I could arrange it sooner, you wouldn't have twenty-four hours.

"Thing Two: This is the biggie. You better start lighting candles to whatever deity you bow to, praying that Jocelyn Farrington never gets another ingrown toenail. That she never has a nosebleed. That she never tweezes her eyebrows too close. Because if I ever find the *slightest mark* on that girl, the tiniest scratch, I will hunt you down and..." He dropped the next four words individually, like single stones into a pool. "Beat. You. To. Death."

He'd bent over as he spoke until his face was level with Styles's.

"We clear, pal?"

Styles nodded his head. Vigorously. But didn't speak. Probably couldn't.

Brice slid into the driver's seat of his cruiser where Bailey'd been waiting for him.

"And...?" she said.

"I just committed a crime, a Class D Felony. Terroristic Threatening. If I have to, I'll take my chances with a jury."

He told her what he had said and done.

"What did Styles do?"

"I don't know. He might have crapped his pants."

That would have been funny under other circumstances, but Bailey couldn't find it in her to laugh.

"So where does that leave us? There is a portrait in my studio of a dead girl who ran away in terror from her murderer before she was beaten and strangled. Was that girl Jocelyn Farrington? Did we prevent a murder?"

"I don't know if we did or not. I do know we did everything we knew to do. The rest is out of our hands."

Chapter Fourteen

BAILEY HADN'T INTENDED to get excited about the birthday party celebration at the Nautilus Casino, had certainly never intended to start looking forward to it! But it'd happened whether she liked it or not, had started renting serious real estate in her head until she finally went out and bought a new dress just for the occasion at the cute little dress shop called the Sassy Fox on Milliken Street. She'd kept the receipt, of course, placed it snug in the zipper pocket of her purse so in the very likely event she was struck by a lightning bolt of buyer's remorse, she could take it back. Of course, she'd tried on so many outfits, she probably wouldn't even need a receipt — the sales lady would definitely recognize her on sight — particularly after she'd selected the shoes, the perfect coup de grâce that sealed the enchantment of the outfit. An exact match to the distinctive green of the dress, the shoes featured *six-inch stiletto heels*, thin as an icepick, made out of shiny chrome with a green rubber tip.

The sales lady had admitted she'd never sold a pair of the shoes because most women couldn't walk in heels that high. Maybe it was being a runner with strong calf muscles, but Bailey had no trouble at all.

When, oh when, had Bailey Donahue last bought anything new to wear? She knew when. Not since … but she was learning the skill of walling off that part of her life, of putting up a barrier with three-foot-thick walls and razor wire on the top, sentries with automatic rifles and attack Dobermans with their sharp teeth filed to razor points. Slowly, painfully, grudgingly, she was beginning to build the semblance of a life on this side of the wall. A *new* life — oh, how she hated that phrase, but it was what it was.

Now, she stood looking at her own reflection in the mirror. The dress was jade green, what her little sister María would have called "slinky" but which she preferred to call "form-fitting"— down to the knee. From the knee to the floor were rows of big puffy ruffles. Like the train on a bride's dress, you could remove the ruffles if you preferred the short version of the dress. Bailey'd picked short because the all-the-way-to-the-floor ruffles completely hid the high heels and she definitely wanted them to show.

She was still a little too thin to maximize the fetching quality of the dress, but she was getting there. No longer rail thin. No longer even skinny. Another five, maybe ten pounds or so and she'd look … yeah, look what? Just like she used to? Not a chance. Her body might one day return to its fundamental shape, but when she looked into the eyes of the face that looked back at her from the mirror she saw a woman fundamentally different from the one who hadn't had a scar on her right temple placed there by a bullet.

She scratched around inside her psyche, trying to regain the excitement she drummed up in her soul for the party, the excitement that'd drained away the instant she saw the portrait she hadn't intended to paint sitting on the easel in her studio.

Now the painting sat behind a closed door, but it might as well have been on display in a lighted frame in her living room.

Was that poor girl Jocelyn Farrington?

Had they found the victim, prevented the murder?

Or not.

She suspected the safer money was on "or not."

She heard a knock on the door — authoritative. Brice was the big Scot even when he knocked on a door. She tried to summon a smile. Nothing. Then she noticed a tear she hadn't cried sliding down her cheek and she blotted it away before she went to let him in.

She'd seen him out of uniform many times, beginning with the day they'd spent in bathing suits, riding jet skis as they searched for the mythical "death boat" that, as it turned out, never existed. She'd seen him in street clothes often as he fought his way back to life after four days on a ventilator, courtesy of a black widow spider. Or maybe a wandering spider. One or the other.

But she had never seen him dressed up. Coat and tie. It was a pretty breathtaking sight.

Six feet six inches of muscle, topped with a face that only missed Pierce Brosnan perfection because the features were stronger than that, the bone structure of his face more angular. The scar on his right cheek from the black widow bite was fading. But it'd always be visible because the skin was slightly indented there.

He looked her up and down and she realized he'd never seen her dressed up, either. His gaze landed on the shiny stiletto heels.

"Those shoes would be considered a deadly weapon in some states. How on earth do you —?"

"Balance. It's all about balance."

"Is it no longer politically correct for a man to whistle at a pretty woman?"

She didn't have time to answer before he produced a ferocious wolf whistle.

"Where did you learn to do *that*?"

"I got skills." He paused. "And one of them is reading people. Not that reading you right now takes any skill. You don't want to go to this party, do you?"

"I have to go."

"No, you don't."

"Yes, I do. T.J. said I did."

"You refuse to let … how did you put it, 'A piece of metal be the hall monitor of your life,' but you let T.J. Hamilton dictate—"

"He's right. Everything in his mother's life was about what she'd painted. Eventually, it destroyed her. I can do the same thing. Or I can … figure out a way to live with it. I'm trying very hard to pick Plan B. Help me out here."

"Maybe I can."

She lifted an eyebrow and waited.

"When I was a little boy, the sweet old lady who lived next door to us found me on the back porch one day, upset about something. I don't remember now what it was, but it wasn't anything that mattered." A look crossed his face she couldn't read because it was there and gone too quickly. But its main component was pain. "I only remember what she said to me about it.

"Li'l Drum …" His face actually flushed. "Middle name's Drummond. You know, when I was a kid …"

Before she could comment, he rushed ahead, mimicking an old lady's voice.

"You need to put that in a garbage bag, pull the strings tight and leave it … oh, by the stairs maybe, or by the door or under that tree you like to climb, just somewhere you can always get to it when you want to.

"I had no idea where she was going. Then she told me, 'The thing is, you *have to* leave it there. You have to put it in that sack and walk away like it doesn't even exist. You can always go back for it, you know where you left it. It'll still be there after you go play ball or ride your bike or chase frogs.'

Then she held out an imaginary garbage bag and had me put my 'trash' in it. 'Now, scat,' she said, and she slapped me on the butt. 'The sack'll be here whenever you want it.'

"And I did. I went out and enjoyed myself … and I went back to whatever I'd been upset about that I'd put in the sack now and then, but … well, you get the picture. She was teaching me how to compartmentalize, how to put the bad stuff somewhere that the stink won't get out and spoil everything else. I've used that technique … often. In Afghanistan, I …"

His face downshifted into grief and loss between one heartbeat and the next.

"All that happened there — it's in a garbage bag … and unfortunately, I go visit it way too often. But I'm not going there tonight. Tonight, I'm going to a birthday party for a pretty lady."

He paused, then extended his hands — holding out an imaginary garbage bag.

"This is where that painting belongs. And after … later, we will *all* get together — all four of us, take it out of the sack *together* and *help you* deal with it."

She took a breath, then dumped very real garbage into his imaginary sack.

Her smile was small, fragile. But it was genuine.

Chapter Fifteen

T.J. AND DOBBS were waiting for them at Joe's Hole Marina, ready to board the launch that would take them across the lake to the Nautilus Casino/Hotel. The complex was owned by W. Maxwell Crenshaw, who also owned Crenshaw Coal Company and, according to T.J., "one out of every two legislators in Charleston, the governor, a supreme court justice or two and the pope."

T.J. and Dobbs, dressed in coats and ties, were a sight to behold. The day T.J. had demonstrated that he could speak without even a hint of West Virginia dialect, she'd told him he was a multifaceted man. Here was another side of the cut stone. Though the suit jacket looked like it probably fit him better when he'd been ten or twenty pounds heavier, he seemed as at home in the attire as he did in the coveralls or jeans and t-shirt he normally wore.

It struck her then, as more a revelation than it should have, that T.J. Hamilton was a man who would be at home in many situations she could not even imagine and — come to think of it — in positions of authority. Yet again, she admonished herself for underestimating the man.

And equally surprising was a debonair Dobbs. Though his

jacket looked like it probably fit him better when he'd been ten or twenty pounds lighter, he wore it well.

"When I bailed out on corporate America, I swore I'd never wear a tie again," was Dobbs's greeting. "These things," he stuck his finger between his tight collar and his neck and grimaced, "were designed by women. Had to be. Not a man alive would think, 'Hey, I know, let's make a garment that cuts off the blood flow to the higher centers of the brain.'"

It was strange, the bond she felt with these men when she knew so little about them. And they knew absolutely nothing about her — nothing true, anyway. She'd given them the Wit Sec rap. Name: Bailey Renee Donahue. Born: thirty-one years ago today, which was the only part of the whole story that was true. Grew up in Phoenix, moved to Oklahoma to live with her grandparents when her parents were killed in a traffic accident, graduated from Ardmore High School, then Arizona State University in Tempe, then landed a job with Timberland Publishing as a graphic artist to illustrate medical textbooks. She'd moved to West Virginia for a change of scenery. All very plausible, and all a load of the wet, sticky substance you find on the south side of a horse going north.

In truth, none of them had ever plied her with questions about her past and she sometimes wondered why not, but it wasn't a scab she picked at. Given that two of the three of them were or had been police officers, she suspected they might have guessed the truth in the very beginning.

All the men told her how lovely she looked. And, of course, T.J. had something to say about her shoes.

"Rubber tip comes off them heels, you gonna poke a hole in the bottom of the boat."

She recalled the woman she'd seen standing in the mirror before she left the house, thought about the portrait of —

Leave it in the sack!

"With the three of you on my arm, metaphorically speaking, I'll be the envy of every woman on the boat." She looked around her. "If this crowd is any indication, that's going to be a lot of people."

"Oh, this isn't the only launch," Dobbs said.

"Launches operate from the other three marinas on this side of the lake, too: Westbrook, Tucker's Landing and Blackfoot."

"I s'pect the crowds won't be on the launches," T.J. said. "Folks drive here from Pittsburgh, even Cleveland — Cincinnati, Louisville ... or from small towns in three states, with the rent money in their pockets and a gleam in their eyes."

"Crenshaw built his own airstrip, ferries guests from the airport by chopper to the helipad on the top of the casino," Brice said. "Which means you're likely to run into just about anybody here. You might be able to add to your Famous-Faces-I-Have-Seen or your Brushes-With-Greatness lists. Movie stars. Politicians. People who are famous for being famous like the Kardashians."

"The lady at the dry cleaners the other day claimed a K sighting," T.J. said. "But she also left a stain on this suit jacket, so her vision is suspect."

"This must be quite a place," Bailey said, genuinely impressed.

All three men rolled their eyes.

"You have no idea," Dobbs said, his voice soft. "No. Idea."

Though Brice had pointed out the casino to her when they were riding jet skis on the lake last summer, it had been a long way away. As the launch drew closer, Bailey's eyes grew wider.

"I never dreamed ..." she said.

"Tryin' to imagine this place is like Wiley Coyote leapin' across a canyon. No matter how hard you try, you always fall short."

The most striking feature of the Nautilus Casino and Resort Hotel complex —though the nearer they got, the harder it was to pick out the most striking feature — was how it had managed not to come off as too flashy. It wasn't garish or tacky. Bailey had once driven down "the strip" in Las Vegas, in the company of two federal marshals who had only hours before swooped down on her in the middle of the night and whisked her out of Albuquerque. The Las Vegas casinos had been tasteless and gaudy —flashing lights and animated figures in tacky neon. The elements added like children tossing tinsel on a Christmas tree. Nothing matched anything, everything was too much, too bright, too glaring, too showy.

Not so the Nautilus. It was spectacularly tasteful. Even with the requisite bright lights, it managed to remain elegant and stylish, aesthetically pleasing. Unimaginable millions had been invested in making it both elegant enough to appeal to the cultured upper crust while seeming accessible to the plebeians who'd come to hand over money they'd actually worked to earn. Clearly, "management" had spared no expense. You almost believed they could pull off the marketing slogan stitched in lights in tasteful calligraphy on the golden archway over the entrance — *Your Every Desire Fulfilled.* Beyond lay the bank of doors that stood open to welcome the world ... and to suck it dry.

The Nautilus Casino and Resort Hotel resembled a gigantic crystalline punch bowl and its walls sparkled like the exquisite cut-glass of a chandelier. There were three floors of casinos on the bottom, topped with three floors of ultra-pricy hotel rooms. The facility was built around a center axis that was transparent and featured snakes of glass-sided elevators speeding up and down like blood coursing to and from the brain.

The casinos and hotel rooms were built in a circle that overlooked the first floor atrium. Hotel rooms on the inside of the circle had balconies where guests could watch kids swimming in a pool, dancers in the Sea Shell Night Club or elegantly dressed guests in the Nautilus Restaurant below. Hotel rooms on the other side of the hall featured balconies providing spectacular views of the lake and the mountains.

Brice had told her that the Nautilus Restaurant was encircled by a ring of "gaming opportunities" ... so it was impossible to walk into the restaurant no matter which of the three entrances you chose, without passing rows and rows of slot machines, blackjack or roulette tables ready to pick your pockets.

Clearly this was a "floating" casino in name only. It might extend out into the lake and be connected to the landward side only with gangplanks, but that central pole structure supported the building and its roots had surely been sunk hundreds of feet into the bedrock below.

Still, in keeping with the pretense of a "boat," the bottom floor where the restaurant was located was surrounded by decking. There were slips for the launches, and spaces for private boats, houseboats and similar large lake craft to tie up for a night on the town. Fifty yards of gangplank led to the shore parking lot where locals from this side of the lake as well as those who'd driven down from Pittsburgh or flown into the airport boarded.

On the other side of the parking lot was an additional hotel with rooms where a night's stay didn't cost more than a month's wages. Brice and FBI Agent Nakamura had questioned a church choir director in that hotel, but it turned out he wasn't the kidnapper they were looking for.

The gangplank leading from the boat slips onto the deck surrounding the casino was covered in red carpet, lighted on the edges with colored beams that shown like light sabers up to a metal rail so they looked like the spokes of the railing. And they pulsed as a heartbeat, keeping time to the music that floated on the cool October air. Beyond it, the deck itself was edged in green light, as if from thousands of shining emeralds imbedded in the floor.

After passing through the first-floor ring of casino games, Dobbs spoke to the concierge at the entrance to the restaurant and the four of them were shown to their table. Aquariums inset in the walls of the circular restaurant were filled with untold numbers, colors and varieties of tropical fish, creating the illusion of dining with Captain Nemo somewhere at the bottom of the ocean.

Seated in velvet luxury, Bailey had to admit that the opulence was the kind that seemed to rub off, that she felt elegant just being here.

"Your Every Desire Fulfilled" was embossed in gold on the front of the menus, which had more pages than the phone books in several towns where Bailey'd lived.

"My desire is for somebody to order for me," she said.

"That's what the waiter gets paid the big bucks for," Dobbs said as if he were totally at home in the environment — which, given the millions he so studiously pretended didn't exist, he probably was. "He will cheerfully direct you to the most expensive items available. You won't know what they are, but for the prices they'll be charging, whatever they are, you'll like them."

"I'm gone tell them this is your birthday," T.J. said, and it seemed he was accentuating his dialect — subtly thumbing his nose at the opulence. "Get all the servers to gather 'round clappin', singin' Happy Birthday To You."

"And then give you miniature cake with a sparkler," Brice added.

"Oh, they know it's her birthday," Dobbs said with an enigmatic smile that made Bailey's stomach clutch. He'd made the reservations, would be paying the tab, and heaven only knew what he'd set up.

Her signature WPPP — Witness Protection Program paranoia — reared its head for the first time in a long while. When she'd first been tossed with a new name into an anonymous pond, she'd imagined every third fish that swam by was a shark, spent a month looking over her shoulder, fearing to see the specter of a man in a fedora, with a gray beard and an eye patch sneaking up behind her. She gradually accepted the truth of the words the marshal used to sooth her: "Relax. Nobody goes looking for somebody they think is dead."

But he nevertheless cautioned against notoriety, against becoming the center of attention with all eyes on her. It was not likely, but it was *possible* that somebody from her own past would spot her — college friend or a former neighbor. That would be disastrous.

"Dobbs, please, please tell me you haven't arranged some spectacular show, with a full orchestra and a cast of thousands performing for my personal enjoyment right here in the restaurant. Please—"

He held up his hands in protest.

"A group picture and a birthday cake — with candles, so you can make a wish."

She thought of Aaron, who'd wished on the candles of Bethany's first birthday cake to be the official candle-blower-outer at her every birthday celebration. Six months later, he was dead.

Leave it in the sack.

She was going to need a bigger sack.

"No banners or fireworks." Brice smiled. "They don't cater to special occasions."

No Easter bunnies or Santas here.

Or Halloween spooks.

This year, you won't need a mask to go trick-or-treating.

She shivered, though there was no cool breeze. Tomorrow was Halloween.

Chapter Sixteen

BAILEY HAD two glasses of "their finest wine," which likely cost more than the gross national product of some Third World countries, and it granted her a pleasant buzz. No sharp edges on anything; the world was painted in a soft, golden glow.

She smiled prettily when the photographer gathered the others around her for a group photo, then listened to the men engage in an unspoken game of can-you-top-this? with stories about coal mining. T.J. had spent "the most instructive year of my life" between the army and college working in the mines. Dobbs had "gone down" every summer after high school "until I made enough money to buy the dad-gum mine."

With Dobbs and T.J. seated across from each other, it was like watching a tennis match.

"The famous Oliver Northfield was just a red-hat miner when I first—" Dobbs began.

Bailey held up her hand. "*Red hat?*" She looked from Dobbs to T.J. "Translate."

"Miners with less than six months' experience have to wear red helmets so the other miners—"

"Can run when they see 'em comin'," T.J. finished for him.

"This is my story and I'll thank you to stop shanghaiing it."

Dobbs cleared his throat like an orator. "Oliver Northfield made his first million—"

"In a dog-hole mine—"

"*Dog* hole?" Bailey asked. "Is there like a *Coal Mining for Dummies* I could download so—"

"A dog-hole mine's no better'n a hole dug by a dog," T.J. said. "Run on a shoestring, cuttin' corners. The methane meters in dog-hole mines ain't no more reliable than an alimony check. I never seen a single meter wasn't stuck in the red zone."

"Methane … hold on while I look that up in my Dummies book."

"Methane gas is released when you dig into coal and it's *extremely* volatile," Dobbs said, wrenching the narrative back to his side of the table. "You can't smell it—"

"That's what mine canaries are for," Brice stage-whispered. "And methane meters."

"You never even know it's there until—" Dobbs began.

"—a spark from a light—"

"The lights are spark-less sodium—"

"A spark from *something* blows pieces of you all over three states," T.J. finished for him. He picked up the surely-it-wasn't-*real*-silver butter knife and stabbed it into the pale yellow dollop on a crystal dish in the center of the table. "But that mine'd a'been a death trap even if it'd been run right. You know there had to be old works—"

"Ding, ding, ding!" Bailey said. "*Old works?*"

"Miners started digging coal in West Virginia two hundred years ago," Brice said, as T.J. smeared butter on a still-warm dinner roll. "The mountains are riddled with mines so old nobody remembers them, hundreds of unmapped shafts you could accidentally dig into."

"And that'd be a bad thing because …?"

"An empty mine shaft don't stay empty, fills up with stuff

and ain't none of it good." T.J. took a bite of the roll. "Explosive gases or ones that ain't explosive but just as deadly."

"Like carbon dioxide," Dobbs said. "And don't talk while you're chewing."

"CO2 ain't poisonous but it ain't oxygen neither and you can't breathe it. You just collapse, flop 'round like a fish on the shore, gaspin'."

Bailey shivered at the image

"Old Works can fill up with water, too," Dobbs said.

"And that water don't trickle all gentle like a leaky faucet into the shaft," T.J. said, swallowed the bite of dinner roll and washed it down. "Hundreds of thousands of gallons of water …" He gestured with his water glass. "You stick a hole in the bottom of it and *whoosh!*"

"I'm having trouble picturing this," Bailey said. "Miners get on this mantrip train thingy," she glanced at Brice and he nodded his approval that she'd remembered his explanation, "and go straight into the mountain through a shaft—"

"Shaf*ts*. Plural, as in more than one," T.J. said.

T.J. and Dobbs exchanged a look, then Dobbs reached out, emptied the sugar cubes in the bowl onto the tablecloth and both T.J. and Bailey stiffened, looked up and caught each other's eye. Bailey'd been drugged once with a sugar cube like the ones Dobbs was arranging in some kind of pattern on the table in front of him.

"If I'd known you still played with blocks I'd a'got you some for your birthday," T.J. commented.

Bailey happened to glance at Brice and his face went rigid at the remark, every muscle tightened so there was no expression at all.

Dobbs quickly built a solid platform of sugar cubes, six across and six down, no spaces in between, and then set the sugar bowl on the platform.

"Instead of a mountain on top of the coal seam," he said

in his made-for-radio voice, "let's pretend it's a building." He pointed to the sugar bowl. "*This* is the building."

"If a mountain was a building, it'd have to be two hundred fifty floors tall," T.J. pointed out.

"Fine. A two-hundred-fifty-floor building—"

"That's twenty miles long and fifteen miles wide."

Dobbs gave T.J. a look.

"You want to explain this?"

"You doin' jest fine, go on ahead."

"If you'll hush up long enough—"

"So this is a two-hundred-fifty-story building …" Bailey prompted, pointing to the sugar bowl perched atop the layer of sugar cubes.

"And let's pretend it's sitting on a base of solid gold, four feet thick." Dobbs indicated the sugar cubes. "How would you get the gold out from under the building?"

"Dig it out from the side, I guess," Bailey ventured.

"Give that a shot," Dobbs said.

Bailey began to carefully remove sugar cubes from beneath the sugar bowl but she'd only taken a few before the sugar bowl toppled over on its side.

"Dig into the gold and just start hauling it away, and pretty soon the building will collapse on top of you," Brice said.

"Point made." Bailey started to replace the sugar cubes and bowl.

"Let's leave the 'building' off so you can see the mine from above," Dobbs said.

He took the bowl and set it aside, then pointed to the solid square of sugar cubes.

"What if you dug into the side but didn't take out *all* the gold like you just did? What if you left big hunks of it behind to hold up the building while you removed all the gold around the hunks?"

He began to remove *every other* sugar cube, leaving an

empty space between them. When he was finished, he set the sugar bowl back on top and it sat stable.

"Bravo!" Bailey cheered.

Removing the bowl again to reveal the sugar cubes, he pointed to the empty spaces.

"These are the *plural* mine shafts. The crossways shafts go from one side of the mine to the other. The longways shafts, which are three times as big, cut through the mountain from the front of the mine to the face."

"A mine has a face?"

"The face is where they're digging. So it gets farther and farther away from the front of the mine the deeper they dig."

T.J. plucked a stray thread a couple of inches long off the front of his seldom-used suit jacket and stretched it out down the middle of the center mine shaft.

"That's the belt line, a conveyor belt that carries the coal from where they're digging it out at the face down 'Main Street' to load on trucks out front."

Dobbs pointed to the mine shaft on the right of Main Street. "That's Broadway," and on the left, "that's Boardwalk."

"They name the shafts?" Bailey said, delighted. "Monopoly. I love that!"

"Just those three, the same in every mine. The cross shafts that run crossways are numbered, starting at the front."

Dobbs looked around on the table, lifted his napkin, scanned the condiments in the center of the table.

"What are you looking for?" Bailey asked.

He sighed, reached into the bowl where the dregs of his salad still resided, picked up a piece of lettuce and tore off several pieces about the size of fingernails.

T.J. wagged his finger reproachfully. "If your mama saw you doin' that, she'd snatch you baldheaded."

"Said the man who talks with his mouth full," Dobbs said as he reached out to the sugar-cube coal mine and placed a piece of lettuce in each one of the crossways shafts all the way down both sides of the longways shaft called Broadway.

"The fans that get air to the miners—"

"Brice already told me, they don't blow, they suck. What does that have to do with the salad that's plugging up the cross shafts along this shaft? The miners ... what? Wanted to spiff the place up, so they hung some *curtains*?"

"Bingo!" Dobbs cried so abruptly it startled her, then held out his fist to hers to bump. "That's exactly right! Huge pieces of plastic sheeting that stretch all the way across a cross shaft *block the air flow*, force the air back into the shaft." Bailey wrinkled her brow, so he explained further. "If it was water, the curtains are little dams that make the water go straight down the shaft to the face; you need the air where the miners are digging, have to suck out that methane. You can move the plastic around," he picked up two pieces of soggy lettuce and moved them to different cross shafts, "to direct the air flow anywhere you want it to go."

"So the air is sucked in the front of the mine, flows around and around the tunnels in the maze directed by the little dams ... the *curtains* ... and then out the back?"

"*In* the front of the mine, yes," T.J. said. "And back *out the other side of the front*. Coal mines is only open on one end. They ain't got no back doors."

"Last Hope #2 does," Brice put in, affecting the tone of a querulous child contradicting the expert.

T.J. rolled his eyes and Dobbs could see Bailey's eyes beginning to glaze over.

"When the coal seam on #1 petered out, Northfield went around to the opposite side of the mountain and started digging #2 there." He was trying to make it simple.

"So like the continental railroad, the two shafts met in the middle and there's an opening on both ends."

"Close, but no cigar," T.J. said. "Last Hope Ollie #2 is

open at both ends, but it's *under* #1, with an elevator that connects 'em."

Brice grinned at Bailey. "See! *There's* that elevator you saw in the coal mine movie!"

Dobbs and T.J. began to argue about the court order only a month ago that had closed both mines — now owned by Maxwell Crenshaw's coal company.

"Froze all the assets — miners workin' that day just got up and walked out, left equipment where it was sittin'," she heard T.J. say before she excused herself and asked the waiter to direct her to the ladies' room. She was *done* with sugar-cube coal mines.

She became aware of the Muzak that'd been playing since they arrived, the musical canvas on which the atmosphere was painted. Like everything else, it was so tastefully subtle you didn't notice, an orchestrated remake of old rock songs. As she crossed the dining room toward the ladies' room, "Hey Jude" morphed into "Let it Be."

The music was muffled by the soft, tasteful whoosh of the ladies' room door closing behind her. She stood in a … what would you call this room? A "parlor" adjacent to the facilities, as richly appointed as any luxury apartment she'd ever seen pictured in *Better Homes and Gardens.* Tasteful wingback chairs, loveseats, delicately carved tables with Tiffany lamps. There was a maid, whisking up imaginary trash off the immaculate carpet.

She admitted to a shade of disappointment that the toilets themselves were not gilded in some way. She'd read that Queen Elizabeth had a special seat made for the royal tush. But the water spigots were gold-colored and the water flowed out of them down a golden trough into your hands.

As she crossed the parlor on her way out, a woman seated in front of a small table she hadn't noticed before asked, "Would you like to freshen up your fingernail polish?"

Seriously?

Bailey was probably in an ever-shrinking population of those-dubbed-not-sufficiently-female because she had never in her life had a manicure or pedicure. She hesitated. The woman pointed to a contraption that appeared to be the love child of a miniature sun bed and a blow dryer.

"They'll be dry in less than four minutes."

It *was* her birthday, after all. By golly, she had a spare four minutes to spend being pampered. She sat down in the chair and offered her hand. The woman placed her wrist on a towel and lowered her fingers into the water in a bowl that was, like everything else within sight, ornate but tasteful, expensive-looking without being gauche, and colored gold. The instant Bailey touched the bowl, the world vanished.

Chapter Seventeen

BAILEY IS SEATED in front of what is clearly designed to be a retro slot machine, a replica of the simpler machines of days gone by, made of metal so shiny you can see your reflection on its surface. Resting on the top is a lone red light that looks like it was lifted off the top of a 1950s-era police cruiser. Across the front are the words Crazy Diamonds.

The screen displays three columns, each with revolving rows of images that have to match across all three columns for a win. The first column shows half a watermelon on top, the center row has two cherries and the bottom row has a big yellow diamond. In the next column, the top image is a cluster of grapes, below it half a watermelon and a lemon on the bottom. The third column displays a bell on the top, matches the cherries in the first column in the center but has a number nine at the bottom.

She can hear "Hey Jude" fade to become "I Want To Hold Your Hand," though it is muffled by the clanging of nearby machines. A sweet scent is barely detectable — perfume, its fragrance rich but subtle. It might not be a cheap knockoff after all.

Then there is a sudden loud Clang! Clang! Clang! Colored lights reflect off the chrome surfaces on the machine in front of her from the revolving light on the machine next to it. A woman's voice squeals in delight and there is the sound of coins gushing out of the machine into the metal tray.

The hand reaches out and takes hold of the red knob on the lever on the right side of the machine — and pulls the lever down. The revolving rows spin ... spin ... spin. Then stop. Three cherries match in two of the columns on the bottom row, but the third image is a cluster of grapes. None of the other images match. The hand puts a token in the slot at the top of the machine. The hand is perfectly manicured and has rings on the index finger and the ring finger with rocks in them the size of raisins. If they're not cubic zirconia ...

She pulls the lever and the rows begin to spin again.

And then the image fades. Bailey can still see the machine — this time isn't a win either — but she can see through the image to the mini table that contains a dozen different colored bottles of fingernail polish where she has placed her own hand.

THEN THE IMAGE was gone altogether and Bailey was back in the real world. She heard the manicurist ask her what color she'd like, her tone implying this wasn't the first time she'd asked.

Yanking her fingers out of the bowl of water so frantically she splattered it into the manicurist's lap, Bailey jumped to her feet and ran out of the bathroom, momentarily disoriented in the huge dining room. When she spotted her table, she raced toward it, turning sideways to edge around chairs, almost colliding with a waiter who carried a tray with drinks balanced on his upturned palm.

"I saw her!" she cried, interrupting an argument about Ben Roethlisberger, the Pittsburgh Steelers quarterback.

"Saw who?" Brice asked.

"The girl in the painting."

"The girl in the painting was in the bathroom?" Dobbs said.

"No, no. I *saw* her, like when I saw Macy after I touched the Adirondack chair."

"Sit down, Bailey," Brice told her in his official, don't-argue-with-me voice. She sat. "And slow down. What did you see?"

She tried to do as directed, but couldn't manage anything after the sitting-down part. Her words continued to pour out in a waterfall torrent.

"I stopped at the manicurist station and when I touched the bowl of water on the table, I saw her. A vision. Like watching Macy Cosgrove get her hand stamped at the carnival. *She's here!* Right now. She's playing a slot machine. We have to find her."

"Some mental patient's here?" T.J. was incredulous. "Her ward at the hospital's takin' a field trip?"

"I don't know why a crazy woman would be here. I just know *she is*! We have to find her."

She started to rise but Brice put a restraining hand gently on her arm.

"Find her and — what?"

"Warn her, tell her she's going to be …" Her voice trailed off as she realized what she was suggesting. Then she shook off the doubt. "Warn her she's going to be murdered." She held up a restraining hand at the protests from all the men at the table, voiced with the perfect unison of a Greek chorus. "I know that sounds crazy. But we have to do *something*. Right this minute, there's a girl playing a slot machine out there," she pointed to the archway that led from the restaurant out to the banks of machines in the encircling casino, "who is going to be strangled."

Dobbs was still stuck on the mental patient part. "How did a patient—?"

"She may be nutty as a Christmas fruitcake, paranoid schizophrenic or whatever. But she didn't *imagine* her own murder. She's going to be strangled, beaten …"

She lost her breath for a moment as some of the images washed over her again. The broken wrist. How bad it hurt.

"Think it though, Bailey," Brice said. "If you find her—"

"I'll find her."

"You know how many slot machines there is—?" T.J. began.

"She's playing a particular kind of slot machine. I saw them when we came in. There's a single row of them right outside the door of the restaurant. They're old-fashioned, vintage, designed to look like historic machines. How many freckled girls the right age and blonde could there be in a row of — what? Twenty-five? Fifty slot machines? I know I can find her."

"So you find her," Brice said. "What are you going to say to her?"

"I'm going to ... tell her she's in danger and ..." She remembered the look on Macy Cosgrove's mother's face when she stood on the porch of the woman's house and told her the dam was going to explode. "And yeah, I'm going to sound like a raving lunatic. You got any better ideas?"

The men looked at each other. No one spoke.

"I didn't think so."

"Bailey, what good will it do to warn her?" Brice said. "What would *you* do if a total stranger came up to you in a crowded place and told you that you were going to be murdered?"

"Even if she did b'lieve you — and ain't no possible reason why she would — what's she s'posed to do about it? What would you do to keep from bein' murdered?"

"I don't know." Then she brightened.

"The man ... the Beast ... he had that skull tattoo on his wrist. And the pinky ring."

She looked at Brice.

"Aren't most murder victims killed by somebody they know? Is that real or cop-show fiction?"

"It's real."

"I s'pect she knows him. Least he knows *her.* What he done to that girl ... that was personal."

"Then a warning *would* matter. If she knows the guy who's going to kill her, she could ... oh, I don't know what ... do *something* to avoid it."

"If she's mentally stable enough to process what you tell her." Ever-reasonable Dobbs reached out and covered her small hand with his big one. "From what you've told us about her, that sounds unlikely. But let's say she is. Let's say she believed you and she knows the guy with the tattoo. A warning might—"

She rose from the table before he finished. The girl had been at the slot machines playing, but how long would she remain there? And if Bailey didn't find her there, in a crowd of people this big, she would never locate her.

The three men started to rise.

"No, you can't come with me. I'm going to sound crazy enough. We can't descend on her like a swarm of bees. I need to go alone."

Chapter Eighteen

BAILEY MANAGED to hold her emotions in check enough not to bowl over the waiter, who was returning to the table to deliver the next in she knew not how many courses of the meal. She didn't recognize it, hadn't recognized the two courses before it and knew she wouldn't be tasting anything else she ate tonight.

Hurrying across the dining room, negotiating a zigzagging path around tables and chairs and servers, she got to the archway that led into the casino. Along the wall on both sides of the archway was a double row of the vintage slot machines she had noticed when they'd passed through the casino on their way to the dining room — Crazy Diamonds. She turned to her right and walked between the rows. Many of the machines were occupied, but not all. The first few machines against the wall were not in use. The ones to her left were, though, with a gaggle of young women — half a dozen or so who were obviously together and in various stages of inebriation. They talked and laughed too loud, squealing in delight every time they got a match, even if it wasn't a win. Beyond them on that side were two men, on the wall side was a woman, older and overweight, and three men. Bailey passed slowly between the rows of machines, scrutinizing every player. Another woman, but she was black, on the wall side. Three women occupied the next two machines, older ladies, two playing, one just watching.

When Bailey got to the end of the rows of machines at the archway on the far side of the casino where they had entered, she heard a clanging bell and an explosion of squealing from the group of young women she had passed earlier. Standing beneath the casino's entrance archway was Brice. He merely nodded at her, letting her know he was there if she needed him.

She crossed the wide aisle in front of him and plunged down between the double rows of machines on the other side of the arch. Almost every one was occupied. Men and women, old and young, staring at the spinning rows of cherries, lemons, watermelons, grapes, numbers and diamonds, feeding the ravenous machines tokens, pulling on the one-armed-bandit's shiny lever topped by a red ball.

And then she spotted a young woman. Blonde.

Time slowed down.

There was a man standing behind her. He was tall and slender, definitely not the man who'd killed the girl in her vision. He appeared to be accompanying this young woman, her date maybe, but he was engaged in an animated phone conversation and paying no attention to her. The machine on the other side of the woman was empty and Bailey sat down there.

"Eleanor Rigby" floated out above the banging and clanging, voices and laughter.

A scent as sweet as a garden of flowers filled her nostrils.

Bailey's heart had slowed with the elongation of time, the stretched-out seconds, but now it became a jackhammer trying to dig a hole in the wall of her chest.

This was her.

She was wearing a flowing white dress of some gossamer fabric that shimmered in the sparkling lights. Achingly lovely, her features were small and delicate, as perfect as if her eyes, nose and mouth had been painted on a china doll. Even though the hair of the girl in the painting had been clotted with blood, it was clearly honey blonde. Just like this girl's. Honey blonde hair and freckles.

THE MAN GRABS her by the hair as she lies on the floor and yanks hard, pulls out a huge handful and drops it on the floor in front of her.

"Stand up or I'll drag you."

BAILEY LOST her breath and felt suddenly dizzy, sick to her stomach. The girl sitting next to her — breathing, heart beating, so very much alive — was going to *die*. Soon. Her only hope of survival lay in Bailey's ability to convince her she was in danger.

The man glanced over his shoulder at the girl as he spoke, and with that one look established possession. She was with him. No, more than that: she was *his*. And he would hear anything Bailey said to her. But she had to say something, do *something*. This moment would pass. The girl would tire of the machine or the man would finish his phone conversation and the opportunity would be lost.

What could she—?

Bailey opened the purse and scratched around inside it for something to write on. She found it in the zipper pocket — the receipt for the new birthday dress, insurance against a flaming case of buyer's remorse.

Her hands were trembling, but she willed them to steady. She took a pen from the purse, flattened the small piece of paper on the slanted area on the slot machine below the rows of not-spinning fruit. Smoothing the paper, she wrote a few lines on the back of the receipt. She had no time to plan out what to say.

This is not a joke. You are in danger. A man who has a skull tattoo on his wrist is planning to kill you — but I can help! Meet me in the ladies' room by the blackjack tables and I will explain.

Then she folded the receipt over, then over again, making it small enough to fit into the palm of her hand unnoticed.

The man on the phone was clearly angry at the person on the other end of the line. He turned his back to the girl.

"… paid for that order to be delivered tomorrow. I don't care if you have to rent a truck …"

Bailey reached out and touched the girl's arm. The instant she did she felt something like … like a current. The hum of a transformer but not as a noise, as a feeling. She saw reactions play across the girl's face, could tell she felt it, too, was *sure* she did. She turned to Bailey, stared at her, pinned her to the spot with the sapphire blue of her eyes. The girl wasn't just beautiful. She was *stunning.* Bailey took her hand and pressed the note into her palm. The girl looked questioningly at Bailey, opened her mouth to speak, but Bailey put her finger to her lips and shook her head violently.

The girl's face tensed and froze. She looked down at the piece of paper, then looked around frantically, a rabbit that's just caught the scent of the hounds. Her eyes widened when she looked toward the corner of the room and Bailey followed her gaze to the amber plastic bubble on the ceiling that concealed a security camera. Fear pulsed off the girl like the heat from a furnace and she shoved the piece of paper down the front of her dress.

"Fine!" the man grunted into the phone. "It had *better* be right this time!" And he ended the call.

Bailey quickly turned away from the girl and toward the machine in front of her. She had never operated a slot machine and even if she had she had no tokens to use in it. So she sat facing it, with the girl in her peripheral vision.

The man touched the girl's shoulder and ran his hand down her upper arm. It should have been an affectionate gesture, but somehow came off menacing. At least Bailey saw it as menacing. The girl looked up at him and flashed him a brilliant smile.

The smile looked like she had learned how to do it from a manual.

"Let's go get a drink," he said. The girl rose instantly. She never cast so much as a glance in Bailey's direction, just took the man's arm and walked away with him.

Chapter Nineteen

BAILEY WATCHED the man and girl leave the room, saw them pass by Brice, who was standing in the center aisle, and after a beat or two, he turned and sauntered off in the same direction. Bailey got up and hurried to the ladies' room by the blackjack tables to wait for the girl, trying to compose in her head what she could say to the girl when she showed up.

And what could she say?

After all, she was not only dealing with a total stranger, but with someone who was mentally unstable. Someone who believed in monsters that ripped open your chest and devoured your internal organs. Still, she was functioning just fine, seemed normal on the outside. Somehow she was managing to live in the real world and keep her own psychotic delusions in check. If she could do that, she'd be able to understand what Bailey was saying.

And that would be …?

She had just blurted out the truth about the soon-to-explode dam to Hattie Cosgrove and she'd thought Bailey was crazy. That part had only lasted seconds, though, before it was replaced by suspicion … then fear … then anger. If it hadn't been for her connection to Macy, she would never have been able to convince the family to run. Well, that and grabbing their baby son and running away with him. But Macy had come, too, willingly, because she'd felt something, some of the connection Bailey had felt for her.

Bailey had used the connection to the poor little girl whose portrait she'd painted two months ago to save her own life and T.J.'s.

But Macy had been a trusting child, intrigued by the wonder of knowing someone, yet not knowing them. This girl had none of Macy's childlike trust. And none of her ordered mental faculties. She'd want to know how Bailey knew she was in danger. What was Bailey to say then? *I painted a picture of you being murdered. I was murdered with you, too, by the way, felt it when the man broke your wrist and* ... Yeah, that'd work. That'd convince her.

No, when the girl came to see what Bailey'd meant by the note, Bailey would have to do better than that. She'd touch the girl's arm, establish that ... whatever it was, the hmmmmm thing. She'd ask her if the girl knew anybody with a skull tattoo on his wrist and a pinky ring with a single stone. This girl had been running in such terror because she *knew* the person chasing her, knew he meant to kill her. Even if she was mentally unstable — which she clearly was! — the girl had felt a connection to Bailey or she wouldn't have taken the note and hidden it to read later.

Bailey looked at her wrist, expecting to see the watch she'd left at home because it didn't match her new slinky green dress. She had no idea how much time had passed. There were no clocks in casinos. She remembered reading that somewhere and now that she thought about it, she hadn't seen one anywhere around. In a casino, they wanted patrons to lose all sense of time.

And so Bailey waited. Other women came and went from

the ladies' room. Every time she heard someone approaching, she tensed. Women entered and left. None of them had pale honey blonde hair and sapphire eyes.

Slowly, the reality that the girl wasn't coming began to seep into her consciousness. And as soon as she allowed in a few drips of doubt, the faucet turned on and filled her up. The girl hadn't read the note yet? That was hardly possible. Even without a watch, Bailey knew enough time had passed for her to read the note.

So she had read the note … and couldn't find a way to slip off to the bathroom? Absurd. A woman going to the ladies' room — that wouldn't be hard to pull off, even with the most possessive date.

Bottom line: if she had wanted to meet with Bailey, she would have. And she didn't.

Finally, Bailey got up and went back to the table where T.J. and Dobbs were seated, looking at plates of cold, uneaten food, and told them what had happened.

Then the three sat in glum silence, the fun and excitement of the evening long drained away. In a few minutes, Brice came back to the table, picked up his napkin and sat down, putting his napkin in his lap.

"I was going to follow them out to their car, get the registration, but they're staying here at the hotel. I got the room number, 387, and went to the desk clerk, flashed my badge and he gave me the check-in information the man had provided.

"He checked in as a single occupancy," Brice said, as if that explained something. When Bailey didn't get it, he continued. "I'd bet T.J.'s pension the girl won't be spending the night."

Then Bailey understood.

"She's … a prostitute, isn't she?"

"Looks that way to me."

"The world's oldest profession," T.J. said. "And likely even more hazardous than coal mining."

They sat together in silence for a beat before T.J. continued. "Anybody want to take a stab at explainin' how the mental patient we been lookin' for turned into a beautiful prostitute at a casino?"

Bailey shook her head. "We jumped to conclusions. I was too eager to find—"

"Wasn't your fault. She b'lieves monsters gonna eat her blue eyes. If that ain't psychotic, I—"

"Her dress." Bailey said. "Tonight, her white dress ..."

Dobbs fit the puzzle pieces together, arranged them to form an entirely different picture.

"We thought *hospital* gown, not *formal* gown. We thought hospital because she was running down a hallway past closed doors. But it was a hotel."

"This hotel," Bailey said.

"Or any other hotel in the tri-state area," T.J. said. "Girls like her—"

"She's wearing the white gown *right now*. Tomorrow is Halloween!" Bailey was heartsick. "She looked so scared. But not of the guy she was with. She was afraid somebody had seen her take the note."

"Her pimp, most likely," Brice said. "They usually keep close tabs on their girls."

"It's him, isn't it? The pimp. He's the guy with the skull tattoo and the pinky ring. He's—"

Brice stopped her. "We've wasted a lot of time running down the wrong rabbit holes already. I'm going to go park in the hotel lobby with a view of the elevators, see if I can catch the girl when she leaves and have a conversation with her."

Bailey started to rise to go with him but he shook his head.

"You'd just get in the way," he told her, all business, a lawman in a business suit. "I'd bet T.J.'s pension—"

"You done bet that," T.J. said.

"Odds are you're right — the murderer is her pimp. Or her pimp's muscle. And I have no authority to force her to tell me anything." He paused. "But she probably doesn't know that."

Brice left Bailey and the others sitting with the cold food at the table. She watched him walk out of the room until he was out of sight.

For the next hour and a half, Bailey, T.J. and Dobbs put as good a face on it as they could, made a show of eating food they could barely swallow, then left the dining room and wandered around the casino. They watched blackjack dealers rake money in for the house, stood with expectant crowds as the roulette wheel spun around and around. The place was full of laughter, but the fun had a frenetic, insectile quality to it — everybody in overdrive, determined to suck from their time here every bit of juice. Because it was likely to be a long, unhappy drive home.

Brice caught up with them watching a steely-eyed poker player who was actually beating the house, and she could read from his body language that it hadn't gone well.

"The guy came out of the elevator and went back into the casino. The girl never came back down."

"She's still in the room?" Bailey asked.

"No, he's done with her." He made an all-encompassing gesture. "She's here somewhere with another john."

"Then we have to find her and—"

"There are thousands of people in this casino and who knows how many more in the hotel."

Brice paused and she knew he was thinking of her futile effort to find the little girl with braids at a carnival — where there were a few hundred people.

"Even if we could find her, then what?"

"We ... we get her out of here—"

"How — short of kidnapping her? If she'd believed your note, she'd have gone to the bathroom to talk to you about it.

She didn't." He stopped, said the next words individually. "Her. Choice."

Brice took her by the shoulders. "We have done all we can do. We warned her, but we can't protect her if she refuses to believe the warning. It's time to go."

Chapter Twenty

"Ever hear of a five-run home run?" Brice asked Bailey as they stood in the front of the launch, crossing Whispering Mountain Lake to the Shadow Rock side. The breeze in their faces was cool, not cold, which it should have been this late in the evening at the end of October. Indian Summer still clung to this part of West Virginia.

"How could you do that? Three bases, one hit. That's impossible."

"Uh huh, but there are some people who spend their lives trying to hit five-run homers. You know anybody like that?"

Then he held out his hands as if he were holding something. It took her a moment to understand. Tonight, what had happened with the girl, had to go into the garbage bag and stay there. Not just so she could enjoy the rest of the evening. This was a *survival* skill. She had to learn it or she would *never* have any peace.

She held up imaginary garbage and dumped it into his bag and he drew the strings tight shut.

They'd arranged in advance for the real "birthday party" to convene at her house after their dinner at the casino. Bailey felt emotionally and physically wrung out, but it was clear the other three were determined to celebrate, whether from a genuine desire to do so or not to let the others down. Injected with truth serum, all four would likely have admitted that they wanted to go home and end the evening, but absent that they partied on.

The first thing she did when she got home was kick off the stiletto-heels. Most uncomfortable shoes she'd ever worn in her life.

While she went into the kitchen for paper plates to use for the cake, she saw the men convene a brief confab, then T.J. went out the front door and it was explained that "he left your present at his house."

That struck her as odd, but she had given up protesting the present thing. They were determined and she knew there was absolutely nothing she could do at this point to dissuade them. And she did appreciate their kindness and thoughtfulness.

As soon as they were seated, Dobbs brought out the cake that he'd asked the waiter at the casino restaurant to box up when they'd lost their appetites. It was only a birthday cake, but as intricate and detailed as any wedding cake Bailey'd ever seen. The frosting was pale blue. Growing up the side of the cake was an amazingly realistic-looking tree trunk, the bark of different kinds and colors of chocolate. The whole top of the cake was covered in the tree's intricate pink cherry blossoms.

What sat amid the blossoms brought a genuine smile to her face. Three figures, the hear-no-evil, see-no-evil, speak-no-evil monkeys, sat on the tree limbs, with hats naming them T.J., Dobbs and Brice. Brice, the speak-no-evil monkey, held a sign in the hand not covering its mouth: Happy Birthday, Bailey.

"We didn't get to pick our own monkey," Brice said. "I wanted to be see-no-evil, but nooooo, Dobbs got first shot because he made special arrangements for this cake."

"I just happen to be on a first-name, close-personal-friend

basis with every baker in town, including the one at the Nautilus. The monkeys were extra, but I splurged."

"Thank you so much. It's *perfect*."

The men exchanged a look.

Brice took a deep breath. "We drew straws and I got the short straw — though T.J. was holding the straws and I'm sure he was cheating. I hope you like the present as much as the cake."

He pulled a small box out of his pocket, gift wrapped in silver paper with a shiny silver bow.

The paper and ribbon came off in one piece and lying on her palm was a flip-top jewelry box. She opened the lid and inside was a set of earrings. Small and delicate, they were striking — an intricate leaf-and-vine design.

"I had help in the selection." Brice was flustered and it showed. "My friend from high school said you would love them. If you don't, blame her."

"They're beautiful, Brice — thank you!" Setting the box down, she took the earrings out one at a time and placed each in an ear.

"Well?" she said, turning her head so the men could get a good look at the earrings.

"I got it right," Brice said, with no discernible emotion that she could detect. "They *are* the same color as your eyes.

"Goody. The kids in grade school used to tease me, called me 'dill pickle.'"

"At least they aren't *Mike-Wazowski green*," Dobbs said, and she wondered how it was that he'd had occasion to see a children's movie.

T.J. had not yet returned, but Dobbs didn't wait for him. He produced a box larger than Brice's jewelry box but still small. It was in bright red wrapping paper with a bow of sparkling gold ribbon.

He sat grinning at her as she tore away the ribbon. She knew as soon as she saw the box. Still, she removed the cellophane wrapping slowly and opened the box, certain that she *had* to be mistaken, that it couldn't be …

But it was.

Lying inside the box was an artisan crafted case. She opened the case with trembling fingers. Inside the case, nestled in white satin, was a majestic, multifaceted bottle, each face catching the light and refracting it into a thousand rainbows. The glass top of the sparkling bottle was hand-sealed. Covering the neck was a fine membrane held in place by a strand of white pearl-cotton thread affixed with a black wax stamp.

A gold sticker on the front of the bottle proclaimed "Coco Mademoiselle. Chanel Paris."

Bailey sat mute. When she finally found her voice, she didn't yet have full command of her words. She was so flabbergasted all she could do was stammer and babble.

"No, I couldn't. Dobbs … *Coco*! Come on, you know I couldn't possibly accept a gift like that." Then she feared she might have hurt his feelings. "I mean, it's not like I don't want … It's wonderful, thank you, but it's *too much*. Please tell me you can see that it's too much."

Brice was looking at her quizzically, didn't understand what all the fuss was about. Dobbs had bought her perfume for her birthday and Brice didn't get why that could be a big deal.

"This is *Chanel*!" she told him, which explained everything in a single word. Except it didn't. She might as well have been speaking Mandarin Chinese. "This sells for … for *three or four thousand dollars an ounce*!"

His face registered understanding and he pursed his lips in a whistle but didn't make the sound.

"See!" Then she turned to Dobbs and said the same word, but plaintively this time. "See?"

"If I'd thought it was too much, chances are I wouldn't have done it in the first place," Dobbs said, the grin deepening in the folds of his cheeks. "You have no idea how much money I have and how little I have to spend it on. Now, either you're going to accept that perfume, or I'm going to have to figure out something to do with it. Guess I'd just have to give it to the first homeless woman—"

Bam! Bailey felt like she had slammed into a brick wall at a dead run. The words "homeless woman" hit her so hard she couldn't draw another breath.

Standing in the torrential downpour at the bus stop, the homeless woman is huddled against the sign, trying to fit her whole body under the small overhang around it.

"... Bailey?" Dobbs's voice penetrated and she refocused, came back to the here and now, trying to shed the tatters of the nightmare that still hung shredded around her.

" ... you alright?" This time it was Brice.

Her face had betrayed her shock and horror.

"I'm sorry," she stammered. She shoved as hard as she could to close the mental door that had come ajar at the mention of a homeless woman. "I ... just ..."

She was done, couldn't protest anymore. Her eyes filled with tears and she looked at Dobbs through the blur.

"Thank you! I can't tell you how much ..." She drew a shaky breath, determined not to cry. She stood, went to where Dobbs was seated on the couch and planted a kiss on his cheek. Her voice was tear-clotted when she spoke. "I've never had a better birthday present in my whole life."

"Oh, yes you have," T.J. said from the door, where he had entered unnoticed. "You ain't seen my present yet."

He turned and stepped back out onto the front porch and returned carrying a cardboard box that was large but didn't look heavy. It was not wrapped in pretty paper, no ribbons or bows. The top wasn't even sealed. It'd been opened, then the flaps folded back together. He crossed the room and set the box at Bailey's feet.

She just looked at him.

"You gonna open it or not?"

When she reached toward it, she thought she heard … *sounds* coming from the box. She lifted the open flap. And then she gasped and both hands flew to her mouth.

"Yap!"

She could only stare, too shocked to move.

"Yap-yap!"

Pulling her hands away from her face with an effort, she reached into the box and lifted from it a puppy. Then she burst into tears.

Chapter Twenty-One

Brice watched emotions wash across Bailey's face as she reached into the cardboard box and gently lifted out the ball of fur inside. Tears first, that quickly morphed into giggles. Then awe and surprise and a hint of dismay and … a half a dozen other emotions, too. It was, indeed, comical.

"T.J.?"

There was such wonder in her voice.

"Had to do something," T.J. said. "Sparky was beginning to forget what I looked like."

The puppy had fur so soft and curly it looked like a stuffed animal. It was black, but its snout and chest were white, and it had a white tip on its tail and white socks on its front paws.

Bailey gathered the fur ball up into her arms and hugged it to her. It began licking her face as furiously as a little kid going after a melting ice cream cone.

"Oh, T.J.!" Then Bailey was all-out crying.

T.J. was caught off guard by her reaction. Of course, he'd known she'd like it, but none of the three of them would have guessed just how much she'd like it.

Brice cleared his throat. "Thousands of dollars worth of perfume. A dog. Sheesh. If I'd known what I was up against, I wouldn't have wasted my time picking out earrings — just a Starbucks gift card."

"No, no," she cried out through tears, trying unsuccessfully to get control of herself. "They're lovely!" She reached up and pulled her long hair behind her ear to reveal the sparkling green. The same color as her eyes. And the puppy matched her glossy black hair. He wondered if T.J. had done that on purpose, but dismissed the idea as soon as he thought it. Not T.J. "It's *all* … wonderful."

The dictionary definition of that word. Wonderful. Full of wonder. Brice considered the implications of that because it did matter. What was happening here was way more important than it appeared to be. Bailey Donahue was chained to an awful "gift," as surely as T.J.'s mother had been chained to the same gift fifty years ago. But right this minute, cuddling the puppy, she had managed to set the burden down for a while. That was no small accomplishment. In the long run, he suspected it might prove to be the single most important ability she possessed. As long as she was able to do that, as long as he and her other friends could help her figure out how to *keep doing that,* day after day … she had a chance to remain whole, her spirit unbroken. She had a chance to survive what had so shattered Eulalie Hamilton that she'd hanged herself from a barn rafter.

Bailey set the puppy down and it proceeded to pee on the floor. There was much puppy-related scurrying around then.

"It's a mini golden doodle like Sparky," T.J. said. "I've had lots of dogs in my life, but I b'lieve this breed is the loving-est, sweetest, smartest …" He stopped himself when he realized he was gushing. "They're hypoallergenic — you ain't allergic to dogs, are you?"

Bailey lifted an eyebrow. "Totally covered in hives every time I'm in the room with Sparky. Itchy red bumps — you didn't notice?"

"Nobody likes a smartass, you know that don't you?" He

continued his spiel. "Doodles don't shed, neither, not so much as a hair." He rubbed the mat of close-cropped hair on his head. "I shed more than Sparky does."

T.J. was babbling, too, surprised by the intensity of emotion his gift had produced. He went out to his car and returned with all manner of supplies Bailey would need. There was a crate — a wire cage where he'd put a doggie bed for the puppy's den — accompanied by a lengthy explanation about how to use it and why it was important. He'd brought a dog dish, a leash and collar, a six-pack of "potty sacks," a bag of dry dog food and a couple of cans of dog food.

"It's a chancy thing, giving somebody a puppy, 'cause you done give them the best present they'll ever get" — he glanced at Dobbs and Brice — "thousand-dollar perfume and sparkly earrings notwithstanding. But puppies is a lot of work! You got to look after 'em and train 'em, clean their poop off the floor, brush 'em and get they shots and—"

"Oh, you'll show me how to do all that," Bailey said with exaggerated dismissal. "I have no idea what I'm getting into — ignorance is absolute bliss."

"It ain't all roses."

"Nothing in life is."

"What are you going to name it?" Dobbs asked.

She lifted the dog up and looked at its underside. "Name *him*. Any suggestions?"

"'Sparky the Wonder Dog' is already taken. In case you was wonderin'."

Though Bailey seemed reluctant to let the puppy out of her arms, she set it down again and it began to sniff its way around the room, growling with what little menace it could summon at the broom beside the fireplace and the kitchen trash basket.

"We've got birthday cake to eat," Dobbs announced. "I've been looking at this thing all night and I'm about to drown in my own spit." Two candles had been provided with the cake, in the shapes of a three and a one. Dobbs produced a packet of matches that said Grand Opening Nautilus Casino Hotel on the front and lit the candles.

"Make a wish," Brice said.

Emotions washed over her face again. He'd never known anybody who wore powerful emotions like hers as transparently as she did, or who was able to hide what she was feeling so completely at other times — leaving them all to wonder what she had suffered that she hadn't shared with them. He was sure Bailey was in the Witness Protection Program, though he'd never done any sniffing around to find out. And you didn't get in Witness Protection for watching a chili bake-off.

She leaned over to blow out the candles.

"Wishes are for tomorrow. Right here, right now. Life is good."

Then he saw a shadow flit across her face before she resolutely drew in a breath and puffed out the candles. She was thinking about the beautiful girl in the white gown, who might at that very moment be running for her life.

Chapter Twenty-Two

Bailey had been hearing music off and on ever since they got to her house. There had been so much going on while the guys were here — a *dog!* — that she had ignored it. But the big old house was more than just quiet when there was no activity. Somehow, the Watford House possessed silence as an entity, a thing that was more than just the absence of sound. Profound quiet ... like she'd felt as she sat at the kitchen table three months ago with a pistol in her hand — that she had no idea how to reload — a gun that felt as cold as death.

It was quiet like that now. Except it wasn't. She could hear the music, but understood it was not breaking the quiet still-ness of the house. The house was silent, the music was playing in her head, the background music at the casino, the canvas on which the atmosphere had been painted, the orchestrated Muzak remake of old rock music. Beatles hits. Simon and Garfunkel.

"Bridge Over Troubled Water" brought to mind Jocelyn Farrington, the pathetically psychotic mental patient they'd suspected might be the girl in the painting. Jocelyn, whose life they might *accidentally* have saved. The rodent-faced little hospital administrator would take great care to ensure she was not harmed.

The real girl from the painting … there was nobody looking after her.

"Yellow Submarine" morphed into Creedence Clearwater Revival. "Heard It Through the Grapevine."

When she'd first heard the music in her head as she and Brice stood together at the front of the launch crossing the lake after the party, she'd thought she must be hearing the actual music. Sound carries a long way over water.

But it was still playing when she got into Brice's car. Softly, in the back of her head. A haunting melody.

She knew where it was coming from then but she'd resolutely pushed such thoughts out of her mind. The guys had tried to help her come up with a name for the dog — Ace, Casper, Bandit/Buddy/Boomer, Scout, Simba, Yoda and Ziggy and two dozen others. Droolious Caesar had been T.J.'s lone contribution. And as they bandied names back and forth, in the background she distinctly heard the clanging of a bell, the kind that sounded when the lights flashed on top of the slot machines for a winner. She hadn't mentioned it. Or that she had gotten a strong whiff of a woman's perfume at the same time.

Both faded.

Now that she was alone in the house … No, not alone. BUND was here. That was the acronym Dobbs had come up with to use as a space holder until she found a name she liked. Bailey's Un-Named Dog. She wasn't going to call the little fluff ball that for long, of course, but Baby Dog, which had been her first gushing response, would have to be replaced by an acceptable moniker as soon as possible. The poor little thing had to have a name!

Bund's yaps and occasional whining didn't mask the music, though. She knew no other sound actually masked it, either, but the presence of other sounds made *that* sound easier to ignore. You couldn't drown out a sound that you weren't hearing with your ears.

She stood still for a moment, listening.

… yesterday, all my troubles seemed so far away …

Her mind added the words to the melody. One of the foster mothers in the parade of foster homes from her youth had purchased a vintage "hi-fi" at a yard sale, the old kind that played vinyl records. When she got it home, she discovered it had one record on the turntable. "Yesterday." Since it was the only record she had, she played it in a continuous loop, all day long, day after day after … Then one day, the record mysteriously vanished. Never did find out what happened to it. Hmmmmmm.

As she mentally sang along with the music, images from her childhood were washed away by an ache welling up in her belly that she had resolutely consigned to the bag hours ago. That girl, the poor lovely girl. And she had seemed a *girl*, as a matter of fact. Obviously, prostitutes came in all shapes, sizes and ages like the rest of humanity, were not confined to stereotypical stiletto heels, dress too low-cut, skirt too short, and eyes way too old for the face. This girl had been elegantly dressed, in expensive clothes. Her perfume had been of the thousand-dollar-an-ounce variety. Still, she looked young, almost childlike. There was an innocence Bailey couldn't reconcile with how the girl had decided to live her life.

"Yesterday" became "I Want To Hold Your Hand." Then, like smoke from a dying campfire, the music grew fainter and fainter until it was only a remembered echo. Bailey fastened the collar around the puppy's neck and hooked a leash to it and took him out into the yard to do his business.

She stood there, trying to be encouraging.

"Go potty!"

She had a treat ready to pop into his mouth as soon as he complied. But he didn't appear to be the slightest bit interested in bodily functions. He went sniffing away across the yard, pausing only to chase an ant and to start frantically digging a hole — for reasons Bailey could not fathom.

Finally, she gave up and led him back into the house. He trotted over to the spot on the floor where he had peed the first time and proceeded to unleash the whole load.

Not good. T.J. had told her about some kind of cleaner that sufficiently removed that kind of odor so the animal wouldn't return to it. She'd buy some tomorrow. That didn't help right now, though. T.J. had also said she would have to take the puppy outside every couple of hours around the clock until he got the hang of things, but he wouldn't soil his bed in his kennel.

So, she needed to …

She occupied her mind with all things puppy, picking the little fur ball up every few minutes to nuzzle him, and get her face licked.

By the time she dropped into bed at well on the south side of one o'clock, she was physically and emotionally wrung out, too tired to dwell on the lovely young girl she had seen tonight, her head full instead of mental to-do lists. And her ears too full of the puppy's pitiful cries from his crate downstairs.

T.J. had been adamant. She *had* to let the puppy cry it out. She couldn't give in to it or he'd never learn. But T.J. had not said the little dog's cry would be so *pitiful.* The poor little thing down there all by himself in a strange place was just a baby, after all. He missed his mother and his litter mates. He was *scared*! And heartbroken. Finally, she couldn't stand it any longer. She rescued the little beast, took him outside where he actually complied with the go-potty request, and then snuggled up with him beside her on the pillow.

The puppy licked her face happily, his tail wagging in delight. She didn't mind having her face licked … if she could keep her mind off what he might possibly have been licking with that same tongue only a few minutes before. She watched the dog go to sleep — quickly and innocently, flipping a switch from awake to asleep.

She'd fallen asleep almost as quickly as the dog.

When she suddenly bolted upright in the bed, she was totally disoriented.

What time was it?

The puppy was snoozing peacefully right where she'd left him, but she was anything but peaceful. Her heart was pounding, her mouth dry and she was breathing like she'd just run the Boston Marathon. She tried to calm herself, steady her breathing. It hadn't been a bad dream, or if it had been, she didn't remember it. But something …

Then she knew. She didn't know how she knew, but she was certain. The bond, the connection between her and the girl had been broken. She hadn't been nearly as aware of the connection as she was now aware of its absence. Like being in a conversation on the phone and the line suddenly goes dead. And you can sense the emptiness on the other end where someone had been only a moment ago, but now was gone.

The girl was dead.

She hadn't heeded their warning and the man with the tattoo had killed her.

Bailey settled back down in bed and began to cry softly. She buried her face in her pillow so she wouldn't wake the sleeping puppy, then felt the warmth of him, snuggled up to her neck, licking her ear. Not the frantic licking from before, excited, his whole body wiggling. He was licking her slowly, softly. It was soothing. Almost like the little dog knew she needed comforting. And maybe he did.

Chapter Twenty-Three

BAILEY TRIED to tell herself it was just because she hadn't gotten enough sleep last night. But she knew that wasn't it. That wasn't what had led her here in her robe and slippers in the early dawn hours to stand in front of the door of her studio, behind which was the painting of the girl.

The nameless girl who died last night.

She stood looking at the door. Didn't reach for the knob, just stood. On the other side of the door … she didn't want to go there. Oh, how badly she didn't want to go there. This time she had *failed.* What she'd painted had come to pass. Poor, delusional Jocelyn Farrington was safe in her bed at Forest Hills Sanitarium, but this girl, the stunning beauty who'd sat at the slot machine next to hers last night had been murdered. Just as the portrait had predicted. And nothing Bailey and the others had done could prevent it.

Destiny had won.

She turned and walked back into the living room, noticing as she did that the puppy had deposited a little puddle of pee in that same spot beside the couch where he'd done his business yesterday. She had to get that stuff T.J. had told her to get or that was going to become a permanent toilet for *Bundy,* who now was happily chasing dust motes in the beam of dawn sunshine that shone through the top of the stained glass window in the living room. Yeah, Bundy. Overnight, Bailey's Un-Named Dog had somehow morphed from BUND into Bundy. And that would do just fine.

She went to the cabinet of cleaning supplies in the hallway, got some paper towels and Windex — it was all she had — and returned to do battle with the puddle on the floor, yawning as she did so, missing the sleep she'd lost courtesy of taking Bundy out every three or four hours … and standing there for ten or fifteen minutes until he was in the mood to do his business. She was not going to tell T.J. that she'd put the puppy in bed with her to sleep so it would stop crying. She knew she would pay for that tonight, and maybe for a whole bunch of nights hence, but she was glad for the company when she woke up knowing, without any idea how she knew, that the beautiful blonde girl with the frightened sapphire eyes was dead.

She hadn't constantly revisited the painting of Macy Cosgrove after she painted it. Oh, she'd "re-engaged" with it when she'd realized she had to paint the child's face if they were ever to have any hope of finding her. So she'd painted it and then she'd left the painting on an easel in her studio behind a closed door. And there it had sat, with the "matching painting" on the easel beside it.

She had left the two of them side by side like that — the painting of Macy and her own portrait with a bullet hole in her temple that T.J.'s mother had painted fifty years ago — for a time after the flood. Then one morning, she knew — maybe it was an impulse, maybe the conclusion her mind had reached subconsciously. Whatever it was, she'd acted on it. She'd taken Macy's picture out into the back yard and set it on fire. She'd had no gasoline to pour over it, so the burning took a while. But eventually it was nothing but ashes.

She decided to keep the portrait T.J.'s mother had painted

of her with a bullet hole in her temple, because … She wasn't sure exactly why, but she couldn't bring herself to destroy the painting that connected her to Eulalie Hamilton, who had been cursed with the strange "gift" as she had been.

As soon as her life had returned to some semblance of order after the horror surrounding the kidnappings two months ago, she'd destroyed the portrait she'd not been compelled to paint but had *decided* to paint. She'd bought lighter fluid to pour over it because she wanted it to burn hot and fast. And it had.

So what should she do with the painting that now rested on the easel in her studio?

She took another sip of her coffee — strong and black — and reached down and picked up Bundy, who had given up on the dust motes and was now sniffing something that appeared to be very interesting on the bottom of her house shoe. She cuddled the dog to her face.

"Aaron would have liked you, Bundy," she said, and her voice cracked a little, hearing the name of her dead husband spoken out loud like that. It hurt to hear the sound, but it felt good to say it, too. To have "someone" who'd listen to her pour her heart out about all that she had lost.

"Bethany would have liked you, too." She stopped, firmed her back and said with more determination than sadness. "Bethany *will* like you when she meets you." And she felt better, somehow, for saying that, too, out loud.

Then she turned from the door resolutely, went to the kitchen and deposited her cup in the sink. If she allowed herself to start the day thinking about Aaron and Bethany, she could end up wallowing in self-pity for the whole rest of the day. Not. She had to — the scraps of a smile fluttered across her face — put her pain, her self-pity and her grief over the lost girl whose shattered face she'd captured in a portrait into a garbage bag and cinch it up tight.

She needed to do something with the portrait. The girl

was dead, the connection broken, their efforts to intervene a failure, game over. Though she absolutely, one hundred percent, did *not* want to go anywhere near it, she had to face it. In the sooner-or-later category of tasks, sooner was always better than later. T.J. had told her once, "If you got to eat a frog, don't look at it too long. And if you got to eat two frogs, eat the big 'un first." This was a big frog.

Maybe if she held the puppy close, it wouldn't be so hard ...

With the puppy snug in her arms, she went to the studio, didn't hesitate at the door. She didn't have to switch on the lights. With the huge windows, the room was well lit anytime the sun was up. She went to the portrait and stood in front of it, discovered that she was gritting her teeth to keep her focus on the portrait itself and not the vision she had gotten when she painted it.

RUNNING AS FAST as her legs will carry her down a dark hallway, so much fear, it threatens to burst out her chest, she will explode from it, fly into pieces in every direction.

A maze of darkened corridors, a rabbit warren of hallways. Soft plush carpet under her bare feet. No sound at all except for her heavy breathing.

BAILEY SHOOK HER HEAD. There was no reason to dwell on this. It was only painful, nothing to be gained. The girl was dead—

THE PAIN in her scalp is ...

Her broken wrist drags along the floor, bouncing down each stair tread.

Pain is her whole world. She can no longer tell where the stabbing agony comes from. It comes from everywhere, every part of her.

Then he drags her over a threshold and tosses her into a room. Her basement bedroom, clothes in a pile, the closet door ajar, the shoes she slipped off so she could run silently lying by the bed. Looking along the floor, she sees … Jeni!

BAILEY'S EYES yanked to the bed that was partially visible on the right side of the portrait, gazing at the darkness beneath it.

The subject of the portrait was so riveting, Bailey had noticed nothing at all in the background. Now she studied the wedge of darkness beneath the bed. The girl had looked there and said, "Jeni" before the man kicked her in the mouth, silenced her, beat and kicked and then strangled her.

But she had said, "*Jeni.*"

Was there someone there, in the darkness under the bed? Was Jeni there?

Bailey's heart began to pound and she set the puppy down on the floor, went to the switch beside the door and turned on the lights. They were glaringly bright, or seemed so after only natural light. That was one reason she almost never turned them on, because the light reflected off the glossy surface of the paint. You had to view the picture from just the right angle or the glare made a shiny sheen that obscured the image.

Returning to the portrait, she moved until the sheen was gone and the right side of the picture was brightly illuminated. The bed hadn't been made. The pale blue bedspread and tangled sheets and blankets didn't reach the floor. There was a slice of darkness beneath them, between the bed and the floor. Was there … a lesser darkness, a dark *shape* instead of just a blob of black? It was impossible to tell for certain, but Bailey found herself filled with the conviction that there *was* a shape there under the bed. A face. *Jeni's face.*

The longer she stared at the portrait, the more convinced

she became. For no rational reason at all — but what was rational about any of this? — Bailey believed that someone, a girl named Jeni, had been watching the scene, peeking out from under the bed, where she'd obviously been hiding.

Jeni — another "working girl?" Probably.

Whoever she was, she had seen. Jeni had witnessed the girl's brutal beating and death. And if the guy with the skull tattoo found out she'd seen? If he discovered Jeni had watched him commit murder ...

Bailey began to shake all over. She knew about that kind of thing, oh, how she knew about that. About monsters who masqueraded as human beings, who murdered casually and then massacred anybody who might have been a *witness* to the carnage.

This man, the one the girl had called the Beast — he'd done this before — *enjoyed it.* And bad guys like him didn't get to be professionals by leaving loose ends.

If the Beast found out Jeni had seen, he'd kill her, too.

Was there really a Jeni ... not just in the room the night the girl was murdered, *but in the painting?* Was there someone else in this portrait, obscured in the dark, but there?

There was only one way to find out.

Chapter Twenty-Four

T.J. STOOD BACK A WAYS, to get the view of the whole painting. Examined it. The pile of clothes, looked like a lady's panties and maybe a camisole. There were shoes beside the bed, another pile of … maybe a towel in front of a closet door that stood slightly ajar. Then he moved forward and examined the right side of it, the part that showed a portion of a bed and bedspread. As far as he could see, there wasn't nothing but black beneath that bed. But Bailey thought there was more than that.

"So you're sayin' you think they's somebody back there in the darkness under that bed? Is that what you're tellin' me?"

"I'm not asking if you see it." Bailey shifted the puppy from one arm to the other. She'd hardly set the little fluff ball down the whole time T.J.'d been here, only long enough to spray the Pee Be Gone cleaner he'd brought on a spot on the floor where the dog had decided made a dandy potty place.

T.J. wasn't a bettin' man. He'd given that up a long time ago, along with most of the rest of his vices — 'cept being ornery, which he held onto with some pride. But he'd have laid down a-hundred-to-one odds Bailey hadn't let that puppy cry in his crate last night.

"I'm just asking if you think it's *possible* there *could be* something there. I don't *see* it either, but I … I don't know how to explain it. I just know there's somebody there. It's like I can feel her. Did anything like that ever happen to your mother?"

"Not that she ever told me about." T.J. reached out and took the puppy out of her arms and set it down on the floor. "God give that puppy legs to walk on and they gonna shrivel up and fall off if you won't let him use 'em."

"I don't carry—"

"Occur to you, did it, that you's naming your dog after a serial killer?"

"I did not! Bundy is just — *nooooo.*"

The puppy had started to squat and Bailey snatched him up and raced out the back door, holding him out from her like you'd hold a mouse by the tail. She deposited him in the grass.

"Go potty," she told him, and he sniffed around for a few moments and then complied. Bailey liked to scared the poor thing to death squealing what a "good boy" he was.

T.J.'d followed her out into the yard, where she was practically choking the poor dog shoving a treat down his throat, and he picked up the conversation where they'd left it.

"You got to remember I's just a little boy and there was lots of things that went on durin' that time she never talked about."

Bailey had told him her connection to the girl in the painting had snapped last night, was convinced that meant the girl was dead and he was sure she was right. Today was Halloween, after all, and the monster'd told the girl she wouldn't need a mask to go trick-or-treating tonight.

When she'd opened her front door to his knock a few minutes earlier she was wearing a look on her face he'd seen so often on his mama's when she'd painted something and then that awful something happened just like she painted it. Bailey was taking it way harder than she let on that this time destiny'd got the gold ring. That's why she was pushing this, sayin' they was somebody else in the painting only they couldn't see her. She wanted to change the future, save *somebody*, and if not the strangled girl, then …

Bailey glanced toward the house and it was like he could see the dark shadow that passed over her face. She shivered and it wasn't cold.

"If you's determined to do it, do it now while I'm here."

Sparky and Bundy had chased a butterfly to the other side of the yard and now the puppy was pawing at something in the dirt there. An ant or a bug. T.J. thought of the letter he'd wrote to Santa for Sparky last year, asking for a box of moths for Christmas.

When he called Sparky, the puppy came loping along with him. He put the puppy in his crate, and the little dog put up a ruckus until Sparky hopped in beside him, lay down and promptly went to sleep. The puppy quieted then.

Bailey looked at T.J., as if begging him to talk her out of this. But she wouldn't listen if he'd tried.

He walked with her to the studio, closed the door behind her and then leaned up against the back wall while she set about mixing paints on the pallet. They'd know pretty quick if—

Bailey touched the brush to the darkness beneath the bed in the picture and he watched her fall down that tunnel his mama told him about, the dark pipe leading down into greater darkness where factories turned out monsters to populate all the nightmares in the world.

She picked up another brush with her other hand, leaned her head back, closed her eyes and painted in a fury that had to be seen to be believed.

Naaaa, even seeing it, he didn't believe.

T.J. shivered and wasn't cold in here, neither.

Chapter Twenty-Five

Seated at his desk in his office, Brice appeared to be pouring over incident reports ranging from a cat stuck in a tree — no kidding, *a cat in a tree* — to domestic violence and a series of bash-and-runs on cars parked overnight in the Joe's Hole Marina parking lot. There'd be twice as many on his desk tomorrow morning — Halloween pranks gone south.

When he was a teenage boy in Shadow Rock, he had been the ringleader of a house toilet-papering ring that had laid waste to a whole street — had plans, and a sufficient stash of toilet paper, for the whole neighborhood ... but it had started to rain.

Kids these days were no less inventive but more destructive. He had a theory about why that was, one that provided him the opportunity to engage in his favorite anti-video-game rant. Last year, kids had dragged old couches out into the middle of the street and set them ablaze, had broken all the windows on the south side of Madison Elementary School and had — he still didn't know how they'd pulled this off — killed the electrical service to the whole south side of town. Kavanaugh County Regional Hospital had operated on generator power for most of the night.

He and his buddies used to dress up as ghosts or monsters and jump out of the bushes and scare the little kids. That was no longer a Halloween entertainment option. Now, small children were escorted from house to house by their parents — who later inspected every piece of candy before they'd allow their kids to eat it. Though there'd never been a single case of tainted Halloween candy in Shadow Rock, the national paranoia had infected even his little corner of the world.

But he wasn't concentrating on the incident reports on his desk. The Kavanaugh County sheriff was thinking about the night before at the casino when Bailey connected to the girl whose brutalized face haunted a canvas on an easel in her studio.

Bailey had wanted so badly to help the girl. They all had. But if the girl refused to listen …

This wasn't as simple as getting people out of the way of a flood. That hadn't been *easy*, of course, but it had been simple and uncomplicated. Convince them, trick them or bribe them — do whatever you have to do because a flood was an event with a beginning and an end and then the danger was past.

He rubbed his right forearm, the arm broken two months ago after Bailey'd attempted what T.J.'s mother never had — she'd tried to *intentionally* paint a portrait of a kidnapped child. No one could ever have predicted the chain of events that painting set in motion, but nothing about it had any bearing on what was happening now because Bailey hadn't *decided* to paint this portrait. She'd been *compelled* to — by what force, nobody knew. Just like all the paintings T.J.'s mother had painted half a century ago.

"Sheriff McGreggor."

Brice looked up and saw his chief deputy, Raleigh Fletcher, standing in the doorway. His tone of voice suggested that might not have been the first time he'd tried to get the sheriff's attention.

"Sorry, I was zoned out on—" Brice gestured at the pile of papers.

"This trumps all that. We got a floater."

"How long?" Recovering the body of a drowning victim was always an unpleasant experience. The degree of unpleasantness was directly correlated to the amount of time the body'd been in the water.

"Not long. Think hours, not days. But there's more. This isn't your garden variety floater."

Fifteen minutes later, the sheriff was standing on the dock at Joe's Hole Marina listening to the near-hysterical rant of a Michigan boat owner who'd only wanted a weekend of relaxation for his wife and kids, he said, and didn't expect to create memories for his children that would haunt them rather than delight them for the rest of their lives.

He was a hound-dog-faced man with droopy eyes and a bulbous nose crisscrossed with a web of tiny red veins.

"The kids were right there, *watching*." His voice shook. "They *saw*." He studied Brice's face to make sure the whole horror of that statement had registered. *"My children saw the body."*

He glanced to where his wife stood apart, children on both sides, her arms around their shoulders, a girl about ten, a boy maybe twelve. She had them crushed up against her. Neither appeared as upset as their parents. Brice suspected that the boy was looking forward to impressing his friends with the story.

"I'm sorry for what you and your family have gone through, Mr. Abercrombie. We don't want to prolong this painful process, so if you'll just start at the top and tell me everything."

"Okay, okay ..." The man took a deep, shaky breath and let it out slowly. "We were out in the middle of the lake, out where it's really deep. Some of the biggest fish are in that part of the lake, but you know as well as I do you can't fish there once the ski boats and the jet skis and the speed boats and all the rest get revved up."

"What time did you—?"

"Before dawn. Still so dark we had to use running lights. When we thought we were out in really deep water, we dropped anchor and started fishing."

"Catch anything?"

"Some. Nothing like we'd been hoping for. And then the sun came up and the wild-eyed crazies showed up, zipping around us, throwing wakes three feet tall. Wasn't long before we felt like the center pole on a merry-go-round and we decided to pack it in."

He paused then, took another deep breath.

"I started to pull in the anchor. For a few seconds everything was fine, but then the motor on the crank started straining. I told my wife, I said, 'Margaret, that anchor's caught on something.' I figured we had hooked onto a tree stump. I was hoping the anchor would pull free, but it didn't. I was sure the rope was going to break and we'd lose the anchor. That thing was expensive and I didn't want … but then …"

He lost his breath again, genuinely shaken.

"Take your time, Mr. Abercrombie."

"There was hardly any rope left and I should have been able to see the anchor coming up through the water. But I couldn't see … then I could tell the anchor'd snagged *a chain*. I couldn't see … thought what on earth is that chain …? I didn't know until it broke the surface. That's when I saw the …"

The man started talking faster, panting.

"It was right up close to the boat and I could tell … Margaret saw what it was and she started screaming."

"What did you see, Mr. Abercrombie?"

"A *dead body*! The anchor'd got caught on a chain … On one end of the chain was a body, with the chain wrapped around and around it. On the other end of the chain was a piece of concrete, the kind builders use to … you know, whatever builders do with those concrete blocks. I made the children go below. Margaret took them and she was crying. Amy was crying. I can't tell you how awful ..."

He began to pant again.

"Get your breath, Mr. Abercrombie. You're doing just fine."

The boy, clutched tight by his mother, was trying to see past the officers to the end of the dock where his father had left their houseboat and its grisly cargo.

"I didn't know what to do. I mean, what do you do when something like that happens? I thought about just cutting the anchor rope, letting it sink. But I couldn't do that. Somebody chained that woman to that concrete block. Somebody *killed* her! I had to come in to the dock, *drag it* in to the dock. So I got on the phone and dialed 911, said I wanted to report a murder."

"You did the right thing, Mr. Abercrombie. Thank you for keeping your cool in a very difficult situation." The sheriff motioned for a deputy. "This is Deputy John Tackett. He's going to take your formal statement."

"I just gave *you* my statement! Why do I have to—?"

"We have to have every detail. I'm sure you understand, this is a murder investigation. He's going to record what you say, transcribe it for you to sign."

"Transcribe? Sign? You mean we have to ...?"

Deputy Tackett ushered the Abercrombie family away and Brice walked down to the yellow police tape that had been stretched across the whole end of the dock. A lone houseboat was tied up there and half a dozen sheriff's deputies, West Virginia State Police troopers, rescue squad and water patrol officers were swarming over the end of it.

He crossed the deck of the boat and stood watching. Water patrol officers had cut the anchor rope and were lifting the whole thing — the anchor, the body and the piece of concrete block it was chained to, onto the dock. The woman was naked and nothing much was left of her face. But Brice could see even from where he was standing that she had freckles. When they rolled her over onto her side, there was a scar on her hip.

This was the girl from the casino last night.

This was the girl whose portrait Bailey had painted.

Chapter Twenty-Six

*H*E *IS the one who always hurts them. Jacko. The Beast. He could hand the task off to one of the others — the ugly one called Vincent. Or Nick, the black guy with red hair.*

But Jacko always does the job personally because he is careful not to "damage the merchandise." No, it's not that. He does it himself because he enjoys it. She can tell by the look in his eyes, the glow there, and the little half smile that parts his lips.

He was smiling when he kicked Poli in the face and broke her teeth. She couldn't see his face, but she knows he was smiling. She could hear the smile in his voice when he told Poli she would need no mask for Halloween. And Jeni had almost cried out then, almost made a sound and he'd have known she was there, cowering under the bed. Watching.

But she had kept silent, had bitten on her lip until the copper taste filled her mouth, watching him lift Poli off the floor with hands as big as shovels around her neck, Squeezing. Squeezing. Then Poli had stopped struggling, hung limp, a rag doll. But he didn't just let go. He flung her across the room and her body made a sick, splatting sound on the wall. But Jeni didn't cry out. She kept quiet.

For all the good it did her.

She had been so stupid. Taking the ring — so foolish. She would pay for that stupidity now. He would hurt her, hurt her bad. They must turn in all "gifts." But he doesn't know the truth. And she must not tell him. If he finds out, he will kill her.

He grabs her shirt and yanks her forward, lowering his face until it is inches from hers and the stench of his breath is overpowering, the feel of his spittle on her face sickening. His voice is raspy, gravelly, sounds like a damaged voice, like he has yelled so long and loud that his throat is raw. It reminds her of the big chains dragging across the metal deck of the ship.

"You will tell me the truth, yes. You will, you know. So tell me now and I will not have to hurt you."

But she knows he will hurt her no matter what she says. She watched him hurt Poli and she knows. She stammers that she has told him the truth, that she found the ring on the sink in a hotel room. Some woman must have left it, and she was going to give it up, was planning to …

"You think I believe you found this ring?" He is holding the shiny piece of sterling silver, tiny and delicate. Poli'd had it on her little toe and they didn't see. So she'd kept it. Hid it away. "Just found it?"

She only nods her head frantically, wants to plead her case, try to convince him, but she has no voice. No words come.

He smiles that little smile.

"We'll see about that."

He tosses her onto the bed, shoves her onto her belly and ties her hands to the post at the head of the bed — with soft fabric, like velvet — so it will not leave a mark. He is careful not to damage the goods.

She is so scared she might be sick, might vomit. It will hurt so bad. Whatever it is he is about to do to her will hurt so bad, but she has to be strong. She can't tell him. If she tells him, he won't just hurt her. He will kill her.

She looks back over her shoulder at him standing beside the bed and sees that he has something in his hand. It looks like a piece of rubber hose. She would beg him, plead with him not to hurt her with it but it will do no good.

She has to be strong.

He hits her with the hose across her lower back, just a small blow, but even that much staggers her and she screams.

Then he hits her again, harder, and she cries out louder. She has to be strong, turns her face away, tenses for the next blow. She has to—

He hits her again and she wails this time. The pain radiates up her back to her shoulders and all the way down her legs to her knees.

When he hits her the fourth time, it hurts so bad she can only grunt and her whole body shakes, like she is having a seizure.

"A boyfriend, too, yes? Like Poli. Did he give you the ring? Were you planning to run away with him like your stupid friend?"

And with what little breath she has, she tells him that she has no boyfriend, no one gave her the ring — she found it. She is telling him the truth.

So he hits her again and again. Does not even ask her about the ring anymore. She writhes on the bed, rolls over onto her side, trying to roll onto her back and draw up her knees to take the blows, but he grabs her hair and shoves her face-down on the mattress.

She can hardly breathe, and he hits her again.

Screaming into the mattress, kicking her feet, struggling to get free, his hand tangled in her hair.

He hits her again. And again.

Sometimes she feels nothing, like her whole body is numb and the room and everything in it are just a horrible dream.

At some point, she is no longer struggling. She tries, but she can't move anymore. The agony has torn loose something inside her. She feels it tear loose.

She will do anything to make him stop, say anything, tell him anything, but she can say nothing with her face smashed into the mattress and he just keeps hitting her.

The world grays out, is almost completely gone, and then he grabs her arm, rolls her over onto her back, gets down into her face.

"Where did you get—?"

He is panting, his breath rancid, and she breathes it deep into her lungs when she gasps in a breath, and speaks as soon as she has enough air.

"Poli's ring. From when she was little. Only I knew where she kept it."

"She couldn't have hidden—"

"The post on the bed ..." It hurts so bad, she can't breathe. *"Unscrew and there is space—"*

"Why would you steal her ring?"

She pauses, but not because she will not answer. She will tell him anything. She just needs air for her words.

"I took ... to remember her."

Jacko never shows emotion, real emotion, but even through the haze of agony she can see that he is genuinely surprised.

Now, she has to do this one last good thing. But she can only do it if he doesn't ask, because if he does, she will tell him. She doesn't want to, but she knows that she will tell him anything he wants to know. So she hurries on.

"I knew her plan. Poli's room ... last night. I went to—"

"You were in Poli's room last night?"

"To talk her from it. To beg her no ..." She drags in another agonized breath. *"Hiding under Poli's bed. You ... strangled her. I saw."*

She wants him to kill her, to put his hands around her neck and squeeze and make the pain go away. Kill her while she still holds onto one truth. One last truth.

Poli wanted to die, too. Jeni saw it when their eyes met and held for that single, brief moment.

He straightens up, turns to the man who has been watching from the doorway, the ugly man called Vincent whose face has little holes in it and whose nose is broken and flat.

The room is swimming now. The lights grow brighter with each heartbeat and then dim again. Though the man is standing right beside her, his words are muffled by a great roaring sound in her head.

Words. Disconnected phrases.

Pictures. Brochure. Video.

" ... no way she knows who ..."

" ... not assets anymore ..."

"... have to cut bait ..."

"... into little pieces ..."

Jacko laughs, cold and grim, turns back to the bed and unties the velvet straps.

"Get up."

She only looks at him. The words make sense, but there is no connection. She can't tie them to any purpose or action because the world is nothing but pain, all pain, everywhere.

"Get up or I'll pull you up by your hair."

Like he did Poli.

He takes her arm and hauls her up to a sitting position. Then he grabs a handful of her hair. She can't let him …

… a pile of bloody blonde curls on the floor.

Somehow she manages to shove herself upward on her numb legs. She stands, holding onto the bed post still encircled by the strips of velvet he'd used to tie her hands. She sways as Jacko speaks.

"I left no mark. She can work until we're ready."

Then the little smile is there again, he says something but the buzzing in her head eats most of his words. She hears only a few clearly and they don't make sense.

" … training video and you'll be the star of the show."

He gets into her face again, his breath unspeakably foul.

"If you will tell me what you saw from your hiding place under the bed, who else will you tell, huh?"

"Nobody!" The word explodes out her mouth so forcefully it carries little sprinkles of spit that splatter on his cheeks, dark spots, red or pink. He makes no move to wipe them away. "Never. I would … I swear I won't tell anybody, would never tell anybody … wouldn't …"

She's babbling, knows she's just prattling on but can't stop. He squeezes her arm in his hand the size of a shovel and the words fail.

"You say that now, yes. And tomorrow and for as long as you can still feel the pain I gave to you. As long as you remember it so fresh it's like you're living it all over again. Yes, for that long, you will be silent. But after that, when the pain is just a memory. Will you still keep quiet, little mouse?"

"I will, I—"

He squeezes again and she shuts up.

"You will squeak one day. It will happen. There is only one way to keep a mouse from squeaking. You stomp the mouse."

His cold eyes reflect the depths of the gray kingdom of his soul where no human emotion has ever lived. And she realizes that she has not been spared death by admitting what she saw and taking the punishment. She has only postponed death. He will not let her live.

Then he shoves her back down onto the bed and she curls into a fetal position there.

"Rest, little mouse. Your beauty is worth a lot of money."

He doesn't ask her any more questions!

He merely turns on his heel and walks out of the room and closes the door behind him. Jeni bleats out a single sob, feeling the brokenness inside her, knowing something is very, very wrong there.

But he didn't ask!

He didn't ask if she was alone in Poli's room when she watched him kick Poli's teeth down her throat, watched him dangle her in front of him until she hung still and limp.

He didn't ask her if there was anyone else in the room, hiding with her. So she hadn't told him.

Chapter Twenty-Seven

THE SHERIFF PULLED his cruiser into the driveway of the Watford House, turned off the ignition but didn't get out. The news he brought wasn't anything anybody wanted to hear, so he sat for a moment, gathering himself.

Other houses in the neighborhood had been festooned with Halloween decorations, but the Watford House remained bare. Bailey wasn't a fan of ghosts, goblins, ghouls or black cats. And spiders? Black, hairy, crawly things were noticeably absent from the whole town's decorations this year. Not surprising, that.

The front screen door was open and he could hear Sparky and the puppy yapping inside. He knocked, then opened the screen door and called inside.

"Anybody here order pizza?"

T.J. came into the living room and didn't take the bait. That was not a good sign.

"Bailey's in the kitchen. I been trying to get some hot tea down her and I think she's finally coming around."

Coming around? Brice's gut yanked into a knot.

"What happened?"

"Another vision.

"She painted another painting?"

"Same painting, different day."

Bailey looked up when he entered the room and he was struck by how pale she was. Her eyes looked like cigarette burns in her face.

T.J. suddenly stepped past Brice, snatched the puppy up off the floor and hurried outside with him. The smile that appeared on Bailey's face was wan but genuine.

"House breaking."

Brice pulled out a chair and sat down across the table from her.

"Would it offend you if I told you that you look like death on a cracker?"

"I certainly wouldn't want to look any better than I feel and I feel like death on a cracker, with a side order of fried awful."

"I don't want to make it worse, but—"

"The girl's dead."

"The connection broke." It wasn't a question, but she nodded slowly.

"Last night ... it was just gone. What ... where did you find ... the body?"

"We weren't supposed to. The killer intended for that girl to just vanish. Chained her body to a concrete block and chucked her into the deepest part of the lake. The chains caught on a houseboat anchor, random fluke. A couple more days and it would have sunk into the mud on the bottom, been covered up and we never would have found her."

"And you're sure ..."

"The rose birthmark." He didn't tell her that had it not been for the mark, and her freckles, there'd certainly been no way to identify her by sight. "We're running her prints, trying to find out who she is."

"Her name is Polly ... *was* Polly."

"And you know that because ...?"

"The other girl, Jeni, the one who saw the murder. That's what she called her."

She must have seen his mind stumble, trying to catch her train of thought, so she told him about the dark space under the bed and the girl who was hiding there.

"And you just … painted her, the other girl? Just like that — painted her into the picture?"

"I didn't *paint her into the picture.* I *found* her there. I couldn't have painted somebody into the picture who wasn't there to begin with. It was a little like …" she paused for a beat, "Riley Campbell. There was a reason I didn't paint him when I tried to. Someone … else was there, in that canvas."

And that someone had very nearly killed everybody in this room.

"Someone else came through this canvas, too. Go see for yourself. And there's more …"

T.J. brought the puppy back into the house before she could tell him about the more. He didn't press her. She didn't appear to have the strength to accompany him to the studio and that was concerning.

T.J. set the dog down on the floor at her feet and she immediately snatched it up into her arms, snuggling it to her face.

"T.J., why don't you show Brice my latest work of art. I think I'd like to just sit here awhile and drink my tea." She picked up the sugar bowl.

"You done got enough sugar in that thing to trot a mouse across," T.J. said.

"If I leave the cubes in the bowl, Dobbs will make a coal mine out of them." Brice could hear her straining for levity she didn't feel.

"You and Dobbs. You both gonna die from clogged up arteries. I mean, if Oscar don't get you first."

Brice cringed at the remark, but wasn't surprised by it. T.J. was determined to demystify the guillotine hanging over her head. Better to laugh at it than to brood over it. Brice was learning that T.J. didn't often miss on such things.

Sitting on an easel in the center of the studio was the portrait of the girl whose body had been dragged out of the lake by a fisherman. Polly. But now there was more to see in the painting. Where there had been only a portion of a bed and bedspread, and a slice of darkness under it, now the darkness had taken over that whole side of the portrait, in the same way the window behind the still-life in all the paintings was disproportionately large to show the image in it. The image in the puddle of darkness was a girl's face, her features rendered in such exquisite detail it was chilling, like it was a digital photograph. She was blonde, too, but hers was the pale blonde hair of a towheaded child, of Marilyn Monroe. Not curly, but hanging long and straight around her face. Her eyes were blue. Not sapphire blue. Robin's egg blue. The blue of a blanket that proclaims "baby boy."

Brice turned from the painting and asked T.J., "What did this girl see?"

"Not saw. Lived through. What she *and Bailey* lived through."

T.J.'s face bore none of the pleasant calm he'd worn in the kitchen, teasing Bailey about the sugar in her tea. His mouth was a thin line.

"They hosed that girl. You know what that is, don't you?"

Brice knew.

"But do you know what that means?" T.J.'s voice was tight, reigned in, like if he let it go he was afraid of what he might say.

"I understand it's incredibly painful."

"I didn't just *hear* it was painful." T.J. dropped his voice to something just above a whisper, though even if he'd spoken out loud, Bailey couldn't have heard him from the kitchen. "I know exactly how painful it is." He took a breath, let it out slowly. "I been hosed. I know."

Brice managed to keep his shock off his face. Most people knew T.J. had won a whole slew of medals when he was in the military, medals he wouldn't talk about. Only a few knew he'd been in Special Forces, too, but even those few didn't put it together in their heads what that meant — that T.J. had done things and gone places he *couldn't* talk about. And in one of those places, he'd been captured. And hosed.

Instinctively, Brice reached out a hand and placed it on T.J.'s shoulder, felt how boney it was. Skinny, but somehow not a fragile old man. T.J. looked at him, their eyes locked, and a world of communication passed between them. Then Brice dropped his hand and focused his attention on the portrait before them on the easel.

Chapter Twenty-Eight

IN A SINGLE, simple gesture, Brice had conveyed his understanding of the horror that T.J. ... *and Bailey* ... had endured. He got it.

T.J. turned back to the painting and tried to get his face and feelings under control.

"I was the one told her to do it. Told her to go on ahead and see was there somebody else in the picture — because I didn't think she'd find anything. Just wishful thinking, her feeling so bad that this awful thing come to pass even though she'd tried to prevent it."

He stopped, ran his hands over his close-cropped hair.

"I's just a little boy, nine years old when I seen how my Mama looked after she painted something awful, how worn out and used-up she looked. She told me once, 'I was there. Inside her.' I knew it musta been awful, understood it musta been awful. But I never really knew until I met Bailey."

He wouldn't let his mind go back to that nightmare on steroids he'd faced as Bailey blinked in and out of the mind of an insane child two months ago. He'd walled off what happened to them that day in The Cedars, put razor wire on the top of the wall. Stationed guards with Uzis every six feet. He figured the others had done the same.

"I only encouraged Bailey today because I thought wouldn't nothin' happen. If I'd knowed, if I'd even suspected she'd really find somebody else in the painting, I'd a'took that thing out into the back yard, chopped it up and burned it."

He paused, lookin' at the face of the girl in the darkness under the bed. She was beautiful, but her face was etched in horror, disbelief, grief and fear. She was watching the monster, the Beast, kill her friend.

"Now, I got to."

"Have to what?"

"Destroy that painting."

"Now? What good would it do now?"

"Bailey didn't tell you?"

"I suppose not because I don't know what you're talking about."

T.J. told him about Polly's plan to run away, about the ring and about Jeni confessing that she'd been a witness to Polly's murder.

"This girl, this Jeni, admitted she'd been in the room, hiding under the bed, seen the whole thing."

He took a deep, shuddery breath.

"He ain't gonna let her live now. He can't, not after what she seen."

"Why didn't he just kill her on the spot? Why'd he let her live?"

"He's got some kinda plan. I don't know what it is, but he's waiting for somethin'. And he don't know the whole of it. She'd a'told him, but he didn't ask."

"Ask what?"

"She didn't tell him she wasn't the *only* one hidin' in that room when he strangled that poor girl. She wasn't the only witness."

Brice's eyes flew to the dark area around the face where the paint was still wet.

"You're telling me there's *somebody else* under that—?"

"Don't stare at it like you might be able to see it. It ain't for eyes like ours."

Then T.J. could see Brice begin to put the pieces together in his head.

"And you think Bailey's going to want to paint the other girl, too?"

"*Girls.* They's more than one. And she sure as Jackson don't *want* to. But will she? Yeah, I'm bettin' she's gonna do just that if we can't find *this girl*" — he gestured to the still-wet face on the canvas — "get her and the others outta there before the Beast makes good on his threats. If we can't find her …"

He could tell Brice was makin' the right connections and nodded.

"Yeah, and if she paints the other girls, what will *they* be livin' through? He's plannin' somethin' awful, maybe for all of 'em. So what kinda torture will they …?" He couldn't go on. He found breath enough to say only one word. "Oscar."

The two men stood together in silence, gazing at the terrified face of the little mouse under the bed.

"Then we have to find her," Brice said. He reached out and almost touched the painting, forgettin' it was wet paint that formed the incredible detail and not points of light on a digital screen. "This girl — we have to find her before that monster kills her."

"And before livin' through some awful torture kills Bailey!"

～

BRICE STEPPED BACK into the kitchen and managed not to stare at Bailey. But when she wasn't looking his way he shot sideways glances, now understanding *why* she was so pale and haggard, with dark circles under her eyes like she'd missed a week of sleep.

There wasn't a mark on her. Of course, there wasn't a mark on the girl who'd actually endured the torturous beating, either. Such was the benefit of hosing as opposed to other forms of torture.

When Bailey looked at him, he said, "What you painted, the likeness is amazing." He managed to keep his voice level. "It looks like a digital photograph instead of a painting."

"I saw."

He included T.J. and Dobbs in what he said next.

"The clarity of that image is going to help us find her — *tonight*."

The others straightened.

"*Find* her—?" Bailey began.

"Tonight?" Dobbs finished for her.

"We know the girl who was murdered was a prostitute working the casino. Obviously, Jeni's a working girl there, too. The guy who hosed her, their murdering pimp, said she was fine, that she could work tonight. Which means she's at the Nautilus *right now*."

"So we're going to go there, try to find her?" Bailey said.

"*We* aren't going anywhere. T.J., Dobbs and I are going to look for her."

"But I—"

"You're going to stay right here with Bundy."

"I could help—"

"I don't need your help. This time, I'm the guy with a badge and a gun. When we find this girl, I'll tell her we believe she has information about the murder of a girl named Polly, whose body my deputies dragged out of Whispering Mountain Lake this morning."

"Can you get her out of the casino *tonight*?"

"I can't take her into protective custody unless she tells me what she saw ... but I'm betting she doesn't know that." He held up his hand. "Legally, I can't *hold* her if she doesn't want to stay—"

"But once you get her out of the clutches of that monster, she'll be *eager* to tell you everything," Dobbs said.

"What about the other girls?"

"One step at a time. We get her, she talks, we bust the pimp. Lock him up so he can't hurt any of them."

Brice deliberately looked away from Bailey and addressed the others as if she weren't there. She was going to sit this one out, whether she liked it or not.

"Take a picture with your phone of that girl's face. Then we'll split up and search the casino, top to bottom."

"Just the three of you? Can't you use your deputies …?"

"Nope." He gestured at the others. "We're on the hook for this one. *We* know this girl witnessed a murder, but *how* we know … I've got nothing I could take before a judge to get a search warrant … *yet.* As soon as this girl talks, I'll march into that place with an army!"

"What if the three of you can't find her?

"We'll find her. But if we don't, we'll go back tomorrow night and the night after. Eventually, she'll turn up."

Dobbs nodded. T.J. did the same.

Bailey didn't protest. Maybe because she had seen the logic — this was a police matter now. Brice was the one to handle it. But maybe it was because she didn't feel up to going to the casino, or anywhere else for that matter.

He managed not to shudder at the thought of her being beaten with a hose. She hadn't been, but she had felt the blows as if she had, and even though she'd suffered no physical injury, the visceral memory was still there. The horror and fear. Those lingered.

He couldn't let himself dwell on what Bailey Whatever-Her-Last-Name-Really-Was had endured. A young woman so small and — okay, she wasn't delicate and frail, but she was certainly too thin and … well, she needed to start working out.

Eulalie Hamilton had dealt with the horror of paintings like these for three years but in the end, she couldn't stand it any longer. Was that Bailey's future — suicide … successful this time? Or would Oscar finally get her when the stress became too much?

He couldn't do anything about all that now. What he could do was *find that girl.* Unless they found her, Bailey would most certainly connect with the other girls, the other witnesses. And God only knew what might be happening that she'd have to live through with them.

Chapter Twenty-Nine

Raymond Dobson moved with surprising grace for a big man. Like some behemoth former linebacker for the Pittsburgh Steelers, he glided around roulette wheels, behind faro tables and past slot machines. He didn't try to hide the fact that he was "looking for someone." No reason to. At any given time, half the people in the casino were likely looking for the other half.

It would have been useless to search for the girl tonight, on Halloween, had it not been for the "no masks" policy the casino rigidly enforced. Halloween costumes were acceptable — *welcomed*! But thousands of people with their faces covered was just begging for a robbery

Even with faces bared, the chances of finding one small needle in the gigantic casino haystack would have been slim, had Brice not plotted the whole thing out in advance and assigned each of them their role when they met him on the launch late that afternoon.

Detailed architectural plans of the casino had been furnished to local law enforcement officers before the establishment opened. Oh, Brice knew the plans weren't accurate, that there were rooms in that huge building — maybe designated maintenance or HVAC or just absorbed into the space of the surrounding rooms — that were really the sites of invitation-only gambling, a hundred, two-hundred-thousand-dollar-ante games. Dobbs had seen those in Monaco. He'd even been one of the players, briefly, though he wasn't by nature a risk-taking kind of guy. T.J. had been the adrenaline junkie in their relationship. He'd joined the Marines, signed up for Special Forces. Dobbs, on the other hand, had gone to college, where he'd made an interesting observation: he was astonishingly good at "pretend risk-taking."

That single revelation had made him a multi-millionaire.

During the first semester of his freshman year, Dobbs fell in love with the challenge of playing the stock market. His father's business had gone belly up right after Dobbs graduated from the fancy prep school he'd been shipped off to that was preparing him for an Ivy League education. Harvard. That'd been the plan. Then Harvard Law School. His life had been totally plotted out for him by his parents. Add water and stir.

But instead of Harvard, that fall, Dobbs enrolled in West Virginia University because he was dead broke and the school charged no tuition to West Virginia residents. And then spent arguably the most important week of his life in the wrong class.

The penniless young man from Kavanaugh County had sat spellbound, listening to the first couple of lectures in a fascinating economics class before he was informed there'd been a mistake in his registration, that he was supposed to be in the 101 class, not in this senior level program. He went once to the 101 class and nodded off. For the remainder of that semester, he'd sat in the back, unnoticed in the senior level class, absorbing every detail that came his way.

In that class, all the students were provided a mythical one thousand dollars to invest as they saw fit. They could buy any stock, sell any stock, throw it all into grain futures — whatever their four previous years of business school training led them to believe would be profitable. At the end of the semester, all the students compared their successes and failures. Since Dobbs wasn't officially enrolled in the class, his numbers were not calculated with the others. It was a shame, really, because he had turned his mythical $1,000 into $58,912.

The next semester, he audited the second semester of the class, *signed up* to audit it, so he could participate in the class activities but would receive no grade or credit. That semester, he turned his $58,000 of Monopoly money into $211,000.

Of course, in reality, Raymond Dobson didn't have three cents to rub together, had to work two jobs to pay for his books. One of the jobs was as a night watchman at a You-Store-It facility. But his day job was at Dunkin' Donuts. Bad choice. He put on weight almost as fast as he made money, but the weight was real even if the money wasn't, and by summer he was fifty pounds heavier — and no richer — than he'd been in September.

During the summer, he worked so hard he lost almost all the weight he'd gained at the doughnut shop. He held four jobs — was a red-hat miner, a stock boy at Walmart, loaded boxes at UPS and cut lawns on weekends. When school started for his sophomore year, he had saved almost $2,000 of *real money.*

He discovered quickly that making and losing a fortune in imaginary money was easy. No psychological pain. No stress. Real money, though … not so much. He'd worked his considerable butt off — literally— to earn every nickel of that money and he couldn't help being careful with it, wasn't inclined to take risks, put it almost exclusively into conservative investments. At the end of the year, he had turned his $2,000 into $3,500 — certainly a profit, but not the killing he had made before.

So he decided to set aside five hundred dollars to use as

imaginary money. He pretended it wasn't real, watched it grow … then lost almost every cent of it in a risky grain futures purchase … but earned it all back and more investing in early electronics stocks. At the end of the semester, Dobbs dropped out of school and got a job as a janitor in a brokerage firm in Pittsburgh to have access to the latest data.

The rest was history. At age twenty-seven, he purchased the brokerage firm. A millionaire before he was thirty, he'd continued to amass a fortune he considered "ridiculously excessive" and was ready to retire before he was forty. By then he was bored out of his gourd, homesick, lonesome and a hundred pounds heavier than he'd been in college.

So he'd gone back home to Kavanaugh County and lived modestly, occupied his time making furniture in his wood-working shop, fishing, volunteering for half a dozen different charities in town, fishing, playing a little golf … and fishing. Only a handful of people in the whole county had any idea he was a multi-millionaire.

It was right after he bought the brokerage firm that he and some other financial whiz-kid friends went on a "sabbatical" to see the world. Specifically, the gambling establishments on every continent. Dobbs found he enjoyed games of chance, and over the next decade, he made something of a name for himself in casinos for the rich and famous all over the planet. As Raymond F. Dobson, III. Only in Kavanaugh County was he Dobbs.

The decade taught him lessons he would use for the rest of his life, though he was not nearly as good at playing blackjack as he had been at playing the stock market. He decided to cash in his chips, so to speak, after he was taken to the cleaners in a $25,000-dollar ante poker game in Monaco, lost close to a quarter of a million dollars. He never told T.J. about it, figured the money was about what he'd have spent on the Ivy League education he didn't get and it had taught him way more than he'd have learned at Harvard.

In truth, it was T.J. who was the gambler. If T.J. hadn't insisted they play for matchsticks in their almost nightly poker games for the past decade, he'd have been the millionaire and Dobbs would have been living on Social Security.

So Dobbs was completely at ease cruising the floors of the Nautilus Casino, searching the faces of the couples at the blackjack tables, standing next to the roulette wheel, not looking at the wheel but at the people looking at the wheel.

He kept in contact with T.J. and Brice by phone every half hour. The three of them had been searching for more than two hours when Dobbs spotted her. He'd been looking for so long that he didn't even trust his identification, called Brice and T.J. to the third floor to confirm his find. Yep, that was the girl, alright.

One reason he'd spotted her was that he hadn't been looking for a girl who was the life of the party. After the torture she'd endured earlier in the day, she'd be in the background with a smile pasted on her face like an airmail sticker on an envelope. Indeed, the girl Dobbs had located standing behind her "date" as he played blackjack looked barely able to stand at all.

Once Brice and T.J. confirmed the sighting, the plan went into phase two. And Dobbs was to be the star of the show.

Dobbs took the first available seat at the blackjack table and stacked up the chips he had just purchased — two big stacks, ten thousand dollars each. Then, he proceeded to play like a riverboat gambler. He bet ridiculous amounts — so he lost ridiculous amounts, but the cards were falling his way and he won ridiculous amounts as well. Pretty soon, casual gamblers stopped to watch him play. He cranked up a fake West Virginia hick accent, acted mildly inebriated and enormously gregarious, and in less than half an hour, he had attracted a crowd. The girl's john was fascinated, went head to head with Dobbs and the girl was gradually pushed to the side. She didn't fight for her spot, and the john never even missed her.

When she went to the ladies' room, T.J. and Brice were in position.

Chapter Thirty

Brice boldly followed Jeni into the ladies' room, wordlessly flashing his badge to the startled women he encountered coming out. The big Scot was an imposing figure, and no one questioned his authority. It would be T.J.'s job to discourage other women from entering, pointing out that they might want to select another restroom. His date was in this one puking her guts out and it likely wasn't the freshest smelling bathroom on the premises.

Brice figured he had three, maybe four minutes before what was going on came to the attention of the roving security forces of the casino. They were prowling lions in gray suits with lapel mics and earbuds, and it was their job to know every time a customer passed gas in the facility. They knew how to read crowds and faces, and the ever-vigilant eye-in-the-sky security cameras provided a real-time picture of the crowd, with zoom-in capacity on any individual. Dobbs had definitely drawn their attention by now, was being watched from several different angles. One of their number would notice the women turning away from the ladies' room quickly and come to investigate.

So Brice had only a handful of minutes to convince this

Jeni to come with him willingly. Or to take her into protective custody, which he had no legal right to do. He had no right to arrest her either, charge her with being a material witness to a homicide or with prostitution — neither of which would hold up in any court in the country because he had not a shred of evidence to prove either charge.

And hauling the girl out of the casino in handcuffs would cause an enormous kerfuffle.

And then he would be the one who'd stepped in it if he arrested her and she flat out refused to cooperate — which she could do. All he had was the belief … the *hope* that once she was out of the clutches of her pimp, she'd open up and tell him what she saw, and be willing to testify to it. But as with the murdered girl with the ruined face whose body he'd hauled out of the lake this morning, this girl would make her own decisions. If she decided she didn't want any help, Brice couldn't force it on her.

But he had to try. For the girl's sake and for Bailey's, too.

She had washed her hands, and when she turned to get one of the stack of fluffy white clouds with the periscope logo of the Nautilus embossed on it with gold thread, she saw him standing in the doorway. She cried out and leapt back, understandably alarmed. What was this *man* doing in the ladies' restroom? Brice didn't have time to pussyfoot around the issue so he came right to the point.

"Are you Jeni?"

Her eyes widened and she stared at him like a rabbit caught in a snare.

"I'm Kavanaugh County Sheriff Brice McGreggor, and I know you witnessed a murder."

He might as well have announced, "Hi, I'm Satan, Lord of the Underworld, here to eat you alive."

In fact, she looked like that's exactly what he *did* say.

And hers wasn't the fear of a call girl facing a night in jail, even of a hooker afraid her pimp would beat her up for getting caught.

This wasn't secondhand terror. This girl wasn't afraid of what might happen to her *because of Brice.* She was afraid of Brice. Terrified of him, in fact. He'd seldom seen such naked terror in anyone's eyes and it literally stopped him in mid-sentence.

Shaking her head pitifully back and forth, she mouthed "no," as she backed away from him until she hit the wall on the other side of the room.

"It is true. You *do* see through walls, hear what is only whispered ..."

This girl was delusional, too? How could that possibly be?

"Ma'am, I'm not going to hurt you. I'm here to help you."

"No." She shook her head, her eyes as big as fried eggs. "The note told Polina to help so she run away and she die."

The girl's accent was so thick he had to concentrate to understand her. Eastern European, he thought, but that was a lot of real estate. Poland, Ukraine, Bulgaria. He didn't know which one it might be, but he did know, for lead pipe certain, that English was *not* her first language.

That and her mental state begged all sorts of questions, which under other circumstances he would have asked immediately. He didn't, though. First, he had to clarify what she had just said.

"Wait a minute, you're saying, you're telling me *the note* ... she got the note and that's *why* she ran away, that's why ..."

"She told me of the note. I went to say her no, but she was gone. Please to let me go. Don't take my heart from me while it still beats. Or my eyes."

"What are you talking about?"

"If they find you illegal, Americans take you to use the parts of your bodies ... to transplant."

"*Organ donors!* Who told you——?"

She started to cry, whimpering pitifully, "I want to go home to Momi and Poppi."

When his stumbling mind put the pieces together, connected everything she had just said — *illegal … Momi and Poppi* — he was almost afraid to ask.

"How *old* are you?"

"Eighteen," came out too quick and practiced.

"How old are you — *the truth?*"

"Sixteen … after Christmas."

That was a conversation stopper.

She looked every day of twenty-five. Of course, the right kind of makeup and clothes could make a four-year-old look sexy these days. Brice's mind fumbled to rearrange all his assumptions, to process the *massive* implications. Romanian, Bulgarian … *a child.* And the other girls, the shapes Bailey sensed in the closet … how many? They were *children.*

International sex slaves!

"Nobody's going to hurt you." He took a step toward her and she cringed so pathetically, he backed up. "You have to understand, I only want to help you."

"The woman with the note said to help Poli. Now Poli dead. They find the note, now the woman will be dead, too."

In spite of the moist air, Brice's mouth instantly went sawdust dry. His heart kicked into a gallop so quick he could feel a delayed drumbeat in his ears.

"What are you saying?" He listened to her reply with his whole body, a tautness in him like a bowstring with the arrow ready to fly.

"The Beast will find. I heard him say to look. Then Jacko will do to her what he did to Poli."

Find. Her.

The sound of those two words was drowned by his own heartbeat, no longer just fast but heavy, sledgehammer heavy, pounding and pounding, slamming blood to his brain to flush out the connections flashing from one synapse to another there between one second and the next.

Find … *Bailey.*

The note. Bailey said she'd written it on the back of a receipt. That little dress shop on Milliken Street, Foxy Lady — no, Sassy Fox. It was a small town — *they could find her.*

"They" being way more than a single homicidal pimp. "They" being people who operated an international sex slave ring, who kidnapped children, *sold fifteen-year-olds* and then murdered them.

Brice snatched his phone out of his pocket. His fingers stone, cold steady, he punched the emergency number at the station.

Fletcher picked up on the first ring.

"Yes sir!" he said, as if Brice had called him by name.

"Dispatch every available unit to the Watford House ten-sixty." Which meant lights and sirens. "Respond to a ten-ten!" Assault in progress. "I repeat, a ten-ten." That part couldn't be true. Whoever "they" were couldn't possibly—

He turned back to the girl.

She was gone.

He took two giant steps to the door where T.J. was supposed to be standing. He, too, was gone.

"Bailey!" Brice whispered. His phone still in his hand, he punched her number.

The phone rang and rang and rang. It wasn't turned off or he would have been sent immediately to voicemail. It was ringing but she wasn't answering it.

"Hi, this is Bailey. Leave me a message and I'll call you back."

T.J. appeared in front of him, winded.

"Lost her," he said. "She come running out of there like her pants was on fire and went," he pointed toward a large crowd of costumed people, where a fat dude dressed as Where's Waldo was engaged in a loud, drunken conversation with the Cowardly Lion, Batman and Princess Leia, "slick as an oiled minnow into that crowd. I got hold of her wrist, but she yanked free … and other than tackling her — an old black man jumping on a little white girl — I couldn't hold her. Then she was just gone. Vanished. Couldn't see her nowhere."

Brice was only half-listening as he punched redial on his phone.

Bailey must be upstairs and left the phone downstairs. Or the other way around. Or in the bathroom, or … just didn't hear the ring. That was why she didn't pick up — nothing more sinister than that!

But she'll see the message light and she'll play it. What can he say?

"Bailey, do exactly what I tell you. Get in your car *right now* and drive to the sheriff's department. Just like you told Macy Cosgrove — *drop everything and run!*"

As soon as he hung up, he dialed again.

The phone rang … and rang … and rang.

Chapter Thirty-One

… THE PHONE RANG and rang and rang …

Well, whatever it was would just have to wait.

The phone was lying on the kitchen counter and Bailey could hear it from the back yard. Odds were ten to one it was a telemarketer. Though she could count on one hand all the people in her life who knew her phone number and would possibly give her a call, every telemarketer for ten thousand miles in every direction had it. She got calls from all over the country. She never answered them, except to yell at a recording that "I don't need dental implants!" or to try to convince an automated attendant that she didn't have the requisite Y chromosome to need a prescription for Viagra. But still they called.

The phone on the counter continued to ring.

Bailey had made herself a tomato sandwich — the only thing that'd sounded good enough to entice her still-tied-in-a-knot stomach to accept nutrition. During the last few weeks of summer, she'd stopped every couple of days at a roadside vegetable stand that was long closed now. When the yearning for a salad had hit her two days ago — as she drove home from the dress store where she'd bought the slinky green dress

— she'd settled for supermarket veg, definitely iffy this time of year.

Though the tomatoes had gotten slightly mushy, she'd cut off two-inch-thick slices, placed them in a puddle of mayonnaise slathered on a piece of bread and added generous portions of salt and pepper. It was good. She'd managed to get down almost all of it before she'd felt the shadow pain in her back from the "hosing" that hadn't really happened to her. Except it had, and remembered pain took her breath and her appetite away.

Setting the sandwich down, she'd picked the puppy up and gone out into the back yard to the designated "potty spot." She'd told him kindly but firmly, "Go potty!" He'd wandered around, sniffing the grass.

That's when her phone had begun to ring in the kitchen.

Maybe it wasn't telemarketers. Maybe it was Brice or T.J. or Dobbs. They were at the casino looking for the girl who'd been … hosed. Maybe they'd found her.

She looked down at the puppy. He appeared to be just about ready to squat. The phone rang again. If she wasn't ready with a treat the instant he complied, the potty trip was wasted. She could snatch the dog up and maybe get to the phone in time … she thought just as he proceeded to squat and a small trail of yellow liquid puddled under him.

"Good dog!" she cried and knelt beside him, telling him he was the most wonderful dog that ever drew breath, petting him lavishly and dropping his favorite bacon-flavored treat onto his little pink tongue.

The phone had stopped ringing.

She started back into the house, but the puppy suddenly pricked his ears up, looked toward the gate in the fence and started barking furiously. Probably the neighbor's cat.

"Bundy, come!" she called, and motioned inside.

The puppy did not yet have … what had T.J. called it — consistent recall. He didn't have any recall at all, as a matter of fact, came when he felt like it and otherwise ignored her. Now, he continued to bark furiously, like a Doberman in an eight-pound body. She went to the back door, opened it and continued to call him. He suddenly lost interest in the back gate and the neighbor's cat that surely was on the other side, but still showed no interest in "recall" either until she waved a treat at him. Then he pranced into the house, pausing long enough to snatch the probably-made-out-of-soybeans fake bacon out of her hand.

She went to the phone on the counter and saw the red light blinking that indicated she had a message. The puppy suddenly bolted out of the kitchen toward the front door, barking furiously. Apparently, the neighbor's cat was playing taunt-the-puppy.

The dog stood in the living room, barking at the door. Bailey picked up the telephone and listened to the message.

And then she couldn't breathe. Or think. Or move. She was in molasses, she remembered the feeling. Remembered it too well.

And this time, the murderer wouldn't be distracted by the poor soaked-to-the-skin homeless woman who had taken Bailey's place in the grave.

Think.

The car. *Run!*

The puppy was still barking furiously.

And it wasn't at the neighbor's cat.

Bailey was suddenly so terrified she couldn't have drawn in a breath if there had been any oxygen left in the room to breathe, which there wasn't.

She couldn't get to the car. It was parked out front. Out the back door? No, the puppy had been barking at the back gate, too.

Survival instinct took over as it had done that night in the rain almost two years ago. It screamed the same word into her mind now that it had screamed then.

Hide!

The hallway and stairs were dark and she bolted up them with no clear idea where she was going, just a panicked run. There were six bedrooms and three bathrooms on the second floor. Only two of the bedrooms had any furniture in them — her bedroom and another one already furnished with a gigantic four-poster bed and matching armoire when she moved in. She'd stored all her unpacking mess in that room — Amazon cartons, huge boxes that contained smaller packages inside. Piles of bubble wrap, a couple of garbage bags full of packing worms. The room was stacked high with all that; her bedroom provided only a closet for concealment. The other bedroom, then. She dashed into it and closed the door silently behind her, looked around desperately in the dark.

A sickening sense of deja vu washed over her.

HIDE, hide, hide — she has to hide!

Looking around frantically, she spots the dumpsters. Without even getting to her knees, she commando crawls toward them across the wet asphalt, gravel and then mud. The nearest is only ten or twelve feet away and the car blocks her from the view of the gunmen in the street.

THE BEDROOM WAS on the front of the Watford House and the streetlight outside the window shined through the crack between the curtains, casting a saber of light into the room, enough for Bailey to make her way among the packing boxes. Some of them were huge, but empty they weighed nothing at all. She pushed the boxes out of her way, dived under the bed, then reached out and pulled the boxes back into place between the bed and the door.

. . .

THERE'S ONLY about eighteen inches of clearance under the dumpster, but she scoots under it, jams herself beneath it and shoves her way through the mud and filth, pushes as far back as she can go.

She can't lift her head to look out. Her right cheek is smashed into the mud and all she can see is the bottom of the front door of her car and her cellphone lying on the rain-drenched street beside it.

WITH HER FACE against the cold hardwood flooring, Bailey could hear nothing but the hammering sound of her heart, exploding with every beat, so fast it didn't seem like there were individual beats at all, just a solid humming sound.

Bundy was barking furiously downstairs.

Then the puppy yelped and fell silent.

Oh dear God, no.

A storm of abject terror blew through her, rattling all the doors and windows of her soul.

No.

She held her breath, waited, her belly alive with winged creatures fluttering frantically through her body and into her bones.

Was that a sound on the stairs? They creak, all the steps creak. Did she hear one make a sound? Her heart was thundering so loud … did she hear … footsteps?

SHE HEARS FOOTSTEPS, sees wet shoes. Someone has come around to that side of the car. The man is only ten feet from her. The panic in her chest explodes like some Navy dinghy when you pull on the strap. If she'd had any air, if she could have breathed at all, she'd have screamed, wouldn't have been able to hang onto the wail as it leapt unbidden out of her throat. All he has to do is lean over and he will see her. But she has no air to scream and remains silent. He stoops down, his back to her, picks up her phone and tosses it into the car on top of her purse. Then she hears scuffling feet.

The other man has picked up the body of the homeless woman and is dragging it across the street. He drags it around the car and the two of them pick it up, toss it into the front seat on top of Bailey's purse and phone and slam the door.

THE STEP DID CREAK! She heard it distinctly.

No! This wasn't, *couldn't be* happening. She was imagining the sound—

She heard the door to her bedroom open down the hall.

Bailey had wanted to die, had put a gun to her temple and pulled the trigger so she would die. Now, she was going to get what she wan—

Bethany!

The name detonated, imploded though, a nuclear reactor creating a black hole in the universe in the center of her chest. They knew Bailey was alive, had come looking for her, had found her before she could testify against the man the federal marshal had said had no soul. She had dared to cross Sergei Wassily Mikhailov. And now he would kill her. But not just her — that was the thing. *He would murder her whole family!*

A small sob escaped her lips, so soft no one could hear.

The door of the room opened. Someone turned on the light. She could see feet clad in clunky black shoes. Boxes were shoved aside, out of the way.

And *this time* the man *would* lean over and look. And he would see her.

Chapter Thirty-Two

The feet approached the bed.

One more second. Two.

The silence was suddenly shattered by the wail of a siren — of more than one siren. *More than two sirens.* The symphony did not sound distant, like it was far away and getting closer. It erupted instantly, so loud the source might be sitting in her front yard.

The feet remained where they were. Big feet — a big man. The shoes were the heavy, lace-up kind, ugly but shined so perfectly she could almost see her reflection in the surface.

Then the feet turned and clunked in loud footsteps out of the room. She could hear the sound of them thundering down the stairs. Heard the back door open. Heard the screen slam shut.

Heard … silence.

Not silence, sirens. But *only* sirens. He was gone.

Bailey slumped on the hardwood floor amid the dust bunnies and began to sob. Relief on top of terror. Then she suddenly stopped crying because she couldn't move or breathe.

Bethany!

They'd found her, they would find her daughter, too. All these months of hiding, waiting for soon, soon, *soon.* All of it to keep her baby daughter safe.

And now …

She slid out from under the bed and raced down the stairs with no destination in mind except to get to her daughter, to hide her, to protect her somehow, to …

Deputy Fletcher, the one who was shot on the Fourth of July — had that been her fault? — was standing in her living room and he caught her as she flew past him. She tried to shake free — he didn't understand, she had to go, she had to get to Bethany.

"It's alright, Miss Donahue," the stalwart deputy said, and didn't let go of her arm. "If someone was here, they're gone now. You're safe."

"Let me go. I have to …"

To what? What could she do?

Another deputy stepped up and handed Fletcher a phone. He listened for a second and then held it out to Bailey.

"The sheriff wants to talk to you."

She took it wordlessly, a robot. It had all been for nothing. All the waiting and the loneliness and the fear … it had been useless. He'd found them anyway. And he would kill them both. María, too.

"Bailey?"

She didn't answer, but a kind of moaning sound came from her throat that he must have heard.

"It's all right. You're safe now."

"Bethany." She whispered the name, caressed it with her mind, felt the sick dread rise up in her with the desperate need to do *something.*

"What did you say?"

He didn't wait for her to answer.

"They found the note to the girl on the back of the receipt."

He wasn't making any sense.

"They who?"

"It is so much bigger and worse than we had any idea. The girl, both the girls, are *teenagers*. They've been kidnapped from somewhere in Eastern Europe and brought here and forced into prostitution. When you gave the girl the note, they thought somebody had found them out."

It took several seconds for his words to register.

And even after they did, the meaning of them lagged behind, like one of those old movies where people's mouths move but what they say doesn't come out at the same time.

Brice was talking again and she tried to focus on what he was saying.

" … use them as organ donors."

"What?"

"The kidnappers told the girls that Americans use illegal aliens for organ donors. The girl, her name was Poli, Polina — I think that's Romanian or Bulgarian — that's what she was terrified of, the monsters who would take her heart and her eyes."

Bailey finally grasped what he was saying.

The girl! The note. It had nothing to do with … she suddenly sagged in relief. Deputy Fletcher caught her before she fell but she dropped the phone. He eased her down on the couch, picked up the phone and spoke to the sheriff.

"He'll be here as soon as he can," he said when he hung up. "He told me to tell you that."

The reality was settling over her and releasing the knot of terror in her belly. Mikhailov hadn't found her. This had nothing to do with the nightmare night and the rain and the dumpster and the rats and her precious, precious baby daughter. *Someone else* wanted to kill her.

And that struck Bailey as funny. The more she thought about it, the funnier it became. She recognized the signs of incipient hysteria but she just went with it. She was in the

Witness Protection Program because one group of organized criminals wanted to kill her, and now she had managed to piss off a whole *different* bunch of psychopaths and they wanted to kill her, too.

It was too absurd to be real. Jessie ... *Bailey* — the first-grader with knobby knees and elbows who'd flunked physical education in elementary school because she was so pathetically uncoordinated. The teenager who'd been too wrapped up in sports to date in high school and too embarrassed in college to admit she'd never learned how to dance. The adult who had never watched a single episode of *Oprah*, the *Academy Awards* or *American Idol*, who'd never kept up with a pair of sunglasses for more than three days, who had — that totally unremarkable human being had managed to earn a coveted spot on not one but *two* different hit lists. That was quite an accomplishment.

She began to laugh. The more she laughed, the more she was struck by the incredible, cosmic absurdity of it all and she laughed even harder. At some point, her laughter turned to tears and that was okay, too. Tears were fine. Cheering was fine. Doing cartwheels was fine. Everything was fine. *Bethany wasn't in danger.* She was safe.

Absolutely nothing else mattered.

And so she sat on the couch, laughing and crying in relief that the officers surely mistook for fear or shock. And then she felt something wet on her leg, looked down and there was the puppy, licking her.

Bundy! He'd yelped. The man must have—

She snatched him up into her arms and examined him. He wiggled and squirmed, delighted by the attention. She could find nothing wrong with him. So she held him, petted him and said stupid baby-talk things to him for some period of time that could have been ten minutes or four hours. Time had come unhitched from reality and she wallowed in that suspended perpetual now moment, her thoughts jumbled beyond easy repair but that was okay, too. Everything was fine. *Bethany was safe.*

And then T.J. and Dobbs were in her living room; Brice was kneeling on the floor in front of her. And there were paramedics. Why had they called an ambulance? Nobody had been hurt. Then she realized they'd come to examine her and when she tried to tell them, to tell Brice, that she was fine, not hurt, nobody was much interested in what she had to say on the subject.

So she performed their little tasks, kept her eyes on a fingertip as it moved back and forth in front of her eyes, remembered how impressed the nurse had been months ago when she'd been able to pull off the miraculous feat of multiplying seven times five. But they didn't ask her that this time. They'd all be gone soon and she could talk to Brice — and to T.J. and Dobbs, too, who had become Tweedledum and Tweedledee at some point in her mind but only in the most endearing way.

She watched the paramedic draw some liquid into a syringe and only connected that he meant to inject her with it when he used the alcohol swab on her arm.

"Hey, whoa, what is that?'

"It's something to relax you, that's all."

"And what if I don't want to relax?" She struggled to move away from the approaching needle. "What if I like to be tense?" She looked beseechingly at Brice. "Come on, Brice, tell them that my very favorite state in all the world is tense and semi-hysterical."

He smiled at that and she could see it was a relieved smile. Apparently, the remark had constituted multiplying seven times five. But if she let them stick her with—

She felt the prick in her arm and warmth immediately flooded her face. Then the whole world smoothed out. She recognized the familiar calming effects of narcotics. Yep, that was relaxed, alright. Not one doubt about it. She considered what it might be about this sensation that grabbed hold of some people, made them so desperate for this feeling they'd do anything — lie, steal — *anything* to achieve it. It was pleasant, in a warm, fuzzy, dopey sort of way, but who'd want to live every day like this?

She was definitely relaxing, though, and then she became tired, an instant tired, an oh-my-gosh-I-just-ran-a-marathon-backwards-carrying-a-Volkswagen exhaustion. Brice told her he would be here when she woke up, and she assumed he meant that she was about to go to sleep, which was just dandy with her at this point.

Two paramedics accompanied her up the stairs, a woman on each side so she couldn't just lie down on one of the steps and go to sleep, which was what she wanted to do.

They passed the guest room. The door was open and she could see the boxes shoved away from the bed where she — she felt terror, surging through her — but on the other side of some kind of gray haze that rendered it surreal, must have happened to somebody else. Then her head was floating down onto her pillow in slow motion, like one of those Sealy Posturepedic commercials where people sleep on clouds. She closed her eyes then and was gone.

Chapter Thirty-Three

SHERIFF MCGREGGOR WATCHED the EMTs lead a now-docile Bailey up the stairs to her bedroom. They'd given her a sedative. She would sleep.

She was safe.

The Beast, Jeni's word for the man who'd strangled Poli, believed Bailey was onto them somehow. What else was he supposed to believe when she'd warned the girl to run away from him or die? He thought Bailey knew who they were and what they were doing.

And so they'd gone after Bailey. Had been here tonight. If Fletch hadn't gotten here in time … Fletch and the other deputies had looked around outside with a flashlight, found a footprint in the mud outside the back gate. Could have been anybody's. But it wasn't just anybody's.

No sense hauling the state police crime lab guys out in the middle of the night. They could dust for prints in the morning, but they wouldn't find any. Even if they did, the prints wouldn't be in any database. These guys came and went like smoke in the wind.

He had stationed a squad car in front of the house and Deputy Tackett in the bushes beyond the back gate. There would be an armed officer with her at all times, from now on, until—

Right. Until what? Brice had to figure out how he was going to play this. He had no explanation for how he knew what he knew, at least not one that he could tell anybody. Before he pulled out all the stops, contacted all the other law enforcement agencies who should be involved in a multinational case — the state police, FBI, shoot, maybe even Homeland Security — he'd have to have more convincing evidence than the painting of a dead girl on an easel in Bailey's studio and a mythical fifteen-year-old who had vanished in the casino.

All he had by way of physical evidence was the body of a Jane Doe resting now on a slab in the morgue. At least now he knew where to look for her identity, the girl Jeni had called Polina. Poli. Probably with an "i" instead of a "y." Maybe Jeni was, too. That was a start. The ethnicity of those names … could have come from half a dozen Eastern European countries. Still, it was more than he'd known about her before.

T.J. and Dobbs had parked themselves in Bailey's kitchen. They all were reluctant to leave, not until they could see Bailey, talk to her. And Brice had no intention of leaving even then. He would be here, on guard, until … until whenever. Bailey was not going to be left alone again.

After the other officers left, Brice went to the kitchen and sat down heavily across the table from T.J.

"Coffee's fresh," T.J. said. "We been downin' it so fast it ain't had time to turn into road tar." Brice got up to get himself a cup and when he sat down with it — steaming and black — T.J. tried yet again to apologize for not stopping the girl named Jeni when she ran out of the bathroom.

Brice silenced him with a raised hand. "Why didn't *I* grab her? I knew who she was, you didn't. What's done is done. We need to figure out where to go from here."

"Where exactly is here?" Dobbs asked.

"'Here' is realizing the girl who was afraid of monsters that would eat her insides was not psychotic — just gullible. They kidnap the girls by making their parents a solid gold promise that they're an employment agency looking for girls to serve as au pairs, or in office jobs in the United States. Maybe the kidnappers even thought the girls were older — their parents could have lied to get them a good job in America."

"I thought they'd given up on straight kidnapping," T.J. said.

"Guess these guys must be old school."

"If they don't kidnap them, how—?" Dobbs began.

"They get around a kidnappin' charge by taking girls old enough to travel with their own passports. Course when they get here, they ain't greeted by the beautiful children whose picture the recruiter showed to everybody in the village. They wind up in some dark basement, bein' 'broken in' by their pimp."

"Kidnapping's cleaner. No paper trail. The girls just vanish and all their parents know is they drove off in a nice car with a nice man who had an American accent and nobody ever hears from them again. Throw them in the bowels of some freighter for a month and they're so psychologically traumatized you get docile hookers who are young, fresh … and disposable. If some rich john goes over the top, the whole problem vanishes without a trace."

"That Poli girl had some stones on her to try to escape," T.J. said.

Brice was silent, then said softly, "Not necessarily."

"Meaning?" Dobbs asked.

"Meaning she didn't run because she had more guts than the rest of them. Jeni said Poli ran because … because of the note Bailey passed her telling her she was going to be murdered."

"Whoa, you sayin' she wasn't plannin'—?"

"She didn't intend to run away, only did it because of Bailey's note?"

"That's what Jeni said." Brice let out a long breath. "And I don't know what to make of any of that."

"I do," said a voice from the doorway. The men turned and saw Bailey standing just out of the spill of light. She looked like she had physically experienced all the trauma inflicted on the two girls she had painted. Her face was deathly pale. Her eyes looked like burned holes in her face. "It means that I'm responsible for her death. She wouldn't have run if I hadn't insisted we go looking for her."

"You can't make them kinds of statements about the future," T.J. said. He got to his feet and went to Bailey. "Come on in here, child, sit down and let's talk."

Bailey allowed herself to be guided into the room, was still dopey from the sedative they had given her. But her mind was clear enough to grasp the implications of what she had overheard.

"Talk about what? What's there to discuss? I thought about all that before, with Macy and the dam. If I hadn't interfered, gone looking for that Adirondack chair, that guy wouldn't have blown up the dam."

"You don't know that," Dobbs said.

"Ain't no way to tell what that man was plannin'. Just 'cause he was down on a houseboat on the lake don't mean he was gonna blow up the casino. He coulda been plannin' to plant a bomb under that dam all along."

"He wasn't. The explosion was my fault. This girl's death is my fault, too."

"We *all* decided to try to prevent the future painted in those paintings," Dobbs said.

"Didn't nobody twist our arms to get us to cooperate."

"And that girl was obviously terrified she was going to be killed," Brice said. "She didn't suddenly decide her life was in danger because of a note from a stranger."

"You can't go poking 'round in that," T.J. said. "Did that first little girl who got strangled — the very first paintin' my mama ever done — was that child murdered 'cause my mama went to the sheriff and tried to save her? Course not. The twisted pervert who'd been molestin' her for months was 'fraid he was about to get caught and *that's* why he killed her. My mama's painting didn't have nothin' to do with it one way or the other."

"But …"

"If you hadn't said nothing, had just took that picture of Macy out in the back yard, made a bonfire with it and cooked marshmallows … Macy Cosgrove would be dead right now."

"Not if that Osbourne guy had intended to bomb the casino, and only blew up the dam because we—"

"Then a whole buncha *other* folks'd be dead. Fact is, didn't nobody die but the sick crackhead." He paused, then added in a soft voice colored with revulsion, "And if we hadn't tracked down that kidnapper …"

He didn't have to say any more. *None of them* wanted to go there.

"I want to believe you, T.J."

T.J. cast a sideways glance at Dobbs before he continued.

"When me and Dobbs was kids, we … we decided we was gonna go watch what one of Mama's paintings predicted."

Dobbs stiffened, his muscles going rigid as if tensing for a blow.

"We ain't never talked 'bout it since that day, never mentioned it, not a word."

"Why not?" Brice asked.

"Something like that — a couple of little boys see …" Dobbs said by way of explanation, which didn't seem to Brice to be an explanation at all. "We pretended it never happened."

"It was a train derailment." T.J.'s voice had a flat quality — either emotionless or so full of emotion he had clamped hold of it to keep it steady. "A trestle give way and a coal train fell off into the river." Again, he looked at Dobbs. "We was close, *watched it happen* just like Mama painted. Then we … heard a man screamin' from the wreckage. So we went runnin' down there."

He seemed to have lost steam to continue, so Dobbs picked up the story, though Brice could tell he didn't know why T.J. had started the tale to begin with.

"At the bottom of the pileup, it was the engineer, I think — he was buried up to the waist in coal, pinned down by the wreckage, and he was hollering, 'Help! Help!' He saw us and begged us to save him."

"But there wasn't nothin' we could do," T.J. took the story back. "The two of us couldn't move that car off of him and pull him out. More'n that, though, the coal — hundreds of thousands of tons of it — was still settlin'. It was slidin' down toward him, toward *us*. If we'd tried to save him, we'd have been buried with him."

"So you were what, eight, nine years old, and you watched this man die?" Brice asked.

"We run from the slidin' coal. But I looked back. I seen."

He took a moment and Brice was trying to figure out where T.J. was going with the story.

"I ain't never told Dobbs the next part." Dobbs had been wearing a hundred-yard stare, his eyes unfocused, and his look snapped to T.J. "After I got home, we run all the way, cryin', both of us. Time I got to my house I's a mess and my mama wanted to know what was wrong and I just blurted it all out, told her what we done. She was horrified that I even knew 'bout the painting, let alone that I'd looked at it and gone to watch it happen.

"I was all tore up, cryin' and carryin' on, sayin', 'We tried to save him. I climbed up there tryin' to get to him, but then the coal started to slide.' I tole her I's sorry I'd sneaked around behind her back and went to see it and now I wished I hadn't seen nothing. She wiped my nose and waited 'til I had a'hold of myself again. Then she took me out to the chicken house and pulled that painting out from under the straw where she'd hid it."

Dobbs had stopped breathing.

"I didn't wanna see it, but she brought it out into the bright sunshine and pointed to the bottom of the paintin'."

T.J. looked at Dobbs as he said the rest of it. Some kind of unspoken communication passed between them.

"I looked, and seen what me'n Dobbs never seen in the dim light inside that chicken house. That man, the one trapped in the coal — *he was in the painting.* It was in the bottom corner of the canvas, a spot not two inches wide. But there he was, stuck under that train car, all that coal in slidin' piles above him."

T.J. took another breath, like it was taking more air to tell the story than he could keep in his lungs at one time.

"The man, he wasn't lookin' at the coal hangin' up above him. He was lookin' at something that wasn't in the picture, facing the river, had his hands out …"

"He was looking at us!" Dobbs gasped. "She painted the man looking at *us.* He was begging us to save him."

"Mama said she didn't understand how the past and the future fit together, how today and tomorrow was 'ranged in the mind of God, but she didn't think it was all laid out in a straight line, one thing after the other."

T.J. wasn't looking at Dobbs anymore or at anything else in the room. He was standing in the bright sunlight beside a chicken house, listening to his mother talking: "It's like life's a parade and we's looking at it through a knothole in a fence and the onliest thing we can see is whatever is in front of that knothole. God sees the whole parade, though. He sees the folks way back at the end, just babies some of 'em, the people we gonna meet next week or next year, a'comin' up toward that knothole. And he sees the people that passed by the knothole 'fore we even started lookin' through it."

T.J. paused and came back to the present.

"She told me 'the painting knowed you was there. So *you was s'posed to be there*. The parade's all laid out even though we can't see but a little bitty bit of it.'"

"What are you saying, T.J.?" Bailey's voice was haunted.

"My mama would have said you was *s'posed* to give that girl that note. You didn't *cause* nothin'."

"Do you believe that? What if you'd warned the engineer before the train left the station, would he still—?"

"I don't do what-ifs!" T.J. snapped, a door slamming shut with a loud bang. "What-ifs will drive you daft."

Then the fierce look left his face.

"I ain't sure even to this day what I b'lieve about how the past and the future's hooked up. I b'lieve we changed what mama painted when I went to your house that night and then you didn't hold that gun steady and that's why you ain't dead like the painting showed. And I b'lieve we kept Macy Cosgrove alive. Just 'cause I can't fit it all into my head and explain it, don't mean it's unexplainable. They's some logic to it that directs forces at work we can't see. All we can do is what we think's best, actin' out of a desire to help people. That's all we's responsible to do. The rest … it ain't up to us."

Bailey shook her head slowly.

"I don't know what I think anymore."

She reached down and picked up the puppy, who was happily chewing on the rawhide lace of her moccasin, and buried her face in his soft fur.

Chapter Thirty-Four

BAILEY SAT at the table as the men talked, not participating, just listening. No, not even really listening, just hearing words but assigning no meaning to them. She could feel the effects of the narcotics they'd given her gradually wearing off and she was becoming more alert as she sat there. Well, that and the coffee were bringing her around.

She had almost been murdered tonight, came within seconds of being dragged out from under the bed and strangled. At least, that's what she'd thought. But the others didn't think so.

"They didn't come here to kill Bailey," Brice said. "What good would that do?"

"What did they want, then?" Dobbs asked.

"To find out what she knew," Brice said.

"And *how* she knew it," T.J. added. "And who she mighta told about it."

"The way Fletch and the cavalry came thundering in to rescue her, they probably figure she alerted every law enforcement agency between here and Nova Scotia," Dobbs said.

"I imagine that is exactly what they think," said Brice dismally.

"Why's that a bad thing?" Bailey asked. They looked a little startled, apparently had just about forgotten she was sitting there quietly sipping coffee and listening.

"They blew it, missed their chance to get answers. So now … they're going to close up shop fast."

A phrase flittered on moth wings through her mind — *have to cut bait* — and was gone before she had a chance to think it.

"How exactly do they close up shop?" she asked.

Brice spread out his hands. "I wish I could read this some other way, but I think it's obvious what their next move is going to be."

"It's the only move they got," T.J. said. "They got to get rid of the girls. All of 'em, however many 'all' is."

"You mean … *kill* them?"

Brice nodded. "Have to. They have to get rid of the evidence."

"And then get the hell outta Dodge."

"So, they're just going to … what?" Bailey was trying to shake off the remnants of the narcotic and think. "You mean, shoot them and dump their bodies in the lake?"

"I wish that's what I thought they were going to do." Brice's face was a grim mask.

Bailey suddenly went cold all over.

"A couple of things he said …" Brice turned to Bailey. "When the guy was through beating Jeni, what did he say to her?"

Bailey didn't want to pull the image back into her mind, but concentrated, trying to get his exact words.

"He told her the only way to keep a mouse from squeaking was to stomp the mouse." As Bailey said the words, the meaning blew away the remaining fog in her brain. "No, before that, when he was talking about a brochure or a video."

That part was too fuzzy to make sense of. The other one, the ugly one, had said something about pictures. A video, too, maybe. Yes, the star …?

"I'm sorry. I don't … I can't …"

"If he's plannin' on making an example of 'em …" T.J. was blunt. "He's gonna kill 'em and video it!"

It was like all the air'd been sucked out of the room. Bailey wanted to protest, to argue, but she didn't. Because she didn't have breath to argue. And because she thought he was right.

"We keep talking about the 'other girls,'" Dobbs said. "How do we know there are others?"

Bailey found herself getting to her feet, discovered what she was thinking when she heard her thoughts come out of her mouth.

"Jeni and Poli weren't the only people in that painting."

"There's a limited amount of space under a bed — how many could there be?" Brice asked.

"I'm going to find out."

She turned and started out of the room toward the studio, knowing if she didn't do this right now, act on what she had realized was their final option, she wouldn't have the courage to do it at all.

"Bailey, I think you ought to—" T.J.'s voice was so full of fear and concern she wanted to hug him.

"Find out?" Dobbs was lost. "How?"

"She's gonna paint them other girls," T.J. said.

"Oh, no she's *not*." Brice stood up in front of her like the giant squid rising out of the sea before Captain Nemo.

She was amazed and encouraged by the strength she could hear in her soft words. "It's not up to you."

Bailey felt a weariness of body, mind and spirit that was not commensurate with her physical exertion for that day. Of course, she had lived through torture and come within a hair's breadth of being murdered. There was that. She wondered how many calories that kind of activity burned. She'd never seen it on any chart.

Okay, her mind was ping-ponging. Get a grip.

She fought the debilitating fatigue that washed over her in waves. It seemed to take all her strength to lift her brush, add dollops of paint and smear them around on the pallet. She tried to gird herself for whatever was on the other side of the doorway that opened up when she painted a picture, the portal through which horror and madness flowed.

Her mind ping-ponged again and she thought about her childhood obsession with ski jumpers.

The Winter Olympics on television had been magical — ice skaters and skiers and that sled-thingy that went so ridiculously fast. But ski jumpers ... *oh, my!*

She'd asked every grownup she knew and never got a satisfactory answer to the question, "How do they *learn* that?" Even a child could figure out they couldn't have merely assumed the position at the top of a ski jump one day — hands on poles, elbows out — slid down the incline and gone flying out into space. How did they *practice* a thing like that?

Her magical paintings — they were ski jumps. She'd been forced to assume the position with a paintbrush in each hand and ... She didn't get to practice, to work up to them slowly, maybe paint a couple in a safety harness just to get the feel of it.

She stood there now at the top of the jump.

The darkness under the bed had taken over that whole side of the portrait, disproportionately large to show the image of Jeni's face, and Bailey looked beyond it into the gloom. The darkness there concealed the girls the Beast hadn't asked about ... so Jeni hadn't told him.

Inhaling deeply, Bailey picked up a brush and took off down the slope, touching it to the dark canvas beyond Jeni's face.

Nothing happened.

She waited. Still nothing.

Bailey'd been prepared to be sucked into a vortex of fear and pain and brutality and violence. But that didn't happen. She turned to look at Brice, who stood in the doorway with his arms crossed over his chest, an unreadable look on his face.

Then she turned to T.J., who was watching her carefully.

The quiet grew uncomfortable. She made a show of looking around behind the portrait on the easel. "Anybody check to see if this thing's plugged in?" Brice came into the room to stand beside her.

"Were you wrong, maybe? Was Jeni alone in the room?"

Not a chance.

"Jeni was in so much pain …" Just saying it took Bailey's breath away for a moment. "She'd have told him about the others, but he didn't ask."

Dragging her eyes over the portrait, she scanned the vague outlines she'd painted of other things in the room and came to rest on the closet door, open just a crack. Bailey had run from an intruder and taken refuge under a bed, as Jeni had done — but maybe the other girls …

Placing the tip of her brush on the slash of darkness between the open closet door and the jamb, she consciously tried to paint it in more detail.

And then it happened.

This was not like the other times she'd had visions or seen whole scenes — as viscerally real as having a hallucination. When that happened, the rest of the world vanished and she fell down into a hole and lived someone else's life. It was like peeking into a cave to get a look at a bat and suddenly the whole flock comes roaring out at you, a black mass, coloring the sky and the world black and you're consumed by that blackness, fall through it into another reality altogether.

It wasn't like that this time. This time the bats were individual.

.   .   .

She sees an image through someone's eyes — one of the girls! The girl is looking out the window of a moving vehicle. A gold archway, with words, instantly gone, then she sees only trees and power lines. Then there's a view out a different window — a different girl — and there's a sign. The sign flashes by so fast Bailey barely catches sight of it.

Someone else … and her mouth is taped shut. She can feel the edge of the tape scraping against the bottom of her nose but it doesn't hurt, not like the pain in her wrists. They're bound together with the zip-lock ties that fasten so they can't be undone. The ties bind her wrists to someone else's wrists, digging into her skin so deep she feels blood and she wants to cry out but doesn't dare.

Big, rough hands grab her arm — the same girl? A different one? — and she's lifted up off the floor of a vehicle, like a cargo van, and tossed out of it onto the ground. She lands on her knees on rocks with sharp edges and they cut into her bare skin and then into her shoulder through the filmy fabric of her dress when the weight of someone shoves her off balance onto her side.

The scene goes dark. But not dark as in nothing there, dark because what the eyes see is darkness; where the girl is, there's no light. Then a shaft of it appears, a flashlight beam.

A wall, just a rock wall. Warmer air. Not warm, really, just air that doesn't have the bite of chill outside.

A sound. A rumble. A lawnmower. No, not a lawnmower. Something else.

A chainsaw.

Someone screams. Shrieks. Wails. Blood splatters on the bare wall, runs in rivulets down the black rock.

Then Bailey isn't seeing through the eyes of one, but the eyes of several, like watching three different movies on three different screens at the same time and the dialogue is garbled.

" … movie stars … "

"…tiny pieces…"

"… have to hose it off … "

Screaming. Crying.

"Oh, God, please noooooo."

Begging and pleading.

Then the images clear. Each one jolted Bailey separately, like when there's too much static electricity and everything you touch snaps and pops and shocks you.

Bailey steps back, not completely gone from the studio this time.

Here but not here.

She is somewhere where the room is dim, the image is indistinct, like she's viewing it through the wrong end of a telescope. There's light at the other end of a long tunnel and Brice, T.J. and Dobbs are in that light. They're calling to her from the light and she begins to run toward it.

A huge rumble roars, sound pounding through her, and the earth beneath her shakes.

She is suddenly terrified, so scared she barely has air to run. She cries out but the sound shatters into tiny pieces against the rock walls of the tunnel. She sees that as she runs toward the light, the circle is closing, the light shrinking, getting smaller and smaller. If she doesn't get to the light before the portal is closed altogether, she will be stuck in the dark tunnel in the absolute black with no way out.

Stuck there in forever darkness.

Dead.

So she dives for it, leaps out of the darkness — "Fight back!" She screams the words inside her mind and hears them reverberate in other minds. — into the light and the tunnel behind her vanishes, disappears with a little sparkle like a soap bubble and is gone.

Chapter Thirty-Five

"BAILEY."

It was Brice. He was holding onto her arm, looking into her face and she knew she had heard him calling her name before, but it had seemed to come from a long way away. From the top of some great chasm and she'd heard it deep in the depths of the darkness there.

"Are you alright?"

"Define alright."

"Are you hurt? Did they do something to the girls?"

"They're taking them somewhere in a van, have them tied up in the back lying on the floor, so all they can see out the windows are passing trees, power lines, tall things like that."

T.J. and Dobbs gathered around as she spoke.

"This was … like Macy and her little brother—"

"Meaning it ain't happened yet."

She hadn't thought about it, but no … these events hadn't happened yet.

"But the images just flashed and were gone. It wasn't a single continuous scene I could watch unfold."

"Sorta like a sketch," T.J. said and gestured at the painting.

Bailey looked at the canvas for the first time, focused on

217

what she'd added to it — which wasn't much. Ghostly shadows now inhabited the dark interior of the closet, pale outlines. Sketches on the darkness that lacked detail. It was clear that someone hid there, more than one someone. The light reflecting off their faces was only barely enough, though. You had to look closely to see them at all, but then it was like one of those dual-image pictures that once you see the second image you can't *not* see it.

"How many girls?" Dobbs asked.

"I'm not sure. More than two. More than three or four, even. I hopped back and forth among their experiences, seeing things from first one girl's perspective and then another."

"Describe what you saw," Brice said.

Bailey knew it was vitally important that she remember every detail of every flashed image. She concentrated hard, but it was like feeling her way back into a dream that was fading even as she tried to grab hold of it.

She described the plastic ties that bound the girls' hands and how they cut into the skin. She recalled the image of lying on her back in a moving vehicle, the floorboard carpet smell. New. It had a new-car smell.

"Trees and power lines and signs fly by."

"Signs?" Brice's attention was intense. "Tell me everything you can about the signs."

"Not sign*s* — sign, singular."

She turned away from them, holding up her hand for them to stop talking. She went to a low shelf and picked up a sketchpad, grabbed a pencil out of the cup she used to hold them — a minion cup, the little guy with just one eye. Sitting down in the small chair in front of the desk with her laptop resting on the top — turned off — she made shooing gestures toward the door. The puppy had accompanied the group into the studio and now plopped down at Bailey's feet.

"Stop asking me questions. Go away and let me jot all this down now while it's still fresh in my mind. It's fading fast."

"I'll make another pot of coffee," Dobbs said.

"And if we don't drink it, we can always use it to pave the driveway," T.J. said.

Bailey jotted down:

Trees — mostly bare, but a few still had some gold leaves. One had faded red.

The end of October was long past the peak of autumn foliage, and the unseasonably warm weather had prevented the brilliant colors a hard freeze and cold weather would have brought.

Power lines. More trees, these bare.

She wrote down what the girls said, how they begged. What the men said, their exact words, trying to capture it all before the images faded away like the smoke from a dying campfire.

When she'd put down everything she could think of, she took the sketch pad into the kitchen and handed it to the men seated at the table.

"Here are the puzzle pieces. You'll have to put them together."

The first thing she'd seen had been a sign. From the girl's view, the sign was upside down and backwards, but it was still clear what it was. "The Nautilus Casino. Where your every desire will be fulfilled."

The van had passed under that archway, had probably left from the back of the hotel parking lot.

"Which way'd they go?" T.J. asked.

"I don't know."

"How long was they in there? How far'd they go?"

"I don't know that either. They were on the highway for a while, then they left it, turned on another road that was bumpy. Then they turned again onto a road — it wasn't like a road at all. They tossed the girls out of the van onto the ground and rocks dug into their hands and knees."

"So they weren't at some building?"

"No. It was dark. The sky was velvet black, big hunks of stars, so they weren't somewhere the lights of the city would have been reflecting. Out in the country somewhere."

Bailey caught the look Brice and T.J. exchanged.

"What?"

"What they's planning … it could be … messy and noisy."

"A chainsaw!" Bailey gasped out the word. "I heard them crank it up. And the walls were made of rock, stone. Somewhere with rock walls. And the girls were begging, pleading. Crying, 'no, don't …'"

Bailey remembered what T.J.'d speculated, that the men were going to kill the girls … and video their murder. Cold nausea curled its greasy fingers through her guts.

"We're playing beat-the-clock here," Brice said. "They're on their way, or soon will be, to a secluded place they've picked out. I don't imagine what they've got planned is going to take very long. Then they're off to Who Knows Where on a Learjet parked and gassed up at Crenshaw's airport."

"Pray for a flat tire," T.J. said.

Bailey turned and left the kitchen, returned to the studio with Bundy tagging along behind, sniffing the baseboards, the rugs, the legs of furniture — everything in his path. She let him in, then closed the door — not because she didn't want the men to see what she was doing but because she didn't want to be distracted by their voices. She'd just thought of something, and maybe …

It was worth a try.

She went to the painting on the easel. The paint of the vague shadowy faces in the closet was still wet, but Bailey wasn't interested in that portion of the picture.

She studied the terrified, horrified face of the girl who had been hosed and hadn't betrayed her friends. Jeni. Evgenia.

Bailey had connected with her as she had connected with the other people whose portraits she'd painted, capturing the ugliness of their brutal deaths in freeze-frame for posterity.

Except Macy Cosgrove didn't die.

And Macy recognized ... *something* ... about Bailey when they met that night as she watched the Fourth of July fireworks high in the sky — just minutes before everything her family owned was swept away. Minutes before she and her family narrowly escaped being washed away with it. Bailey had reached out to the little girl, had touched her and when she turned around, the bond went *snap,* like a stretched rubber band going back to its original shape.

She had asked the little girl, "Do you know me?" The child had smiled and nodded. So the connection didn't just go *one way.* It was not just that Bailey was connected to the little girl, Macy had been connected to her, too.

Macy'd been the only other image Bailey'd painted that she'd been *compelled* to paint, where the magic had reached out through the canvas and created the image of a future event. The painting she *decided* to paint had shown an image from the past. And that image had led her and the others into the worst nightmare of their lives. But even then, Bailey had *connected* to the subject of the painting.

So was it possible that there was some way for Bailey to use that connection? Was there a way to communicate with Evgenia?

And if there was, what should she try to communicate?

The whole idea sounded impossible, of course. She barked out a burp of sardonic laughter. *Impossible?* Like anything about her ability to paint the future was *possible!* Nothing in her life existed between the fences of possible and impossible anymore, not since she woke up in a hospital bed with a ceiling tile as her best friend and Oscar in her skull.

Bailey reached out to the face in the painting, touched it. It wasn't like there was some kind of electric current, no connection of energy that she could sense. But she closed her eyes anyway, and concentrated.

What could she say, what could she try to communicate that would do the girl any good? She certainly couldn't communicate some complicated message, instructions on how to escape from plastic hand ties — if, indeed, there was any way to escape them. It wasn't like this was some open phone line where she could chat, or maybe drop a text into the system and it would show up with a smiley-face emoticon at the other end.

What could she tell Evgenia that would help her and the others?

Delay.

Bailey whispered the word aloud, concentrated on it. Blanked out every other thought and image.

DE-LAY.

Slow them down.

Stall.

She waited to feel … *something.*

Nothing.

If there was any communication going on, she was unaware of it.

"Bailey," Brice called.

"Coming," she replied and went back down the hallway to the kitchen. Bundy followed along happily.

"What can you tell me about the sign you saw?"

"It flashed by so fast I didn't see all of it. Couldn't make it all out." She pointed to where she had jotted down what she could see of the sign. "There were some letters in front of the **W** that I didn't get. They were above the other letters. The **W** on top and beneath it was **OH7**."

She crossed the room to lean over Brice's shoulder to point out the sign on her sketchpad.

"OH7," he mumbled the words to himself. "A road sign, maybe? Ohio Route 7?"

Out of the corner of her eye, Bailey saw the puppy squatting, preparing to do his business in the middle of the kitchen floor.

"Nooooo."

She leapt around the chairs, picked him up before he could get in position and hurried out into the back yard with him, holding him out from her in case he decided to let it fly anyway. Depositing him in the grass, she told him to "go potty," and reached into her pocket for a treat so she could pop it into his mouth the instant he let the liquid flow. Bundy sniffed the grass as if it was the first time he'd ever encountered such a phenomenon.

Chapter Thirty-Six

THE PUPPY STOPPED SNIFFING the grass, turned toward Bailey and began to bark furiously.

She sensed rather than saw, felt a presence and started to turn around. But before she had a chance to move more than her head, a gloved hand grabbed her upper arm in a vice grip and she felt the cold metal of a knife at her throat.

"Move, squeak, so much as breathe loud and I will slice *your* throat all the way to your backbone." It was a low voice, full of pebbles, harsh and grating.

For emphasis, the man pushed the knife into her neck and the blade sliced as sharp as a scalpel into her skin, releasing a river of warm blood to slide down the front of her neck into the V of her blouse.

"Move!" he whispered, holding her tight against his body, his face beside her ear. The smell of his breath was gagging, the stench of garlic and onions and rotted teeth.

Bundy continued to yap, standing in front of Bailey, looking past her at the man, who kicked at the dog but the puppy danced out of his way and kept barking.

Not man, *men.* When she turned she saw the other one. He was carrying two guns — some kind of big rifles, automatic weapons. One on a strap over his shoulder and the other in his hand.

Dragging her, half-carrying her, the men moved with remarkable speed across the back yard, gliding through the shadows, around the huge maple and oak trees. Bailey only briefly considered shouting for help, but she had no doubt that if she made a sound, it would be the last sound she ever uttered. If she cried out, the men would have to run, and they couldn't do that dragging her along. He'd kill her, drop her body in the grass and be gone.

The old board fence had been built the same time as the Watford House and extended out from it on the north and south sides before making right-angle turns at the edge of the property and stretching down the back sides of the yard. It was obscured along most of its length by ancient vegetation, box-trimmed shrubbery, thick and impenetrable, overgrown bushes and vines, morning glory and honeysuckle, that stretched up over the top and down the other side. The gate was in the center of the fence line that stretched across the back of the property. You could see it from the back porch. Brice had stationed a deputy in her neighbor's back yard on the other side of the gate. What had hap—?

The men didn't drag her toward the gate, but made for the back corner of the yard instead.

Swarms of terror, black shrieking harpies with horror faces flapped their bat wings in the pit of Bailey's belly, clawed at her bones and stole her breath. Her racing heart slammed blood through her veins, pounding a stake of panic into her chest.

The puppy followed them, out of range of the man's kicks, barking furiously.

At the fence, Bailey saw how the men had entered, how they'd pried out the nails where one section of the slat fence was attached to the post and then pushed the section inward far enough to make a space to pass through. When they got to the opening, the second man went through, turned and the first shoved Bailey into his arms. She couldn't see in the darkness beyond the fence, into the back yard of the house that faced the street that ran parallel to Sycamore.

The man who'd held a knife to her throat was big, had to squeeze through the opening in the fence with the puppy on his heels, barking. But he must have closed the opening in the puppy's face because as Bailey was dragged across the neighboring back yards, through pools of dark and shadow, she could hear the puppy's barks fade into the distance.

This can't be real!

It had happened too fast. Had it even been a minute ago — no, maybe thirty seconds — that she'd been telling Bundy to go potty and a heartbeat after the words left her lips she was hauled away into the night by the man who'd murdered Poli and tortured Jeni. Bailey had already been strangled to death by this man once and the thought of it happening again, to her own body this time ... no waking up later on the floor, feeling all the sensations of being strangled to death, but still alive.

There'd be no waking up at all.

A tiny voice in her head whispered that dead was not such a bad thing. It had been so appealing three months ago that she'd tried to put herself in the grave. But that time was a lifetime of experience ago and life had become infinitely precious. That parade of terrifying moments — lying on the wet pavement looking under a car as a one-eyed monster murdered her husband, hearing the roar of flood waters thundering toward her, blinking in and out of the tortured mind of an insane child — all seemed puny compared to this. She was so afraid now she thought she might be sick, might throw up, or pass out, or start screaming and not be able to stop until someone silenced her.

She kept the nausea at bay and held onto the frayed edges

of her panic with her fingernails. And tried to think! What could she do?

The answer was grim: absolutely nothing. These men were practiced killers and they wouldn't blink at blowing her guts out her back or slicing her throat.

But they hadn't killed her when they had the chance. The man could have sliced her throat and even now she'd be bleeding out on the grass of the back yard. He didn't.

If he'd wanted her dead, she'd *be* dead. Clearly, he wanted her alive.

And she knew why. He wanted to know how she had known the girl named Poli was "in danger," that a man with a skull tattoo on his wrist was going to try to kill her. And when they asked her how she knew, what could she say?

Well, it's like this, see — I paint pictures of what hasn't happened yet ...

She had no explanation they would believe.

And what would they do to her when they didn't believe her?

What would they do to her to make her give them answers that made some sense to them?

She heard the remembered sound of the chainsaw, its rumble echoing off rock walls.

The men hauled her stumbling, dragged, *carried* her across the back yard of the neighboring house toward a dark car that was parked a couple of houses down beneath a burned-out — or otherwise disabled — streetlight.

When they approached the car, the driver, a small, Middle-Eastern-looking man hopped out and opened the back door and the man who had held a gun on her shoved her into the car, pushed her down into the floorboard behind the driver, jammed her painfully into the small space and slammed the car door. Seconds later, the knife-wielding man got into the back seat on the passenger side. The driver and the third man leapt into the front seat and the car began to move forward. Not in a hurry, slowly, drawing no attention. Every second, they were moving farther and farther from any hope Bailey had of survival. How long had she been gone? Two minutes, even? Three, tops. She considered trying to leap across the car, open the door and dive out of the moving vehicle. But that was absurd. She'd never even make it up off of the floorboard.

When she lifted her head, she saw that the man seated on the other side of the car was looking at her. His face was washed in rhythmic splashes of light and shadow as they passed beneath streetlights.

"I come to take you and you're served to me on a silver platter." The voice was too rough and ragged to be natural. It'd been damaged somehow and now came out in a human growl. "Scared, are you?"

Then he slapped her, backhanded — casually sent hot pain searing down her cheek, knocking her sideways so her head connected with the back of the front seat with a force that blurred her vision. There was no reason for him to slap her, and he had done it offhandedly, with no clear intent of any kind, like a man might reach up and flick a ladybug off his shoulder.

"You don't know what scared is, little mouse. But you're about to find out."

Bailey could only draw quick, shallow breaths, her heartbeat a single, prolonged hum, a hammering blur of sound so loud it drowned out the rest of the world. But she saw his wrist when he slapped her, saw the skull tattoo. She'd been right. This was the man who had murdered Poli, had yanked out a bloody chunk of her hair, kicked in her teeth and then strangled the life out of her.

Bailey was, indeed, a mouse, hypnotized by the dead black eyes of a snake.

Chapter Thirty-Seven

Brice concentrated on the letters and number on the sign Bailey had seen through the eyes of one of the teenage girls who'd soon be dumped into the back of a van and hauled away. Maybe already had been.

"Ohio Route 7 runs right along the riverbank," he said. Outside he heard the puppy barking.

Whispering Mountain Lake was in West Virginia, but the western shore was only a couple of miles from the Ohio River which formed the whole length of the boundary between West Virginia and Ohio.

"Some letters before the W." Brice repeated Bailey's words, willing his mind to figure out the puzzle.

T.J. and Dobbs leaned close. The puppy's barking was softer now. "And the W is on the line above."

"With some letters in front of the W ... " T.J. said. "It might be S as in SW, southwest Ohio Route 7."

"Think about what she said — how it was dark," Brice said. "Outside the spill of light from any town. And rocks. When the girls were shoved out of the van, they landed on rocks. So this wasn't a field or a barn, anything like that."

Brice heard the puppy scratching on the back screen door.

"And a rock wall," put in Dobbs. "What's that tell us?"

"If the letter in front of the W was N, then we might be onto something." Brice's mind was moving fast, skipping from one thought to the next. "A rock wall — like in a cave. Nothing more private and soundproof than a cave and Rock Creek Cavern is on *North* West Ohio Route 7 … what? Ten, twelve miles from the casino?"

The puppy scratching on the screen door was annoying and Dobbs was closest to it.

"Open the screen and let the puppy in," Brice told him.

And even as he said the words something felt hollow and empty in his belly.

No.

He leapt to his feet, dropping the sketchpad where Bailey had jotted down what she had seen through the eyes of the girls in the closet.

In two strides he was at the door. When he opened it, Bundy trotted happily inside.

"Bailey?" he called out.

Nothing.

He switched on the back porch light, which flooded the porch and the area directly in front of it in light, but left the rest of the huge yard in shadow.

"Bailey!"

T.J. and Dobbs caught his tone.

"She took the puppy out to pee, couldn't a'been more'n a couple of minutes ago," T.J. said.

Brice stepped out onto the porch, calling urgently, "Bailey! Bailey, where are you?"

He flipped the switch on his shoulder mic.

"Unit Seven, this is Unit One. Report position and status."

Unit Seven was Deputy John Tackett, the officer Brice had stationed at the back gate of the yard.

Brice let go of the button. Silence.

He pushed the button again. "Tackett — position and status!"

Still silence.

"Unit Four, do you copy?" he said into the mic, but he was already moving out the back door, across the porch and into the yard. Unit Four was the deputy in a cruiser parked at the curb in front of the Watford House.

"Affirmative, Unit One. All cl—"

Bundy had hopped back outside when Brice opened the door and the puppy was racing across the yard, not toward the gate, but toward the back corner, yapping. The fence there didn't look—

Dobbs stepped out onto the porch behind Brice.

"She must be inside," he said. "Came back in by the front door. I'll go check."

That was absurd, of course, but even more absurd was the fact that she wasn't in the back yard with the puppy. She hadn't been gone five minutes. Not even three. Dobbs had started the coffeemaker before she left and the decanter was less than half full.

He heard Dobbs calling her name in the house and felt the dread solidify into a lead ball in his belly. His heart knocked so hard his vision pulsed, and the carotid arteries thumped in his throat as if jolts of electricity slammed through them.

"Tackett, position and status!" he commanded into his shoulder mic as he raced across the back yard, looking around in the shadows beyond the porch light. Silence. He punched the button again. "Four, did you see anything, anybody in the yard beside the—"

He stopped cold. The back fence wasn't right. He ran to it and a quick examination told him everything he needed to know in one sickening glance. The nails connecting the fence to the post had been pulled out, and the fence had been shoved inward, across the grass, bending it down. There was dirt beneath where the fence had been and as he knelt down to take a closer look, his mind was already three steps beyond where he sat crouched down.

Bailey was gone.

She'd been kidnapped.

The words slammed into his consciousness individually, each one with the force of a wrecking ball.

That's what the puppy had been barking at!

With a sheriff in her kitchen and officers front and back. These guys had ice in their veins. Snatching her out of her own back yard … but he instantly calculated they hadn't come expecting to do that. That'd been a lucky bonus. They had come prepared to take on all of them — kill everyone *except Bailey.*

Where was Tackett?

When he stood and turned toward the back gate, he saw that T.J. was already there. He had opened the gate and was looking at something on the other side.

Something on the ground.

No!

He knew from the look on T.J.'s face what he'd find when he got there.

The sick feeling, the awful sick feeling …

T.J. stepped aside wordlessly when Brice got to the gate. Tackett was lying on the ground just beyond in a puddle of blood. His throat had been slashed. Even from where he stood, Brice could see that the wound went all the way to his spine.

Moth thoughts, fluttering around a back porch light:

MARJORIE TACKETT WAS pregnant with their third child. John was hoping for a girl after two rowdy boys, but had chosen not to be told the baby's sex.

"We'll wait until the baby's born to find out … we're old-fashioned like that."

. . .

John had taken the statement of that poor fisherman who'd hooked onto the dead body of the girl in the lake.

He keyed his mic. *"Officer down!"* It took a great force of will to bar the entrance to his conscious mind, banish memories of the *last* time he'd spoken those words. "I repeat, officer down. All units respond to the Watford House."

He drew a breath.

"Dispatch, I need a bus."

He didn't need an ambulance. It was too late for that. Tackett was dead.

But Bailey was *alive*. At least for now.

Sam Henderson, Unit Four, who had been stationed in a cruiser in front of the house, was suddenly standing beside him and Brice didn't know when he'd arrived.

Brice turned to him.

"You're in charge here," he said. Sam stood gawking at John's body, in shock. Brice grabbed his shoulders and got in his face. "I said, you're in charge."

Maybe Sam nodded, maybe he didn't. Brice didn't know because he was running across the lawn back to the house as his mind was forming plans. He pushed past Dobbs and stepped into the kitchen.

He paused.

Get a grip!

Took a breath.

Then he punched the button on his shoulder mic.

"Dispatch, this is Unit One. Notify the Weatherford County Sheriff and the Ohio State Police Post in Lewiston of a ten-thirty-one." Ten-thirty-one was the code for major crime in progress. "A confirmed 207." A 207 was a kidnapping. "Repeat, *confirmed* 207. Suspects headed from the Nautilus

Casino toward Rock Creek Cavern on north West Ohio Route 7. Armed and extremely dangerous, at least two subjects suspected in the" — there was a heartbeat pause; he needed a full breath to continue — "the *murder of a police officer* and the death of the Jane Doe we dragged out of the lake this morning."

The dispatcher repeated his message back to him, her voice strained, her words terse and clipped. He was proud of Sylvia for her professionalism.

"Dispatch Units Five and Nine Code Three to the Tucker's Landing Marina to take the launch across the lake. Contact Water Patrol — Dan Witherspoon's on vacation, call dispatch and advise … *whoever!* … that I need a boat at Joe's Hole Marina — Code Three." Code Three meant haul ass!

Again, the dispatcher repeated his message back to him.

He'd get the West Virginia State Police to meet him on the other side of the lake to take him across the Ohio River Bridge and on to Rock Creek Cavern. But the Ohio officers would get there sooner. He needed to call Gail Miller, the Weatherford County Sheriff — on her cellphone, let her know what she and her officers would be walking into.

Gail and John Tackett's wife … weren't they cousins?

Brice paused then, looked at T.J. and Dobbs. There was nothing to say.

"Keep going over those notes she left. There may be more information in there that we can use. If you find anything, call my cell. Or dispatch will relay messages."

Then he was running again, out to his cruiser. He could hear the mournful wail of sirens ripping open the night air. Pulling out of the Watford House driveway, he slammed the car into gear and peeled out, leaving rubber smoking on Sycamore Street, his lights flashing and his own siren joining the symphony.

Only then, when he had done all that he knew to do, did Brice allow himself to suffer the onslaught of guilt that he wouldn't allow himself to feel before, with his game face on. Now, as he flew down the streets, ignoring stop signs and passing cars on the right and left, he considered the reality of the situation.

Deputy Sheriff John Tackett — *a friend* — had been murdered. Had died *only minutes* ago! His body was probably still warm.

Bailey was in the hands of *the men who'd killed him.* Murderers who wanted information she couldn't give them, information they would stop at nothing to get.

His grip on the steering wheel was so tight his knuckles turned white.

John had been killed in the line of duty. But *Bailey* — that was on Brice. He never should have let her out of his sight for a second.

Whatever happened to her was — *His. Fault.*

Chapter Thirty-Eight

T.J. STOOD with Dobbs in Bailey's kitchen. Silent. Not companionable silence. *Nothing-to-say* silence. They needed to get to work, do something, go back over Bailey's notes. Search for other pieces of the puzzle in the random images she'd been able to see through the eyes of them girls who was being hauled away to be murdered.

Of course, Bailey was being hauled away to be murdered right along with 'em!

T.J. swore, let fly a string of the most colorful expletives in his vocabulary, and he'd collected many of them over the years, collected and stored but never used.

Dobbs looked at him and made no comment, though the explosion of profanity constituted more cursing than he'd ever heard come out of T.J.'s mouth in the going-on-seven-decades of their relationship.

T.J. didn't curse. Not even in the military. It was a self-discipline he ruthlessly imposed on himself, one of many. Discipline built strength and T.J. was determined to be strong. He'd long since traced that determination to its source: the weakness he'd felt watchin' his daddy beat his mama, helpless to do anything about it. He understood that the violence had hardened his childhood, turned it to stone, and he'd had to carve from it the shape of his manhood. But *understanding* it was as far as he ever got. He never mastered it, rose above it or worked through it or came to terms with it or whatever other psychobabble term shrinks used. He just incorporated it into his life.

That's why he had joined the military, why he'd chosen Special Forces. Heat, cold, back-breaking labor, sleep deprivation — T.J. had switched it all off, stopped attending to it, assigned it no value. It flat out didn't matter how bad conditions got, T.J. went on.

A blind determination to be strong was the reason T.J. pushed himself relentlessly in everything he did, constructing strength from the bricks of small acts of self-discipline, mortared together with the belief that if he always forced himself to do things the hard way, it would toughen him.

That's why — and how — he had eradicated his West Virginia dialect.

And why he refused to allow himself to curse. Obscenities were a crutch for the lazy. It was mental release. T.J. didn't want to vent — what was inside he *kept* inside, to make him strong.

But he cursed now, fouled the air around him with every obscenity he could think of. Cursed himself and Brice for their stupidity. Cursed them both for their colossal failure as law enforcement officers to assess the threat and guard against it.

Dobbs returned to the table, but sat down opposite where Brice had been seated when Bailey was leaning over his shoulder, showing him the notes she had made — when they were figuring out that WOH7 stood for North West Ohio Route 7.

T.J.'s mind was racing, constructing survival scenarios — ways Bailey could somehow — and discarding them immediately. He wasn't yet able to stare the naked truth in the eye, grasp the implications of it. He couldn't make himself admit that Bailey—

"Uh … T.J. …?" Dobbs said.

"What!"

He was immediately sorry he'd snapped at Dobbs. He and Brice were to blame. They should have known better, but none of this was on Dobbs. He was the only one among them who hadn't screwed up.

"Look at this." Dobbs handed T.J. the piece of paper where Bailey had jotted down the characters she had seen on the sign through the eyes of one of the kidnapped girls.

"WOH7. What about it?"

"The girls were lying on their backs in the floor of a van, right? They wouldn't have seen what was outside the window from the same angle as somebody in the front seat."

"Yeah, and …"

"Would have seen it cockeyed — maybe even upside down."

"Maybe. What's your point?"

"This is my point."

Dobbs took the paper with WOH7 written on it and turned it upside down and slid it across the table to T.J.

It took T.J. a moment to see what Dobbs was getting at.

Upside down, WOH7 became LHOM.

"What are you getting at …?" But something was already fluttering around the outsides of T.J.'s consciousness as images rearranged themselves in his head.

"She said the W was *on top* and had some other letters with it but she couldn't see what they were, right? Letters that would have been *in front of the W* so we figured it was *north* west or *south* west."

T.J.'s mind was stumbling toward a destination Dobbs had already reached.

"So you're saying if—?"

"—the sign were upside down, the W would become an M. It wouldn't be on the top, it'd be on the bottom and the other letters would be *after the M*, on the right side instead of the left."

It was there. T.J. almost had it.

"What if the letters *after* the M were *ine*? That would make the word *Mine.*"

T.J. looked from the piece of paper to Dobbs and back to the piece of paper.

"You're saying it could be LHO on the top line and 'Mine' on the bottom." It wasn't a question.

"LHO, as in *Last Hope Ollie* … Mine."

The two men looked at each other across the table. Neither spoke.

T.J. began to back up from the idea so fast he almost tripped and fell backwards over his own thoughts.

"It couldn't be … there's no way …"

"Why not? It's as reasonable a deduction as North West Ohio 7."

T.J. took a breath. Then another.

"Are you sayin' you think Brice is marshaling all the forces of law enforcement at his disposal to go crashin' down like a hammer on Rock Creek Cavern in Ohio when the bad guys is actually in a mine in West Virginia?"

"Give me a good reason why not."

T.J. tried.

"Well … North West Ohio 7 … Ohio roads are designated 'OH.' But the Last Hope Ollie Mine would have been written out that way on a sign. All the words."

"Not necessarily."

"Are you sayin' you seen a sign where it was abbreviated LHO Mine?"

"Are you saying there couldn't possibly be one we haven't seen?"

The men were silent again.

"We can't just sit here," Dobbs said.

T.J. threw in the towel then.

"No, we can't. We got to go out there to the mine and make sure that it ain't where they've taken them girls and Bailey."

"And if it is? Do we call Brice off the hunt in Ohio?"

"If it is … it'd be too late for that."

Chapter Thirty-Nine

BAILEY TURNED her face away from the man in the back seat who had slapped her, the Beast who had strangled Poli and hosed Jeni. Jammed into the floorboard area behind the driver, she struggled to grab hold of her runaway panic, tried to order her thinking, to make some kind of plan, figure out …

What was there to figure out?

Something. *Something!*

Her thoughts were water spiders on a still pond, flitting here and there so fast it was impossible to catch one long enough to think it.

Her feelings, though. What she felt was not some tangled jumble of ever-changing emotions. Just one, only one — abject terror.

But undergirding her terror was a deeper, more familiar emotion. Despair.

The despair of being utterly alone, vulnerable and totally helpless. She recognized *that* feeling. It was an old friend.

· · ·

BAILEY WALKS SLOWLY around the empty house, going from one room to the next. She stands in the doorway of each one. Just stands. The only furniture in the house is what's absolutely necessary, the bare essentials. A bed, a dresser and a nightstand in the bedroom. A couch and two chairs in the living room, and a flat screen television that isn't hooked up yet. There are dishes stacked in neat piles on the kitchen counters. Plates, cups, saucers, glasses and silverware. There are basic cooking utensils, too — a pot, a frying pan, a set of muffin tins. A meager assortment. If she wanted to do anything more elaborate than make a sandwich and heat up a bowl of soup she would have to go out and purchase more utensils.

With what?

They'd talked to her about all of it when she was still in that safe house where she'd thrown up her breakfast after they told her about the murderous Sergei Mikhailov. That day, the man she had never seen before had explained to her how the Witness Protection Program worked. She hadn't heard a word he said, and then they'd tucked her into the back seat of a nondescript Honda for the road trip. The first of many.

At the end of the trip was this house.

Another man whose face she could barely recall had told her all over again what the first man had told her about Wit Sec. This time, she listened. She would be given a whole new identity, he said, with the whole paper trail of driver's license and school records and social security card to back it up. He'd said the government would rent a place for her to stay and provide a vehicle for her to drive and would bank transfer into her account a monthly living allowance, though they had never specified how much that would be and she hadn't had the slightest interest, at the time, in finding out. He'd said they did not expect her to have to get a job to support herself, that she would not be isolated here in scenic Albuquerque for long enough to need employment. She would just be here for a short time, because soon *— ah, yes, the mythical* soon *— they would capture Mikhailov, arrest him and his drunk son, Ivan, she would show up at the trial and testify, and then she could have her life back.*

Could have her daughter back!!

But for now …

What furniture there was she had picked out of a catalogue. It had been delivered this afternoon. She didn't know why she'd had to select from a catalogue. She supposed she couldn't be trusted to go into a store and buy a bed or a lamp. Were they afraid she'd burst into tears and tell the clerk that she was being hunted by the madman who gunned down her husband in the street, the old man with a black eyepatch and a gray fedora?

The federal marshals here had been as dour as morticians. They were not the same ones who had driven her across the country. She had learned their names — Jeff and Danny — and a little about them. They had become people to her, not that she had felt particularly chatty as she sat in the back seat of the car, watching the hills and fields and trees streak past the window, packing one mile on top of another, getting farther and farther away from her world, her life — and from Bethany.

The marshals who had driven her had turned her over to the other two men at the house. They had left the rental car they had driven here, told her she would be driving that while she was here. Which wouldn't be for long, they assured her. They had told her goodbye, wished her good fortune, and then left to be taken to the airport to fly back to wherever it was they had come from, their job done. Back to their wives and children. Back to their lives.

The other marshals had looked around the place, making sure there were locks on all the windows, dead bolts on the doors. As if a locked window or door would stop Mikhailov if he ever figured out she was alive and came after her. The fact that there was only meager furniture and only the barest essentials of food and drink in the cabinets and refrigerator, didn't seem all that important to them. As soon as everything that had been ordered was delivered and set up in the house, they had given her the keys to the rental car in the driveway, a bank debit card with the pin number 12345 and two hundred dollars in twenty-dollar bills.

"Is there anything else you need?" one of them had asked.

Such an incredibly absurd and obtuse question. She just shook her head.

Then they had left. Since their departure, she has wandered from one room of the house to another, looking at what is now her home.

Eventually, she realizes that she has been aimlessly pacing for … for some amount of time, it doesn't matter. It is late afternoon now and she should be hungry. She isn't. She needs to put the sheets, the brand new ones in a plastic package, on the bed, and the bedspread. She doesn't. She needs to begin putting things away, what little there is, the dishes in the cabinets, the linens — four towels, four washcloths, four hand towels — on the shelves in the bathroom.

She does none of those things.

She finds herself wandering again, room to room, in a daze that degenerates gradually into utter hopelessness. She sits down on the couch in the living room, looks at the picture-less walls, shades drawn on curtain-less windows, and discovers she is crying. What she feels is so tangled and confused and intense, she can do nothing but cry. She doesn't sob, though. Not the gut-wrenching sobs that wrecked her body like seizures in the days right after Aaron's murder.

She just cries softly, forlornly. This is her life now and it is more utterly miserable than any bad dream.

The only thing more powerful than her misery is her fear of the one-eyed man who killed her husband. If she let it, that fear would grow in her chest until it stole her breath, stopped her heart, took over her mind and annihilated the person who had been Aaron's wife and still was Bethany's mother.

She had to learn how to deal with raw terror or it would consume her. She began that day — as she sat crying on the plain couch in the nondescript living room, of the not-home where they'd parked her — teaching herself how to deal with fear.

As SHE LISTENED to the hum of the tires on the highway, Bailey called on what she had figured out that day and learned in the hundreds of days since. Panic would destroy her.

"Boss, you want me to call Vinny?" asked the man in the front seat, the one who had held a gun on her and shoved her into the car. From her position, she could only see the side of his face illuminated in the occasional streetlight. His hair was white and the back of his head was as flat as a dinner plate.

"Tell him we're about fifteen minutes out," said the man in the back seat, the man the girls called the Beast, who was obviously the man in charge. His gravelly voice reminded Bailey of — an image formed in her mind: huge chains dragged across a metal floor, the deck of a ship. Then the image was gone.

Fifteen minutes from where? Where were they going?

When she grabbed hold of her thoughts and tried to concentrate, she didn't like the conclusions she reached. She'd left the kitchen to take Bundy out to potty — it couldn't possibly have been more than fifteen minutes ago. The men at the table had been trying to figure out the puzzle of images, had been connecting the letters and numbers she had given them to a road in Ohio. They appeared to be coming around to the conclusion that it was somewhere on that road that the girls in the van were being transported.

She didn't know where she was, but she definitely knew where she *wasn't*.

Ohio was on the other side of the lake from Shadow Rock and they had *not* crossed the lake. Wherever they were going, they were driving, and if that was the case, whatever forces Brice could muster to come looking for her would be looking in the wrong place.

The car swayed as it wound around tight corners and her ever-sensitive ears were popping. They were *not* on some flat road in Ohio. They were in the West Virginia mountains, going deeper and deeper, higher and higher.

She was so jammed down into the floorboard, her legs folded unnaturally under her, that her legs and feet had gone to sleep. But she didn't dare wiggle to get more comfortable. She didn't want to draw the attention of the man who'd slapped her. She tried to concentrate on calming her breathing, slowing the jackhammer rate of her heart. Panic was an enemy almost as dangerous as the man seated beside her.

Eventually, the car began to slow. Had it really been only fifteen minutes? It had seemed like hours to Bailey — time had elongated and stretched out. The car turned off the highway onto another road, an unpaved road. She remembered *that* — the bumpy road. They jostled along it for what seemed like another eternity. Her strained muscles were cramping, sending shocks of pain up into her thighs, but there was nothing she could do to relieve the pain. The bouncing made it worse.

Then the car ground to a stop. The driver rolled down his window and spoke to someone in a language she didn't recognize. It sounded like crackling flames. Then the man seated beside her grabbed her by the hair — she cried out in pain — and yanked her up onto the seat. The Beast got out of the car, came around to her side, opened the door and barked, "Get out."

She would have complied, would have done anything he told her to do but she had no voluntary control over the four feeling-less stumps that were her arms and legs. They'd gone numb. He reached for her again and she steeled herself for the pain of being yanked by the hair. But instead, he just grabbed her arm, dragged her out of the car and threw her to the ground where rocks dug into the skin of her hip and thigh.

What she had seen out the eyes of the girls ... when they were taken from the van and dumped out on the ground, there were sharp rocks like these.

Feeling the tingling pain of blood flowing back into her cramped arms and legs, she lay on her side and looked around at what she could see without moving. She was afraid to move.

Out in the country.

Away from prying eyes.

Chainsaw!

For the first time in months, she tried to think of a way to dislodge the bullet in her brain and send it out to do its dirty work in the tissues around it. Was there any way to get the bullet to kill her before these monsters began to question her, to ask her questions for which she had no answers they would believe? And since she couldn't answer their questions, what lay ahead for her was an ugly painful death. But maybe there was some way to get Oscar to kill her first.

Chapter Forty

THE MEN WERE SPEAKING among themselves in a language Bailey didn't know — short blunt sentences, guttural sounds, and then silence. She thought she might have caught names, but she could have been mistaken. The gunman in the front seat with the flat head was Sanderson, Sandy. Besides "Boss," the others called the Beast Jacko.

It was dark except for the headlights of the vehicle and Bailey wasn't facing the front of the car and couldn't see what the headlights illuminated. She lay frozen where she was, fearing any move would draw unwanted attention. She could see only darkness around her, knew it was probably forest. Above, the sky hung in a black velvet drape sprinkled with stars as big and cold as chunks of ice.

Before long, she heard the vehicle, coming up the dirt road they had traveled, then saw the illumination from approaching headlights. A van pulled up next to the car. With the men's attention drawn to the van, Bailey risked a quick look around. In the splash of light from its headlights, she saw that the car was parked on the side of a wide spot in the dirt road where it terminated in a gate and a chain-link fence.

The spill of headlights also illuminated a sign and Bailey

felt her heart fall out of her chest down into the pit of her stomach. The sign read *"Last Hope Ollie Mine. Closed."*

There were other signs around as well, on the fence and against the gate.

No Admittance. There was text under the large words but she couldn't read it.

No Trespassing. Smaller words warned that all violators would be prosecuted.

Risk of Explosion: Flammable Gas. Beneath, in smaller letters but large enough to read: *No flames, no sparks.*

Keep Out.

Danger: Poisonous Gas.

Bailey was not tied up and none of the men who'd been in the car were paying any attention to her. Should she try to slip away? Make a run for it? But the feeling was just beginning to return to her feet and arms and she probably couldn't have gotten to her feet unassisted, let alone run off into the darkness.

When the van pulled to a stop, two men got out of it. The van driver was a big, black man whose hair appeared, in this dim light at least, to be naturally red. He had the freckles to match.

Brice had freckles. He'd told her "Brice" in Gaelic meant "spotted."

She was never going to see him again.

The stab of pain that realization brought her made a statement about her feelings for him … that didn't mean anything at all anymore.

The man riding shotgun in the van, whose chinless, flat-nosed face was so ugly it was memorable, opened the passenger side door, sliding it along the side of the vehicle. She could hear the sound of crying as soon as he opened it.

"Shut them up, Hollywood," the man said, and Bailey heard what sounded like a slap from inside the back of the vehicle and there was instant silence. The man stepped out of the back of the van then, and she saw why they called him Hollywood. He was tall, blond and strikingly handsome. He was dragging two girls with him. Their hands were bound behind their backs and they were tied to each other, as well. Bailey didn't have to see to know that the plastic ties holding them were tight, digging into their skin.

Their feet were free, but their mouths were sealed with large gray strips of duct tape. Both were dressed in evening wear, like the "white gown" Poli had been wearing. The one with red hair had lost a shoe, tottered on one high heel. The other's brown hair stretched down her back in a single braid. It was hard to tell with the tape on their faces, but she had no doubt they were startlingly beautiful girls. These people specialized in beauty. She also had no doubt that they were young, teenagers, though you couldn't tell that either from looking at them.

Hollywood dumped them onto the ground and stepped back into the van. When he stepped out again, he was dragging another set of girls. They were bound as the others were, their hands but not their feet and their mouths taped shut. One girl was black, with short-cropped black curls, the other's short hair was multicolored — pink, blue, gray — cut in a stylish punk boy cut. The black girl was wearing a sweatshirt and sweatpants, the "tropical fish" wore a black designer dress with a miniskirt covered in sequins that sparkled in dim light, and above-the-knee black boots. He dumped them on top of the other girls, making a pile of them, and the top girls moved off the others and sprawled beside them in the dirt.

The other man, the ugly one, had climbed into the back of the van and emerged with another set of girls. *How many were there?* Bailey had no idea. One of the girls, whose hair was long, blonde and curly, was dressed in an evening gown, but the other, a tiny, black-haired girl was dressed in jeans and a t-shirt. The blonde in heels, and the tiny girl in sneakers, were such disparate sizes it was hard for them to move as a unit.

Bailey's heart began to hammer. Some of these girls had been hiding in the closet in Poli's room, had witnessed the girl's murder. How many of them? Two? Four? Surely not all of them, but Bailey didn't know that for sure. What she did know was that she connected to the girls who'd hidden in that closet — in a vague way, flashing through their minds, just blurred images. She wondered if she would feel anything now that they were so close. That hadn't happened with Macy Cosgrove. Yet when she touched the little girl, there had been a connecting of some sort that she still couldn't explain and certainly couldn't describe, as if they knew each other well, though she couldn't have told a thing about the child except what she had seen through her eyes on those two occasions.

She stared at the tangle of girls on the ground … and felt nothing. No connection of any kind.

The ugly man returned to the van and brought out a single girl. It was Jeni, pale blonde hair, Nordic blonde, long and straight. Bailey couldn't see it, but she knew Jeni's eyes were blue. Not startling sapphire blue — pale blue, the color of the sky on a hot day. She was wearing skinny jeans, a button-down shirt and a denim jacket.

Bailey recognized her instantly, of course. She had painted her face in such vivid detail the men were able to take digital photographs of her and find her in the casino. Bailey had had only a flashing connection to the other girls, but she had been inside Jeni's head, had suffered through a brutal torture with her, was connected intimately to her. She was sure that if she touched Jeni, she would feel the same connection she had felt to Macy Cosgrove, but the girl lay on the top of a heap of six other girls fifteen feet away. And what was the point of connection? It wasn't like she could communicate with her in any way. And what would she communicate if she could?

Apparently, Jeni was the last one because Hollywood pushed the van door closed behind her.

Bailey sat up in the dirt, the feeling having returned to her arms and legs so she could control them, and *stared* at Jeni. At first, the girl was unaware of her, looking around at everything and nothing in abject terror just like the other girls. But eventually she noticed Bailey and their eyes met and locked.

If Bailey had expected some kind of connection, it wasn't there. But then, she hadn't connected to Macy Cosgrove either, until she put her hand on the child's shoulder.

When the men spoke now, it was in English. Perhaps the men in the van didn't speak whatever language they'd used before. The metal gate in the chain-link fence had a padlock on it and Jacko turned to the small, Middle Eastern man.

"You got the key, don't you, Akeim?"

The man nodded, put his hand into his pocket and removed a single, small key and inserted it into the padlock. He snapped the lock open, then tossed it aside and walked the gate inward to open it. Then the men went to the girls on the ground. The man who had opened the gate grabbed Jeni and hauled her through the opening. The other men grabbed the other bound girls, dragged them to their feet and shoved them into the darkened area beyond the gate.

The men also removed from the van four plastic barrels with sealable lids. The barrels were light, apparently empty, and the men carried them easily. They also unloaded several duffel bags, heavier than the barrels.

Jacko came to where Bailey sat and she struggled with all her strength not to cringe away from him. But he wasn't interested in terrorizing her right now. He simply yanked her up off the ground and shoved her in front of him through the gate.

Once inside the enclosure, it was clear that they were in the open area in front of a hole in the side of the mountain. The men who'd been hauling the girls threw them back down in heaps up against the fence, then began shining their flashlights around, apparently looking for something.

"S'posed to be on a pole," said the white-haired gunman.

The men shined their flashlight beams on the fence, the posts, and the front of the entrance to the mine, their backs toward Bailey and the girls.

"Turns all the lights on," Hollywood said.

Bailey saw Jeni sit suddenly upright on her knees, and watched in fascination as the girl raked her cheek across the side of the chain-link fence next to her, dragging it sideways — must have been *painfully* — along the links until the piece of duct tape on her mouth began to peel back. She only pulled it back far enough so she could open her mouth, then she tottered on her knees six or eight feet to a spot behind where the men stood searching the darkness. Then she leaned over, put her mouth to the ground and appeared to pick something up with her teeth. Whatever it was, it was small, and the girl tilted her head back and swallowed it. Then she fell over on her side and rolled back to the fence, sat up, shoved her face against the links and smashed the duct tape back across her mouth.

The whole operation had taken only a few seconds. The men saw nothing.

"There it is," said the ugly man called Vinny who'd driven the van, pointing to a panel box on a pole near the entrance to the opening in the front of the mountain. They shined flashlights on it. The sign on it warned Danger and Electrical Something.

Jacko turned to the man who had opened the padlock. "Unlock with the padlock key," he said, and the man reached into his pocket. He felt around, then reached into his other pocket.

"Come on!" Jacko was not happy. The small man who had unlocked the gate was searching all his pockets now, clearly unable to locate it.

Then Bailey understood!

Jeni had seen the man drop the key on the ground and she had picked it up and swallowed it! That's why she'd rolled back to where she'd been sitting — to remove the tracks she had made in the dirt with her knees.

Bailey's heart was pounding so hard her vision was pulsing. There was only one reason for Jeni to do a thing like that — *to delay them. To slow them down!*

Then Akeim began to look around on the ground, shining his flashlight around his feet.

"You dropped it?" Sandy, the flat-headed one who'd shoved a gun into her belly, was incredulous.

"I had it. It's here somewhere."

The other men trained their flashlights around the man's feet, searching the ground.

It was clear Jacko was losing his patience.

"Find the key!" he said, his voice thunderous.

He used his flashlight, too, searching the ground around them, then tracing the path they'd taken through the gate.

"It's gotta be here *somewhere*," Akeim said.

It wasn't long before the men were frantic and furious.

"I don't know what could have happened to it." Akeim sounded pathetic now. He shot a glance at the girls, shoved up against the fence and Jacko followed his look.

"What — you think *they* got it? How'd they manage that — telekinesis?" He got in the man's face then. Didn't yell at him. Yelling would have been far less intimidating than the harsh whisper. "Their hands are *tied behind them*, moron. And they got shoes on so they couldn't have used their toes. Now, find the key!"

The men searched and searched. But, of course, they could have looked for the rest of the night and never located it.

After a long search, Bailey couldn't be sure how long, the men gave up on finding the key and began considering how to get the box open without it. One of the men went to the van and returned with a tire iron and began trying to pry open the metal box. It was slow going. The box was made of heavy-grade steel and it didn't give easily.

As they worked, Jacko's rage reached epic proportions.

Half an hour, maybe forty-five minutes later, the man who had lost the key finally managed to move the mangled door away from the control panel on the box far enough to reach inside and flip a switch, and the front portion of the mine was flooded with light.

Akeim's shoulders slumped as relief flooded over him. Jacko raised his gun and shot him in the face.

The girls' screams were muffled by the tape across their mouths, but Bailey let out an involuntary shriek at full volume. Even the other men jumped back.

"Drag him in there," Jacko said. Hollywood and Vinny grabbed the dead man's arms and hauled the body toward the lighted mine entrance.

Chapter Forty-One

As the men dragged away the body of the dead man, Bailey looked at what the bright light now revealed. It was just as T.J. and Dobbs had described it. The multiple shafts of Last Hope Ollie #1 were carved into the back of the cave in front of them. Last Hope Ollie #2 lay under #1. Oliver Northfield had started digging on the other side of the mountain — but the shafts had not "met in the middle" as Bailey had suggested. Last Hope Ollie #2 was sixty feet below Ollie #1, the face of the mine reached by an elevator that ran down the cave wall through a hole in the floor.

When the Beast flipped the last switch, turning on the last bank of lights, Bailey thought about what the men had said about sparks. These were spark-less sodium lights but still ... there was poisonous gas here, wasn't there? That's what the signs all around said. Methane in the air. This was an *abandoned* mine.

Of course, gas wouldn't build up here, in this open cave mine entrance. But down below, in the mine beneath it ... maybe. Since you couldn't smell it, perhaps they'd all go in and then drop over dead. That seemed a far better end than the one Bailey could see out there in the future waiting for her.

The men hauling pairs of girls into the cave had to double up, now that one of their number was lying in a dead heap against one wall. They brought the captives into the cave, then went back to the van and brought the barrels, and duffel bags that looked large enough for a set of golf clubs, though that wasn't likely what was inside. Bailey refused to speculate, wouldn't let her mind go there, but there was no denying what she had heard when she was listening to the flashes of conversation from the girls in the van.

And the sound she'd heard in the vision. It hadn't been a lawnmower.

The elevator on the wall looked rickety. Made of wood, not metal — its size and shape were suggestive, and someone had carved a half moon on the solid wooden door. The frame from which the elevator was suspended was constructed of wooden beams. No metal there, either. Even the pulley wasn't a steel cable but a length of rope thicker than Bailey's arm. The elevator was too small for all of them to fit in one trip, so they went down in shifts. As the elevator with the last of the kidnappers and captives slowly sank out of sight into the hole in the floor, Bailey was left alone with the Beast — Jacko. He studied her, a predatory half-smile on his face. Perhaps it was just natural intimidation, the body language of a dangerous man, but it seemed to Bailey an intentional thing. The big man built an air of menace around him with his glowering, cold silence.

"You are a mystery, little mouse." He walked slowly in a circle around where she sat in the dirt, like a man appraising a backyard barbecue grill. "Who are you and how did you come by the information in your little head, huh? I have checked you out — nothing remarkable." He then parroted the high points of the made-up story of her Witness Protection Program identity.

"So, how did you get messed up in my business?" It wasn't a question to which he expected an answer. At least not now. That would come later. "Not just how ... *why* would you do such a thing, a woman who makes a living painting kidneys and livers and gall bladders?"

He shook his head in genuine bafflement.

"It makes no sense. My men found the note on Poli after ... let's just say she could no longer tell me where she got it. On surveillance video, I watched you pass it to her. Poli didn't know you! So how did you know her? How did you know she planned to run off with that—?" He used a word in another language she was sure was a curse.

His lips formed an approximation of a smile, stapled to his face like a yard sale sign to a telephone pole. "I am looking forward to the tale and I will hear it soon. Very soon you will be begging me to ask more questions so you can tell more of your story."

"I didn't get mixed up in your business." Bailey hated that she sounded as frightened as she felt. Her voice was thin and reedy, and it trembled. "I know nothing about—"

"Wait." He stopped her before she could spew out more of a story he was not for a nanosecond going to believe. "*I* decide when you speak and when you are silent."

Someone below had pushed the button and the elevator rose slowly from the open area in LHOM #2 below to the cavern that formed the entrance to LHOM #1. She briefly considered making a break for it, and this time she didn't have the excuse that she couldn't feel her arms and legs. If she ran, he'd shoot her ... not a kill shot. He wanted her alive.

But she might get lucky. He might miss and actually kill her. It was worth a try.

She didn't leap up, though, and dash out into the darkness. She sat where she was, staring up at the monster, paralyzed with fear. It wasn't panic — panic was white-hot rocket fuel that propelled you into action without thought. This fear glowed with a cold blue flame that burned away resolve, left you unable to form an intent to do anything, much less the will to carry it out.

She thought of T.J, who was a decorated war hero. He seemed like a peaceful old man, wouldn't hurt a fly. But you could sense a strength in him that hadn't been diminished by age. More than that — she could sense courage. In T.J. and in Brice, too. These were men who had been in battle, had lost friends, had done what was required of them even at the risk of their own lives.

Some foster father or other who'd been pontificating on a subject about which he clearly knew nothing, had handed out a platitude as if he'd earned the understanding of it. His ignorance didn't make it any less true, though. Being brave didn't mean you weren't afraid. Bravery was doing what you had to do anyway.

The Beast took her arm and pulled her to her feet.

"Pick that up."

He indicated the duffle bag one of the men had left lying beside the elevator. Bailey obeyed. It was heavy, with all the weight on one end. The size and shape, yeah, she knew what it was and the understanding momentarily paralyzed her.

She wanted to scream *stop!* As she had wanted to do when she sat in the anonymous chair in the anonymous police station, trying to wrap her mind around the reality that her husband was dead and her daughter lost to her. She had wanted to call out to the universe, point out the mistake: "Hey, Fate, you got the wrong girl here. You must have been looking for somebody else. I'm just a young mother with a beautiful baby daughter and a husband who loves me and we have a life."

But the universe didn't right things. She'd just been a leaf in a stream then, being carried along by the current, taken wherever the river wanted her to go. And she was being swept along now by an equally mindless stream.

Jacko picked up the remaining duffle bag and shoved her into the elevator, closed the door, punched the green button.

As the wooden contraption began to move slowly down into the mine below, she screamed in her head, *Nooooo, it's not fair.* And heard T.J. reply, *Sugar, the only fair I know gives prizes for livestock.*

It was what it was. The very best possible outcome was for her to find a way to make her death less horrible. The people in the twin towers on 9/11 were ordinary people just like she was, whose fate was no more fair than hers was now. They hadn't *wanted* to jump out the windows of a skyscraper! But burning to death was worse and they'd jumped. If she could figure out any way to get the Beast to kill her outright, she had to jump.

She had a bullet in her brain, for crying out loud! Not everybody had a get-out-of-jail-free card like that. Oscar. Dislodge him, game over. Surely, a severe head trauma would do it. Well, then she had to orchestrate a severe head trauma. The death the Beast had planned for her was definitely worth dying to avoid.

Chapter Forty-Two

THE ELEVATOR DESCENDED through the rock ceiling of a ten-foot-tall space hollowed out of the face of LHOM #2 into a mine that was just as Dobbs had described it with his sugar-cubes/sugar-bowl illustration. Fifty-foot pillars of coal — left behind to hold up the mountain — were separated by fifty-foot-wide shafts of empty darkness where the coal had been removed around them, eight black tunnels that stretched a mile, maybe farther through the center of the mountain to the opening on the front of the mine on the other side.

Back there in the darkness were cross shafts eighteen feet wide that cut across the mine from one side to the other, creating a grid of shafts around black "sugar cubes" of coal.

She finally understood the problem of "tall miners." She was five feet, five inches tall and even she would have to bend over to enter one of the mine shafts. The roofs were only fifty-two inches off the floor, shoulder high on Bailey, a little over four feet.

... because that's how thick the coal seam is and no coal company on the planet is going to dig out the rock above the seam just so guys like me can stand up.

Brice had told her that in another lifetime as they drove through the mountains in the fall sunshine.

"The miners in *Lord of the Rings* were dwarves — there's a reason for that," he'd said.

She couldn't think of Brice. Not now.

Looking around, she tried to remember why they'd hollowed out this open space in front of the shafts, made it a cave with a ten-foot ceiling stretching across the whole face. But either the guys hadn't explained that part or she hadn't been listening. She *had* been listening when T.J.'d placed the string off his coat on Dobbs's model, though, and there in the center shaft — Main Street! — was the belt line that hauled out the coal, extending twenty feet out into the open space. When the mine closed, the miners must have just flipped a switch to turn off the conveyor belt and walked out — because there was coal still loaded on the belt bound for the front of the mine.

A piece of equipment with a shovel on the end was sticking out the nearest shaft and Bailey assumed it was the scoop the machine used to scoop up coal and pieces of the roof when it caved in, and there was a continuous miner around somewhere, she supposed, since it was the piece of equipment that cut into the coal. It wasn't here in the hollowed-out space, which was empty, except for instruments of some kind on a post on the wall opposite the elevator. Methane meters, she supposed, *about as reliable as an alimony check.*

Bailey had to admit this was the perfect place to ... to do whatever you wanted to do. Sound would not even carry up into the cave above. Whatever happened here ... no one would ever know.

Hollywood crossed to them when the elevator door opened and took the two duffle bags they carried. Jacko shoved Bailey out the door and she stumbled to the ground and remained there. He looked at the man who'd ridden shotgun in the van, Vinny, the ugly, chinless wonder.

"Go back up and keep an eye on the car and van."

As Vinny went up in the elevator, Jacko instructed the other men to "get the barrels set up," and they arranged the barrels along the back wall and pried off the lids. From the duffle bags, they retrieved bags of someth—

Bailey understood and horror stole her breath.

Jacko caught her looking at the barrels.

"We might as well get started — with me asking questions and you answering them." He crossed in two steps to where Bailey sat on the ground, yanked her to her feet and grabbed her by the neck with one hand.

"Tell me … what do you think I'm going to do with these barrels?"

She could barely speak with his clenching fingers around her throat, but she managed to croak, "You brought them to … put the bodies in."

"And whose bodies would those be?"

Bailey nodded toward the girls, who had been dropped in heaps on the floor.

"Their bodies."

"And what will happen to the bodies?" He didn't wait for her to answer, just indicated the sacks the men were opening. "Plop, plop, fizz, fizz. In a week, there will be nothing left in these barrels you couldn't pour down your sink without stopping up your drain."

The girls cried out, and one girl, who had hair as black as the coal in the walls of the mine, began to sob, big gulping sobs like an inconsolable child. Jeni looked shocked and afraid. But she wasn't surprised. Perhaps she hadn't shared her suspicions with the other girls, but it was clear she had known all along that they would not leave the mine alive.

"And who else's body will be turning to mush very, very soon?" he prompted.

"Mine."

The crying of the girl obviously annoyed him. He said nothing, just gestured toward her with his chin and the red-haired black man stopped opening the sacks of whatever the chemical was — not simple lime, she didn't think, sodium hydroxide maybe — and advanced on her. She saw him coming and stifled her tears, almost choking on the effort. The Beast let go of Bailey's throat and she staggered backward, almost tripped over the pile of coal at the end of the conveyor belt but didn't fall. Her heart was pounding, her vision pulsing with each beat and she felt lightheaded. Her hands went to her throat and she coughed.

"It was a stroke of good fortune for your friends that you … wandered away from the herd."

Bailey got the implication — they'd planned to take her by force. Her shock must have shown on her face.

"What, you don't think I could have killed the big sheriff and the other buffoons?" He scoffed. "They sit there so complacent, believe they are safe. They are *prey*." He gestured toward the girls, lying where they'd been dumped on the floor. "Prey! And prey is always stupid. A single wolf can take a whole herd of sheep. They are many, he is one. But they are too stupid to join together and fight so he kills them all."

Bailey looked around the room, searching for any way she could take her own life before he had a chance. Any way to inflict a head injury. But there was nothing. The chunks of coal lying about were jagged, with sharp edges, like the smaller pieces that had cut into their hands and knees when she was dragged out of the car. But she doubted she could grab one and clock herself in the head with sufficient force to dislodge Oscar to do his job.

The Beast stepped up in front of the girls and made a speech.

"I have not been at all satisfied with your job perfor-mance." He stopped and smiled wickedly. "Oh, I don't mean your performance with your customers. From the comments I have heard, you have done a remarkably good job satisfying them, particularly for amateurs at the trade. But being an amateur, not a professional, was what they were willing to pay so dearly for."

He began to pace, affecting a professorial tone, as if lecturing a group of students who had done particularly poorly on the midterm exam.

"But in other areas, you have not lived up to my expectations."

He whirled around to face them so fast it was startling.

"One of you," he paused, then whispered the words for effect, "*has a loose tongue.*"

He continued in a normal voice, shaking his index finger at them. "You cannot say you did not know. You were warned. The most important rule? Keep *our* business *our* business." He paused, looked each girl in the eye, his gaze lingering before he moved on to the next. "But *one* of you, or perhaps all of you — that remains to be seen — have broken the rule. Now you will pay."

It was clear that he delighted in the girls' terror, thrived on it. His was, indeed, calculated intimidation. He had kept the girls in line with the threat of his retribution, and now he was very much enjoying the chance to make good on his threat.

"I have invested enormous time, effort and spared no expense to make you profitable commodities. But I am first and foremost a businessman, and a good businessman must learn from past mistakes. Obviously, I did not impress upon you in sufficiently forceful terms that there was a penalty for disobedience. I will not make that mistake with the next group of girls."

He smiled the snake's smile. In this light, his eyes could have been any color or no color at all. They were just black holes under his eyebrows, desolate wells in the lonely depths of which something small and feral had drowned.

"So I am going to kill two birds with one stone, so to speak." He turned back toward Bailey. "No, *three* birds. First, I will make of you such an example that the next group of girls fortunate enough to take your places will be sufficiently impressed with the consequences of transgressions that they will keep their mouths tightly shut."

He had been pacing and he turned back the way he'd come with almost military precision.

"Two, in the process of making you an example, I will find out which one of you it was whose loose lips got all of you into such terrible, terrible trouble." He focused his gaze on Bailey. "When you see what is in store for you if you are not honest with me, you will be anxious to give me all the information I require."

He turned back toward the barrels.

"We all agree that you are *stupid* girls, yes?" He seemed to be waiting for a reply, so some of the girls nodded. None dared speak. "But even stupid girls must be looking at these barrels and wondering — how does he intend to fit the bodies of *eight dead girls* into only three small barrels?"

At the words "dead girls," the black-haired girl burst into sobbing again. Two of the others followed suit, crying and shaking their heads, their eyes and faces pleading, their voices muffled by the duct tape across their mouths.

He walked to the duffel bag Bailey had carried down in the elevator for him. It was fastened shut with Velcro and the sound of the pieces separating set Bailey's teeth on edge. Then he reached into the bag and pulled out what Bailey had guessed was in there.

A chainsaw.

As soon as the girls saw it, they began to scream and cry in earnest.

The Beast rumbled, "Quiet!" and the volume decreased, but the girls were now past the point that they were capable of controlling their tears.

"I will not be jamming bodies into the barrels. Just *pieces* of bodies."

He held the chainsaw up in front of their faces.

"Messy work, yes." He smiled. "But we—" he gestured at the other men "—are prepared."

Jacko's performance had commanded the rabid attention of all the girls, and they'd not noticed what the other men had been doing. Now they turned as one to look.

The man called Sandy, who had helped Jacko snatch Bailey out of her back yard — the one with white hair and a flat head — had put on coveralls.

Hollywood had taken out his phone and held it in front of him.

Nick, the red-haired black man, merely stood by Jacko's side. The two of them would be the muscle.

The smile never left Jacko's face as he wrapped up his speech. It hung there, an old rug left on a clothesline.

"We will be making a … recruitment video." He nodded at Hollywood. Then he turned his gaze on Jeni. "As I promised, you will be the star."

The smile finally drained off his face. Without it, his features were all sharp angles. His soul sat there, naked and proud. A predator.

"You serve as an example to future girls, a word-picture of the price of disobedience. You will give of yourselves totally to the lesson I am teaching. With this," he held up the saw, "you will be cut into pieces — a hand, an arm, a leg — while you are pleading with me for a mercy that I will unfortunately be unable to show."

Bailey felt the room sway around her. The edges of her vision grayed out and blackness threatened to slam in from all sides and take her. But she remained conscious, though the man's voice, shouting above the girls' hysterical crying, seemed to come from a long way off.

"You. Will. Be. *Silent!*" It was the roar of an angry lion. "Or you will go *first!*"

The screaming cut off like water from a turned-off spigot. He dropped the next words into the ocean of dark silence.

"That's better."

Holding the handle of the chainsaw in his left hand, he took hold of the pull chain. One yank and the motor would spring to life.

A voice suddenly came from out of the darkness of the tunnels that opened into the hollowed-out area where they stood. It was impossible to tell which tunnel, since sound bounced around like a ball in a racquetball court in the enclosed rock-walled space.

"I wouldn't do that if I were you," the voice said.

It was T.J.

Chapter Forty-Three

THOUGH T.J. HAD BELIEVED he and Dobbs ought to check out the Last Hope Ollie Mine, he hadn't never seriously considered the possibility that it *really was* where the men was takin' the girls and Bailey. He'd believed the better interpretation of the flashes of images Bailey had seen through the eyes of girls being transported in the van was that the kidnappers were making for a cavern off North West Ohio Route 7.

Even Dobbs, whose idea it'd been to go to the mine to look for 'em in the first place, was stunned speechless when they rounded the last curve and seen light ahead. Dobbs had slowed down then, drove past the entrance to Last Hope Ollie #1 carved out of the back of a cave. A car and a van were parked there, inside the fence, which meant somebody'd given them a key. No one was in sight. The men had already taken their captives into the mine.

Dobbs had looked at T.J., his eyes open too wide, and T.J.'s heart'd locked up in his chest. He'd learned a phrase in the military — doin' the necessary — the Marine Corps way of sayin' soldiers had to set aside their feelings to do whatever it was the mission required. T.J. had to concentrate on doin' the necessary now. There was no help coming. They couldn't summon law enforcement. Even if they could get cell coverage — which in this hollow wasn't likely — there wasn't nobody to summon. Brice and the troops were in Ohio. T.J. had texted Brice as they were leaving Bailey's house, told him their take on the mysterious sign. Once Brice came up with a handful of nothing in Ohio, he'd come blazing back into West Virginia 10-60 — lights and siren. But he couldn't possibly get here before whatever was going to happen was long done.

No, T.J. and Dobbs was on the hook for this one. They was all the hope the captives had and the soldier in T.J. recognized dispassionately that the flame of that hope was a flickerin' candle on a dark, stormy sea.

The man with the skull tattoo had at least one, maybe two men with him in the car. Added to two or three men in the van, they were facing at least four, maybe as many as eight armed, trained assassins. Those men had brought the teenagers to this secluded spot so no one could hear the girls' screams when they were murdered. The one Poli'd called the Beast would torture Bailey until she gave him a believable explanation for why she'd warned Poli, and since she had no explanation he'd believe, she would suffer a slow, painful, brutal death.

He and Dobbs were all that stood between her and that fate.

T.J. had to come up with a plan. Fast.

They were armed, had stopped by T.J.'s and picked up weapons. They could hide in the woods and capture the unsuspecting men when they came out of the mine. Or they could — and T.J. *would* — simply drop the men where they stood, without warning, firing out of the darkness before they had a chance to respond. He'd likely get most of them, and the ones he didn't would be returning fire at an invisible enemy. Even with the automatic weapons he was sure they were packing, T.J. would have the advantage.

But if they waited until the men come out of the mine, all the captives would be dead.

Comin' at 'em from *inside* the mine, T.J. would still have the advantage of surprise, could get the drop on 'em while remaining in the darkness. But he had no illusions about his ability to capture that many armed assailants. Sure's God made little green apples, one of 'em would go for a gun, and the resulting gunfight would be lethal in such an enclosed space. With bullets ricocheting off the walls, ceiling and floor — automatic gunfire — the captives stood little chance of survival. If he simply opened fire on the kidnappers without warning, he'd have to drop maybe half a dozen men with one shot each. Not likely. And they'd almost certainly be hostages in the line of fire, anyway.

Dobbs pulled over to the side of the road about a quarter of a mile past the mine. He said nothing, just waited.

"Get out," T.J. told him. "I want you to go back there and disable those two vehicles, any way you can. Take whatever you need out of the toolbox."

Dobbs obediently got out from behind the wheel of his Jeep and began to dig around in the toolbox on the floorboard in front of the back seat in the extended cab.

"Take the gun." T.J. was trained to use all the weapons they had brought, but Dobbs'd never fired anything more powerful than a deer rifle. But he was a crack shot with it.

"Any of them men come out of that mine ... shoot him."

Dobbs held his stare for a moment, then nodded. He was no a soldier, but T.J. knew he'd drop any man he got in his sights.

Without a word, Dobbs picked up the gun and tools and headed back down the road in the darkness.

T.J. slid over behind the wheel. Dobbs had brought hisself a brand new Jeep Renegade to replace the one the flood washed away in Turkey Neck Hollow last summer. With its 1.4-liter turbocharged engine, that baby could fly. T.J. knew the roads, and if you was lookin' to speed, it was a whole lot safer at night than in the daytime 'cause you could see headlights coming at you over a rise or around a corner. He was expecting no traffic. This was a mine access road and the mines was closed.

When the mining industry hit the skids, W. Maxwell Crenshaw had been the last man standing. He'd been paying off mine inspectors for years to keep the Last Hope Ollie #1 and #2 open and likely would have gone sailing merrily along … but he'd been slapped with a lawsuit by a miner injured in a rockfall. The story had hit the media — a David-and-Goliath tale of one lone miner against the biggest coal operator in West Virginia — and it had gone viral. If it hadn't, Crenshaw'd have tried to buy the miner off, and if he'd refused to settle, well … But with all that media attention focused on the case, a federal judge had issued an injunction just a month ago closing both mines and freezing the assets. The way T.J.'d heard it, the miners who'd been working that last day, just got up and walked off the job.

As soon as they'd discovered Poli'd been only a teenager, that she and — *how many?* — others had been kidnapped as part of an international operation on a grand scale, he knew Crenshaw was involved somehow. He'd availed himself of the services of teenage sex slaves to make good on his guarantee, "Your Every Desire Fulfilled." The Beast hadn't taken the girls to Last Hope Ollie by coincidence. They'd needed a place to commit brutal murder and Crenshaw had provided it — had obviously given them the key because T.J. could see that they hadn't had to break down the fence.

Careening around hairpin turns at a ridiculous speed, T.J. raced around the base of the mountain toward the *front* side of Last Hope Ollie #2. He was sure the open area at the face of #2, sixty feet below the cave opening that formed the front of #1, was where the monster intended to commit his crimes. T.J. intended to come up behind him. Which meant he'd have to travel the whole length of the mine. Oh, he could take a mantrip, the vehicle that transported miners inside the mine. He was sure there were several sitting unused in the back of the mine. None of the mining equipment — the mantrips, scoops or the continuous miner — required a key for operation. But a mantrip would make noise and all T.J. had going for him was the element of surprise.

He slid to a stop in front of the entrance to the front of Last Hope Ollie #2. There was a fence around it and the gate was locked. Shifting Dobbs's Jeep into four-wheel drive, he backed up fifty yards and slammed into the gate, knocked it off the hinges and sent the lock pinging off into the darkness.

He needed light, not to find his way in but to direct him back out again. The light switches were in a locked breaker box on a pole out front — and W. Maxwell Crenshaw hadn't provided *him* a key. But if his memory served him, there was a second set of switches that turned on only the one bank of lights set just inside the mine entrance. That set of switches was on the first coal pillar on Main Street right above where the conveyer belt dumped its load of coal from the face.

Leaving the Jeep lights shining on dark shafts at the mine entrance, T.J. jumped out of the vehicle, grabbed his weapons and raced toward the end of the belt line. When he flipped the switches there, the whole front portion of the mine leapt out of the darkness. He ran to the nearest mantrip, searched around on it, couldn't find what he was looking for and ran to another mantrip sitting in the mouth of the Boardwalk shaft. There! A helmet with a headlamp.

It was a red helmet, and that was appropriate because T.J. fully intended to be a red-hat miner, *unpredictable and dangerous.* He donned the helmet, flipped on the headlamp and without a backward glance plunged into the interior of the dark mine. Dark. Black dark.

This far away, there was obviously no spill of light to be seen from the other side. He ran as fast as he could through the black tunnel, bent almost double, shocked back into the intimidating reality of an environment he hadn't entered in almost forty years.

As he ran, he rounded out the plan he'd put together as he flew down the dark mountain roads, a 'wish and a prayer' plan. Daring and creative, but dangling by a single thread. Everything would hinge on T.J.'s poker-playing skill, specifically his ability to run a good bluff.

Chapter Forty-Four

RAYMOND DOBSON HAD NOT BEEN afraid very many times in his life. There had been that horror-filled afternoon when he was a child that he and T.J. had gone out to watch the train derailment T.J.'s mother had painted. A monumentally bad idea from the get-go, but it had taught him a valuable lesson about thinking through his actions all the way to the end.

There'd been times when he was working as a miner when he'd been so scared he'd been grateful for the darkness so the other miners couldn't read the terror on his face. He had made the whole experience sound exciting and glamorous when he was explaining it to Bailey. In reality, mining was working bent-over in a dark, dirty, miles-deep hole under a mountain. He'd come within inches of being crushed once when he was a red-hat because he strayed too close to the back of the scoop. And he'd almost been chewed up and spit out by the continuous miner — the piece of equipment that actually ate into the coal seam with its spinning, teeth-like blades. That day, he hadn't realized until it was over how close he had come to dying.

But as he crept along the side of the road in the moon-light, heading for the area in front of the Last Hope Ollie mines stacked one on top of the other, he felt a kind of elemental terror he would never have admitted to his childhood friend. T.J. was the brave one. He was the soldier. He was the man who had fought and killed others, had survived imprisonment after his capture on an unofficial mission the government pretended not to know about.

Dobbs, on the other hand, had never faced real danger — *on purpose*. No accident. No surprise. Straight up. And he was terrified.

T.J.'s was the dangerous part of this operation. Dobbs just had to get in and get out without getting caught.

He was still terrified.

Dobbs's job was something he could do in his own garage in a few minutes. Easy peasy.

He was still terrified.

Keeping to the shadows, he moved silently from one tree to the next, approaching the vehicles parked in the area in front of the gate in the fenced-in mine property. His job was to disable them. He stood for what seemed like an eternity, studying the car and the van. The area was deserted. Obviously all the kidnappers had gone inside the mine with the girls. And with Bailey.

To do what with them … Dobbs definitely couldn't let his mind go there.

Finally satisfied no one had been left behind to guard the vehicles, he slipped silently out of the trees and hurried to the van. He carefully tried the door handle. Locked. He figured that'd be the case. Making his way around the van, keeping the van between him and the gate in the fence, he knelt beside the back tire, took a long, flat-head screwdriver and carefully loosened the hubcap. Sticking the screwdriver down in his belt, he picked up the tire iron out of the knapsack and popped off the hubcap. It came off with a clunking sound and Dobbs froze, his heart hammering louder than the sound the hubcap made. He sat frozen, held his breath. Waited thirty seconds. A minute. When nothing happened, he used the lug wrench to remove the five lug nuts, grunting from the effort with the third one, which seemed to have been welded in place. He threw each lug nut into the woods as he removed it, then pulled from the knapsack the mechanic's jack he'd taken from the workshop in his garage where he worked on his collection of antique and classic cars.

He and T.J. had considered the best way, the quickest and easiest method to disable the vehicles. Remove the battery or some other key component of the engine was first in line, but you couldn't get the hood up if the vehicles were locked. Dobbs removed the jack, inserted the lug wrench into the slot to serve as the handle, and scooted the jack under the frame. When he began to jack the vehicle up, every *crank-crank, crank-crank, crank-crank* sounded as loud as a smoke alarm. Or so it seemed to him. In truth, this was the best jack money could buy and its operation was almost soundless. When he finally had the van up high enough, he wrestled the tire off the axel, set it on the ground and rolled it ahead of him back toward the woods, then shoved it off into the trees.

He hurried back to the van, let off the jack and pulled it out from under the vehicle. Now the van axel rested on the ground. It wasn't going anywhere. He made his way silently to the car, tried the door handle. And it wasn't locked. But if he opened the door, the dome light would come on. Wouldn't take but a couple of seconds to pop the hood release and close the door again, though. The light would blink on, then off again. Still …

It'd be easier and faster to remove the battery than to take off one of the tires.

The light would only be on for a couple of seconds.

He thought, vacillated, then set down the tools he was carrying. Taking a deep breath, he pulled open the door and searched frantically. Where was the — there it was, the hood release. He popped it and quickly closed the door, dousing the light. Then he leaned against the car, panting. It took maybe a minute to get his breathing under control, to stop gasping, and he went to the front of the car and pushed up the hood. Taking the adjustable wrench from his pocket, he leaned in and felt around. The brief flash of light had messed with his vision and he couldn't see as well as when his eyes were adjusted to the darkness. But he found the battery, took the wrench and removed the first cable.

"Looking for something?"

The voice came out of the darkness behind him. He jerked immediately erect and banged his head painfully on the hood.

Then he felt the jab of a gun barrel into his back.

"Move, fat boy, and I'll blow you away."

Dobbs didn't move.

A hand grabbed Dobbs by the shoulder and shoved him violently to the ground.

"You just boosted your last battery, hillbilly," said the man standing above him, through crooked, blackened teeth. His face was strikingly ugly, no chin and a nose smashed flat between pockmarked cheeks. Obviously, he hadn't yet noticed the wheel missing from the van and believed Dobbs was merely a thief. He brought the barrel down to within inches of Dobbs's nose, and thumbed back the hammer.

Dobbs had two, maybe three seconds to live.

Chapter Forty-Five

For a big man, Jacko was surprisingly agile. The shock of a voice coming from the depths of the mine paralyzed him only for an instant. Then, in a single fluid movement he grabbed Bailey, yanked her in front of him, a shield, as he drew a weapon from a shoulder holster and pointed it at the shaft openings, swinging it back and forth in a sweeping motion. The empty space at the face of the mine offered no cover except the bodies of the hostages, and the kidnappers followed their boss's lead, dragging the girls to their feet and hunkering down behind them.

Bailey could tell the Beast was shocked and surprised, but there was nothing that even resembled fear on his face. A lifetime on the delivering end of violence and brutality would make Jacko a hard man to intimidate.

"Whoever you are, you better—"

"Shut. Up!" The words boomed out of the darkness, harsh and loud, echoing against the rock walls, coming from everywhere and nowhere. "Here's how this works," T.J. said. "I talk, you listen."

"You're making a big mistake. You have no idea who you're—"

"I know exactly who I'm dealing with — a stupid city boy so dumb it must take you two hours to watch *60 Minutes.*"

While T.J. was talking, the Beast had motioned to his three men. Shoving the girls in front of them, two advanced with weapons drawn on the tunnels to the left of the center belt-line tunnel. He and the blonde called Hollywood started toward the tunnels to the right.

"Forget trying to get the drop on me." The men's attention yanked to the tunnel at the end on the right where it now seemed the voice was coming from. "You ever even been inside a coal mine?"

The Beast didn't answer, just shoved Bailey a few steps in front of him, leaned over and grabbed a flashlight out of one of the duffel bags.

"Flip the switch on that flashlight and it'll be your last act on this earth. When the dust settles after the explosion, they won't be able to find enough of you for a DNA sample."

The Beast stopped.

"Think you're a tough guy, don't you. Can do anything you want — the law doesn't apply to you."

The voice seemed to be coming from the shafts on the left side now. The men exchanged glances, confused by the ever-changing location of the voice coming at them from the darkness.

"Well, let me tell you something, moron. The laws of the state of West Virginia, of the United States — even international law — might not apply to you, but if you flip the switch on that flashlight or try to crank that chainsaw the *laws of nature* are going to …" He paused, said each word individually. "Punch. Your. Ticket."

Then T.J. sounded frustrated.

"Can't you *read?* Those signs on the fence — 'Danger', 'Poisonous Gas' — you think they're a joke? Maybe a bluff, like a 'Beware of Dog' sign when the dog's a chihuahua. You ever heard of coal mines *blowing up?* Happens all the time, and

I'm about to explain to you why that is. It's okay, I'll use small words so you won't have to take notes with your crayons."

T.J. paused, only for a second or two, but when he started talking again his voice appeared to be coming from only a few feet away, from the belt-line shaft right in front of them.

As he spoke, it dawned on Bailey. There wasn't a hint of a West Virginia dialect in his words.

"Methane gas — you can't see it or smell it — is released when you dig into coal. The stuff that kills all those mine canaries. Add in particles of combustible coal dust floating in the air — the combination's more volatile than nitroglycerin. A cubic centimeter has ten times the explosive power of a stick of dynamite. You with me so far?"

By unspoken command, all the men had been converging on the center shaft and the black guy literally jumped when the next words came from a shaft three over to the left. They didn't seem to have put it together that there must be connecting shafts back there in the dark!

"There's a gigantic fan that sucks bad air out and good air in when miners are working. You see a fan here? Go ahead. I'll wait while you look around. Hear one running, do you? The fan on this mine hasn't been turned on *in a month.* Methane's been building up in here day after day. That's why there are warning signs, idiot!"

The lone word "idiot" seemed to come from the tunnel against the left wall. But it couldn't have, because the next words clearly came from the one on the far right. T.J. was playing with the echo. "There's a meter that measures methane on the back wall over there. Why don't you go take a look at it — you don't have to be a rocket scientist to read it. There's a dial — green, yellow and red. First-grader stuff."

The Beast didn't move.

"What's the matter — afraid to see what it says?"

Jacko gestured with his chin and the black man turned and went to the methane meter on the wall.

"The portable one I'm carrying isn't as accurate as that one. Read the sign next to it — the part where it says if the needle leaves the green, moves even a hair into the yellow, federal law requires you to *evacuate the mine*." He thundered the next words, "You think that's a *joke*?"

He spoke softly then.

"But that needle's not in the yellow, is it? I can't see it from here, but the needle on *my* meter isn't." He paused for a beat, then said even softer, "It's in the *red*. Take a real good look at it, because not many men have ever seen a methane meter in the red ... and lived to tell about it. You better hope there's no static electricity in your pants. When this blows, it'll take out both these mines, the road and the first hundred yards of the mountain on the other side."

The look on the black man's face when he turned away from the meter, along with the careful way he moved, said all that needed to be said.

When T.J. spoke again, it was measured and slow.

"Use your brain, idiot. *Think*! Who gave you the key to that gate out there?"

T.J. let the words hang like coal dust in the air.

He scored with that one. Bailey could see a vein in the Beast's temple begin to throb.

"Mr. W. Maxwell Crenshaw the third, Billy to his friends if he had any, told you he had a dandy place for you to do your dirty little job." T.J. let that lie. The Beast didn't argue. "He did, didn't he ... and he *does* know what happens in a mine when you don't run the fan for a month."

The Beast and the others had stopped trying to figure out where the voice was coming from. They just stood there, listening.

"You provided a valuable service for Mr. Crenshaw's special clients, but the minute that houseboat anchor line dragged up the body of that girl this morning — the one *you strangled* — you became a liability. Murder, kidnapping, prostitution ... and the trail leads right back to his front door."

He made a *tisk-tisk* sound.

"So I'm Maxwell Crenshaw and I've got a serious problem on my hands. I may be a criminal, but I've made my fortune with cunning. Lying, cheating, stealing — but *not* violence. I don't have an army of professional killers to make witnesses and evidence go away. What do I do?"

Then T.J.'s voice became harsh and sarcastic. "Well, duh, I give a dumbass like you a key to the fence and send him down into a coal mine full of explosive methane gas, tell him, 'Go ahead — crank up that chainsaw!'"

Bailey could actually feel the sudden fear in the air.

"Problem. *Solved*."

"Who are you and what do you want?" the Beast called out. There was no emotion of any kind in his voice. But he didn't continue toward the mine shafts and he didn't try to turn on his flashlight. And the other men were standing absolutely still, not moving, the way you'd stand if ... well, if you had a bomb strapped to you.

"Who I am doesn't matter and what I want is obvious. Those girls. Unharmed. All of them."

The Beast let out a bleat of sound. Disdainful laughter, maybe. Bailey wasn't sure what it meant.

"Mexican standoff," T.J. said, pleasantly. "We're *both* screwed. You can't let any of us walk out of here alive, not with what we know. What could those girls testify to? Oh my. Death penalty, needle-in-the-arm material — kidnapping, rape ... murder."

T.J. lost it then. "They're *children*!" There was raw rage in the words, but when he continued, he'd gotten control of his voice and again became a negotiator.

"You *have* to kill us — you have no choice. So we have absolutely nothing to lose. You kill me or an explosion kills me. I'm just as dead either way. And those girls — blown instantly into red mist is a more merciful death than what you have planned. You have nothing to threaten any of us with. No leverage."

"I asked you what you want from me."

"This isn't about what I want you to give me … it's about what *I'm* willing to give *you*."

Suddenly, the belt line, the conveyor belt that made a continuous loop through the shaft called Main Street sprang to life. But it wasn't moving forward, carrying the coal to the front of the mine. It was moving backwards, dumping the chunks of coal that'd been loaded onto it into a growing pile on the floor a few feet from where Bailey stood. Its rattle and clunk rumbled loud in the stillness. All eyes were fixed on it, instantly saw the cleared-off space where some small, red thing was lying on the belt. It looked like … a Pez dispenser? T.J. stopped the conveyor belt right before the red thing dropped off onto the floor in front of them.

"Ever bought a Bic lighter in a convenience store?" There was a heartbeat of breathless silence before T.J.'s voice echoed again off the rock walls. "Don't know about where you come from, pal, but here in West Virginia … convenience stores sell butane lighters in a *two-pack*."

Chapter Forty-Six

T.J. SAID NOTHING ELSE, let the silence hang there, full of restrained violence, a mighty storm before that first crack of thunder. Either the guy'd bought the line of crap he'd been hawking or he hadn't. Firing out of the darkness, T.J. could pick his shot, would probably be able to drop two of the gunmen without hitting the girls. He'd gotten a bead on the Beast. He'd die first.

"So what is it?" Jacko said. "What you're offering?"

Hooked him!

"Escape," T.J. moved quickly down the cross shaft — as quickly as it was possible to move bent over like an old man hobbling behind a walker in a fifty-two-inch hole. After all these years, he'd forgotten that part, how hard it was for anybody taller than a fire hydrant to get around.

His next words came out a different shaft.

"Right now, just about every human being with a badge in the whole state of West Virginia and Ohio — oh, and the state water patrol, too, maybe even the FBI — is out there beating the bushes looking for you — *in the wrong place.* When they don't find you *there,* they'll come *here.* I left a voicemail with directions." T.J. paused. "I'd estimate you have less than half an hour to get in your car, beat feet to the Triple C Airport, hop in that Learjet sitting on the runway gassed up and waiting, and disappear out of the lives of this county forever."

"If the police know about us, why didn't they come here in the first—?

"You want me to tell you the whole long story or do you want to haul ass out of here? Me, I got all the time in the world. You, on the other hand ..."

Suddenly, the motor on the piece of equipment that was sticking out the front of the shaft next to the far wall sprang to life. It rumbled like a freight train inside a kettle drum — stunningly, *disorientingly* loud for somebody not used to it.

"Don't worry, the engine on this scoop won't set off an explosion, but this Bic lighter ..."

"You're bluffing!"

"Think so? Fine. You got a flashlight in your hand, a dumb civilian flashlight that'd never be allowed in a mine. I'm standing here in the dark right in front of you. Turn that flashlight on and shoot me. Or don't. Just stand there, trying to decide what to do — while every second the cavalry is getting closer and closer."

The pregnant silence settled around them again, broken only by the rumble of the scoop's engine, the sound echoing off the walls until it seemed to come from everywhere. That's why T.J. had started it, to dump noise into the silence, confuse and distract.

Then he called out to Bailey.

"Bailey, honey, I want you to know that seeing you painting that day on your front porch — seems like a lifetime ago, now — was one of the best things that ever happened to me. If these are the last few seconds I'm going to draw breath on this earth, I want you to know that I love you like a daughter."

His voice actually cracked. Hadn't meant for it to, but it

was good it did. When he spoke again, the steel was back in his words.

"Now *you*, tough guy. Call. My. Bluff!"

T.J. let the rumble of the motor fill the empty silence. After he let it drag out for what seemed like a minute, maybe two, but which was probably no more than thirty seconds, he spoke again. Ran bent over three shafts down so the words would issue from a different place.

"You won't — because you're a coward and cowards are always afraid to die. Now put your weapons in a pile way over there in the back corner room and untie those girls. Move slow and careful. One spark of static electricity — that's all it'll take — and where you're standing will look like Hiroshima after first pass of the Enola Gay."

"You know this isn't over." Jacko ground out the words, sounded like gravel in his throat. "I will find you. I will come for you and I will—"

"Put a sock in it. You don't scare me. I'm a Marine, Special Forces. Wimps like you … snack food."

"You are a dead man! Now, as you stand there. A *dead* man! You understand."

"Tick. Tick. Tick."

All the men looked at the Beast. T.J. had only once in his life seen such raging hatred on a human face, and that face hadn't been human at the time. The Beast looked at his watch, then met the gaze of his men.

He said nothing, just turned and walked to the back corner of the hollowed-out space at the mine face and set his weapon down on the floor, nodded to the others and they did the same.

"Now the *other* weapons you think I don't know about. Backups. You first, tough guy. The shoulder holster and the ankle." The Beast unloaded two more firearms onto the pile, the others made offerings as well, though T.J. was sure a couple of them were still holding out. "Open those coats, gentlemen. Pull up the pants legs." Three more firearms were added to the pile.

The men went to the hostages, cut their bonds and roughly ripped the duct tape off their mouths. The girls cried out in pain. Then they all ran to Bailey — T.J. couldn't have said why — and huddled around her where she stood in front of the end of the conveyor belt. Jacko reached out and grabbed the girl whose punk-cut short hair was colored like a tropical fish.

"Christina, you stay with me for a little while." He held her between him and the mine shafts, unwilling to stand unarmed and unprotected.

Jeni, the blonde girl they'd found in the casino, was the last and she paused in front of Bailey, stood looking at her.

"Delay?" she said.

Bailey sucked in a breath.

"Yes!" she cried, reached out and enveloped Jeni in a hug.

Before T.J. could order Jacko to let the girl go, there was a noise — and it wasn't another piece of mining equipment he'd cranked up. It was the elevator descending from the cavern above. No one spoke. When the elevator reached the bottom, the door swung open. Dobbs! A white-haired man stood behind him and shoved. Dobbs stumbled and fell to the ground.

T.J. saw the gun the same time Jacko saw it.

"Vinny, put that thing away!" Jacko yelled.

"He said he knew the ladies. I said they could watch him die."

The man lifted the gun then and pointed it at Dobbs.

"No," roared the Beast. "Don't—"

Bailey cried out, "Dobbs!"

A shot rang out, the roar of a cannon in the confined space.

Chapter Forty-Seven

T.J. WAS MAYBE a minute away from pulling the noose on his trap!

It took only seconds for the whole thing to fall apart.

The man holding the gun on Dobbs looked up quizzically before he crumpled to the ground, blood squirting in arterial bursts from the hole in the front of his neck.

T.J. had intended to take the weaponless kidnappers hostage as soon as he could pry that last girl out of Jacko's clutches. Or shoot the men where they stood if they tried to resist. He was fully prepared to do either.

But in an instant, they scattered like roaches on a kitchen floor. He didn't dare fire at Jacko, even though he let the girl go when he raced toward the pile of guns. He did fire at the blonde man, who'd dropped to the ground, and missed. And at the black man and heard him cry out, wounded, not dead.

Then T.J. called out to Bailey.

"Boardwalk! Run!" praying she'd remember Dobbs's description of the layout of a coal mine.

The instant his shot rang out, he saw Dobbs leap up and dodge into the Broadway shaft. After that, it was utter pandemonium. The world was alive with gunfire, rattling, ricocheting bullets flying everywhere. And with screaming — the girls either scared or hit, T.J. couldn't tell which. As soon as the gunmen reached their weapons, they began firing indiscriminately into the shafts.

T.J. crouched behind the edge of the coal pillar as bullets knocked out hunks of coal all around him.

"Kill them all," Jacko roared in rage. "Not one left alive."

T.J.'d seen a continuous miner sitting behind the coal pillar in cross shaft #79, halfway between the belt line and Broadway. He ran to it, bent over like an old man with a walker, climbed into the seat, hit the beam of his headlamp just for an instant to light up the dashboard and cranked the machine to life. Its motor emitted a rumble twice as loud as the scoop that sat idling three shafts over. T.J. needed all the distractions he could get, so he shoved down the lever that turned on the revolving blades on the boom sticking out the front of the piece of equipment, vicious whirling knives — like the propeller on a boat — that cut through coal like butter and could turn a human body instantly into a Slurpee. Then he put the miner in gear and got out of the seat. The big machine with blades whirring out in front began to move ponderously down past the coal pillar and out into the Broadway shaft. Hopefully, it would provide cover for Dobbs, who knew how to avoid getting killed by it. Bullets pinged off the machine. As he'd hoped, the kidnappers assumed somebody had to be driving the thing and they were determined to take him out.

T.J. turned then and headed in the opposite direction. Spray-painted in white on the back side of every coal pillar in that cross shaft was the number 79. Which meant that the front of the coal mine — and their only way out of here now — was 78 cross shafts south.

The plan T.J. was making on the fly was to gather up Bailey and the girls somewhere along the Boardwalk shaft. Bailey would go there, take with her as many of the girls as had survived the barrage of gunfire. Seven girls, seven kidnapped teenagers! He had figured three or four, never that many. He trusted that Bailey would remember the location of Boardwalk, that it was the shaft on the *left* of Main Street, the shaft with the conveyor belt. She'd laughed at the Monopoly names. She *had* to remember that!

Once he found the girls, T.J. would lead them in a zigzagging route south, dodging out of sight behind the plastic curtains that hung between the coal pillars to direct the flow of air when the fan was on. He hoped that when the gunmen running down the shafts got to the first cross shaft … and realized all the shafts were connected, a maze of them out there in the darkness, they'd give up and leave. But in truth, he had no faith they'd show good judgment. They'd seen he was bluffing, and now Jacko surely figured the whole thing had been a con — including the part about the approaching armada of police officers, the only part of the elaborate story that was true. They'd hang in, try to find and kill their prey, not daring to leave all these witnesses behind.

Gunshots continued to ring out. The kidnappers had moved down into the shafts now, blasting with automatic weapons, lethal ricocheting bullets. The barrage of gunfire made it impossible for T.J. to return fire. They would kill anybody they found, any girl who fell behind … but the girls could move fast, like baby rabbits. They were small, wouldn't have as much trouble as the men were having with the low ceilings.

And the mine was a big, long, dark place where T.J. felt at home and where the men following him were clueless. He'd win a game of cat and mouse here. There were eight shafts leading longways down the mine toward an exit they didn't even know was there. Only four kidnappers remained, one of them wounded. They couldn't cover all the shafts, and the way they were shooting, they'd soon run out of ammo. He'd bide his time, pick them off one by one.

But first he had to *find the girls*!

When he finally got to the Boardwalk shaft, one of the kidnappers with an automatic weapon was lumbering down it, spraying the air in front of him with a hail of bullets. Bailey might have brought the girls here but she couldn't have stayed.

So where had they gone?

T.J. couldn't protect them if he couldn't find them! He had a headlamp — light. The girls had nothing. The girls would be just as lost as their pursuers!

… unless Bailey remembered Dobbs's description of a coal mine, recalled the grid of numbered cross shafts, used it to her advantage. If she did, they had a chance. If she didn't, they'd get hopelessly lost, double back, stumble into the line of fire and the gunmen would mow them down.

There was only one way for T.J. to help them now. He had to do whatever he could to distract the gunmen, keep them busy, give Bailey a chance to lead the girls away.

But the darkness itself would soon become the enemy. The light from the face would fade quickly the deeper they went into the mine. Soon, there would be nothing but darkness all around, a profound darkness hard for the human mind to countenance, the utter sightlessness of one born blind. Only someone who'd been inside a coal mine could understand the power of the horror that kind of darkness produced. Eventually, the girls would run deep enough into the mine to encounter it, a blackness where they would have to feel their way along.

Their pursuers had flashlights. The psychological advantage of that was incalculable. With light in your hands, you could chase away the shadows. With light in your hands, the oppression of the darkness could be held at bay. With light in your hands, you were the master, you were in charge.

But with no light at all, the darkness became a sea of ink, drowning you. Darkness that profound was disorienting. Even with your feet on the ground, or crawling on all fours, you could experience vertigo with no light reference points. He prayed Bailey wouldn't panic, race off with the girls down the shafts in a madness of flight, deeper and deeper until the darkness overtook them.

As long as they could see the light from the face, even if it was only a distant spark ... they could orient themselves, know where they were going, where they'd come from, keep moving around the grid, stay hidden. And he'd turned on the lights in the front of the mine when he came in, so there would be light ahead. But LHOM #2 was so deep there was a space in between the front where he had come in and the face where they had come in that there was *no light at all.* Total, absolute blackness. If Bailey and the girls ran that far, with no light behind or in front, they'd become paralyzed, unable to go forward or back, huddled together, afraid to move. They would be like a deer in the headlights in the glow of a flashlight beam then, unable to run away.

T.J. could only protect the girls now by becoming a target, goad the gunmen into firing until they'd emptied their automatic weapons. With only handguns left, he would pick them off, one by one. Sitting ducks, they were, with flashlights in their hands. T.J. would stalk them and kill them all.

Chapter Forty-Eight

IN THE SILENCE that followed the gunshot, Bailey froze, believing that Dobbs was dead. Then she saw the gunman collapse and heard T.J. call out "Boardwalk!" Grabbing Jeni's hand, she covered the few steps past the belt line, snatched up what was lying on it and headed for the shaft entrance on the left. She ducked into it and ran as fast as she could — bent at the waist — down it.

Behind her, the kidnappers were scrambling to get their weapons. She and the girls had to make it all the way to a cross shaft where they could duck out of sight before the shooting started. Shorter and smaller, it was easier for them to run crouched over than it was for the men chasing them. A flashlight beam shot out of the darkness behind them and a bullet flew by Bailey's face so close she could feel the air rearrange itself around it. She dropped to the ground, crawling, crying out in an urgent whisper, "Come on, this way."

The girls behind her stumbled, fell, too, and crawled frantically.

Bailey reached the cross shaft and dived behind the coal pillar. A flashlight beam swung back and forth in the shaft behind her. Searching. When it swung away from where she crouched, she leaped out and grabbed the girls still crawling and scrambling and yanked and shoved them behind the pillar.

An automatic weapon of some kind spewed gunfire down the shaft along with the light, sweeping back and forth with it. One girl was lagging behind. The girl with the brown braid got her feet tangled up in the long skirt of her evening gown and tripped. When she staggered to her feet, a bullet tore into her. She flew forward, blood spewing out her mouth, and collapsed into the dirt.

"Rayna!" one of the other girls cried out.

Bailey turned away instantly, grabbed Jeni's hand. "Follow me. Hurry."

She ran in a duckwalking crouch down the cross shaft to a piece of plastic sheeting stretched all the way across — iridescent orange, not lettuce green— shoved it aside, herded the girls through the opening, then shoved it back in place and led them down the cross shaft to the next large shaft, knowing the gunman would be right behind them. Peeking out around the pillar of coal, she saw no flashlight beam in this shaft so she dashed across it, ran down the cross shaft to the next curtain and leapt behind it.

They *had* to find T.J.! And he had directed her to Boardwalk. She knew where it was — the shaft on the left of the belt line shaft called Main Street. But that's where the gunman was. They couldn't go that way. She had to lead the girls in the opposite direction, off into the maze of shafts. Maybe they'd be able to double back and find T.J.

As soon as the last girl crawled through the opening, Bailey replaced the curtain and ran to the next shaft, saw no flashlight, but instead of racing down the cross shaft, she turned right and ran down the main shaft, past one cross shaft, two, three, four, then she dived behind a coal pillar, yanking the girls around it, too, and sat where she was, panting, listening to their whimpering and labored breathing.

"Shhhh," she commanded, and the whimpering ceased.

Somewhere in the darkness, she heard an engine rumble, the sound echoing and pounding, directionless. T.J. had started some piece of equipment. Then she heard the grinding, whirring of the spinning head and knew he had cranked the continuous miner.

What should they do now?

Continue to run?

Hide here?

Try to double back and find T.J. on Boardwalk?

She ached to find T.J.! He'd protect them. He was a coal miner!

But no matter how much she yearned to be "protected," it didn't make sense to chance running into the gunman on the way to the Boardwalk shaft, and by now, the gunmen had likely forced T.J. away from it, too.

It was always possible they would stumble upon Dobbs — she refused to believe that any of the bursts of gunfire she'd heard had cut him or T.J. down. That was happy talk, though. Reality still in the husk, as T.J. would put it, was that they were on their own. But they had their own ace. The Sugar Cube Coal Mine, which she could vividly picture in her mind — with its lengthwise shafts and crossways breaks and lettuce leaf curtains. She could picture where she was going, would know how to zigzag — the cross shafts were *numbered* so she could double back. The gunmen were big, hulking men trying to run bent over and shoot at the same time. If she was careful, she and the girls could stay one step ahead.

They had to keep moving — which was good because it allowed her to give in to the terror bursting in her chest and obey the accompanying command to *run*!

"Hold hands and stay with me."

And so they ran. There was no destination, no *to*. Only the urgent *from* that sent them scrambling off into the darkness. Bailey had no intention of trying to lead the girls all the way out the front of the mine. That awful forever-darkness lay between them and where T.J. had come in. So she stayed where she could see light.

Zigzagging. Doubling back. A deadly game of cat and mouse.

Even bent at the waist, their backs scraped painfully across the rough stone ceiling of the fifty-two-inch shafts. They stumbled and fell on the floor littered with sharp chunks of coal that bit into the skin of their knees and palms until they were scratched and bleeding. Three of the girls were dressed in formal evening wear, one of them in a long gown. They'd been in heels and had lost them; now they ran barefoot over the sharp rocks.

When they paused for a few moments, Bailey addressed the girl in the long skirt of blue satin.

"Get rid of that," she said. "Tear it off so you don't trip over it ..." She didn't add "like the girl who was shot" but they all got the message. The girls used long, fashionably manicured nails to rip the fabric and tear it away at the waist. Now the girl was wearing only the top part of an evening gown — with long sleeves — and pantyhose.

And it was cold in the mine.

That was one of the few things Bailey had already known about coal mines before she moved to West Virginia. They remained a uniform temperature year round — fifty-seven degrees.

Jeni took off her denim jacket and gave it to the red-haired girl she called Lora.

The girl in the black-sequined dress turned her back to Bailey. "Unzip. Is too shiny." She was right, of course, in the beam of a flashlight, the sequins would twinkle.

When Bailey touched the girl there was ... *something* Some connection. Not as sharp as a pop of static electricity, but a shock a little like that.

"I'm Christina," the girl said, and Bailey knew she felt it, too.

Bailey helped her out of the dress. Then she turned it wrong side out and put it back on. The black girl, who was the warmest of the lot in a sweatshirt and sweatpants, ripped off strips of fabric from one of the gown skirts and wrapped it around and around Christina and tied it so the unzipped dress wouldn't fall off.

The girl in the torn-away evening gown had started making a whining, mewling sound as the girls ripped the fabric. She was looking around, her eyes open too wide, shaking her head.

"No ... I can't ... I have to get out." Her breathing was hitching in and out like a child after a crying jag. She squeaked out a little sob and Bailey feared she was about to break, start screaming or—

Jeni slapped her — *hard*. Then spoke to her in a harsh whisper, a language Bailey couldn't understand. She caught only one word, the girl's name — Nikolina.

Nikolina held her hand to her cheek and stared at Jeni, still looked like she was seconds away from bolting. But they'd all stayed here too long, had to move. Bailey whispered, "This way," and they all took off again, having figured out how to crouch-run beneath the low ceiling. It was like ducking under a kitchen table ... and running beneath it for miles.

Though Bailey couldn't have said exactly where she was, she wasn't lost. The light from the face they'd run from was an orienting beacon. She kept track of the numbers spray-painted in white on the cross shafts they ran through. She didn't want to stray too deep, too far away from the face light, or they'd be plunged into utter darkness. But the very nature of running away was inexorably driving them deeper and deeper into the shafts.

They stopped often to listen, to catch their breath, struggling not to cough in the gagging black coal dust that slathered every surface. In one space, they turned from a cross shaft to run down a shaft and the roof above their heads vanished. Roof fall. There was no debris on the floor so it'd been cleaned away, and they were glad to be able to stand upright as they ran. Still, Bailey hurried through that part, back down a cross shaft. Roof fall meant roof *fall.*

Time came unhooked from the universe and they were captives in a forever-now moment. Had it been an hour since T.J. shot the kidnapper who was going to shoot Dobbs?

Two hours?

Ten minutes?

Forever?

They continued to hear gunfire. Sometimes it sounded so near Bailey was sure the gunmen couldn't be more than one shaft away. Other times it was distant. But the echoing sounds lied and Bailey didn't trust them. During a brief stop hunkered down behind orange plastic sheeting, Bailey glanced up and saw the white, spray-painted number of the cross shaft — #71. The number on the last cross shaft before the face had been #79. They had come a long way into the mine. If the lights at the face hadn't been so bright, they wouldn't be able to see them. As it was, there was only an orienting glow in the distance.

The girls and Bailey had said almost nothing to each other, though the girls had whispered back and forth in a language Bailey didn't understand. But she held fast to Jeni, and Jeni held fast to her. And there was some kind of bond there she couldn't have explained, but it was real and true and she experienced it, knew Jeni did, too.

Bailey hurried to the orange piece of plastic across a cross shaft, moved it aside for the girls to pass through, replaced it where it'd been and hurried to the edge of the coal pillar — and only escaped detection by seconds. A light saber of flashlight beam flashed in the dirt of the shaft she'd been about to lean into.

She froze. Backing away, she ran back to the orange plastic and darted back to the other side of it, and ran to the edge of that pillar. When she peeked down the shaft she and the girls had just run down she saw light there, too.

One of the gunmen was crouched at the intersection of the next shaft and this cross shaft, deciding which way to go. If he picked this way, she and the girls would be trapped. With a gunman coming down the shafts on either side of them. She waited, held her breath. There was a sudden rattle of gunfire. The gunman with the flashlight coming down the shaft behind them was spraying the shafts in every direction.

"You can't get away," he yelled. "I'll find you and I'll strangle the life out of you."

"Fiara," Lora whispered. The Beast.

Any second, bullets would rip into the plastic sheeting that lay between them and the gunman. Bailey shoved the girls down onto the floor, hunkered down as low as she could. Bullets stitched the plastic on the far side, ripping it apart, the line of bullet holes coming right at them.

Then there was a rumbling sound and the ground beneath them shook like an earthquake. Black coal dust filled the air and small pieces of coal fell down from the roof into their hair.

Someone began to scream back up toward the face of the mine and the rumble grew louder. What on earth …?

Chapter Forty-Nine

Dobbs raced down the Broadway shaft, his back and shoulders scraping painfully across the roof, unconsciously falling back into the coal miner's duckwalk he'd used when he worked in the mines. But that had been fifty years and maybe a hundred pounds ago. And even then, he always left the mines with painful cramps in his legs and his back so sore he couldn't stand up straight even when there was room above him to do it.

He'd never played football — had been big enough but his mother would never have considered such a thing! But the boys who did play said the coaches made them perform an exercise in practice called a "bear crawl" that was exactly how you had to move beneath a low coal mine ceiling.

When a roof bolt tore into his shoulder, he felt it, knew what it was and that it ought to hurt. But he was pumped so full of adrenaline from being milliseconds away from death, that he didn't feel a thing. He couldn't run fast enough to get to the first cross shaft and behind the coal pillar unless he stood up as straight as possible. So he dragged a bloody snail trail along the roof, heard his gasping breaths, cringed away from a bullet he knew any second would rip into his back, strained every muscle, and let out some kind of wimpy whine when he got to the cross shaft and dived into the space behind it. Seconds later, a hail of bullets ate up the coal beside where he'd been standing.

Scrambling as fast as he could, he crossed the distance to the yellow plastic curtain — he'd used a chunk of dressing-slathered lettuce leaf as a curtain on his coal mine model at Bailey's birthday party … a lifetime ago.

He ducked behind the curtain and crossed to the other edge of the coal pillar. Seeing no flashlight beam, he stepped out into the shaft and ran down it instead of continuing along the cross shaft, duck-walk-bear-crawl staggering as fast as it was humanly possible for him to move.

He made it to the next cross shaft, crossed it immediately to the plastic, slipped behind it and scrambled to the edge of that pillar.

Then he doubled back toward the face, down the Board-walk shaft, hurrying from one cross shaft to the next, hiding behind the plastic, knowing he had to keep moving.

Sweat poured down his flushed face. His breathing was so loud and labored he couldn't imagine it wouldn't give his position away. With his protruding belly, he flat out couldn't keep leaning over and lumbering along. The back of his head, his shoulders and back were soon gouged raw. Blood flowing down his forehead mingled with the sweat to sting his eyes so all he could do was squint.

He had heard T.J. start the continuous miner, could tell by the sound of it that T.J. had put it into gear. It was in the next cross shaft up, rumbling along behind the coal pillars and out into the shaft. He followed the sound, one cross shaft away, sometimes two, as the machine lumbered across the mine toward the wall. Its roar used to intimidate him, but now the familiarity of it was comforting somehow in a way he wasn't in any position to pick at. All his mind could process was that he couldn't keep running, would drop dead if he did, and other than behind the miner, there was nowhere else in a mine for a man his size to hide.

Eventually, the machine crossed the whole width of the mine. The boom on the continuous miner finally ran into the mine wall and the whirling blades began to cut into it, as easily as a drill into the side of a chocolate cake. In seconds, there was a hole and the blades kept digging. An operator using the continuous miner would have moved the boom arm up and down and side to side, across the face of the mine, digging shallowly, uniformly cutting away the face as the scoop operator came up on the side and men shoveled the coal into the scoop. Without an operator, the boom arm would simply dig a single hole deeper and deeper into the coal the whole length of the cutting arm until the miner itself ran into the wall. Dobbs stopped and listened, feeling in his teeth the rumble of the miner's engine and the cry of the coal as the rotary blades dug deeper and deeper. He had in mind to hunker down on the front side of the miner beside the boom, when he stepped out into the shaft.

Standing beside the miner was one of the gunmen, who must have crossed in front of the miner before it hit the wall. He didn't see Dobbs at first, shining his flashlight longways down the tunnel past the miner. He must have thought someone was operating the machine and had come to kill him. Dobbs tried to turn and hurry back into the cross shaft but he was exhausted and stumbled over his own feet.

"Stop right there, fatboy."

Dobbs stopped. It was the big blond kidnapper. He was taller that Dobbs and he had trouble bending over and leveling the gun at the same time.

"You're coming with me — out of this hole — and we'll see if your friend wants to save your butt *again* bad enough to show himself."

Dobbs got up on his hands and knees facing the man, who focused his flashlight into his eyes, blinding him.

Before Dobbs could make a move toward the man the world exploded around him.

The force of the water that suddenly spewed out the hole the miner had dug in the wall was so fierce it knocked the miner back down the shaft like a kid's toy, throwing chunks of rock as big as refrigerators along with it. Dobbs dived back into the cross shaft as boulders flew past him in the shaft.

The roar of the water was deafening, but not so loud that it drowned out the screams of the man who had moments before been holding a gun on Dobbs. The flashlight had been knocked out of his hands and it had rolled into the shaft toward the cross shaft where Dobbs crouched. He crawled out, picked it up and directed it into the shaft where roaring water was shooting out a hole in the wall with such force it was splashing off the side of the coal pillar fifty feet away. The flow of water down the shaft was so swift even behind the coal pillar it would have knocked Dobbs off his feet if he'd been standing, was a foot deep and rising in seconds.

The water pressure was ripping the hole in the wall bigger and bigger and Dobbs thought of the movie *Titanic*, the scene where the edge of the iceberg collides into the hull of the ship, slicing it open. The water behind the wall was doing the same thing, creating an ever-widening gash in the coal.

Dobbs turned the flashlight beam on the screaming man.

The man had been knocked into the miner, which was now lying on its side, the boom arm whirring in the empty shaft. A boulder the size of a washing machine rested on top of him, like a beach ball in his lap, and the force of the water against the boulder held him fast. He was screaming so loud his voice could be heard above the sound of the rushing water.

Dobbs directed the flashlight beam downward to the man's legs, sticking out beneath the rock. The force of the water had torn the flesh off both of them — skin, fat, muscle, *everything*. From his mid-thighs down was *bare bone* — knees and shins. His left leg ended in a jagged bone where his foot had been torn off. The bone of his right leg ended at the top of his running shoe, which tore away as Dobbs gaped in horror.

Too late, Dobbs realized that the man who'd dropped his flashlight had managed to hold onto his gun. In what felt like slow motion, Dobbs watched the man lift the gun, point it at him and pull the trigger, spraying bullets indiscriminately as Dobbs dived back behind the coal pillar. He felt a fire brand of pain on his upper arm, his thigh and calf, but he didn't know if he had been wounded by the gunfire, or by pieces of coal shrapnel that sprayed where the bullets tore into it. But he had been hit with *something*, more than once, and the pain seemed so all inclusive he wasn't sure exactly where or how many times.

The gunfire continued, bullets and coal shrapnel flying around as thick as moths around a backyard light. Off balance, Dobbs floundered in the water, couldn't duck down far because the water was already up to his elbows and rising rapidly. But the force of it shoved him away from the gunfire, and he didn't try to get control of his retreat, just floated along with the water, trying to keep his head above it. The gunfire stopped, though the screaming continued. Then there was a final burst of gunfire and the screaming stopped abruptly.

Now, Dobbs tried to regain his footing, but the force of the water kept him off balance and he was pushed farther and farther away from the face. He finally managed to get his feet under him, stagger and dive into a cross shaft that was rapidly filling with water, too, but the force of it was not so strong. Dobbs staggered down the cross shaft, leaning for support against the coal pillar. The water rose up his legs. The water was frigid, as cold as if it'd melted off a glacier. How much water was there in the old works the miner had cut into? Was it enough to flood this whole mine? Yeah, it probably was.

Staggering along the cross shaft, Dobbs crossed one shaft after another, the force of the water diminishing the farther he got from the gushing geyser of it on the far wall. But the water level continued to rise. Dobbs felt weak, dizzy. He knew if he ever went down, was swept off his feet again, he might not be able to get back up.

He shook his head, trying to orient himself. A wave of vertigo overtook him and he went down, face-planted into the water, the cold of it a slap that revived him as he washed out of the cross shaft into the next shaft — where his legs connected painfully with something — the *belt line*! He grabbed it and held on with all his strength, the river of water parting around him. If he could manage to keep a grip on the belt line, he could follow it out.

He wasn't the only person who'd figured that out, though. Between him and the face he could see the form of a man, also clinging to the conveyor belt. He hadn't yet seen Dobbs, but if he lost his grip on the piece of machinery, he'd wash right into him.

The man was not armed, had obviously lost his weapon in the water. Any second now he would notice Dobbs and … yeah, and what? He'd try to kill Dobbs, of course. With his bare hands. Dobbs wasn't armed, either. Well, except for the flathead screwdriver he'd stuck down in his belt.

T.J. HEARD the rumble from the mine wall and horror stole his breath. He knew instantly what had happened. The continuous miner had dug into old works full of water and now it was pouring into the mine. He heard the screaming then. It was a horrifying sound, unnerving in its intensity. But it was a man's voice, not Bailey or one of the girls. So unless it was Dobbs … No, it wasn't Dobbs. T.J. decided that and wouldn't let his mind countenance another interpretation.

Then the gunshot silenced the screams. That meant there were only two gunmen still pursuing them and once they were left with only handguns, T.J. could quickly dispatch them to the hell they deserved. But there was no time for that now. The men with guns hunting them was no longer the most life-threatening danger in the mine. The girls couldn't play a cat-and-mouse game, hiding in the labyrinth of tunnels until T.J. was able to pick off the remaining gunmen. Those tunnels were filling up with water. The mice were about to drown.

The only safe place in the mine right now was the open area at the face, with its ten-foot ceiling and elevator leading up to LHOM #1. The flood waters would only rise up fifty-two inches, the height of the mine shafts. The gunmen were the closest to the face of the mine. If they had the sense to retreat to it, they could escape. But the girls couldn't go back to the face. They could only run from the rising water deeper into the mine, into the disorienting darkness. On the other side of the blackness, the lights at the front would guide them out.

Could they make it through the darkness?

Would they panic and freeze, unable to move forward, so disoriented they were unable to determine which direction "forward" was?

Actually, even that was no longer an option. They couldn't hunker down somewhere, unmoving, paralyzed.

Soon, the force of the rising flood waters would knock them off their feet, carry them along.

In a dark hole. Washing down a drain pipe. Freezing water all around, getting deeper and deeper.

Could a group of teenage girls survive that?

Could Bailey?

It was a race against time. If they couldn't get out of the front side of the mine before the flood waters filled all the shafts to the roof, they all would drown.

T.J. reached up and flipped on his headlamp and the shadows leapt away from him. He saw the water crashing into the coal pillars, turning in his direction down the shaft. With his headlamp on, he was a sitting duck. If the gunmen were still searching for him and the girls, he had just lit up their target. But he had to chance it, had to give one more effort to finding Bailey and the girls. With him to guide them, they might have a chance.

He slogged his way down the cross shaft and shined his headlamp up and down the shaft at the intersection. Nothing. He slogged to the next cross shaft, turned his head—

Shots rang out. Hunks of coal from the coal pillar beside him sliced into his skin. The light from his helmet as it flew off arched over the ceiling and down the coal pillar to the floor. The light shone out along the floor as it was washed away by the foot-deep water.

Then there was only darkness.

Chapter Fifty

AT THE SOUND of the inexplicable rumble, the gunman stopped firing. The line of bullets ripping through the plastic ended only a few feet from where Bailey and the girls lay. Then the gunman was gone.

Accompanying the rumble was a sudden high-pitched screaming, a horrible sound, one voice that echoed and bounced and became two. Three.

Who was screaming and what would make someone scream like that?

T.J.? Dobbs?

No, it wasn't. They were both fine. *Fine!*

A gunshot. Maybe two or three. Echoes bounced everywhere. The screaming stopped.

But the rumbling sound continued. In fact, it was growing louder. The girls lay where they were, huddled together, afraid to move. The pile of bodies was trembling almost as one. Cold and fear. Bailey was wearing jeans, so she was warmer than—

Suddenly, her pants were wet.

Water? Where had—?

Her heart locked up, stopped beating altogether, then took off in a mad gallop. The rumble was *running water.*

The girls squeaked in surprise as water flowed under the yellow piece of plastic, water as cold as ice.

There was only one horrifying explanation. The continuous miner T.J. had cranked up had dug into the mine wall. It had hit old works full of water!!

The implications of that hit Bailey like a blow to the belly. They were in a hole under a mountain with a fifty-two-inch ceiling. There couldn't possibly be enough water to flood the whole mine all the way to the top!

But maybe there was.

Mindless panic threatened to take over her legs and propel her in a wild-eyed run away from the incoming water. Already, it was more than an inch deep, and getting deeper. She could hear the rumble continue to change tenor. The water was obviously kicking the hole in the mine wall bigger. More water. Rising faster.

Now there was no strategy to contemplate, nothing to figure out. No game of cat and mouse to play. She couldn't count on finding T.J. or Dobbs. She was on her own. They had to run, now. *Out of the mine.* They had to run through the darkness to the other end.

If they couldn't get out in time, they would drown.

There was some light where they were now. The bright lights at the face lit up the shafts, stretching out bright fingers into them. An ambient glow carried farther than that and with eyes adjusted to the darkness it was possible to see shapes and images in the gloom. In this faint light, the girls had been able to keep together and stay with Bailey. But where they were going there would be no light at all. She had to keep the girls together and they had to understand what was going on.

"I'm Bailey. Do all of you speak English?"

"Yes," said the red-haired girl. "I'm Lora."

"We do, yes," said the tiny girl with long, black hair. "My name is Sophia."

"Ana, I am Ana, and I speak not so good, but yes," said

the black girl. She looked so young and frightened. They all did.

"And you're Jeni," Bailey said to the girl whose hair was the color of Marilyn Monroe's. Whose face she had painted peering out from under the bed. Who had been hosed. And had heard *delay*.

"You have to listen to me and do exactly what I tell you or you will die here. Do you understand?"

The water was rising where they sat. It was several inches deep now, moving fast and absolutely frigid. When it got deeper, when they were wading in it, the cold would be numbing. How—?

"The rumble you hear is water. It's flooding the mine and if we don't get out of here fast, we will drown."

A girl with curly, honey-blonde hair squeaked out a cry of fear.

"Hush, Nikolina," Jeni said. "Listen to Bailey."

"This mine has two entrances. We came in the one on this end and there's another one on the other end. But it's a *long way* from here through the mine. You have to understand — as we go deeper it will get darker and darker ..." She paused because the thought literally stole her breath and she couldn't speak. "... until there is no light at all. *None!*"

Nikolina gasped and whimpered. "I'm afraid of the—"

Bailey blew by her. In truth, Bailey was afraid of the dark, too, but that was irrelevant right now.

"We have to stay together, hold onto each other. Anyone who gets separated from the rest of us is lost."

"We will hold hands," said the girl with short, multicolored hair. "Hold tight."

"Not good enough ..." Bailey didn't know her name. "You are ...?"

"Christina."

"Okay, Christina ... everybody — when our hands get wet, they'll be slick. We have to have something we can *grip*."

The girls looked at each other and back at Bailey, shaking their heads.

"Take off your underwear," Bailey told them.

There was the silence that shouted incomprehension.

"Your panties, take them off. Do it *now,* there's no time!"

The girls wearing skirts lifted them and slipped their underwear down their legs. Bailey and the other three girls wearing pants wiggled to get out of them, wet now and clingy, then hastily put them back on.

As she had guessed, most of the underwear was made of nylon. Nylon was strong. Bailey'd read somewhere that the nylon used for underwear had basically the same molecular structure as Kevlar, the material used for bulletproof vests. But it was the shape of the underwear that mattered. It provided *hand holds* you could grip.

Bailey reached out and put the fingers of her right hand through one leg hole in Jeni's panties and gripped tight, then held the underwear out for Jeni to wrap her fingers through the other hole.

"Make a chain."

Jeni grabbed her own panties with her right hand, turned and took hold of Lora's panties with the left. All the other girls did the same. When all seven of them were linked together, she told them, "We have to get as far away from the source of that water as we can. We're going all the way across the mine to the far wall. Then we'll feel our way along the wall to the front of the mine."

That idea had struck her in a bolt of insight. She'd been desperate to think of some way not to get lost and disoriented in the darkness, twisting and turning in the maze of shafts and cross shafts. As long as they stuck tight to the wall, they could find their way through the absolute darkness until they could see light from the other side. They had to move fast. When the water got high enough, it would wash them wherever it wanted them to go.

Nikolina had begun the hiccupping cry again, probably unaware she was making the sound, her eyes wide, looking around like a terrified rabbit.

With the roaring rumble of the water now echoing against the walls of the mine, there was no danger one of the gunmen would hear her and find them. Bailey suspected the gunmen didn't care anymore, anyway, had written them off, gone back to the face and left the girls to drown.

"Remember, you have to hold onto the chain! You can't let go — no matter what."

Nikolina was on the end. Bailey almost moved her up in the line, but didn't. She seemed to be the one most likely to panic and let go, breaking the chain. Bailey didn't want her to carry any other girls away with her if she did.

The water had risen now to about four inches deep, moving so fast it was already slippery.

"Come on now. Everybody ... *hold on*."

Bailey got to her feet and went to the edge of the coal pillar and looked around it. There was no one in that shaft, but the water pouring down it was flowing faster than Bailey'd thought it would. She hurried across the shaft to the next coal pillar, leading the train of girls behind her.

Slipping past the plastic curtain, she went to the edge of the coal pillar, prepared to peer down the next shaft. But a flashlight beam washed across the shaft and she froze.

"Go back," she whispered, and the girls hurried back, retraced their steps to the shaft they had just crossed. Bailey looked up and down it and saw nothing, so she led the girls down it toward the darkness. She couldn't keep going that way for long, had to find the wall before the light failed.

The water was six inches deep now, flowing so fast it was hard for the girls not to lose their footing. Finally, the absolute darkness ahead stopped Bailey. She turned around and could barely see the glimmer of light from the face shining down this shaft. She had to cross the mine here, not go deeper into it. She had to find the mine wall and follow it out.

Bailey'd had time to consider that whoever'd been carrying that flashlight might come up with the same escape plan, might be heading for the mine wall as they were. But she had no choice but to continue. They crossed another shaft, behind the pillar, then another shaft, and another. After two more shafts, the cross shaft they were traveling down came to a dead end. The mine wall!

Bailey peered back toward the face, saw nothing except the faintest glow of the lights there, and nothing in the other direction but absolute black.

She put her left hand on the wall, held onto the link to Jeni with her right, and headed out into oblivion, the light behind them diminishing with every step.

Chapter Fifty-One

It grew darker and darker. There was no ambient light at all anymore, only inky blackness ahead of them, and now, when they looked back, not even a pinprick of light from the open area at the face of the mine.

Feeling their way along in the darkness. One step. Another and another.

For a while, they outdistanced the water. It was flowing out a hole in the eastern wall near the face of the mine. They were running away from it toward the front of the mine along the western wall. But it caught up with them eventually and kept rising.

Bent over, Bailey trailed her left hand along the wall and with her right clutched tightly to the nylon daisy chain. Soon, water rose over her feet.

With the roar of the water diminished, Bailey could hear Nikolina now, sobbing, making squeaking sounds, almost screams. The other girls were silent as the water rose over their ankles.

Up their calves.

Toward their knees.

It was so *cold*! And the current was strong.

After a while, Nikolina stopped crying.

Suddenly, Ana, who was next to last in line, lost her footing and fell, dragging Christina and Nikolina down with her. The three of them washed forward with the water and bowled Lora, Sophia, Jeni and Bailey off their feet. The water was almost to Bailey's knees by then and the current was too swift for them to get their balance and stand back up.

In the total, absolute blackness, *which way was up?*

All the girls screamed, cried out when they tumbled down into the frigid water. Then they were washed down the shaft in a tangle, going under, coming back up, sputtering and choking. Fighting the water. Disoriented. Sobbing.

Drowning.

It's all Bailey can do to keep her head above water and hold onto the piece of nylon. Jeni is still holding onto it. Bailey can feel her.

Black and cold. Everywhere is water, moving water. She is carried along, trying to keep her hand out trailing along the wall to her left. It's all that orients her. But now she needs the hand to keep herself upright in the flooding water, too.

It feels like shooting the rapids in a mighty river. Except the river is in a drain pipe and there's no light.

If the water rises higher, Bailey knows she will die, in the dark, drown here.

She has drowned before, with Macy Cosgrove in the black water of a flood. She remembers how it felt — the agony of holding her breath, her lungs desperate to let the air out, knowing there's no air to breathe back in.

No, please, not that!

She bangs her head on the roof of the tunnel again and again as she's washed forward. Suddenly, there's no tension on the piece of nylon in her right hand, the one she's grasping with all her strength. Jeni has let go. Bailey can hear her behind, though, thrashing in the darkness. Coughing as she, too, begins to strangle on the water. Bailey is on her back, washing feet-first down the tunnel, using both hands now, her left on the wall of the shaft, her right feeling along the roof, which now seems to be right in her face.

Jeni's behind her, alive. She feels her bare feet kicking her in the back of the head as she, too, washes along. But the other girls …? The shaft is fifty feet wide. If they strayed away from the wall, were washed out into the center of the shaft, they could pass right by Bailey and she would never know.

Oh, please no! No, no, no! Not like this, drowning in the dark. No light, no air.

Where's Jeni?

She cries out in her head in anguish, Jeni! Jennnni!

And there's an answer, soft but clear. Here, I'm here.

BAILEY's right hand on the mine roof above her head was suddenly no longer touching stone. The roof was gone and she reached up into nothingness. A few seconds later, her feet hit something. Her left hand that'd been touching the wall clawed at empty air. What did she hit?

Then the rest of her was washed along with her feet into … rocks. A pile of rocks. She smashed into the rocks, rough edges, but *not* sharp. What …? There was no roof above.

Lora crashed into her, pinning her body against the rocks. Bailey wiggled out of the tangle of arms and legs and scrambled — up? Yes, she was moving out of the water, crawling, squirming, dragging her body up onto rocks, a pile of rocks.

Rock pile. *Roof fall!*

She reached up and could feel no roof above.

The other girls crashed into her and Lora and the rocks. Someone — Sophia or Ana — cried out in pain. Christina was choking and gagging, half-drowned. Jeni landed next and the world became all wet arms and legs, crying, coughing, gagging, scrambling to find *up*.

Up was out of the water. *Up!*

"Climb!" Bailey coughed out the word, sputtering as she

scrambled to pull herself up, her body tangled with the others. She was out of the water from the waist up, then she dragged her legs out, too, collapsed on top of dry rocks and lay coughing, gasping for air.

"Up here." Her words were ragged and hoarse, as if she'd been cheering too loud at a ball game.

Coughing, gagging, crying, the girls felt their way up onto the island in the absolute blackness.

"Lora!" Bailey cried. "Lora, are you—?"

"Here." Lora coughed, then sounded like she was vomiting up water.

"Sophia!"

"Sophia, where are you?" The voice was Jeni's.

There was no answer.

"Nickolina!" Bailey called, dread in her throat.

"Ana?" Lora's voice then.

"Where's Sophia?" Ana asked.

"Sophia!" several voices cried out.

There was no answer. Bailey couldn't countenance that the tiny, black-haired Sophia had washed past her in the dark.

"Nickolina!" Jeni cried. Bailey called her name, too, but the only answer was the rush of water past the rockfall.

Then Lora said, "Here. I think this is … Sophia's here in the water, but she's not moving."

"Get her up here out of the water," Bailey said.

The girls were tangled in a pile, trying to find Sophia's arms or legs or something to pull her out of the water. Something hard smacked Bailey in the cheek, an elbow maybe, and she cried out. The girls were feeling around for each other in the dark, trying to get their own bodies upright, out of the water, and then help the others do the same.

"Drag her up," Bailey said, and felt the others pushing and shoving an unmoving body, arms, legs and torso up and over themselves to the top of the pile where Bailey was. Bailey felt the girl's leg, her body, found her shoulder, her neck, put her hands on the girl's face

"Sophia!"

Nothing.

Bailey slapped Sophia's cheek.

"Sophia, answer me!"

She hit her again and the limp form moved and groaned, and Bailey could tell she was breathing. They were all here, then, all alive.

Except Nickolina.

Nikolina had been on the end. Had been so terrified. Had she panicked and lost her reason, unable to control her desperate need to get out of there, the enclosure and the flood. Had blind terror driven her …? Or had she just lost her grip? Clearly, for some reason, she had let go of the daisy chain and the current carried her … where?

"Nikolina!" Bailey cried. The others called her name, too. Over and over again.

There was no answer.

"Everybody, stop wiggling for a minute. Let me feel around up here, see how high, how far I can get out of the water."

Feeling her away along in the dark, Bailey moved to the left, her hand out, searching for the side of the shaft, the wall of the mine, but there was nothing but air, so the rock fall had taken out a piece of the wall with it, wasn't right next to it. But it could have been only a few feet away, just out of her reach. There was no way to know. She climbed up, scrabbled, slipped. The rocks weren't sharp. Broken coal created sharp edges so these rocks had fallen down into the shaft from above the coal seam … the rocks no coal company would remove just so a miner could stand upright when he worked.

She could feel Lora behind her, holding onto her foot, could hear the others gasping and coughing, the sounds of their life music to Bailey's ears.

She could think of only one fate worse than drowning here in the dark and that would be to drown here *alone.*

Bailey tried to imagine the shape and size of this pile of rocks. On the top of it, she was completely out of the water, several feet above it. The rocks were dry. Since the water in the shaft was at least three, maybe three-and-a-half feet deep now, the pile of rocks was a big one. She turned around carefully on the rocks and eased herself into a sitting position, lifting her head and shoulders up carefully, expecting at any time to bump her head on the roof. But she didn't. Sitting upright, she raised her hand and felt around above her head. Nothing. The hole made in the roof of the mine when the rocks crashed down into the shaft must be at least five, maybe even six feet above the top of the pile of rocks in the shaft.

"Jeni," Bailey said, reached out in the dark, feeling around, until she connected with a wet body, an arm, Jeni's arm, and they found each other's hands and squeezed.

"Everybody, wiggle around until you're completely out of the water. Scoot over, there's plenty of space. Hold hands, form a circle."

With much maneuvering, finally all the girls were out of the water, up on the rock pile, gasping and coughing, getting their breath. The water had numbed Bailey's fingers but the feeling was coming back into them now. She heard someone's teeth chattering. Once they got their breath, felt around until they got a sense of their surroundings and where each of them was in the dark, she needed to gather them all close together, hugging each other to conserve body heat. Hug Sophia, too, who still had not regained consciousness. Perhaps she had hit her head, perhaps she'd almost drowned and the lack of oxygen had … had something. Bailey didn't know.

Bailey had hold of Lora's hand on the right and Ana's hand on the left. Jeni and Christina were across from her, facing her, holding the girls' other hands. Sophia was lying on the rocks next to Bailey, out of the water but unmoving.

"What are we to do?" Lora was crying, shivering, her words stuttering out of her throat.

"We're going to stay right where we are," Bailey said. "The water will go down eventually. And they'll … somebody'll … T.J. and Dobbs and Brice will come looking for us. "

How she hoped the girls couldn't hear the desperation in those words.

"Everybody, listen. Try to concentrate on being quiet and just breathing, get your lungs cleared and let's listen. I don't know how far we are down the shaft, how much farther it is to the front of the mine. But once we calm down, get quiet and still, maybe we can hear … the fan at the front of the mine."

They *wouldn't* hear the fan! There was no reason in the world T.J. would have turned it on before he plunged into the mine. But getting them to pause, to listen, was a way to calm them, to get them to concentrate on something, soothe their nerves.

The girls coughed, sniffled and tried to still their breathing. Slowly, they grew quiet and there was only the sound of the water rushing past. Bailey breathed deep in the silence, let out a slow sigh.

And then the hair on the back of her neck began to stand up.

A cold terror gripped her for which there was no explanation. She was simply so suddenly afraid she could barely draw in another breath.

Something was wrong, very very wrong. Every fiber of her being was responding to some danger out there in the darkness, in the wet silence.

It came over her slowly, the suspicion. Then the suspicion became a certainty for which there was no rational explanation. There was no possible reason to believe what she now believed, but she knew with that part of her soul where all truth lies, that what she sensed was correct.

She and the girls were *not alone* on the pile of rocks.

Chapter Fifty-Two

BRICE STOOD beside the open door of his cruiser parked on the shoulder of the road that led to Last Hope Ollie Mine #2, standing still in the midst of the storm of activity around him, watching the torrent of water squirt out the holes in the mountainside. The flooding water had ripped away the fan from the shaft on the eastern wall of the mine and carried it a quarter mile down the road, had washed three mantrips and two scoops up against the single remaining piece of ten-foot fencing that once encircled the whole front of the mine. In a tangled heap of mangled chain that resembled the autopsy of a robot was Raymond Dobson's Jeep, which had obviously been used as a battering ram.

The surging water had gouged out a chunk of Bethel Church Road and washed it down the hill. Now, there was a rip down the center of the highway where the asphalt had been torn away. Seeking its own level, the water had gushed out across the road and cascaded into the little creek bed on the other side of it, then tore out everything on the creek bank in a pell-mell rush downstream. He had sent units down the road, warning/evacuating anybody who lived close to the creek, which had never flooded before, at least not in Brice's lifetime.

The world was decorated in what Brice had come to think of as "disaster festive," aglow with red and blue lights — the gumball machines on the state police units, the red bar of lights on sheriff's department cruisers and the revolving red ambulance lights painted the mountainside and the fifty or so rescue workers in alternating hues of color.

The state police had set up huge lights, the kind used for nighttime road construction, two on each side of the front of the mine. But beyond that, there was nothing for the "rescue" workers to do, because right now there was nobody to rescue.

All around him was organized pandemonium; the arriving rescue squad units usually trailed a fire truck from their station, and Brice had summoned a herd of ambulances. How many … *injured* people would there be? He didn't know. He'd started with half a dozen ambulances and could call out more if he needed them.

How long the flood waters would rampage out of the mine and down the creek was impossible to guess. What exactly had happened here was hard to know, too, but Brice had pieced together his best-guess scenario from what he had found in front of the Last Hope Ollie Mine #1 on the other side of the mountain.

What he had figured out took his breath away.

He had stood here looking at the floodwaters for the past ten minutes, desperately trying to concoct some scenario that would explain it *other than* the only reasonable explanation — the one that he believed to be true, but that he could not force his mind to accept.

He had listened to T.J.'s message before he and the other units even got to Rock Creek Cavern on Ohio Route 7 and the words had made him nauseous. What if he *had* been wrong? Made a terrible mistake? He'd confirmed his mistake as soon as they arrived at the cavern. It was deserted. He had misinterpreted the road sign Bailey had seen in a flashed image. He had been in such a hurry, so … okay, so *desperate t*o find her, that he had leaped on the first explanation and run with it.

As he stood watching water gush out the mine shafts, sickening certainty settled in his gut, a lead ball of horror that so weighed his whole body down it was hard to stand upright: he had likely gotten the people he cared most about in the world killed.

He looked away, out into the red-and-blue-spangled darkness, trying to grab hold of his emotions.

They had found the two vehicles inside the open gate of LHOM #1. A van with one missing wheel, a car with the hood up and one of the battery cables disconnected. And a dead body, a man shot in the face. The lights were on in the front of the mine. The elevator was down at the face of LHOM #2 and the lights were on there. The face was a bubbling, rolling pool of water fifty inches deep, within two inches of the ceilings of the mine shafts that tunneled away from the face, through the mountain to the front of the mine.

T.J. and Dobbs had found the kidnappers, disabled their vehicles and gone in after the girls and Bailey.

And then …? Somehow, a continuous miner ripped into old works on the east wall of the mine. The current was strongest in the eastern shafts when he'd arrived. But it quickly spread out. Why a miner would have been running at all, why it would have been cutting into the wall, why …?

Though he didn't understand the why, he couldn't deny the what. His friends — *Bailey!* — the kidnapped girls and the kidnappers, too, were somewhere inside that mine. And if they were, they would drown.

"Sheriff McGreggor," Fletch called out.

Brice turned to see Deputy Fletcher and a state police trooper rushing through the flowing water, chasing something that had floated out of the mine shaft. The men grabbed it —

the body of a girl — before it floated all the way across the pond that had formed in front of the mine shafts, and dragged it through the three-foot water to higher ground where the other police officers and the rescue squad and the ambulance had parked.

It was clear the girl was dead. Brice got there as they were turning her over, revealing the wounds where bullets had torn into her back. Two had gone through and exited the other side. Two EMTs, emergency medical technicians, and one paramedic were all over her, of course, but moments later one looked up at him and shook his head.

"She's gone."

Chapter Fifty-Three

BAILEY DID NOT WILL her mouth to open, did not consciously form the words or provide the will to speak them. Some other autonomic part of her had taken over and was making the conscious decisions she was incapable of making.

"Who's ... who's there?" Her voice was the quavering voice of a terrified child.

No one replied.

The darkness responded, though, with a soft, ugly chuckle.

The quiet cavern exploded into hysterical screaming. All the girls shrieked in terror and the more they screamed, the louder the Beast laughed. What had begun as a sinister chuckle became a rumbling, almost maniacal roar.

The constant stream of laughter made it possible to figure out his location. He was somewhere behind where Jeni had sat in the circle, before all the girls had fallen back toward Bailey, retreating from the horror.

"You thought you got away from me, didn't you," said the horrifying, gravelly voice out of the darkness. Yes, he was facing her. Bailey'd never been any good at judging distance, but he was at least fifteen, maybe twenty-five feet away.

Not still, though. Because he continued to chuckle, she

could tell that he was creeping slowly forward — on all fours. The voice wasn't coming from a man standing up. There was nowhere for Bailey and the girls to retreat from him except back into the water. If they got back into the water they would drown.

If they couldn't run ...

From some deep reservoir — of fear or anger, maybe that was the place where courage lived — Bailey began to feel calm settle over her.

"You. Will. Die!" The voice rumbled at them like thunder, even deeper and more ragged than Bailey remembered. "You are sheep ... and the wolf is coming to eat you."

Instant terror shocked the wailing, screaming girls into silence.

And into that silence Bailey dropped words.

These sheep fight back!

She spoke the words *inside her head* without making a sound.

She, Jeni, Christina, Lora and Ana were uninjured. Five of them. There was only one of him.

He had two hands. They had ten.

They weren't unarmed.

Rocks! She spoke the word inside her mind.

If they all charged him at once, five of them, hammering his head with rocks from all sides at the same time ...

If they could catch him off guard ...

Surprise!

She knew Jeni could hear her. Could the others? Had they *all* been hiding in the closet? Bailey had made only the barest connection to the shadowy figures when she'd painted them. But she'd gotten flashes, multiple images from their minds in the van.

How many of them had been in the closet? Which ones?

"I will strangle each of you ... like I did Poli." He was

closer now. "I choked the life out of her, squeezed ... and squeeeeezed."

He was enjoying this. Eagerness slathered the evil in his vicious voice.

Together! She wanted to *shout* the word in her head but she didn't know how to do that. Or maybe she *was* shouting. All the girls were near her, only a few feet away — not driving down some road, separated by miles. Would that matter?

"Jeni watched me, saw me kill Poli. Tell them about it, Jeni." When he was speaking, she could get a bead on his location. He seemed no more than fifteen feet away.

My signal.

She had to give the girls a target so they could locate him in the dark.

That was the only card she had to play. She had no idea if it would work now, soaking wet. Picking up the biggest rock she could find with her right hand, she reached into the back pocket of her jeans with her left, pulled out what she'd stuffed in there, and held it out in front of her.

"Come and get me," she said aloud, striving for bravado but missing by a mile. Her words sounded every bit as terrified as she felt.

"Oh, I *will*."

He was right in front of her, in grabbing range. She thumbed the striker. Prayed.

Bright light filled the tunnel from the flickering flame of the Bic lighter she'd grabbed off the belt line and only now had a chance to use.

The light imprinted an image on her cornea and into her brain that would be there for the rest of her life.

The Beast was on his hands and knees, only a few feet away, a leopard crouched to pounce. The girls — soaked, scratched, dirty and bleeding — had surrounded him. Jeni and Ana were on the left, Lora and Christina on the right. They all had rocks. Ana and Christina had rocks in both hands. Lora's was a hunk of coal as jagged as an ax blade. Jeni held a single rock, but it was the size of a toaster and she had it raised high above her head.

"Now!" Bailey screamed, her voice a shrill shriek.

The Beast pounced at her.

She slammed the rock in her hand down into his face. He was moving, though, diving at her and she could only land a glancing blow on his forehead as he batted it away, grabbing her other arm and twisting it viciously. She screamed in pain and dropped the lighter before he flung her away into the darkness.

In that millisecond before absolute black erased the world, Bailey saw the movement all around, saw blows from half a dozen rocks raining down on his head.

He bellowed in pain and rage, grunted, too — the way you cried out when a solid blow has landed. Bailey splashed into the water, the current threatening to rip her away from the rock pile. She scrambled, clawed at the rocks, her left wrist in agony. Held on, crawled up, dragged herself out of the flood.

All the girls were crying out — words in a language Bailey didn't know, but mostly just sound, inarticulate, guttural sound, a communal growl. One of the girls began to scream. Lora, maybe. There were scuffling sounds and her screams were cut off with a grunt. He was strangling her.

Bailey dived back up onto the rock pile, felt his arm or maybe his leg and hammered it with a rock as hard as she could.

The man was cursing, roaring filth into the air, but there was great pain in his cries, too. Now, Bailey could tell where his mouth was, where his head was in the darkness. She struck in the direction with her rock, connected solidly with something. Heard a sound like … like breaking teeth.

Now there was so much sound it was hard to tell anything. The other girls were crying out, too, screaming and grunting as they struck him. Christina suddenly shrieked, a wail of agony — he had gotten to her, hurt her badly somehow. Bailey felt something hard slide past her ear. His fist had missed but his elbow caught her in the upper arm. His elbow … meant his upper arm was here, his back must be …

Clawing her way up, grabbing his clothes, she hauled herself onto his back, hammering at him with the rock. He lurched upward, like a bucking bronco, reached to grab her, got her shirt but her arm was slick and he couldn't hold on. She grabbed a handful of his hair — the pain in her wrist a distant agony she acknowledged but couldn't really feel — yanked his head backward and brought the rock in her right hand down with all the force she could muster on his face. He screamed and lurched upward and flung Bailey off his back. She flew into the darkness but landed on the rock pile behind him instead of the water.

He was yelling now, grunting, just sound, lurching around all over the top of the rockfall, staggering, a wounded bear, striking out. Another girl screamed. Scrambling in the dark, Bailey's hand found his bare foot and she smashed a rock down on his heel. He kicked out at her, but the other girls were hitting him as well and he was fighting them, too, punching them, grabbing them. She clawed her way up his leg, rose up and brought a rock down as hard as she could on what she hoped was his back. But she'd caught him on the hip instead and he kicked out at her again, caught her in the thigh, knocking her sideways. She had a sense of where he was now, leapt on his back and collided with someone already there. A rock came down hard on her upper arm and she cried out, bringing her own rock down on whatever might be below it. As she struck the blow, her fingers felt his ear, and she hammered at it again and again. He was wiggling, squirming, moving and all she and the others could do was rain down blows in the dark, striking each other sometimes, but most of the blows fell on him.

He was hurt now, badly. She felt his fist connect with her shoulder, but there was no force in the blow. Then she felt him staggering to his feet, throwing the girls off. Someone hit the water. Bailey found his leg and sunk her teeth into his calf, tasting blood, biting as hard as she could. A blow caught her and hammered her aside, knocking her to the ground on her back in front of him. He was almost upright now, and Bailey drew her knees up to her chest and struck out with both feet with all the strength in her body — all the horror and pain and rage in a single blow.

He'd been straddling her and she got him in the family jewels.

He didn't even cry out, just grunted and fell forward, but she rolled to the side before he could collapse on her. Then she was on top of him, they all were, grunting and crying and screaming. Hitting him — and each other — but he was below them all now, they could feel him there and the blows landed on him. They hammered him again and again. She got her hands into his hair as someone landed a painful blow on her fingers and she screamed, but still brought her own rock down on his head. Hit him again and again.

He was all the way down now, not moving anymore. Still, she kept hitting him and hitting him — they all did. Finally, her arm was too tired to lift the rock and she fell over on her side, panting, gasping for air. She heard whimpers, groans, cries all around her, finally found the air to call out.

"Jeni!"

There was a groan on the other side of the form of the man.

"Is that you — Jeni?"

I'm here.

It was Jeni, but she didn't say the words out loud.

Then she did speak, called out, "Lora!"

No response.

"Lora!"

Still nothing.

"Ana!"

"I am ..." Ana didn't finish, just groaned and whimpered, "Where's Christina?"

"Christina is here," Jeni gasped. "He knocked her into the water but she grabbed my leg, held on."

Bailey could hear the moaning near Jeni. Christina was injured. The groan ended in a word ... "Lora?" Christina's voice was pain-thin. "Lora, where are you? Where's Lora?"

There was still no response.

"Is he dead?" Jeni gasped.

Bailey didn't know if he was dead, but he was obviously unconscious.

"We need to make sure."

She felt around in the darkness, felt his head, his face where the nose was crushed, his mouth was open, teeth were shattered.

And Bailey felt something like animal triumph, then. He had done that to Poli. Had punched her and kicked her, knocked out her teeth and then strangled her.

Bailey felt around for a rock, picked it up, and began to pound his head with it. Hammered it into his face until she was slick with blood and had no more strength.

"Is he dead?" Jeni pleaded again.

"I think so."

A hand came out of the darkness — Jeni's hand, feeling for Bailey, for the man.

"Move!" she told Bailey and Bailey rolled away. She heard Jeni hitting the man as she had done. Again and again.

When Bailey caught her breath, she told Jeni, "We have to push him into the water. Over here, from this side."

Feeling for each other in the darkness, Bailey knelt beside Jeni.

"Push!" The two girls shoved with all their might, but were

only able to move the massive body a few inches, and Jeni cried out in pain from the effort.

"Maybe ribs broken," she said.

Bailey was sure the little finger and ring finger on her right hand were either broken or dislocated. Her left wrist had been twisted so badly that surely it was broken, too. She felt the pain of it now, the agony no longer masked by the adrenaline of the fight. And there were cuts and bruises on her upper arm, her legs, her back — all over — where she'd been pummeled by the other girls' rocks.

"Not all of him," Bailey gasped. "Just his head. I want his *head in the water*!"

For Poli. When he'd strangled Poli, he'd strangled Bailey, too.

Until his head was in the water, under the water, for a long time … only then would Bailey believe he was dead, that he would not suddenly regain consciousness and kill them all.

"Use your feet."

They scooted backward on the rocks on their butts and used their feet and legs to shove the body down toward the water. It wasn't far and he was already lying with his head downward. But Bailey was almost utterly spent, knew she did not have the strength for more than one more shove. The two of them heaved with all their might. The body scooted downward a few more inches.

Bailey got to her knees, felt around, felt down his back, his neck … and felt water. His face was in the water, she felt around to make sure. His whole head wasn't under, but his face was. All of it.

He wasn't going to come back to life. He was dead.

She collapsed backward, on her side, suddenly loath to touch the body, didn't want to feel him anywhere near her.

Who was left?

A voice out of the darkness gasped, "I found … Lora is

here." The voice was Ana's. "She's breathing but she's not moving."

Bailey, Jeni and Ana appeared to be the least injured. Christina was hurt bad. Lora was unconscious.

Sophia. Where was Sophia?

Bailey and the others felt around, called her name.

She was gone.

Sometime during the battle, her limp body had been shoved off the rocks into the water and washed away.

No one actually said it, but it was an unspoken agreement that they all wanted to get as far as possible from the body of the Beast, which had ended up — if Bailey's mental picture of the rockfall was accurate — on the far end of the island very near the spot where the monster had been crouching in the dark.

Together, Bailey, Jeni and Ana helped Christina move to the end of the island where they'd washed up on shore. Though she was awake and aware, Christina was in great pain. Her left arm — Bailey could *feel the jagged bone!* Compound fracture.

Then the three of them dragged Lora, who was now semi-conscious, to the same spot.

"We need to huddle together close," Bailey said. And they all squirmed and wiggled, crying out when someone bumped an injury in the dark. "Don't lie down, sit up. The rocks are colder than the air."

They pulled the unconscious Lora into the pile of bodies and all shivered together. Finally, silence returned to the shaft, broken only by the sound of running water and the whimpers and groans of the injured.

"What is to happen to us?" Jeni asked.

Bailey was too tired and in too much pain to sugar-coat the truth.

"The water is still rising. I don't think it's all the way up to the roof of the shaft yet, but if it's not, it soon will be."

"Will it cover us, will we drown—?" Ana's voice sounded so small and frightened.

"It can only rise up to the top of the shaft — we're higher than fifty-two inches. But if it fills the shaft, it will cut off the air supply. Then the air in this hollow space — that's all the air we'll have to breathe. I don't know how far up it goes. Higher than I can reach my hand."

"Will someone look for us, try to find us, to help us?" Christina asked. Her teeth were chattering so hard she could barely form words. She would go into shock soon unless … "The man who shouted out of the darkness? And the other one?"

Bailey didn't say, "if they didn't drown" because she couldn't think a thought that scary and painful.

"Yes."

"So we just … wait for help?" Jeni asked.

Bailey felt around for Jeni's hand and squeezed it. "They'll come for us."

Chapter Fifty-Four

BRICE SANK to his knees beside the body of the dead girl, in part because they seemed suddenly unstable. He reached out his own hand to feel for the carotid artery in her neck. There was no pulse, and her body was cold, lifeless. She was a pretty girl, with long brown hair stretching in a wet braid down her back. Her clothing was torn, but the dress was some kind of filmy fabric that clung to all the right places, expensive, the kind of garment you'd expect on someone who was out for a night on the town at the casino. Brice got slowly to his feet and turned his back and the men loaded the body onto a stretcher, covered it with a sheet and moved it toward the waiting ambulance.

How many girls were there? He didn't even know.

"Sheriff!"

Brice turned to see another body float out of the mine; this one came from the shaft that ran along the east wall of the mine, where the current was the strongest.

This body was alive.

T.J. Hamilton shot out of the shaft and down into the mini-lake in front of the mine like a kid on a waterslide into a swimming pool. He was struggling to his feet with the help of two deputies, coughing out water, choking, gasping for breath when Brice slogged out into the water to him.

"T.J." It was all he could say.

T.J. was looking around frantically and spotted the body of the girl lying on the stretcher by the ambulance.

His look of fear and pain matched Brice's.

"Is she …?"

He couldn't finish the sentence.

"One of the teenagers. How many girls were there? What happened?" Then, because he couldn't help himself, Brice added, "Where's Bailey?"

He could hear the anguish in the question but he couldn't mask it.

T.J. turned back toward the mine, coughing.

"In there."

EMTs approached and he waved them away, while he explained to Brice in clipped sentences what had happened.

Brice didn't look at him. Partly because he couldn't take his eyes off the water flowing out of the mine shafts and partly because he couldn't look at anybody right now, didn't dare make eye contact, not until he got better control of himself.

"… were four kidnappers," T.J. said. "I shot one before he could shoot Dobbs …" T.J.'s voice trailed off. He wasn't looking at Brice, either, his eyes devouring the water spewing out of the shafts. "And I killed another one. In the dark, broke his neck."

Brice noticed then that T.J. was bleeding. The water had washed the blood away, but it was appearing again now, from multiple small wounds all over him, his face and arms, his back, and from a larger wound, a deep gouge across his upper arm.

"You need to sit down, let the EMTs—"

"I'm fine." The point was non-negotiable. "So only that one body. The two men …?"

Brice shook his head. Anything that was in that mine could have gotten hung up on any number of things and not washed out. Water pressure could hold … whatever … against a coal pillar in a cross shaft.

"They're not full yet," T.J.'s eyes swung back and forth across the streams of water pouring from the shafts. "There's still air left in them."

Brice could hear the hope, the desperate hope in his voice.

"I went looking for the girls, for Dobbs, got my head-lamp knocked out. Took the flashlight from the man I killed, but it went out soon's it got wet. Then I couldn't see any better than they could. By then the water was so high, you couldn't cross the current. There was nothing to do but float out. But I thought … *hoped* … when I got out here, they'd be …"

They both saw the body shoot out of the shaft at the same time. Both hoped. Both instantly realized it was one of the kidnappers. The two of them slogged over to the body as the rescue squad members dragged it out of the pond.

The body had a flathead screwdriver buried up to the hilt in its back.

"Dobbs?" T.J. gasped in wonder. He looked at Brice, his face the definition of astonishment. "Had to be. Who else …?"

The deputies dragged the body up onto the high ground and as Brice was turning around, T.J. shouted, "*Dobbs!*" and took off running toward Main Street, where the conveyor belt had been torn by the current but still dangled out the hole.

Through that hole, the water had just spit out a man. T.J. reached him two steps ahead of Brice and was already calling over his shoulder for the EMTs. Dobbs was limp, blood poured from a gunshot wound in his right shoulder.

"He has a pulse," T.J. cried and began to pull him out of the water. The rescue squad swarmed over him, carried him quickly to the shore, where the paramedic examined him.

Brice could see that he wasn't breathing. T.J. must have imagined the pulse.

While others rushed to the ambulance for the gurney, the paramedic and one EMT began CPR and mouth-to-mouth, working quickly and efficiently. T.J. and Brice backed away to let them do their jobs. It took four men to lift Dobbs's limp body onto the gurney, and they continued to work on him as they shoved the stretcher across the bumpy ground to the open back door of the ambulance.

"Charge the paddles," the senior paramedic called out before they'd even reached the vehicle. One of the EMTs not working on Dobbs spotted T.J.'s wounds and started to treat them but T.J. shoved him roughly away, all his attention focused on his friend, on the big chest that only moved up and down when air was forced into it.

T.J. started to step up into the ambulance after they loaded the gurney but the paramedic stopped him.

"We got this," he said. "You'll just get in the way."

Brice watched T.J. bristle, knew he could chew the man up and spit out pieces no bigger than raisins.

T.J. said nothing, stepped back, watched the medics slam the ambulance doors shut behind Dobbs and roar up the hillside, bouncing over rocks and chunks of dislodged asphalt to the piece of highway above the mine that was still intact, lights flashing, siren wailing. Brice watched the lights until they disappeared around the first bend, listened to the shrieking siren until it, too, fell silent in the distance.

"I got no idea what that miner hit." The two men had returned to the vantage point of Brice's cruiser and stood scanning the water flowing from the mine.

"Something big. More than a mine shaft full of seepage water. I'm thinking an underground aquifer. And if it is, then—"

"There could be ..." T.J. stopped, then continued, his

voice firmed up. "… millions of gallons of water in it. And through that one hole, it could take—"

"Days for the mine to empty."

Both of them were watching the water levels in the shafts. Brice had noticed, was sure T.J. had, too, that the shafts were filled completely to the top. Neither said a word, just stood there, helpless.

Chapter Fifty-Five

"Who are you?" The words came from only a few feet away in the darkness. It was a whisper, the way you whisper when you're scared even if there's nobody to hear you. "Why you help, not want ... our bodies like the others?"

It was Jeni, and at first Bailey thought she was talking about the johns who had ... had *raped* these girls over and over, night after night.

Then she realized the girl was talking about "American monsters."

Bailey had to concentrate to speak through her chattering teeth. She spoke aloud. Wanted to hear the sound of her own voice. "They lied to you! Everything they said to you was a lie. They lied about ... whatever they told you to get you to leave your homes with them—"

"To find good jobs, take care of children, but then ..." someone said, maybe Ana.

"That was a lie. So was what they told you about Americans using illegal immigrants for organ transplants — that's crazy."

"Is ... is not true?"

There was such wonder in her voice Bailey had to remind herself she was talking to a child, a naive child.

"Not one word! Americans don't ... would *never* ... they just said that so you'd be scared to run away."

Bailey moved when she spoke and Lora moaned. She must have touched somewhere the girl was injured. But who knew where any of them were injured? She wouldn't allow her mind to dwell on her own pain, wouldn't try to move the fingers. She had broken ribs, too, probably. Who knew how badly or where the others had been hurt. Best not to think about it. In the darkness, everything was exaggerated. All she could think to do was huddle them all together as best she could. They had set Lora up, then wrapped their arms around her and each other.

"They said you could see us from the sky ... and hear what is whispered in secret ..."

"That part might be true — but it's not magic. It's satellites. And some gizmo microphone. Americans aren't monsters."

Jeni said nothing then.

Ana spoke. "You are American, yes?"

"Yes."

"Then is true, Americans *aren't* monsters."

"Why is it you help us? And why did I hear you when you did not speak?" Jeni asked. "I did hear you. We all did, yes?"

"You told us to fight, to use rocks," Christina gasped, her voice pain-ravaged. "How is that ... possible?"

What could Bailey say?

"It's a long story. I will tell you someday, I promise. But now ... it's too complicated for now."

They fell silent and Bailey felt the cold, the pain, the darkness ... and the *fear* more intensely in the silence. She should keep them talking.

"How did you all get ... here?" she asked.

In broken pieces, from different girls, she pieced together

the story of small villages in Bulgaria, very poor, very backward. Technology did not yet rule there. More than anything, parents wanted better lives for their children. And when the big car had driven into town ...

"The priests, the elders, said not to listen," Ana said. "But my parents, my family ... wanted so much ..."

Quiet settled back around them except for the water rushing by and the sound of Lora, squeaking out little cries of pain now and then. Or maybe it was Christina.

Bailey closed her eyes. It was no darker with her eyes closed than with them open. And somehow she felt like the darkness was inside her if her eyes were closed, so she opened them again. She was shivering violently, they all were. Now she tried to still herself to calm her breathing and slow her heart.

Then she looked out into the blackness and conjured up the image of Bethany's face — which wasn't really her face, of course, because the image was of a baby and Bethany was three. Bailey wanted so desperately to know what she looked like now, wanted to live every bit as badly now as she had wanted to die a few months ago.

"Are you ... afraid?" Jeni clamped her teeth almost closed to still the chattering.

"Yeah, I'm afraid."

More silence. Then Bailey heard her own thoughts as she spoke them aloud, and believed what she was telling the girl.

"I was terrified in the water, and when I heard him laugh ..."

She shuddered and the movement seemed to confuse her trembling body and gradually she grew still. "I don't know how I know this ... but I do. I know that ... I don't believe we were meant to die here. We, all of us, we're *survivors.*"

"On the ship to America, I always want to know the day, what day it was," Jeni said. "And then one morning, I opened my eyes and realized I did not know. And I was, I panic. It was most awful fear to rise up in my chest, I could not breathe. Where we were, deep in a ship, was no windows, was no way to tell time, but for when they come to feed us. I was so careful to count, but that day somehow, I was confused, couldn't remember the number."

She paused and took a breath. The effort to speak had stilled her shivering, too. The other girls still shook, but not Jeni.

"Is hard to explain in English, the fear was bigger than being locked up in a metal box on a ship in ... some ocean somewhere. On my way to ... I not know then where."

She paused, said something in a language Bailey didn't know. Then started over.

"If I do not know the day, some part of me is no longer there. When I knew, as long as I knew, I could hold that one thing ..."

"You could control that one thing."

"Yes! I think to myself, I count the days and think — where could you go in five days? Or nine days? Poli and Rayna, they didn't care where they were. How did they expect to get back home if they couldn't retrace their steps?"

She stopped then and the sound of the rushing water pounded in the silence. When she spoke again, her voice was quiet.

"But that was the thing, I knew. They are huddle in a corner of the room. They *didn't* expect to get back home." She paused. "But *I* did!"

They both were silent then. Their breathing was measured, all in the same rhythm. Inhale. Exhale. Inhale. Exhale. In such profound dark there was no passage of time except that measured by their breathing. Like Jeni holding onto what day it was, Bailey was aware of every individual breath. Otherwise, time would have come completely unhooked from the world and she would have lived in the forever now of that one, black empty moment.

Gradually, and she was probably imagining it, Bailey began to sense a stuffiness in the air. Bailey moved, carefully and painfully, a few feet and slipped her hand down toward the water below her. She grabbed hold of herself in time not to gasp. The water had risen as high as it could, now filled the mine shafts from the floor to the ceiling.

They were in a bubble now that only had a finite amount of air. How much? She had no idea. Dobbs had told her once about the formula all miners knew — how to figure out if they could survive if they were trapped. All miners knew the simple cave-in principle: one cubic yard of air will last one miner one hour. Even if she could have done that kind of math in her head, she didn't know how tall the hole was above their heads. She should probably stand now, reach up, see if she could touch …

No. There was no sense in that. She didn't want to know that the roof hung just a few feet above their heads. If they were going to suffocate … well, there were a whole lot worse ways to die. As she understood it, when you suffocated, you just got sleepy from lack of oxygen, closed your eyes, and never woke up.

She would rather not know that was happening to her. And she definitely didn't want the other girls to figure it out. She crawled carefully back up the rock pile to the others and settled back in beside them. To wait.

But as she huddled in the darkness, she couldn't deny the reality — the air really was getting stuffy.

Chapter Fifty-Six

T.J. stood next to Brice, staring at the water gushing out of the mine shafts. Nothing else come out of the mine after they hauled Dobbs away in the ambulance. T.J. shoved his mind away from thinkin' 'bout Dobbs. Wasn't no sense in it. It was what it was. He couldn't imagine a world without Dobbs in it. So he didn't. Dobbs was gonna be fine and T.J.'d b'lieve that until he found out different. End of discussion.

No more bodies floated out — alive or dead. Not the kidnappers. Not the girls. They were all still in there. In shafts that'd been completely full of water for — he looked at his watch but it had stopped. El Cheapo brand watch, can't get it wet. Whatever happened to Timex watches that took a lickin' and kept on … he realized his mind was ping-ponging off one inane subject after another, an escape mechanism. And wasn't no sense in grabbin' hold of it now, forcin' his mind to face the reality that it was comin' up on an hour and a half since the shafts had flooded all the way to the top.

There was nothing to say so they said nothing, just stood watching, waiting.

Then more bodies came — two of them almost at the same time from opposite sides of the mine. One of the bodies was a horror, both legs were only bones. His feet were gone and so was the top of his head where he'd put a gun in his mouth and pulled the trigger.

There was no explanation necessary. It was obvious what had happened.

The other body was a tiny girl, could have passed for ten years old, dressed in jeans, a t-shirt and sneakers. She was dead, long dead. Her body was cold.

Then ... nothing.

T.J. and Brice stood together after the bodies were taken away, just watchin' the water.

"When I's a little boy and my mama was paintin' them pictures, I was tore up 'bout it all the time, didn't ask nothin' more from life than for my mama not to have to paint them things. Some days, I wanted to run out and warn everybody I seen in one of her pictures and other days I didn't b'lieve it'd do any good if I did. But it never did occur to me back then that interferin' would *cause* them awful things to happen."

He turned to face Brice. "I don't know what to think about that. Do you?"

T.J. had watched the sheriff climb into a shell of professional detachment, saw him close up all the windows to who he really was, slam the door shut, and then lean with his back against it. There was no light in his eyes now, nothing there but pain and longing and T.J. felt those things, too. And guilt. Oh, yes indeedy, guilt.

"I don't know what I think about the people Bailey tried to save, but I do know if she'd stayed out of it, she wouldn't be in there now." Brice turned to T.J. "And *I* urged her to do it."

"I's the one cranked up that continuous miner."

"I ... went to the wrong place." Brice's voice was as emotionless as a recorded announcement at baggage claim in an airport.

"Maybe Dobbs was right when we was little kids — that you can't change the future. Maybe all you do when you try is make matters worse on everybody, put other folks' lives in danger."

They said nothing more then, just stood together watching the water shoot out of the mine shafts. The water pressure was as intense as it had been when that continuous miner poked a hole in the mine wall. It'd never occurred to T.J. that the thing would hit a wall, dig a hole in it, hit … He was just trying to create noise, distraction, put the thing in gear so the noise'd move and they'd think somebody was operatin' it, maybe get lucky and one of the kidnappers'd walk into the blades.

But *old works*?

T.J. glanced at the big watch on the sheriff's arm. Yeah, it'd been an hour and a half now, just like he'd guessed. He felt despair well up in his chest and it took all his strength to beat it back down. No, he wouldn't go there.

BAILEY HAD INTENDED to stay upright so the cold rocks wouldn't suck away their body heat. Though they were still huddled together as close as possible for warmth, they were stretched out on the rocks now, and she didn't know how they'd gotten there.

Ana and Bailey were on one side of the heap, Jeni and Christina on the other, with a semi-conscious Lora between/beneath them. They were a pile of clinging arms and legs and shivering bodies. Still desperately cold, their combined body heat had made it possible to stave off hypothermia, at least for a while.

It didn't matter. They wouldn't live long enough to die from it.

Their breathing was becoming more and more raspy. Bailey didn't want to gasp, but when she drew in a normal breath, it didn't seem like there was enough air in the air. She couldn't help sucking in another one, seeking the air she hadn't found in the one before.

The absolute darkness had been so terrifying when she first encountered it that she could only barely hold onto her panic. That initial fear had passed. She couldn't see, but it felt more like being blind than like the darkness itself was some malevolent force, some monster with an open maw waiting to devour her. And in the last — what? Half an hour? Five hours? Three days? — she had begun to regard the darkness as … well, not her friend, but not her enemy either. It felt almost inviting now, the empty blackness, and when she died, when she breathed her last, it would be easier to pass from this life into the next if this life were dark. She believed, she *knew* there would be a next life and that it would be brilliant, full of sparkling light. Here, like this, it would be possible to watch the glory of it happen, watch the passage from absolute darkness into absolute light.

That would be a sight to see!

Maybe it was a result of the fuzziness of her brain, but she couldn't seem to hold onto her anguish anymore, her pain over losing Bethany. All she could feel now was gratitude for the time she'd had with the precious child and with Aaron. They'd been happy, and though that happiness had been ruthlessly snatched away from her, she could feel the golden warmth of where it had been in her soul, like crawling into bed between warm sheets.

She knew that the monsters who had taken her husband and daughter from her would never awaken in light. They were doomed to remain in some form of darkness forever — and for them, it would not become a friend.

"You were … in my head." Jeni's breathless voice. "When he beat me with the hose, you … how you did that?"

"I painted your picture, your face." She didn't have the air or the will to explain what that meant, so she just left it there, hanging in the darkness between them. "I lived the beating with you." She paused for more air. "You were very brave."

"Who are ... *what* are you?" Jeni sounded so achingly young it broke Bailey's heart.

She couldn't have answered that even if she weren't suffering from hypothermia and oxygen deprivation.

"The air is to be gone soon. I ... I thank you for trying."

The darkness began to pulse with her heartbeats. It felt like every breath drew darkness into her lungs now instead of air. And soon her lungs would be full. She would be full.

She squeezed Jeni's hand. But Jeni didn't squeeze back. Maybe, she had already left.

"I'm sorry," Bailey whispered. Or thought she did. But even if she hadn't spoken, if Jeni was still here, she had heard.

Chapter Fifty-Seven

WHEN THE WATER level in the mine began to drop, it dropped quickly and dramatically. Brice and T.J. instantly saw it when a small space appeared between the rushing water and the roof of the mine shafts. Then the velocity of the water diminished, only a little at first, then quickly. It went from a raging torrent to water flowing fast, to water merely flowing. The water level dropped and dropped again. Whatever the source of the water that had gone tearing through the mine, it was finally emptying.

Brice wanted to go in as soon as there was even a foot of clearance between the water and the mine roof. But that was too dangerous. He couldn't lead a rescue team into the mine at the risk of their own lives. The Scotia coal mine explosion in 1976 had been a devastating but effective object lesson in mine safety. Caused by a spark igniting methane and coal dust, an explosion rocked the mine one spring morning and killed fifteen miners. Tragically, another eleven rescue miners died in a second explosion because they'd gone dashing madly into the mine before it was safe.

It was probably dawn out there on the flatlands, but the sun would not crest the mountain to the east until midmorning. Still, West Virginians knew the look of the sky when it began to turn, could read the subtle changes as it transformed from black velvet to dark blue, could see above the mountains the blue become pale blue, then watched pink and gold capture the sky.

Brice had organized the rescue squad members, firefighters and deputies into teams, three each. They would move in tandem, one in each of the shafts. Besides headlamps, each team carried a high-powered light — flashlight or LED lantern — and they'd be connected to each other with walkie talkies. They'd cross the first cross shaft — the one with "#1" in white spray-paint on all the coal pillars — then the second, and all the rest at the same time, searching behind the curtains as they came to them. Brice didn't even bother to try to convince T.J. to stay behind, though he had finally managed to talk him into allowing an EMT to treat his wounds. The lead paramedic spoke to Brice, said T.J.'s bullet wound wasn't life threatening, but it was serious enough to need stitching and he'd lost a lot of blood. He belonged in a hospital.

"You want to tell him that," was all Brice said.

He didn't.

Brice forced himself to wait until the water was only a foot deep and the level still falling before he'd led the teams into the dark world of Last Hope Ollie #2. It was particularly hard for Brice and a couple of the other men. The female EMTs and rescue squad members and his three women deputies were all considerably smaller and had an easier time beneath the low roof. Brice had to perform a modified duckwalk/bear crawl. He had only been in a coal mine a half dozen or so times in his life, had always admired the miners willing to go miles underground in a hole and work bent-over all day, knew he could never have survived that kind of life. But right now, he would have crawled down into a two-foot pipe filled with three feet of water if it meant rescuing the girls who'd been locked up inside a water-filled, airless mine for hours.

He wouldn't admit it was hopeless, though. Still, he was steeling himself for the emotional hammer blow of discovering the lifeless body of the woman he loved …

The woman he loved.

When had he decided that? He didn't know, *did* know he'd never hung words on it until now. It was more an acknowledgement of a long-held reality than a discovery of some strange new thing. Yeah, he loved Bailey. What did that mean to a man who *could not* become involved with a woman, *could not* have a relationship, could not … he didn't know. All he knew was he had to find her. And when he did, he was certain that whatever he found would change forever the course of the rest of his life.

Brice took the west wall, with Fletch a step behind him. T.J. took the east wall — the one that had filled first with water gushing out of the hole ripped in that wall of the mine on the other side of the mountain near the face.

The water level and the force of water pressure they were striding against as they entered the mine diminished almost with every step. By the time they had reached the dark interior of the mine, the space beyond the reach of the lights from the open area at the face and in the front of the mine, the water had fallen to about six inches deep, flowing fast against their progress, but not gushing, not threatening to sweep them away.

At cross shaft #35, the team two shafts over called a halt.

"We've got a body," said the voice from the walkie talkie on Brice's shoulder.

He kept himself from shouting, "Who?" Just waited.

"It's a man, must be one of the kidnappers," he said. "Looks like a gunshot wound in the front of his neck."

They'd mark the location, but continue. This was a *rescue* mission. It would switch to a body retrieval mission only if they could find no live survivors.

Another team found another one of the kidnappers, his

body floating in the shaft between the wall and cross shaft #41, where it had obviously been held against the coal pillar by the force of the water until the water level dropped. The leader reported that the man was black, with red hair, and he could see no apparent cause of death. The man could have drowned, of course, but Brice suspected his neck had been broken. That left one more kidnapper — the Beast.

Brice was in front, his headlamp scanning the dark corridor in front of him, formed by the mine wall on the right and the coal pillars and shafts on the left. At each intersection, he shined the light down toward the team members who were in the same cross shafts all the way across the mine, could see the glow of their headlamps through the ones with plastic curtains.

Then Brice began to notice that he could not see the sheen off the top of the water in the shaft ahead of him. The shaft appeared to be blocked. He was still thirty feet away before he realized the shaft had been blocked with rockfall, which was now an island with the water flowing around it down the tunnel.

He edged out from under the low roof and stood upright in the shaft around the pile of rocks, the cramping in his back and legs easing instantly.

The first thing he saw as he approached the rockfall was the body of a man. He was lying on his back, head dangling down, no longer in the water, but it would have been underwater until the level receded. The front of his head was a train wreck. It looked like he had fallen off a three-story building and landed on his face. It was beyond unrecognizable. His forehead was crushed inward — nose, mouth, eyes — gone. His whole head was nothing but wounds and protruding bones and … gray matter.

He had died a grizzly death.

Brice leaned over and picked up the dead man's right arm and shined his headlamp on it. When he turned the arm over, he saw the skull tattoo on the wrist. The stone on the small pinky ring sparkled in the light.

The Beast.

Dropping the arm, Brice straightened and began shining his headlamp in a sweeping motion over the rockfall. Fletch and the state trooper with him had crawled out from under the low roof of the shaft and stood beside him, shining their—

A tangle of wet bodies.

Even from where he stood, Brice could tell they were female.

He pulled in a gasp of air that'd suddenly gone thick as pudding. There were two — three, no *four*, maybe five — bodies lying together on top of the rocks. But they weren't in a tangle, as if they had been washed there by the current. They were lying longways beside each other, their arms—

He dropped to his knees on the rocks, reached out and took the arm of the nearest girl. She fell over toward him when he pulled on it. Her face was a mess, wet and dirty, her lip split, cuts and … it wasn't Bailey.

It was Jeni, the girl he'd spoken to in the ladies' room of the casino. These girls had been huddled here together on the rockfall. They'd been alive, had *climbed up here.*

He felt Jeni's neck. Nothing. The girl's skin was cold. No, wait. Weak. *A heartbeat!*

"She's alive!" he roared, the first words he had spoken since he entered the mine. He had been unable to produce a sound when he first saw the mound of bodies, unable to form the horrible words.

He saw a horrible injury, a compound fracture. Was that …?

Then he spotted her.

Bailey was on the other side of the pile of girls, her arms draped across a small black girl with close-cropped hair. Her face was a mess, too. Dirty, bruised and bleeding.

He was kneeling beside Bailey then, didn't know how he'd

gotten there. He took her arm, felt her wrist. Was there …? His own hands were trembling. Please …!

No … *Yes!*

There was a pulse!

"All units, west wall, four — *five* victims. *Alive.*"

Then his voice broke and he couldn't continue. Fletch was right there to finish for him as Brice leaned over and gently lifted Bailey into his arms.

Chapter Fifty-Eight

BAILEY KNEW she'd regret adding her special treat to the traditional Thanksgiving menu. The guys would make jokes and she'd laugh and her ribs could still launch rockets of pain into her chest if she wasn't kind to them. Of course, the No Wisecracks rule hadn't stopped T.J. and Dobbs from "doing what they do" in the four weeks since she'd been released from the hospital, so why should today be any different?

When she extended a steaming mug of amber liquid to T.J. and told him what it was, the look on his face was worth the pain laughing caused her.

"Underwear cider."

He just said the two words and looked at her with what appeared to be concern that she'd sustained a head injury along with the cracked ribs, broken fingers, sprained wrist, dislocated thumb and uncounted cuts and bruises. "Surely, I didn't hear you right."

"What did you say this was?" Dobbs looked suspiciously at his own drink.

"I just want to know whose underwear you used," Brice said. She laughed so hard, her ribs protested loudly.

Pointing to the bag of spices — cloves, brown sugar and

stick cinnamon — that floated in the crock pot full of cider, she explained that in one of her many childhood "homes," her foster mother had not had the cheesecloth she needed to make the bag. So she'd cut out the back side of a pair of underwear to take its place.

"*New* underwear!" she cried, over the chorus of *ughs* and *ewes* that followed. "Still sealed in plastic. She'd bought one of the boys the wrong size and hadn't gotten around to taking it back to the store. After that, it became a tradition — every Christmas, she'd go to the store and buy a new pair of underwear."

Bailey'd been in that home for a couple of years — it was where she'd met and bonded with her "little sister," María — so she'd carried the image of the floating bags of "underwear" with her when she left.

"It's a tradition in my family."

She turned away quickly, so the guys wouldn't spot the momentary longing that washed over her face every time she dropped the "F-bomb." Family. Her only real family, Aaron and Bethany, had enjoyed underwear cider the two Christmases they were together. That's why Bailey was serving it now, *at Thanksgiving* instead of Christmas. She'd learned to avoid the emotional triggers that sent her into that dark, empty place of loneliness and despair, and underwear cider coupled with Christmas carols would be an express ticket on a fast train there.

Now, at Thanksgiving, she could enjoy it with what had become her new family: T.J., Dobbs and Brice. Thanksgiving was a celebration of gratitude, and given what the three of them had been through in their brief acquaintance, they had a lot to be grateful for. Brief acquaintance — yeah, it was brief if you only counted elapsed time. Only a few months. But Bailey measured their relationships in dog years. One human year equaled seven dog years. That was about right.

Even though Dobbs had been injured far worse than she

had in the mine a month ago, he had joined the other two in an adamant refusal to allow her to help prepare the meal. Her dislocated fingers and sprained wrist were fine now, but the men wanted the whole celebration to be "their treat."

The fragrant aroma of roasting turkey filled the whole first floor of the Watford House. Bailey hadn't realized how hungry she was until she'd started smelling it about 6 a.m. There was no sleeping after that. T.J. had said he'd come in quietly at 2 a.m. to put into her oven the masterpiece he'd been doing who-knows-what to at his house all day. In and out, he'd said, wouldn't disturb her. Right, like Bundy wasn't going to announce his presence as soon as he pulled up in the driveway. Maybe even before he turned off the street.

So she'd watched, bath-robed and slippered as he slid the beast into the oven, listened as he admonished *again* that she was not to get out the dishes, that the rest of them would set everything up when they got there.

"My turkey, I carve," T.J. had announced when the four of them were seated around the festive table in the kitchen of the Watford House ... where all those years ago Sophia Watford had died, Eulalie Hamilton had hit her head and ...

Bailey let the thoughts go. No images of nightmare paintings ... and the quest the portraits had sent the three of them on. Not now. Now was thankful time.

Brice had shielded her from most of the prying and questioning by the federal agencies that got involved in the "international sex trafficking case." He'd told them Bailey had been dragged into it when a stranger slipped her a note at the casino, saying she was afraid she was about to be murdered. The next day, the stranger's body was fished out of the lake, and when Brice started asking questions, the kidnappers had come after Bailey because they thought she knew what they were doing. Everything had mushroomed from there.

The girls had answered all the questions put to them with

innocent honesty — said they had no idea how Bailey and the others had gotten involved in the effort to save them.

Yeah, eyebrows probably went up in the offices of several federal agencies when they put it together that this was the same Shadow Rock, West Virginia that just a month ago had been the site of three kidnap-murders and a strange infestation of spiders.

It was likely they suspected more was going on than they were being told. But they had nothing to back up that suspicion — and all the bad guys were dead so there was no reason to chase that rabbit down a hole.

They had celebrated with Jeni, Lora, Ana, Christina and their parents with a quiet dinner when all the girls were ready to go home earlier in the month, then put the reunited families on flights to London Heathrow, and then "home" where their whole villages awaited their return. Jeni and Ana had remained with Christina and Lora after their release from the hospital. Christina had required orthopedic surgery to repair the compound fracture she'd suffered, and Lora had remained hospitalized an extra couple of days because of her concussion. So Dobbs had paid for tickets for the parents of all four girls to fly to Shadow Rock to be with them — and they had all stayed at the Watford House, cared for by a crew of local people hired by Dobbs to help out.

It had been a glorious madhouse, filled with laughter and tears that had done more to heal Bailey's mind and spirit than the splints on her fingers and thumb and the brace on her wrist had done to heal her body. She showed no one the portrait of Poli — with Jeni's face peering out from under the bed and the shadows of the other girls in the closet. Bailey had asked Brice to burn it the day she woke up in the hospital. She'd promised Jeni the story, though, and she'd told it … in bits and pieces. It was too much to absorb in one sitting. She hadn't been surprised that the girls had so little trouble believing what she said. Regardless of the nightmare they'd endured, they were in many ways as innocent as Macy Cosgrove had been.

The emotional bond between Bailey and the girls would last a lifetime. But the strange connection she'd had to them vanished when Brice burned the painting.

The bodies of the other girls — Poli, Rayna, Nikolina and Sophia — had been shipped home for burial.

When Dobbs was released from the hospital shortly after the girls returned home, Bailey had insisted, would not take any answer but "yes ma'am," that he come to the Watford House to stay while he recuperated from the bullet wound in his shoulder and from the particularly nasty case of pneumonia he came down with from the water in his lungs. He'd only gone home a few days ago and Bailey missed him. He had always seemed to be standing in T.J.'s shadow, absurd as that might seem, given he was twice T.J.'s size. Still, T.J. was such a firebrand, so full of piss and vinegar that he sometimes left Dobbs in the shade. Not that Dobbs minded. She could tell the two of them had worked out the yin and yang of their relationship before their ages were two-digit numbers. Not only were they supremely comfortable with what they had forged half a century ago, they had grown into each's image of the other in the way of men secure in who they were and who love each other more than brothers.

"I want a leg," Dobbs called out as T.J. set knife to bird.

"Me, too," said Brice.

"The leg is my favorite piece," Bailey moaned.

T.J. gestured with his carving knife to the carcass of the bird on the platter.

"This is a *turkey*, not an octopus. Work it out."

The three had adjourned to the living room with mugs of cider, and Brice settled on the couch beside Bailey after he took Bundy outside to "do his business."

"I've got something you're all going to want to see," Dobbs said and reached into the manila envelop he'd left on the mantle. "Maybe you don't remember, but we had a group picture made the night of Bailey's birthday celebration at the Nautilus. I found it when I finally got around to going through the stack of my unopened mail."

The three gathered around where he sat in the wingback chair. He held an eight-by-ten photo that grabbed a moment from the past and dragged it into the present, the moment when the four of them had assembled on one side of the white-table-clothed table in the dining room of the Nautilus Casino. Bailey in her green dress. The three men looking suit-and-tie handsome on both sides of her. They were all grinning into the camera.

"You've got your eyes closed," Bailey told T.J.

"I don't think I've ever seen a picture of him with his eyes open," Dobbs said.

Bailey studied the picture, each face, thinking about—

And then she couldn't breathe.

Couldn't think.

She snatched the picture out of Dobbs's hands and turned to the lamp, holding it up beneath the shade into the bright light.

"Bailey, what's—" Brice began.

She let out a little piece of a cry then, a strangled sob that expressed an uncountable number of emotions all detonating like military ordinance in her chest.

"Sit down, child." T.J. took her by the shoulders and guided her to the wingback chair that was the mate to the one where Dobbs sat. She collapsed into it, her knees bags of water, her eyes riveted to the photograph she clutched in her hand.

Then she began to cry, not great heaving gulps of sobbing, but a condensed, airless cry that spoke of pain too deep to express with any sound she possessed.

Brice knelt on the floor in front of her and took one of her hands.

"What's wrong?"

"It's ... *him.*"

She somehow gasped out the words and continued to cry at the same time, pointing to an older man in the background of the photograph. He was with a group of people standing only a few feet behind where the four of them were mugging the camera. His face was clearly visible.

"He's *back.*"

And she was instantly transported to the night almost two years ago that had changed her life forever.

Chapter Fifty-Nine

AARON GETS OUT of the car and fishes the big golf umbrella out of the back seat as Jessie calls out "We'll give you a ride!" to the homeless woman standing in the rain at the bus stop.

Hurrying to her with the umbrella, Aaron ferries her back to the car under its protection — as if she weren't already soaked to the skin. She slides into the back seat behind Aaron, the smell of wet clothing — not very clean clothing — wafting into the car with her, babbling her thanks.

Aaron opens the back door on the other side, collapses the umbrella and tosses it into Bethany's car seat, which occupies the whole right side of the back seat behind Jessie, then hops back into the car. Even in his brief rescue mission, he'd have been soaked to the skin if he hadn't been wearing a rain jacket. As it is, his shoes, the new Rockports she had given him for Christmas are oozing water all over the floor.

"Thank you sooooo much," the woman gushes from the back seat. "I was near about to drown out there!"

She's younger than Jessie had thought when she first spotted her huddled under the awning, holding a plastic grocery sack over her head. She could be any age from twenty-five to forty. Her face is lined and worn. She looks used-up in a way that only the homeless can look. The rain has rendered the color of her long hair indiscernible — brown, maybe black like Jessie's. Her face is so thin she looks anorexic, or like she's just been released from a concentration camp. She's wearing a soaked denim jacket, jeans and running shoes, carrying a soaked sleeping bag under one arm and a trash bag jammed full — with probably every item she owns — in the other. Every garment she's wearing is holding maximum density of water, which is now oozing out and onto the back seat of the car.

"I'm getting water all over everywhere," she bemoans. "I'm so sorry. I was trying to get to the shelter before the rain started but I didn't make it."

She must be talking about the Overland Street Homeless Shelter. Jessie glances at Aaron and he meets her look. If they take the bypass to the airport instead of the interstate, they'll go through the industrial park and pass the shelter on their way. No sense dropping the woman at the next bus stop and let her wait there in the rain for a bus when they could take her all the way themselves.

When Aaron offers a lift all the way to the shelter, the woman beams and relaxes back into the seat.

"The good Lord'll bless you for doing this," she says. "He'll shine his light of good providence down on you this day. You'll see!"

Less than five minutes later providence strikes.

Jessie had been taught that all good gifts come from God, so this stroke of providence has obviously been conceived in some other, darker region.

It happens so fast it's hard to track the exact sequence later. Sometimes, when Jessie — or Connie Bradshaw or Amanda Prichard or Alexis Stevens or Bailey Donahue — lies in bed at night, her pillow so soaked with tears she has to turn it over so she can put her face on the dry side, she's able to see the events in a kind of slow motion, frame by frame, like a series of still photographs.

Other times, the handful of minutes that will forever change every day of the rest of her life fly by in a frenetic fast-forward that looks like a herky-jerky video from a convenience store surveillance camera.

The rain has let up, ratcheted down from a monsoon to a steady downfall. They have crested Blanchard Hill and the empty street narrows at the bottom at the Akron Street traffic light. On the right corner is a collection of big green dumpsters, obviously repositories for trash from the warehouses and storage facilities that line the streets of the industrial park, and behind the dumpsters is a vacant lot, overgrown with waist-high weeds and littered with piles of trash.

The only other vehicle in sight is coming down Baxter Street toward them. It is white, one of those sport utility vehicles, a Honda CRV maybe. The traffic light is green. The CRV enters the intersection as she and Aaron are still approaching it when suddenly Jessie sees something on the right, out of the corner of her eye. There is a flash of red — so fast you can't follow it. Another car comes roaring down Akron Street, through the intersection, flying, never makes any attempt to stop at the red light, plows into the side of the CRV with a horrible whump, a sound of screaming, protesting metal and breaking glass that awakens Jessie in the midnight dark every night after that for months, panting in sweat-tangled sheets, a silent scream on her lips that hadn't been silent that day.

She shrieks, wails as the red car rips open the white car like an ax has sliced into it, hacks it apart at the driver's side door, tears the vehicle in half, flinging pieces of it in every direction. The force of the impact drives the two conjoined cars, red and white, fifty feet down Akron Street until the tangled mass of twisted metal slides off the asphalt and slams into a utility pole.

Two seconds, maybe three.

The world as Jessie has always known it comes completely apart in seconds.

Screaming.

Jessie realizes she's the one screaming and clamps her mouth shut. The silence that rushes into the car with the slushing of the rain is broken by a car horn honking, a long, mournful cry that goes on and on.

Then she's out of the car in the rain, Aaron at her side, running toward the tangled mass of metal where steam rises up into the rain to form a halo of mist around the ruins. She gets to the portion of the white car where the driver's side door is caved so far into the vehicle that the top of the car has exploded upward from the compression and the undamaged sunroof window, torn from its moorings, stands upright in the rain.

Inside, beneath the crushed door is … a woman. Jessie thinks so because long blonde hair hangs in curls on her shoulders. But her face, above the bridge of her nose, and the whole top of her head is … gone.

Jessie sucks in a gasp, turns away, thinks she is going to be sick, staggers backward. After that, she's never able to order her memories sequentially. Several things happen, but it's like they are individual events totally unconnected in time and space to each other. The order in which they happened remains forever unclear.

Aaron is beside the red car pulling on the door, and it comes off in his hands. He reaches out and the driver of the car takes his hand and Aaron pulls him out of the wreckage. The car, it's some kind of small sports car, is as collapsed as a stomped Pepsi can, but somehow the man unfolds himself out of it and steps away. His face is bloody from a cut on his forehead and he's staggering, takes a couple of steps and then trips and Aaron has to grab him to keep him from falling.

That's when Jessie sees the car seat in the street. Or maybe she had seen it before that. She must have run right past it because it's between her and her car, where she can see the homeless woman out of the car now, standing beside the open back door on the driver's side, the umbrella Aaron had dropped on the back seat open and over her head.

Aaron is talking to the man he pulled out of the sports car, seems to be shouting at him, but the sounds are coming from a great distance. Everything feels indistinct, slowed down. Each raindrop that splats in her face is an individual event, falling independently of every other raindrop, slowly moving through the air to make contact with her skin, hitting it with a tiny stinging sensation, and she feels each of them, one at a time. Aaron's words are garbled, slowed down and elongated.

"... think ... you're ... doing ...?"

"... red ... light ..."

"Drunk!"

Jessie doesn't run to the car seat, which lies face-down in a puddle. She hurries to it — it's face-down in the water! — but it's an incredible struggle, fighting her way through air that has taken on substance, air that resists like water, like molasses, air that tries to hold her back, keep her away, not let her see.

Then she's standing beside the car seat, watching someone's hand, it's her hand, reach down and turn it over, lift it out of the puddle and lay it face-up on the street so that the rain splats down on the baby strapped into the seat. Washes the blood slowly down the baby's face. Tiny baby. Three, four months old maybe. Dressed in a blue terrycloth sleeper with footies, the kind that has snaps on the bottom so you can open it up to change the baby's diapers. Bethany had had an army of those, in all colors, pink, white, yellow, some with flowers on them, daisies, and bees, and she'd outgrown them so fast. Jessie would try to fasten it around her fat little bootie and the snaps wouldn't meet—

None of them had been blue, though. Not like this one. Blue. But the red blood running in a rivulet out of the baby's right ear and seeping up out of the baby's chest is slowly soaking into the fabric, turning it purple.

The baby's eyes are open, but he isn't looking at Jessie. He isn't looking at anything at all, and as she watches, his open eyes begin to fill with rainwater. It puddles there in the indentions his eye sockets make in his face until they are full and begin to overflow—

"—hear me?" Aaron's voice. She turns, sees him looking at her as he holds the guy from the red car upright by his shirt. "I said get your phone, call 911!"

She doesn't want to leave the baby. Leave him lying there like that. She should unbuckle him, pick him up, comfort him, get him out of the rain—

"Now! Call 911!"

Then Jessie's running through the rain, splashing through the rain back to the car, where she and Aaron both had left their doors open and where a woman — who is this woman? — stands beside the closed back door of the car holding an umbrella over her head.

Maybe that's when it happened, when Jessie got to the car, knelt down to get her purse out of the front seat. No, it had to be before that because she saw it.

A big gray car, not a limousine but the kind of big car that has a driver, like a chauffeur, coming from the same direction as the red car, screeches to a halt in the intersection under the traffic light and men, three of them in dark suits, jump out of it.

Jessie's hands are wet and she fumbles with her purse, drops it into the street. She gets down on her hands and knees beside the open door and digs through it. Her hands are numb, though, and she can't feel what she's *touching. In frustration, she sets it on the front seat of the car, intending to upend it and dump out the contents, but her fingers find her phone. She pulls it out of her purse, tries twice before her shaking hands hit the right numbers.*

9. 1. 1.

"Nine-one-one dispatch, what is your emergency?"

Jessie can't remember how to talk, can't form words.

She wants to tell the dispatcher there's been an accident, but her tongue is dead in her mouth. They'll want to know where! But Jessie isn't sure where she is. On her knees behind the open passenger door, she has to lean over and peer around the door to see the street signs.

Two of the men from the gray car are half-carrying, half-dragging the young man from the red car back toward the gray one. Aaron is in the street, yelling at the third man. He is older, wearing a fedora — nobody but older men wears hats like that, older men with money. He has a neatly trimmed beard, steel gray, and it comes to a ridiculous point at the base of his chin. And there's an eyepatch covering his right eye, the kind held in place with a piece of thin black elastic, like a pirate.

She looks from the men to the street signs. Akron Street. It's the intersection of Akron and ... what street had they been on? She can't read that sign from this angle.

Baxter, she thinks. Yes, Baxter Street.

She opens her mouth to force those words out, to tell the 911 dispatcher there's been an accident and to tell her where. But before she has a chance, there's a sudden bang, like a firecracker.

Then a scream. The homeless woman, standing on the other side of the car screams, not just once but in a continuous shrieking wail. Jessie swings her vision back and looks at Aaron. He's holding his belly and he slowly drops to his knees like he's praying. The man, the older man with the eyepatch is standing in front of him ... pointing a gun at him.

The phone clatters to the pavement out of Jessie's suddenly lifeless fingers. She can't breathe.

The man shouts something in a language Jessie can't understand and one of the men who was helping to shove the man from the red car into the back seat of the gray car stops what he's doing and turns toward her car.

He reaches into his coat, like he's going to take a wallet out of a breast pocket and pulls out something — it's a gun! — and starts forward.

"Jessie ... run!" Aaron's voice cries.

Another gunshot rings out. The eyepatch man has shot Aaron again. Shot him! He flies backward onto the wet street and lies still.

Jessie screams, shrieks with every fiber of her being, but can't make a sound. She opens her mouth, but nothing comes out except an awful, guttural grunt, like she had been kicked in the belly with a pointed-toe cowboy boot. The homeless woman screams, though, makes enough noise for both of them, drops the umbrella and goes running back up the street trailing a high-pitched wail behind her like the tail of a kite.

There's a third gunshot and the screaming cuts off and Jessie hears the woman's body hit the street with a sick, plopping sound.

Jessie drops down onto her belly and looks out under the car. Between the wheels she can see the woman lying face down on the street. She turns back toward Aaron ...

Aaron!

The old man shouts again more unintelligible words, harsh, staccato words. She can only see his feet, but the man who'd shot the homeless woman rushes to Aaron's body, grabs his arms and begins dragging him up the street toward their car.

That's the first time Jessie is afraid. It comes all at once. Confusion and horror morph into a panic that hits her with the force of a wrecking ball square in the chest.

Hide, hide, hide — she has to hide!

Looking around frantically, she spots the dumpsters. Without even getting to her knees, she commando crawls toward them. The nearest is only ten or twelve feet away and the car blocks her from the view of the men in the street. There's only about eighteen inches of clearance, but she scoots under it, jams herself beneath it and shoves her way through the mud and filth, pushes as far back as she can go.

She can't lift her head to look out, her right cheek is jammed into the mud and all she can see is the bottom of the front door of her car and her phone lying on the street beside it. She hears footsteps, see shoes. Someone has come around to that side of the car. The man is only ten feet from her.

The panic in her chest explodes like some Navy dinghy when you pull on the strap. If she'd had any air, if she could have breathed at all, she'd have screamed, wouldn't have been able to stop herself, and he'd lean over and see her. But she has no air and remains silent. He stoops down, picks up her phone and tosses it into the car on top of her purse. Then she hears scuffling feet, can't tell ...

The other man has picked up the body of the homeless woman and is dragging it across the street. He drags it around the car and the two of them pick it up, toss it into the front seat on top of Jessie's purse and phone and slam the door.

Then she sees Aaron.

Aaron!

A man is dragging him by his arms. One shoe has come off. She can see a bloody snail trail behind him that the rain is washing away. Aaron!

She makes a noise, an involuntary sob, but the two men are on the other side of the car now, helping to shove Aaron's body into the driver's side of the front seat, and don't hear her. Then the car begins to move. The engine isn't running but it's moving. The men are pushing it, the man beside Aaron's open door leaning in to steer — pointing it down the hill toward where the mangled wreck still sends tendrils of steam or smoke into the rain falling softly from the sky.

It isn't hard, the incline is steep enough that once they get it moving, the car rolls easily, gathering speed as it goes.

The man piloting the car steps back and the car continues to roll until it hits the tangled mass of wrecked cars pushed up against the lamppost. Jessie can't see well now since she can't lift her head to—

Something brushes against her leg!

There is a squeaking sound.

Jessie would have thought it impossible to be more horrified than she already is but she's wrong.

Rats!

There are rats under the dumpster and Jessie is lying in the middle of them.

The panic that steals her breath and takes complete control of her body is primeval, there is no thought to it, she plans nothing. Horror hijacks her and she scoots frantically away, only barely able to apply enough reason to her retreat to shove herself out the back side of the dumpster rather than the front. The rain hits her, splashing cold, as she clears the dumpster and leaps to her feet, holding onto a scream with her fingernails, looking around on the ground — there it is, they are, crawling out from under the dumpster toward her—

And then she's running into the weeds behind the dumpster, tall weeds that reach almost to her shoulders. She only makes it a few steps before she trips, falls into the mud, and then crawls as fast as she can, mindlessly, blindly, not looking back, crawling in terror.

The crash of an explosion tears open the world while she's still in the field of weeds. It's a blast like a bomb. Only then does the car horn, that had wailed nonstop as a mournful accompaniment to the carnage, fall silent. The explosion is followed a few seconds later by another blast, as loud or louder than the first. The sounds come from behind her, from beyond the dumpsters and horror from which she fled. She leaps to her feet then, looks back. She has crawled … thinking, if she had thought at all … only of away, get away, not considering a direction or a destination.

Standing in the chest-high weeds, she is disoriented, can't make out where she is. She doesn't recognize any of the buildings, but when she turns around she can see boiling black smoke rising up into the rain and she realizes that she has crawled back up the hill parallel to Baxter street, crested it and gone down the other side.

There is no sound now coming from the other side of the hill beneath the pall of smoke. Only silence.

Then she hears another sound that makes her knees weak and she sinks back down into the weeds.

Sirens. A symphony of sirens.

She puts her head in her hands then and collapses into the mud, sobbing.

Chapter Sixty

"Who is that man?" T.J. asked.

"He shot Aaron. Twice. Killed him!"

"Who's Aaron?" Brice asked.

"My husband." Then she let go and did sob, cried so hard she lost her breath. Cried for all the times she'd swallowed tears. And some part of her tears were tears of relief. Finally, after all this time, she had admitted the truth to her *friends*.

When her tears had finally ratcheted down to the hitching breathing of a little kid who'd just thrown a tantrum, she looked up into the concerned faces of the three men who had come to mean so very much to her in the past few months. Men she'd lied to every breath, pretending to be somebody she wasn't. Men who had helped her forge a new life ... to replace the life the monster with the gray beard and the eyepatch had stolen from her.

Only maybe now ... now he was back.

"You's in the Witness Protection Program," T.J. said matter-of-factly. "We all knew that. Is this" — he pointed to the man in the photo — "is he why?"

Bailey was so surprised she looked from one man to another, unable to speak.

"You knew?" she said.

T.J. managed a smile.

"Of course we knew," he said. "Mountaineers ain't near as dumb as we look." His face softened. "Your real name's Jessie Cunningham, the name you gave me the day I stopped by your front porch to see your kidney painting."

"The day we came barging into the rest of your life," Dobbs said.

She looked at Brice.

"You … you checked me out, found out—?"

"No." Brice's voice was decisive. "It wasn't any of my business." He looked around at the others. "We figured you'd tell us when you were ready."

The revelation that they'd known all along should have been no revelation at all. Of course, they did. She pointed to the man in the photo. "It's a long story."

"We ain't got plans."

She told them. Every horrible detail. Cried through most of it.

At some point while she was telling them about that night, someone had refilled her mug of cider and T.J. urged her to drink when she was finished with the tale. The slow, rhythmic act of swallowing calmed and centered her.

Pointing to the man who'd been standing *not ten feet behind her,* she said, "His name is Sergei Wassily Mikhailov. It was his son, Ivan, who was the drunk Aaron pulled out of the red sports car."

She took another long drink of the cider — underwear cider. Only a few minutes ago, they'd all been laughing about the name. How quickly life changed.

"According to the federal marshals, he has no soul. He's a Russian mafia boss who makes his way in the world by killing anybody who gets in his way and—"

She discovered it was hard to say the words out loud.

"—and by *murdering their families*, too."

"But he thinks he got rid of all the witnesses," Brice said, putting it together. "He shot your" — there was a hesitation there, or Bailey thought there was — "husband and believed the homeless woman was you."

"Nobody looks for somebody they think is dead. That's what Bernie said."

Bernie. U.S. Marshal Bernard Jordan. She had heard the other officers refer to him as Bernie, but she'd never used the name. Didn't know why it had popped into her head just now.

"He said I'd be safe while a hush-hush grand jury issued super-secret indictments against Mikhailov and Ivan and the henchmen. Then I'd come out of nowhere and testify, they'd stick a needle in the monster's arm and I could have my life back. Bada boom, bada bing. But before they could serve the indictments, Mikhailov returned to Russia. And vanished."

"And you've been stuck ever since … waiting," Dobbs said.

She saw understanding dawn on T.J.

"And because you're supposed to be dead," he paused and looked at her tenderly, "you had to leave your … little girl *behind.*"

Bailey bleated out an involuntary sob.

"Yes," she said. She whispered the name, "Bethany."

Said her name, actually said it, "Bethany!"

"And … Oscar was because …?"

"I couldn't stand the thought of missing another of her birthdays. She … turned three June 27."

The room grew quiet then, each of them digesting what she'd said. She realized that it felt like she'd shed chains that had been around her chest for so long she'd forgotten them. Telling these guys the truth unlocked the chains and they fell away. She felt light without them. Like she might float away, Forrest Gump's feather on a breeze.

"And now …?" Brice asked.

"I ... don't know. I guess I call Marshal Jordan." His was the number she'd been given to call in an emergency. U.S. Marshal Bernard Jordan. She felt disoriented. "It's just ... I don't call *them;* they call *me.* Actually, they don't call. They just show up and tell me ..."

She realized she was babbling but couldn't seem to grab hold of the bubble of pure joy that had swelled up in her chest so big she could barely breathe.

Inhale.

Exhale.

She spoke slowly. "Now I call the marshals and tell them ... Tell Wit Sec *I want my life back!*"

And what exactly did that mean? *This* was her life, too. Here with these three. Somehow she would fit it all together. She'd figure that out ... work it out somehow.

She took a long, slow drink, drained the last of her cider and set the cup on the coffee table. Then, she let it wash over her, watched the urgent message flash in red letters on an LED screen in her mind: *BETHANY! BETHANY! BETHANY!*

T.J. LOOKED at the brilliant smile that lit Bailey's face. He had never seen her look so happy.

And he was happy for her.

Happy and scared.

He glanced at Brice and saw unnamable emotions play over his face, too. Their eyes caught and held. They were both thinking the same thought.

Bailey had watched a ruthless Russian Mafia boss commit murder.

He thought he'd killed all the witnesses. Once he found out different, that he'd missed one, he'd come looking for her hidey hole. He'd pull out all the stops, turn over every rock, look under the chewing gum on the bottom of the picnic tables.

Would the federal marshals really be able to keep Bailey alive long enough for her to tell a jury what she saw?

THE END

A Special Request

Thank you for reading *Gold Promise*.

If you enjoyed this book would you please consider writing a review of it on your favorite bookseller's website so other readers might enjoy it too. Just a couple of sentences would mean a lot to me.

Thank you!
Ninie Hammon

About the Author

Ninie Hammon (rhymes with shiny, not skinny) grew up in Muleshoe, Texas, got a BA in English and theatre from Texas Tech University and snagged a job as a newspaper reporter. She didn't know a thing about journalism, but her editor said if she could write he could teach her the rest of it and if she couldn't write the rest of it didn't matter. She hung in there for a 25-year career as a journalist. As soon as she figured out that making up the facts was a whole lot more fun than reporting them, she turned to fiction and never looked back.

Ninie now writes suspense--every flavor except pistachio: psychological suspense, inspirational suspense, suspense thrillers, paranormal suspense, suspense mysteries.

In every book she keeps this promise to her Loyal Reader: "I will tell you a story in a distinctive voice you'll always recognize, about people as ordinary as you are--people who have been slammed by something they didn't sign on for, and now they must fight for their lives. Then smack in the middle of their everyday worlds, those people encounter the unexplainable--and it's always the game-changer."

Cornbread Mafia

Fire In The Hole

Blown' Up A Storm

Ridin' For A Fall

So Shall The Tree Grow

Nowhere, USA

The Jabberwock

Mad Dog

Trapped

The Hanging Judge

The Witch of Gideon

Blown Away

Nowhere People

Through The Canvas Series

Black Water

Red Web

Gold Promise

Blue Tears

The Taken Saga

The Taken

The Changed

The Hidden

The Saved

The Unexplainable Collection

Five Days in May

Black Sunshine

The Based on True Stories Collection

Home Grown

Sudan

When Butterflies Cry

The Knowing Series

The Knowing

The Deceiving

The Reckoning

The Fault

Stand-alone Psychological Thrillers

The Memory Closet

The Last Safe Place